W9-AJN-448

INVITATION

INVITATION

Shehryar Fazli

TRANQUEBAR

TRANQUEBAR PRESS
An imprint of westland ltd
Venkat Towers, 165, P.H. Road, Maduravoyal, Chennai 600 095
No. 38/10 (New No.5), Raghava Nagar, New Timber Yard Layout, Bangalore 560 026
Survey No. A-9, II Floor, Moula Ali Industrial Area, Moula Ali, Hyderabad 500 040
23/181, Anand Nagar, Nehru Road, Santacruz East, Mumbai 400 055
47, Brij Mohan Road, Daryaganj, New Delhi 110 002

First published in India in TRANQUEBAR by westland ltd 2011

ISBN: 978-93-80658-65-0

For sale in the Indian subcontinent only

Typeset in Sabon Roman by SÜRYA, New Delhi
Printed at Manipal Press Limited, Manipal

For Nanu

Contents

Acknowledgements

I am indebted to Ikram Fazli, Rehana Fazli and Faisal Fazli for a lifetime of encouragement; my MFA peers and faculty at UMass Amherst for giving me the support and several deadlines I needed to complete this novel, in particular to Chris Bachelder, Stephen Clingman and, above all, Sabina Murray for her critical eye from the earliest drafts; and my colleagues at the International Crisis Group, especially Samina Ahmed and Bob Templer, who often made me feel that this book was as important to them as the work I owed them.

Capturing 1970 Karachi is not easy, especially for one who wasn't around at the time, and I am grateful to Farouk Dosa, Kamran Noorani, Zahid Murad, and many others on whose extensive descriptions I've depended.

The friends who've made me feel like this novel was partly their mission, too, are too numerous to list, but I would like, especially, to thank Fahd, Nada and Emad for their crucial interventions. Finally, I thank Ayesha for her dedication, persistence and honesty; and Renuka for her steady hand and meticulousness.

A tragedy was taking place all right, a national tragedy on a grand scale, but those of us who played our parts were—let me put it bluntly—clowns. Clowns! Burlesque buffoons, drafted into history's theatre on account of the lack of greater men. Once, indeed, there were giants on our stage; but at the fag-end of an age, Madam History must do with what she can get.

—Salman Rushdie,
The Moor's Last Sigh

He stalked like an assassin through the town,
And glared at men because he did not like them,
But trembled if one passed him with a frown.

—W.H. Auden

PART ONE

Karachi, 1970

1

'What's so funny?'

I must have been chuckling, or smiling. I turned my head. It was Mona Phuppi, my aunt, her pants rolled up to her calves like mine, exposing thick white ankles. She carried a purse in one hand, her sandals in the other, and walked the sand with laborious steps, her shoulders hunched, looking me dead in the eye as if she was coming to attack me. Which in a sense is what she did.

'Haan? Kya, what's so funny?'

'Oh, I was just looking at those.' I pointed to the little island next to ours, the island of old Indian boats, captured in Pakistani waters over the years ever since Partition and stockpiled here. I don't know if I ever saw the boats myself as a child, or whether the image I carried was based only on my father's descriptions. But I did carry that image, a museum of decaying Indian boats in the middle of the sea. 'They're probably haunted,' my father used to say. 'Ghosts of the Indian boatmen, all over the place.' This was how he forced impressions of the old country on a child's mind once in exile. And now here they were.

Mona Phuppi, standing next to me now, gazing at the boats, asked me to hold her sandals. I held them by the straps. She removed a cigarette box and lighter from her purse and lit a cigarette. I caught a glimpse of two bottles of pills in the purse. According to my father, his older sister had to be medicated every day to keep a mental illness, the root of their bitter relations, at bay. She blew smoke that flew apart in the wind. 'Come, let's sit,' she gestured towards the rocks behind us. Sitting down, she played the wet sand with her toes, bunching it up, digging. I set her sandals on the rocks. We watched the sea together in silence. Two men, minute figures, were sailing, making a line towards the beach, but then one of them pulled the rope to point the sail in the other direction, his friend holding another rope, and then they urgently swapped places. The boat went in the opposite direction. This was how they'd make it back to land: sailors had to always come back at an angle, I remembered, from the side and not head on, so that one had to sail more or less parallel to the shoreline, and come closer to it by making that repeated cursive 'm' or zigzag. Mona Phuppi puffed on her cigarette. Sandy layers coated her toenails and formed particularly thick clumps on the big toes. 'I'm going to sell the orchard.' She said this very calmly. Momentarily, I was emptied of thought.

The family orchard, our dearest possession, confiscated by the government years ago, and now ours again.

'Why?' I asked. 'Why sell?' She puffed smoothly on her cigarette. 'You know Abba will never agree. He loves that orchard.'

'Ha ha ha. He *loves* that orchard. *Loves* the orchard, eh? Then please tell me why your father hasn't been back in the country in what, twenty years?' Nineteen. 'If he loves it so much . . . no-no, it's time to sell.' She put out her cigarette against the rock and flicked it away. 'I'm expecting your *full* cooperation. Now come, lunch is probably served.' She left her sandals behind, walked back to the Yacht Club without looking to see if I was following. I watched her go.

The property was one of the things I remembered, or thought I remembered, well. Every spring, a two-hour train ride to Hyderabad, a switch and another hour to Mirpurkhas. From there, a tonga to the orchard. For the grown-ups it was a place to rest the soul, for us kids a very different affair, and to these thirty-six acres of peace and discovery we'd go, the mango season just beginning. During daytime we explored the innumerable little pathways that led to other pathways, climbed the trees, picked the mangoes. We created bases in the trees, bases and code names and acronyms, allowed and denied access to others at whim. We dug holes that the elders told us to fill up unless we wanted to go back to Karachi this-minute-now. And at night the children slept on charpoys outside while the elders slept in the small single-room house at the centre of the property. I hadn't seen the place in two decades, and it had acquired a certain charisma in my reflections of Karachi.

We'd lost the property under Ayub Khan's land reforms in the late '50s, along with much of the six hundred and fifty acres we'd been given by the government to compensate for the estates the family had left behind at Partition. But Mona Phuppi had fought and fought in the courts, and now we had some of it back, including this most cherished part. When my father heard the news, his astonishment at his sister's success soon changed to panic: pacing up and down the drawing room of our Paris apartment, face to the floor, he said, 'She'll keep the orchard to herself.' A few days later he entered my bedroom, remained silent when I said salaam, before saying, 'You've got to go back. Make sure she doesn't do any hanky-panky with that orchard. I'm telling you, she'll keep it to her bloody self.' Back? Back to *Karachi*? Yes, he said. Back to Karachi.

I didn't doubt that Mona Phuppi would try to claim the orchard for herself. But the thought of *selling* was absurd.

I picked up my aunt's sandals, and returned to the Yacht Club veranda. Mona Phuppi had arranged this visit as a homecoming party of sorts, to welcome my return after nineteen years. The elders—Mona Phuppi, her husband Phuppa Jaan, another man who was bald except for a single curl on his pate, and this man's wife—now were eating chicken sandwiches and floppy fries, talking politics. The coming elections, the military giving up power, Bhutto and his Bengali rival Mujib, East Pakistan and West Pakistan, things it was far too late, in 1970, for me to trouble myself about. Nobody at the table seemed particularly joyed or trusting about General Yahya's decision to hand the country back over to civilians. Mona Phuppi, least of all. She sat at the head of the white baroque table. 'Hopefully the elections will be enough of a mess that the army will remain in power,' she said. 'They talk of democracy, in twenty years we'll be ruled by these people, these kids who aren't taught anything, who don't know a single poem. I mean, what poetry we learned in our day. "The fireflies light/Is a flame for which science has no name/It must be mighty peculiar to go about with an unknown flame attached to your ... *posterior*?" Something like that, na?' Someone was about to say something, but Mona Phuppi began keenly again. 'Achha, achha! Then there was: "They brought back her warriors dead/She neither wept nor uttered cry/All the maidens watching said/She must weep or she will die." What was the next part? Or was that it? Ahh, and: "The dew of the morning felt chill on my brow/I felt like the warning ... the warning ..." Haan, remember that one? "The dew of the morning felt chill on my brow/I felt like the warning of what ... I feel now"? Aisah kuch, isn't it? You think they're teaching these lines *today*? Ha! *Dee-mawk-rassy*.'

The waiters brought us cold drinks. Dressed in white Yacht Club uniforms, they were darker skinned than average, giving the place a relaxed colonial feel, and I imagined older days filled with white men in white navy uniform, enjoying cocktails in the sun, taking a break from a horrific war.

Mona Phuppi set her manicured toes against my seat; moving them inwards and then outwards, the way my father did to keep the circulation going. But in her I was convinced that these little movements betrayed a disturbed biology underneath. The temperature alternated between warm and windy. The sea didn't make a single sound, but something of it, perhaps its very silence, enveloped us. From where I sat I could still see the island of boats. Once again it took me a few moments to adjust to the sight. Whether I'd seen them myself years ago or not, with all the stories my father used to tell about them, of Indian pirates and ghosts, these boats had an element of myth to me, belonged too deeply to the child's mind to exist in the real world. They were covered in dust and cobwebs and looked haunted just as my father had said.

The air above seemed more grey and toxic. I felt the unease of someone who's just learned that what ayahs tell you about poltergeists or dakus who attack you in the middle of night, announcing themselves with loud drums, had turned out not to be tall tales after all. Yes, there the boats were, ghoulish, exquisite. Not just covered in decades of dust, but seemed *made* of that dust, or of something equally insubstantial, the boats not really boats but sculptures erected from ash, which one prick of a pencil would collapse into a big heap of powder, slowly blown back to the sea. And then ghostly men would come out, first a few and then a hundred and then a thousand, dead Indian boatmen, covered in ash, invading the beach, walking the earth again.

Phuppa Jaan sat at the other end of the table to his wife. My memories of him, too, were vivid. I'd always been fascinated that he wore a hearing aid in one ear, hidden behind an unwieldy black mane; if close enough, you could hear it buzz with your own distorted syllables. As children we'd always be amused when at soirees he dozed off on his seat. I'd once reached out to remove the device from his ear, probably to try it on myself, but with eyes half-open he'd slapped my hand away and shouted, and I dashed away, shocked by his first display of temper. Whether because of his deafness or not, he was an insignificant man, a non-actor. 'Not-a-man,' my father would say, 'not-a-man.' Under his wife's fat thumb.

After lunch, the bald man and his wife said they wanted to walk on the sand. Mona Phuppi encouraged her husband to join them—he got up abruptly to follow them when he finally heard his wife repeat the instructions a third time—leaving aunt and nephew alone again.

'Abba won't agree,' I said. She blew smoke from a fresh cigarette in my direction. I raised my finger. 'He simply *will not agree.*' My tone was curt, and I saw the old rage rise in her face. It made her look more natural, discarding the polite charade of old poems. *This* was Mona Phuppi: pale, combustible, a face full of hate.

'Just!' She leaned forward and lifted her own finger, right in front of her eyes, and while she searched for the words to accompany it, the finger, and the arm it extended from, took on a separate life, not quite pointing at me but upward, quivering tensely like the string of a bow just shot. She was silent, her eyes seemed trapped in panic, desperate that the words come soon before the moment was lost. 'What does he think,' she finally said. 'Does your father think it's *easy* to fight the government? Over *land*? Ha! Two lawyers—no, three. I've been through *three bloody lawyers.* And what has your father done? Not much. Not much and minus two! But I'll tell you what it really is: being away from this country has made Ghazanfar whiny. Arrey bhai, just come back. But no, Ghazanfar on his high bloody horse. *I'm never coming back.* But now he wants his share, doesn't he?' I could see the momentum, the rhythm of prosecution, gather in her face, her eyes protruding, deep breaths as she leaned her frame forward. Her voice was becoming coarse. 'Sitting in Paris for the last, how many years has it been, fifteen, twenty? Meanwhile I'm going to court in the bloody heat. And he should know this is just the beginning. It will take forever and a day before the government hands over ownership. But when it does I *will sell it.* If you or Ghazanfar have a problem with that . . .' She took a breath and relinquished the thought. I was grateful. A moment passed and in a more tranquil tone, she said, 'Come with me tomorrow. I'll take you to it. See for yourself, bachai. I'm sure you'll give me your full cooperation.' She smiled a closed, unconvincing smile, and then she put her hand to the side of my neck, tapped me, and got up. She walked back to the beach, joining the others.

An image kept reappearing from childhood: my aunt, standing with her arms crossed, her head down, one foot ahead of the other, and rocking her torso back and forth—whether she was listening to music, to someone speaking, or lost in her own thoughts, in my recollections this was Mona Phuppi at rest. Despite moments of kindness, I recalled an unpleasant, abrasive figure, a detractor searching for signs of the decay of civilization. And in this she'd often single me out as the first exhibit: 'Ghazanfar, this boy doesn't even say adaab when he greets me. Can you imagine us never saying adaab to Phuppi or Chacha, any of our elders?' At the same time, she seemed to draw strength from the spiritual peril that surrounded mankind; there was an excitement in her eyes when she'd cry to me, 'You see how people are today!' And now I had to meet her on adult terms, about the most adult things. Land matters. How I resented my father for not coming back himself!

∾

'Came her nurse of ninety years/Put his child upon her knee/Like summer tempest came her tears/Sweet my child I live for thee.' Mona Phuppi announced this last poem on the boat back to the Karachi mainland. Was it because she was mad that the people here indulged her like a child, let her recite half-forgotten poems from her

schooldays? Looking behind us as we made our way, I
thought there should be a poem about them, too, Indian
boats on a pirate island. I had an impression that this
was not an island at all, just a pile of boats reaching all
the way down to the seabed. However much I tried to
take it in that afternoon, today, back in exile, this island
of dead boats recedes back into the fantastical.

The boat ride smelled of a polluted sea, of childhood,
the smell of my clothes and young skin when we'd get
back from a trip to the beach. Whenever Mona Phuppi
and I made eye contact, she developed a devious half-
smile, tongue squeezed between her top teeth and lower
lip. As if she was in secret communication with me, the
poem a diversion for the others, to obscure what was
really happening. As if she'd achieved a triumph,
snookered us, and now eagerly watched for my father's
next move. She was going to sell the orchard, she said,
and with the smile she was giving me now I almost felt
as if the decision was *our* secret, *our* great project. There
was a sudden intimacy between us on that boat. As she
sat facing me, I imagined reaching down, holding her
thick white ankles and upending her into the sea.

2

My aunt and uncle dropped me to the Khyber Hotel, insisting once more that I leave this dump and stay with them, to which I could say nothing more than that I appreciated the offer and would certainly let them know. Up the stairs waited Doli, the receptionist with a wild moustache over mustard buckteeth. Behind him, a portrait of a dictator, a former dictator, Ayub Khan, gone since a year ago, 1969. The hotel had the air of a hospital, the smell of disinfectant, the walls painted two shades of blue—mostly aqua, with a navy belt at the bottom—and a first-aid box on the wall where the corridor began. My father had talked to people he hadn't seen since the start of his exile, requesting accommodation for me while I was here. By no means, he said, should I stay with Mona Phuppi. I picked this old hotel myself. My room was on the same floor as the lobby, small, a fat swamp-green cabinet constricting the space further. An arched door-length shutter led to a balcony I shared with two other rooms. The toilet was a porcelain hole-in-the-ground, and the shower had no tub nor curtain to separate it from the rest of the bathroom. Curiously, the sink was outside the bathroom itself.

I washed my hands, as I did whenever I returned from the outside. My father's instructions. I turned the lights off and lay down. The sounds of the marketplace in Saddar—screaming shopkeepers, light metallic rings of bicycles, car engines and brakes—came sheerly into my room as if through pipes. I'd already dozed off by the time Ghulam Hussain knocked fiercely on the door, and whispered my name, 'Shahbaz bhai,' as if the whispering compensated for the knocking. I got out of bed, opened up, and his fat face appeared like a smudged thumbprint against the hallway light. 'Asleep, Shahbaz bhai?' He slipped a portly foot out of his chappals and propped it against the opposing calf muscle. Ready to serve. He spat a pellet of spit, punctuating his presence, onto the floor of the hallway.

Three days ago, the International Arrivals area at Karachi airport had been crawling with eager cab drivers, fighting each other for clients—'Nahin! That one's mine ... okay then, I have the Angrez sahib ... no the one with the two children ... nahin, chalo-chalo, they're mine!' And in the tumult of their sport, as one cab driver after another stood shoulder to damp shoulder with me ('Taxi, bhai jaan?'), I saw Ghulam Hussain for the first time. He had a cardboard sign with my name written in thin black letters, which he held in one hand, discreetly below the waist. It was only when I signalled to him that he smiled and held up the sign with both hands. I was prepared to like him.

Now, three days later, he led me down the steps of the Khyber, whispered, *Bismillah*, as I took my seat next to him in his sandy brown Morris Minor. Despite his immense frame, he kept the seat forward so that all the leather and metal seemed to tear from the pressure of his expanding limbs. His thigh constantly got in the way of the stick whenever he switched gears, and he drove roughly through Saddar and into another part of town, which except for an occasional lit window in a residence was dark. The streets were uneven, cracked and glossed with puddles from recent monsoons.

'How's your father sahib?' Ghulam Hussain asked. 'He's happy over there? Why didn't *he* come back?'

What was the Urdu word for 'exile'? Was there such a word? 'Not yet,' I said. Not ever. But he did try to ensure that I could survive Karachi without him (money, addresses, phone numbers), and when he sent his old cook word about my visit, he, the former employee, offered this nephew as guide and chauffer for as long as I needed one.

Ghulam Hussain opened his door slightly, collected the phlegm in his throat with a loud animal noise, and spat out. The black skeletons of two burnt cars lay abandoned on a roundabout. 'Did I show you my scar, from the riots?' he asked, using the English word for 'riot'. He lifted his hand from the gear stick, shook back the baggy sleeves of his kameez to reveal a thin scar, the length of a little finger, on his forearm. 'See this? This is from the riots.'

'Yes, you did show me. Very ... hala.' The word meant nothing, but it expressed approval, it was one of those terms that helped fortify my weak Urdu.

He parked outside a tall black gate through which we passed on foot. Ghulam Hussain had a lazy walk, sandals skating the ground, and he was intent on letting me walk ahead of him. The house we'd come to was unfinished, the second storey covered in cement, with two large square spaces yet to be filled by windows. He pointed me to a flight of stone steps that led down. 'One minute,' he said, and finally overtook me. He took time on every step, adjusted the balance of his heavy frame before moving to the next. 'My brother's quarters.' He tapped the bolt of his index finger against the wall. 'Very fat walls. People could be screaming in there and we wouldn't hear it.'

Ghulam Hussain opened the wooden door to the quarters, and left his sandals at the entrance. I left mine next to them. The room was crammed with bodies—a bunch of men and two women, the latter of whom lay together on a thin mattress, one of them on her back, the other on her side, using one hand to support her head, and one hand to play with her friend's corkscrew hair. Ghulam Hussain introduced me in Bengali. In the dimness of a weak, naked bulb, the men's faces were all the same: thick moustache, fat inquisitive eyes, copied from one face to the next. Most sat in a loose circle, arms encircling or resting on raised knees. One man lay sideways, naked to the waist, behind the circle. He sipped a clear liquid from a clear bottle, and leaned over a battery-operated radio that projected a female singing voice in a melee of static. In the centre of the room was a rusty old hookah. Ghulam Hussain sat next to the man who was sucking from it, and gestured me to sit with him. The scent of hash mixed with the odours from these men's baking glands.

'These days, we often get visitors from outside,' the shirtless man said, switching to Urdu. He had a long wily nose. 'They come and spend some time with us, smoke some hash with us, talk about socialism with us, and then go back to their big homes and their big lives. Without us.' The others laughed. I smiled, not sure whether I was being implicated. I lowered my eyes. When the hookah finally came into my hands, I sucked in and reflexively coughed an untidy patch of smoke. 'Nahin, nahin, bhai jaan!' the same shirtless one blurted. 'You're doing it wrong.' He placed his bottle on the floor next to him, and crawled over to me. He was thin at the chest, the bones of his ribcage protruding from the dark skin, but developed mass at his belly. He took the hookah from me, lifted its mouthpiece up to my face, told me to put my mouth to it. 'Now, from *here*.' He placed his hand against my abdomen. From his tongue came the tinny stink of local liquor. 'Hard!' I sucked in again; his hand pushed into me, 'Keep going, keep going,' he said. I was running out of strength but the man held the hookah, and my stomach, firmly. 'Keep going, keep going ... now, slowly ... breathe out.' He relaxed his hand. I let out a thin line of smoke towards the ceiling, and followed it with a furious coughing fit. My guide laughed and returned to his original place. I was relieved to have him away from me, to pass the hookah on. I turned to the two women and offered one of them the pipe, but the man on my left took the hookah from me, shaking his head. I could still feel the warm patch on my stomach where the hand had been.

Ghulam Hussain soon took over the conversation with a loud Bengali discursion that his friends responded to with studious nods. Any attempts at rebutting or interrupting him were met by hard choruses of reproof from the others. I listened to him with a small sense of comfort, as if his authority somehow validated my presence here. The shirtless man was quiet now. Occasionally he mumbled to the two closest to him. Did the murmurs relate to me, there was no way of knowing— the Bengali people weren't well-liked in this part of the country, and as a child I'd never been encouraged to learn their language. But Ghulam Hussain and his friends interspersed their conversation with occasional words of Urdu and English—'Government', 'Army', 'Elections', the names and titles of the country's powerbrokers, 'Bhutto', 'Yahya'—and I seized on these almost desperately. The coal of the hookah died down, temporarily recovered in small red sputters as I sucked in more hash. The others had stopped smoking. I put the mouthpiece on the floor. I wanted to lie down, or to at least put my head against the end of the mattress, if it wasn't for the two women. I lowered my face, stocky toes in the corners of my vision like hordes of beetles.

'Shahbaz sahib!' The man across from me called out. 'Kya mehsoos?'

I looked up, not knowing the word he used.

'Theek hain, aap?' the man asked.

'First class,' I replied. I looked at Ghulam Hussain. He was grinning. He picked up the hookah and again held it out to me. 'Still a little there. Finish it.'

I raised my hand. 'I've had enough.'

Ghulam Hussain laughed. 'It's no problem, Shahbaz bhai, take it, take it.' I took it and inhaled again.

❧

I opened my eyes and found the quarter empty. Their voices came at me from outside, and through the door's wire netting were vague human forms on charpoys and large amber waves of a fire. The women weren't on the mattress anymore, but who knew, maybe my lying on it would still breach some custom, provoke outrage and wounded honour. I placed my head on the soft end and closed my eyes again.

I couldn't sleep here. I walked outside. Ghulam Hussain lay on a charpoy in shalwar and undershirt. The radio was now with him.

'Haan ji. You want to go back, Shahbaz bhai?'

'Yes,' I said. 'Let's go.'

He was still in his undershirt, and he brought the radio, humming softly to the tune that came wafting out from it, and set it on the front seat between us. Back in Saddar the streets were abandoned except for one cyclist, a trio of men walking hand-in-hand-in-hand, and a tobacco kiosk that was still lit. The Palace cinema hall with its large, hand-painted poster of Sean Connery holding a thin Walther PPK, whose grand lights and long queues gave it life earlier in the evening, now looked vacant and on the verge of decay. The tobacco man's eyes caught mine as we drove by, and remained fixed on me until we were out of range. Tomorrow morning, he'd be too busy selling something to stare like that. In front of the Khyber, Ghulam Hussain rejected the five rupees I removed from my wallet. Following our daily ritual I insisted and he eventually gave in. I climbed the long flight of steps to the reception, where Doli, still awake, sat behind his desk with red resentful eyes, rubbing his teeth on a miswaak twig. Another man, in a champagne-coloured shalwar-kameez lay sleeping on his back on the leather sofa in the hallway by the reception, one hand under his head, the other around his crotch.

'Sirji, your father.' Doli removed the miswaak from his mouth. 'He called again.' He threw my room key onto the counter.

From the window of my room I noticed that Ghulam Hussain was still there, sitting in his car downstairs, doing apparently nothing. Just waiting. The next time I checked, after pissing and washing, he was gone.

∾

It was more than just liking him. I was drawn to him from the start, before and even after I understood the threat I posed to him. This thing, this being-drawn-to-him, was something I wish I could have explained, especially when I'd committed my crimes against him, but my Urdu was and still is far too weak. So that if I saw Ghulam Hussain again today, his injuries healed or not, and he asked me, why did you do what you did, I would still be unable to describe my special affection for him. All that would be left would be to explain the bigger picture.

3

My driver's sleeves were rolled back. He sat across the table, at a café on Burns Road, and as we waited for our breakfast I couldn't help stealing glances at the scar he got from the riots, a discoloured strip of tissue, the mark of the state on flesh, that looked like a worm or leech half dug in. Drawing blood from his fat forearm. No such marks on me. The waiter brought over an aluminium jug, filled Ghulam Hussain's glass with water, and after he filled mine, Ghulam Hussain said, 'No bhai jaan, sahib has an English stomach!'

'Achha?' the waiter said, squinting and smiling. 'Then he won't drink our water.' His voice was rich with ridicule. When he moved to take my glass, I stopped him. 'No it's okay,' I said. I took a tiny sip and let it sit in my mouth before finally swallowing, as if that would kill the toxins. Ghulam Hussain gulped his down without a thought. He eyed my glass for a moment, and once the waiter had left us, said, 'You have bottled water in the car, right? I'll get it for you.'

'No, no,' I pleaded. 'This is fine. I don't drink much water when I eat.' This was a lie.

'I drive a lot of foreigners around,' he said. 'I always have to stop somewhere where they can buy mineral water.' He laughed disparagingly. 'What, over there you don't drink tap water, only Evian-shevian? That's what the foreigners always ask for, Evian-shevian.'

I took another small sip, my rite of passage, as it were. What resentments these people must have harboured for me, like foot soldiers' for the civilian.

'Ah-haa!' he exclaimed at the appearance of our parathas and tea, brought to us in aluminium plates and mugs. The table, with its asymmetrical legs, tilted this way and that as Ghulam Hussain shifted his arms, rubbed his hands. He had a muggy smell, too, which spooled across to my side. 'In France what-what did you eat for breakfast, Shahbaz bhai? My uncle wasn't cooking for your father anymore, so, what, you ate those sausages and things?'

I shrugged.

'Omelettes?'

'Sometimes,' I said.

'What-what do the French put in their omelettes? Masala? I'm sure they wouldn't, na? When I first came to Karachi from East Pakistan, that was my business.'

'What?' I asked.

'My father used to cook for a woman, a Pathan woman, in Clifton. She'd be asleep by ten at night. Then my business would start.' He dipped a wedge of paratha into his tea and chewed noisily, producing a thick *chup-chup-chup* from behind his buckteeth. 'My friends would come at around eleven, twelve at night. I'd take out charpoys and put them in the lawn. Take five rupees from each of them for the night, and for breakfast in the morning. The begum didn't know a thing. She unlocked the front door at around eight in the morning. She used to sleep lots. Oof, that lady needed her sleep.' He laughed, half-chewed morsels of paratha hanging on his tongue. 'My uncle would go inside by eight. Begum-sahib would be taking a bath and getting ready upstairs. I used to rush in and take some eggs and milk and bread, make my friends breakfast. And I would throw everyone out before begum-sahib came down. By then I'd fed those sisterfuckers all the omelettes they could eat. She had no idea where all her eggs were disappearing. She thought my uncle was eating them. Bhainchod, how many eggs can one man eat!' *Chup-chup-chup*.

How long did he continue this scam before getting exposed?

'I don't know, some neighbour mentioned it to her, just by chance. Meaning, some neighbour was talking to her one day and said something like, "Yes, and your back lawn is full every morning." That bastard-woman ruined my business. And everyone missed my omelettes. But I still make the best. Whenever you want to eat an omelette, Shahbaz bhai, you ask Ghulam Hussain.'

'Certainly,' I smiled.

'Not just omelettes,' he raised his voice. 'Anything. When you need to buy a car, you ask me. I'll get it like that,' he snapped his finger, 'first-class, guaranteed.' He licked the grease from his fingers. 'I make life easy for money people, Shahbaz bhai. Cheap car parts, gun licences, mujhra dancers, at a day's notice, like that.' A press secretary for the black market, he sipped his tea thoughtfully. 'Now, Shahbaz bhai, this land problem of yours. What-what is happening?'

'Land problem?'

'My uncle says you are here because of a land problem. Tell me the full story.'

I didn't like him knowing this. But I felt he'd shared a part himself just now and that it was only right for me to give back. But how to explain? The *full* story? Even half the story was too intricate for my exhausted Urdu. I poured water into my driver's glass. 'Bas, it's a big problem,' I said. 'I don't even understand it myself.'

'*Land* matters, Shahbaz bhai,' he laughed, shaking his head from side to side, as if those two words alone were enough to explain everything. 'Land matters.'

He drove me back to Saddar. The city was in a period of calm, the riots that my father followed from Paris with post-patriotic zeal in the foreign news had ceased, the dictator Ayub Khan was gone, and shopkeepers had taped sheets over their broken windows. Saddar was as I remembered it, with Empress Market at its centre, more like a cathedral than a market, European Gothic with its own tropical adjustments, where the British in their day could monitor local commerce, policemen and health inspectors always on alert, ready for quarrels and the spread of local infections. When they taught us this at Grammar School I remembered thinking, who's keeping the order now, now that the British have left? We drove past a series of apartment buildings, square yellow, green, and grey blocks. I was meeting Mona Phuppi at noon to take the train to the orchard, and I was damned if I was going to spend the intervening time in the Khyber. I asked Ghulam Hussain to wait for me outside the hotel while I did a round of the market. I walked deep into Bori Bazaar, where the market shut out the rest of the city. I paused at a junction that led to four lanes, a third-world Amsterdam, pedestrianized, tourists and locals on cobblestone, lane after lane. Arbitrarily, I chose a lane. Everyone was bargaining, promises of the best price, best quality. 'Ya Allah!' wailed a beggar whose eyes were pale and seized my image for an instant before he walked on. Where did this mad theocrat fit in the scheme of things? I turned around and hurried ahead, out of the lane into an open boulevard. I could see, on my left, the mud-yellow walls of the Khyber Hotel. I walked back towards the Morris. As Ghulam Hussain drove me to Cantt Station, humming his Bengali tunes, my head and chest filled with anxiety— the same anxiety I used to feel as a child before every new encounter with my aunt.

At five to twelve, she shuffled through the door of the station's waiting room with a handbag strapped around her shoulder, and the male servant trailing her with a picnic bag of water and chips and fruits and greasy Irfan Bakery boxes. We greeted each other according to standard: I put my hand to my forehead and said, 'Mona Phuppi, adaab,' and she responded with, 'Jeetairaho,' a condescending hand to the side of my face. She was tall for a Pakistani woman. Her skin looked stretched and pasty, her hair short-shiny-stiff, which meant she might have resorted to wearing a wig. Or perhaps she'd always had one. Out of breath, she instructed me to wait while she bought our tickets.

'Chalo, chalo!' she exhorted when she returned from the booth, called to the servant, 'Munir!', and the three of us rushed to the train. It wasn't terribly hot, but Mona Phuppi had bought First Class A/C tickets for me and her. She took the picnic bag from Munir, handed it over to me, and sent the servant off with his Third Class ticket to the rear. Our compartment had two green velvet sofas for three facing each other. A couple shared the compartment with us. As the train started—how strange, we were going to the orchard—Mona Phuppi lit a cigarette, despite the look of denunciation from the neighbouring couple at a Muslim woman smoking in public. And despite my occasional coughs and fanning the smoke away from my face, she didn't make any effort to aim her exhalations.

'Here.' She passed me a box. I started on the two patties in them. 'Next time we come here, we can take the Super Highway to Hyderabad,' Mona Phuppi said with an indulgent smile, as if she were promising her nephew a special treat. The window didn't yield much of view, save for telephone and telegraph poles and wires cordoning the Sindhi desert. My aunt stretched her legs and put her hard grey heels on my seat next to my thigh. She rotated her feet at the ankles. We sat watching each other.

'Years ago,' she began, 'before the government took it away, I wanted to plant banana trees in the orchard. You and your father were already in Paris. Bananas are lucrative, so why not? So. I had some bananas planted, and then Ghazanfar finds out. Aaand . . . he *throws a fit*. Throws a *fit*!' She looked up towards the ceiling, and raised her hands in wonder, beseeching a higher force. 'Arrey bhai, what's wrong with planting bloody bananas in the bagh. But no, Ghazanfar is angry because I didn't consult him. He's sitting in Paris, and he wants to be consulted on every bloody thing.' She put out her cigarette in an ashtray. 'Achha, *then*. The mangoes we had weren't really good quality. We could barely sell them in any good market. So I thought, high time to get rid of these mediocre ones and plant some *good* mangoes. Again, Ghazanfar says nothing-doing. What do you mean nothing-doing, it's *done*. I mean it's just . . .' She slapped her tongue against her palate in loud smacks, followed by sips from her bottle, the attack on my father having dried out her mouth.

She put her head back and closed her eyes. I wanted to tap my fingernail against the hard grey heels to see if she noticed. She leaned forward and spread her shawl to cover her feet, without opening her eyes. She emitted an occasional complaining bleat from her gullet. The gentleman next to us turned the pages of a newspaper roughly, persistently, and with almost every crackle Mona Phuppi opened a censorious eye.

We had more than an hour's wait in Hyderabad. A People's Party jalsa was taking place near the station, and we sat silently through the exhortations against the army, the pledges that Zulfiqar Ali Bhutto would restore all the ground lost in the '65 war against India, that he would redistribute land and wealth in the country. The closing exchange between speaker and crowd had the latter screaming 'Zindabad' to a list of proper names:

Zulfiqar Ali Bhutto?—Zindabad!

People's Party?—Zindabad!

Pakistan?—Zindabad!

'You know,' my aunt said. 'If Bhutto comes to power, we won't get our hands on one more acre of our land. With his Mao cap, promising a home for every bloody commoner in the subcontinent.' She slept some more during the hour to Mirpurkhas. My adversary, calmly leading me to the site of skirmish. She awoke briefly, and in half-sleep offered me a pear from her basket. Mirpurkhas was far more urban and busy than I remembered it. Munir found us a tonga, and sat in front, while Mona Phuppi and I sat at the back, fighting against the sloping seats as the horse traversed pebbly

ground. Two boys ran alongside, throwing scraps at the
horses; the tongawalla swiped at them with his stick—
'Chalo, dafa ho!'—to which the kids laughed from their
safe distance from him. Munir found something to
throw at them and, still laughing, the boys left us. We
got off at the entrance to the deputy commissioner's.
Across the street was the orchard's boundary wall. It
was an odd sensation, standing here again, after so long,
being so close to it. After the confiscation, there'd been
a sense of melancholy and of the abstract in my father's
conversations about the orchard, as if it were a lost
vision or a forgotten language. Now it was real again,
breathing right across the street.

'We'll just see if the DC is in,' Mona Phuppi said, and
led me through the government compound's gate. Munir
waited on the pavement outside. The deputy commisioner
had visitors, whom he interrupted when he saw my aunt
at his door, and came to greet us. He invited us for a late
lunch in his office, once we were done with the orchard.

My heart sped as we crossed the street, apprehensive
of the rush of the past, of things better left alone. I
wanted to turn back, but my aunt walked quickly, large
rather than small steps, her arms swinging confidently.
The outer wall was soiled, and with chunks broken off
along the top, revealing old grey underneath. The entrance
gate, rusty and unused, was beaten out of shape on one
side. We walked through, but stopped only a few feet in,
as if the rest was forbidden to us. No matter how
romantic my memories of it, the orchard certainly
couldn't have looked like this: there were dwellings
everywhere, most of them loosely put together, with logs
holding up corrugated tin roofs, and large sheets of
cloth hung across to form walls; other roofs were made

from hay and all kinds of twigs piled atop beams of wood; from some of the trees hung ropes with tyres tied at the end, and children sat swinging on them. 'You see?' Mona Phuppi said, and the two words seemed to echo and echo. Some of the little homes were made of mud bricks—one was being built as we stood there. Clotheslines criss-crossed across the plot, with wet kurtas and shalwars strewn on them. *You see.* Her gaze as she looked at me standing by her side was merciless, she was gloating like the overseer of some torture who didn't herself have to touch bones or blood. A woman climbed a bamboo ladder to the rooftop to say something to a man hammering something. A few of the homes had light blue water geysers outside.

Everything was brown and hazy. A part of my childhood had been smashed and this is what remained. *You see.* The place was smaller than I remembered it. I remembered the distance between the opposing boundary walls being endless, but now, though it was still far away and indistinct, the opposite wall was visible. The orchard was big but not as immense as the heavens. It wasn't like seeing the place nineteen or twenty years later, but seeing it in an earlier era, an earlier century. 'Look at it. It's been this way for years,' my aunt continued. 'This is what happens when a nice property goes into government hands. When they hand over the deeds, they'll hand over these bloody haris, these squatters, as well. If your Abba wants them, he can be my guest.'

'Who'd buy this?'

'Oh, there's always someone to sell to. Whatever price we get we should just be happy and take it.'

Two labourers came out from inside. They stared at

us menacingly as they exited the compound. Many of the children were also staring at us now. Until then, there seemed a safe distance between us and them, as if we were in a separate area that absorbed the awfulness of the place, but now we were exposed to the savage looks and sounds—metal, brick, loud illiterate Sindhi speech. 'I'll talk to Abba,' I said.

In his office, the DC gave us tikkas from the nearby market; I ate only half of mine, claiming a bad stomach. Mona Phuppi dominated the conversation, which was almost entirely devoted to the elections, how Yahya should arrange it just right so that neither Bhutto nor Mujib would win a majority, the army would stay on.

'Bhutto will win majority in the West, Mujib in East—'

'But not enough for a majority, DC sahib.'

The thought of squatters overrunning the orchard had never crossed my father's mind.

'This country doesn't need politicians,' Mona Phuppi declared. 'For the first ten years we had them and where did it get us?' Our host made an effort to respond but she cut him short, 'Abhey chorain, DC sahib! Mohajirs are the only ones who can run the country. If not them, better the army.'

I wondered, still, whether my father would agree to the sale.

At maghreb, Mona Phuppi asked the DC for a prayer mat. He directed her to his own bathroom for wahzu, and once she was out a peon gave her a mat, which she took to a neighbouring room. 'Aap bhi . . .?' the DC asked me. I shook my head. I hadn't prayed in years, the last time being at an Eid assembly at the Pakistani embassy, off the Champs-e-Lycees. When we finally left the DC's compound I wanted to have a final look at the property to see if, with the initial shock now gone, it would appear just as treacherous. But it was getting dark, and immediately Munir found a tonga that we mounted.

4

The electricity at the Khyber went off in the morning. As the fan teetered to silence, the heat settled on and around me like cement. The sheets were soon soaked through with sweat. In between dream and consciousness, when it was already early morning, I thought that the woman from last night was still in the room with me, felt her presence like the heat, so that I was relieved to open my eyes and see nobody.

When we were done I'd stared at her naked back, its thin region of hair at the start of her spine and tiers of flesh around her waist. After orgasm, I was confronted again by the black beneath her fingernails, her hard feet, the small tyrannies of her body and profession. It was an offensive vision, and I'd wanted to lean in, put my hands around her neck and expel the last breath from her body, from our little crime. She'd turned around and rottenly flashed me a smile, and I told her then to put her clothes on and leave.

'I should leave? But you paid for the whole night.'

'I know. But it's okay. You can go. Tell Doli I said you could go.'

'What's wrong bhai jaan, you don't like me?' She'd said this teasingly, looking down at her chest and cupping her breasts. 'But you moaned like a girl.' She sat up in bed, her feet tucked under her, her arms hanging loosely along her torso, meeting between her thighs. How I hated the way she was so comfortable in her nudity. I reached for my shalwar, told her I was tired. 'Chalo! Five minutes and the guy's tired! You reading-writing people, you should stick to your books.'

The fan started again. But the noisy Saddar streets wouldn't allow me any more sleep. My stomach was tender, but wanted food. The mattress had given me a backache. I opened my door and picked up the *Dawn* on the floor in front of it. I picked up the Urdu newspaper too, even though I wouldn't read it. I'd given Doli fifteen rupees for the month to bring me an English paper every morning. He'd agreed, then asked, 'What, you don't read Urdu, sir?'

I wanted to use the bathroom, but I didn't want to squat over a hole-in-the-ground toilet; I held the shit inside me, showered and changed and went to the small dining hall, past the first-aid box attached to the wall. I greeted Doli in the dining hall. Neither of us mentioned last night's woman. His parathas and egg this morning revived me a little. I didn't have anywhere to be yet, but I wanted to be out of the Khyber as soon as possible. I walked up one block into the pits of Bori Bazar. My first stop was a bar on a street corner. The seating arrangement comprised three columns of wooden booths with green and red back supports of artificial leather. I sat at one of the booths in the middle column, with my back to the street, and ordered a Murree beer. One booth in front of me was occupied by three men, two sitting in the seat that faced me who both eyed me, sipping a clear local liquor. My beer arrived in a tall green bottle, the Murree label wet and peeling off. 'For beer, it's not too early?' the waiter said. I asked for a glass (I'd been advised never to drink straight from the bottle because of the places where these bottles were stored). It *was* too early in the day for beer, but I went on drinking.

My father had called last night and said he wanted me to find a man, an old friend of his, a retired brigadier. Brigadier Alamgir. This was the first I heard his name. He—this man, this brigadier—owned a hotel, the Agra, and I should find him there, my father said. Last he heard he was still running the place. Might be a better place to stay, my father said, funny I didn't think of it sooner, I'm sure he'll put you up at a special rate, an old-old friend. When I asked my father why he didn't call this old friend himself, at least to let him know I'd be coming to see him, he said no no, it would be fine, I should just show up and tell him who I was. I wasn't particularly keen, but it was after all something to do.

The news of the squatters hadn't affected my father the way it should have. I suppose one would have to see it for oneself, the poor haris eating away at the land like salt into leather, to know how irretrievable the orchard of old times really was. He was incensed by the idea of selling the property, not realizing, not having *seen*, that the orchard was lost already. Beta, he said in his old-fashioned patronizing tone, that property has been with us since the beginning. So he insisted that I stick around and block his crazy sister, that eventually she'd give up, that it was vital for me to be there when the ownership deeds were handed over.

I drank my beer and a filial anger warmed inside me

like a fever. Through his twisted strategies and his twisted life, my father had dislocated me even within Karachi. I was a gatecrasher in Ghulam Hussain's world, without the stomach for it. And now I had to fight my aunt. This battle was part of my father's effort to keep a part of Pakistan in him, it was the failed idea of exile and I was being made to endure it. I nursed this feeling for hours, several beers, in that hot booth. When I came out, I hailed a cab and asked the driver to take me to Clifton. There was a long, single-lane road to Clifton, surrounded by sand, where if a car came from the opposite direction, one would have to get off the road. Nothing in itself here was recognizable, but there was a smell and something else less distinguishable that compressed nineteen years into a fierce couple of moments. I felt I'd still find our old house, one storey, three bedrooms, mine to the left of the entrance, the window looking out into the garden and street. 'Try that road,' I told the driver. I remembered it was somewhere behind the Mohata Palace, and we tried a side lane, a main road, another street off the main road, where I saw someone who could have been the grown-up form of the mongoloid boy who lived a street away from us. But we didn't find the house, and after several minutes even the cabbie's indulgence was ebbing. 'Ask someone from home,' he said.

I got off at the Clifton promenade, and the cabbie said he'd wait. Shirtless labourers relaxed under or around the red sandstone pillared kiosk of the Jehangir Kohtari Parade. I walked on the pathway towards the sea, and in my path a tall white man in a white suit had one leg trapped in the obstinate arms of a beggar girl, who'd glued her whole upper body to the leg as though it would save her from drowning in the warm concrete. The man's female companion smiled, but the man's expression showed more and more grief. From trying to disentangle himself with his hands, he resorted to using his free leg against the girl with a genuine force. The white woman took some notes out of her bag and showed them to the girl. After some attempts at rejecting the sum for too little, the girl reached out with one hand. The lady let her have one of the notes, held a second one just beyond the girl's reach until she let go of the man's leg completely. With the negotiation complete, the visiting couple—she still with an expression of amusement, he of scorn—walked on. As they passed me, I smiled at them, but got no response. I, too, walked on. A small boy, squatting in my path, made an attempt at my legs but missed. I increased my pace to be out of the beggars' province.

The Parade's colour darkened, the clouds filled with red and looked themselves like sandstone, suspended miles above us. Small groups collected around the pavilion. So much of a city's value depends on what it offers the lonely. In Paris, at age thirteen or fourteen, I'd walk along stretches of the famous Bois, where hookers waited for customers in their parked vans (you could always identify these vans by their blinking lights). The thrill of summoning the courage to knock on a window, even if only to be told, 'T'es trops jeune, mon petit,' was enough to make an afternoon. When I'd see men go into those vans, I'd stand only a few feet from the van, awed by the situation, that behind that silly door, was . . . what? Sex. Life. A kind of freedom. And sometimes, when I was feeling bold, I'd go right up to the side of the driver's seat and see if there was a small parting in the drape that would give me a bit of a view.

Once I was sixteen or so the women were slower to dismiss me, asking my age, looking sceptical, like cops, at my claim of eighteen. On occasion one of them would smile and give in (even if not finally convinced), invite me into the back of her cold, bedded van where she'd free my quivering legs from my trousers, bring me to erection, and, just as quickly, back to limpness. In the beginning my heart used to beat with terror as the van's side door would open. My thoughts would fill with possible conspiracies—a pimp arriving on cue to harass me for more money, a policeman to take me to a juvenile facility and inform my father. But I came out every time, unharmed.

As I grew older, I sought the darker corners of the city, the streets of Pigalle and Rue St. Denis. The women were cheaper than the ones in the vans who, under the same underworld edicts, all charged the same rate. But the areas around Rue St. Denis and Pigalle were entirely ungoverned. Men and women fucked you to bankroll their habits. One night, a girl looked at me from the corner of her eye, smiled as we passed each other. I stopped, turning my head to keep her in sight. She'd walked on a few feet but when she realized that I'd stopped, she walked back. 'Salut,' she said. Her hair was short, bluish, and she couldn't have been out of her teens. 'Salut,' I replied. A man with dirty blond hair and a thick Jewish nose approached me; the girl moved back a couple of steps.

'Tu aimes ma pièce?' *Ma pièce*, he called her. His property. 'Tous ce que tu veux,' he said. 'Vingt francs. Puis cinq francs pour la chambre.'

I followed the girl to a small motel, paid the concierge five francs for the hour. Once we were inside the room,

I gave the girl her twenty francs. She then pulled out a syringe from her hand bag. I objected to her using it, but she said she couldn't do what we were about to do without. 'This scares you?' she asked, rolling up her sleeves, forcing me to watch.

'No,' I replied. I tried not to avert my eyes as she sank the needle into her arm.

She put her equipment away, took a moment to absorb whatever she'd injected, and then sat on the bed in front of where I was standing. There was blood on her sleeve. She unzipped my pants, pulled my penis out and stroked it roughly.

'You're not going to take your clothes off?'

'Not for twenty francs,' she said.

'But your friend said—'

'Non,' she said. 'Pas pour vingt francs.' She was still stroking me, angrily. I bent down and stopped her.

'Your friend said sex. If not, give me my money back.'

'Already spent it,' she said.

'You've spent it?' Switching to English, I raised my voice, 'When the fuck did you spend it? How the fuck could you have spent it?'

'Yes, fuck, fuck, fuck.' The familiar English word had provoked her, her voice now was full of venom. 'I told you I spent it.'

Switching back to French, I said, 'Then take off your clothes.'

'No.'

'Take off your clothes. If not . . .'

She leaned back in bed to give me a fuller view of herself, stretched out her palms. 'What are you going to do?' She smiled, daring me to violence. And gaining confidence from my immobility, she said, 'You treat me like a bitch, I'll act like a bitch.'

'I don't think you're a bitch.' I said that out of a short-lived faith in the sentiment, believing that all she was looking for was a man who wouldn't treat her like a whore, and that I could, through my kindness, salvage our agreement. How I'd wanted for months afterwards to go back to that scene and scream, 'Oui, t'es une putaine, une salope!' But all I did, when she remained there with her arms outstretched, outlasting me, was zip up my pants and rush out of the motel. I was still shaking with humiliation and rage when I took my seat in the metro home.

Weeks later, on that same corner, in daylight, I saw the girl's pimp with the Jewish nose crossing from the opposite side. Many times I'd daydreamed about meeting him again and getting justice. But our only interaction was a moment's eye contact as we passed each other. I was sure he recognized me. And I knew that when the daylight subsided, he'd transform back into the raider who sifted and trapped men like me.

After that encounter I came to see the ladies in the vans on the banks of the sixteenth arrondissement as my only friends, ministering to my solitude without intermediaries and collaborators. That was their function, to console me, to console the immigrant. Their higher fee was the price of amity and safety. Now, as I stood at the far end of the Clifton Promenade, I missed seeing those vans. For the twenty or so minutes that I spent in the back of them, under the maternal attentions of the older proprietors, I forgot the unstable city that waited outside. Even during the demonstrations of May '68, when history enfolded Paris, when the young embraced it without fear of the harm it would inflict on their bodies, making the city less comprehensible to me, it was to the solace and security of those vans that I'd escape, where the smell and sting of teargas, the sounds of bodies and metal and glass clashing, was far, far away.

And it was to one of those vans that I now wanted to go. The clouds above the Parade looked worn out, like abating foam. In Karachi I could find no retreat; even when Doli brought a woman to my room it wasn't an escape from the city—the woman carried its pathos to the place where I slept, to my naked body. This idea suffocated me. Even the sea in front of me felt like a barricade. My stomach tightened. I knelt down, my hands against my knees, ready to vomit. But nothing came out and the ache remained. At that moment I wanted so frantically to be back in Paris, away from Karachi. Even away from my father. Back to a place where land didn't matter because there was never hope of owning much of it. Back where I could seek the therapy of an anonymous woman.

By the time I got back to my room at the Khyber, I had the city's filth under my fingernails, the smell of high tide, which brought the sea right up to the roads, on my clothes. I undressed and lay on the bed in my underwear. The rough wool of the blanket scratched against my back. Someone upstairs was taking a shower, the water so loud and close that it seemed to be cascading around the walls of my room. When two or more guests showered at the same time, the water was colder than usual. I waited for the sound to stop.

❧

The air of the Agra Hotel's cabaret was chalky with cigar and cigarette smoke. The tables were small and round and covered in carmine cloth; the crowd was middle aged, brown and white. Their dress was modest but elegant, mostly fitted shirts and bellbottoms on the men. Dancers loitered around, waiting to be courted. Others stood on the wooden spot-lit stage, behind them the band members sitting or standing with silent instruments. I sat down and signalled to the waiter, asked for a vodka-lime. In the microphone the master of ceremonies cleared his throat, announced: 'This next one, friends, is from Bobby Short.' The band's jazzy rendition and a male baritone filled the saloon, two dancers awakened into a jerky routine. A Pakistani-looking woman staggered across the saloon from her table to another, occupied by three men, all foreigners. She shook hands with two of them, then dropped into the lap of the third, laughing and wiping his sleeve and thigh where his drink had spilled. When the Bobby Short piece finished, the master of ceremonies bantered in his laboured British accent, then announced, 'This next one, my friends, is in German. By Marlene Dee-trish. Dee-trick, excuse me. The lovely, famous Marlene.'

'You are okay?' said a woman at my side.

I looked up.

'No more drink?' she gestured to my empty glass. Her light-green eyes were remote and calculating; below them a round, almost masculine nose. She was shorter and thinner than the other dancers, small breasts behind the Mediterranean clatter of her cabaret outfit.

'Not yet.'

'Can I *sit*?' The last word was stretched impatiently, as if I'd already violated some custom.

'Actually, could you tell me where the brigadier is, the man ... the gentleman who runs this place?'

She stayed where she was. Then, she narrowed her eyes and in theatrical, slow motion extended her arm toward me and raised her middle finger. She prolonged the gesture—I absorbed it properly—and walked away smiling like a child proud of some delicious, wicked deed.

Before the next song, this woman, who the master of ceremonies introduced as Malika, Malika from Cairo, replaced her colleagues on stage. While there was something loquacious or excessive in the other two, there was a cool detachment in her. She didn't look at the audience at all, seemed contained within her performance, and wore an impudent smile as if she was enjoying a private joke at everyone's expense. Her front teeth sloped inward, giving her that look of a child. I was moved by the possibility that, at a price, I could have this woman. When the song finished she went straight to a grey-haired man in a dark corduroy blazer, who whispered something to her; she responded with a frown and quick shake of the head. She went back to the stage, and the band began again. I asked my waiter whether that was the brigadier, in the dark blazer. It wasn't. And where was the brigadier? He usually came in around this time, the waiter said. So he *was* still here, still in charge? Point him out to me when he gets here, I told the boy.

When the brigadier finally did show up, he was with three foreigners in shiny suits. He had thin grey hair, combed back, a large rosy forehead. There was a neat economy to his actions—closed smiles, restrained laughs—while his white companions communicated in more eager gestures, competing for his attention. He watched the performance with his elbows on the table, his arms crossed, a fixed, superior expression on a red handsome

face. I told the waiter who'd pointed him out to bring
me a bottle of Chivas Regal. When he came back with
it, I asked him to take it to the brigadier's table. He
looked confused, and only after I insisted, 'Chalo, bhai!'
did he deliver it to them, pointing in my direction. The
four men inspected me. I raised my glass. They looked
at each other, and then back at me. The white men
nodded. The retired brigadier remained still, arms crossed,
inquiring eyes fixed on me. A man in the front row, full
of booze and hope, had stood up, wobbling like a
toddler to his own awkward clap. The brigadier and his
three guests rose and were soon out of the cabaret. I
checked my watch. It was late. The waiter brought the
unopened bottle of Chivas back to me and asked what
I wanted to do with it. The song had finished, and the
dancer, too, was gone.

'Is that dancer, the one who was just on stage, done
for the night?' I asked the waiter.

'I don't know sir, maybe.' He held the bottle to me
expectantly. I told him to keep it at the bar, that I would
take it from him the next time. I left the bar and walked
into the hotel's lobby. I wasn't sure what to do. Leaving
now meant going back to the Khyber Hotel, which I
wasn't ready for. At this late hour, the Agra Hotel
seemed full of possibility, a theatre of intrigue for the
privileged, and I wanted to commune with it somehow,
join whatever indiscretions were afoot.

I approached the exit, opened for me by a midget in
a uniform and turban. I bent down and asked him, 'Did
Brigadier Alamgir leave?'

'I did not see him,' the midget replied, in a woman's
voice.

'Thank you,' I said, and placed two rupee notes in

his miniature palm. As I walked back into the heart of the lobby he said, 'Check the conference room. Maybe he's there.'

In the lobby men in black and beige suits sat on sofas. Beyond them were steps leading up to a mezzanine. I walked up the carpeted steps, to a large double door. The gold plaques on the door, one word on each wing, read 'Conference Room'. I could hear talk and laughter behind it. But as I put my ear to the doors, a male bass sounded in Urdu behind me, 'Yes sir? Is there something you want?' I turned around. A heavy man with a menacing face, like the actor Anthony Quinn's, stood over me. He had the Karachi moustache, a law enforcer's gravitas, and a lazy eye frozen in one direction—a mild deformity that carried its own threat.

'No,' I replied. 'On my way out.' I moved past him, back down the carpeted staircase. Unsatisfied, I again approached the midget in the turban. 'Excuse me. One more question for you. There's a . . . a dancer (I used the English word) here, her name is Malika. She danced this evening.' His expression was blank. 'Not very tall, a nose like this—her name is Malika. Malika from Cairo. She stays here, I think.'

'Ji, sir.'

'I need to know her room number.'

At first the midget gave me an uncomfortable grin . . . Then his small face and figure relaxed, more poised now that the truth of my character had been revealed. 'Sir,' he sniggered. 'That I wouldn't know.'

I moved a step closer to him, using my height for leverage. With a smile and a lowered voice, I said, 'But you can find out.' He tilted his whole frame back to look up at me; I thought the turban would fall from his mini head. I took a ten-rupee note from my pocket. 'I come here a lot,' I continued. 'You've seen me, right? I'm a very good customer.' He seemed unstable again. This devious negotiation would have its own inevitable course. I slipped the ten into his palm. 'Malika,' I repeated. 'Please, for me.'

His uncertain fingers closed around the money. 'Come back in five minutes,' he said.

I sat in the lobby, near the men in the beige and black. Above, on the mezzanine, Quinn walked to and fro, with an occasional glance in my direction. What went on behind those doors that a man like Quinn was charged to protect?

I went back to midget. As stealthily as I'd put the money in his hand, he now placed a piece of paper in mine. I thanked him, looked at the number he gave me as I walked away. I took the stairs past the mezzanine to the second floor. The wall-to-wall carpet there was olive green, and gave off the clammy smell of rain. The walls were painted white, the outlines of every brick showing, as a matter of style. The hallway was lit with yellow orbs in a straight line descending from the ceiling by thin golden chains. Going over the numbers on the doors, I finally stood at the last door. I put my ear to it, hearing enough to know that the occupant was in. What would I say? Why would I be at her door? I didn't want to go back to the Khyber. What gesture was there to signal my intentions? I knocked on the door. *'Kaun hai?'* I froze. She opened the door, appearing in a sleeveless, dark blue caftan. 'Yes?' Her mouth remained open in the shape of the last word.

My clothes filled with sweat. 'I'm sorry,' I coughed. 'Wrong room. Excuse me.'

She frowned, shut the door. I turned to walk away, but approaching me with quick, furious steps from the far end was Quinn. I slid back from Malika's door. With my aggressor a few feet away I tried to go past him, hugging the wall, but he took hold of my elbow in an uncompromising grip. 'Sir, sir, sir, *where* are you going?' he said. I became more aware of my own body, its limitations—organs, bone, blood. Was it biological? Was my body hardwired to cowardice? His grip relaxed, but still held me, a small grin on his face that revealed he was more familiar with conflict and bodily threat, came from a more ruthless world.

'Abhey, let go of my arm, bhai.' The words sounded even to me like forgeries from the argot of Ghulam Hussain's world, betrayed by a tentative Urdu accent. But if my opponent noticed, he didn't make an issue of it. He let go. With a wider vocabulary I would've been more capable of bargaining my way out, but my years abroad had stripped my Urdu down to a formal tongue. Now this deficiency was under special stress.

'What are you doing here?' he asked. *Goddamn you, I thought, what a waste of both of our bloody time.*

'*So?*' he persisted.

I switched to English. 'Why couldn't you be a midget?' I asked. Then it dawned on me that if he *was* from some underworld, he might also be for sale. I pulled out loose notes from my pocket, twenty in total. I stuck to English. 'Why don't you take these, and we'll call it even.' I dropped the bills to the ground. And to this he finally took offence. I heard him mutter *haramee*, before his first punch struck my face, followed quickly by a second. I fell against the wall and then to the floor with a series of thuds that were louder than the pain. I heard a door open behind me and a female voice lifted in alarm. It was Malika's. My ears still readjusting, I couldn't make out much of their exchange. But it was clear they'd come to some understanding. Quinn looked down at me, unsatisfied, and walked away. Malika helped me up, examined my face.

'Come inside, I get you ice.'

'It's okay,' I said, and tried to walk away but she gripped me in the same place the man had, and said, '*Just ...*' She asked my name. 'Shah-baz,' she tried it. 'Shah-baz. Shahbaz. Okay.'

Her room had a frayed green carpet, a darker shade than the one in the hallway, yellow walls and ceiling, with damp patches on both. A mosquito coil burned on a plate in one corner, coating the air with harsh smoke. I passed my tongue over my teeth—rigidly fixed. 'I would have hated to have lost a tooth in that,' I said.

'Sit,' she said, pointing to the bed. At the foot of the bed was an issue of *Illustrated Weekly*, with a cover picture of Zulfiqar Ali Bhutto, the leader of the People's Party of Pakistan, and the Bengali leader Mujib, both vying for civilian control of the country. I picked it up. I massaged my cheekbone, disappointed that there was no cut, no blood. Malika picked up the telephone receiver.

'Yes, it's me—yes, one-o-two—one bucket of ice, please.'

I was still shaky. I'd offered Quinn a bribe. What a craven act! When the ice arrived, Malika wrapped a few cubes in cloth and put it to my cheek.

'Hold it there,' she said.

On her bedside table was a tall glass of lassi, moist on the outside. I lifted it and gulped down the contents, which were strangely bitter. Malika lit a small gas burner that lay on the floor by the bathroom. 'I make green tea. You want?' Her voice was stretched by exhaustion and irritation, the dancer in post-production. She looked up and saw the empty glass in my hand. 'Oh, I . . .'

'I prefer this,' I said. 'I hope you don't . . .'

'Hmm.'

'Thank you,' I said.

She approached me, lowered my hand and looked at my cheek, scrunched up her face in pity. 'You're *swollen*.' She separated her syllables, unsure of her English.

'I'm okay,' I said.

She returned to her little burner. 'So why you were following Brigadier Alamgir?'

'Who?'

'*Brigadier Alamgir.*'

She came back to bed with a cup in her hand, stirring its contents with a spoon. She sat beside me, raised her delicate feet onto the bed, and held the cup on her knees. 'Men like him don't like it when men they not know buy them drinks and follow them.' There were small stains on the side of her forehead, reverberations of a childhood of skin trouble that promised they'd eventually disappear but hadn't. I imagined her hiding them, like misdeeds, behind her bulky brown hair. She blew into her cup and cautiously took a sip. High on her right arm was the circular mark of a smallpox vaccination.

I emptied the ice into my glass. 'So that charmer downstairs is a brigadier, huh?'

'Why you were following him?'

I looked around her room. 'Malika from Cairo,' I said. 'Do you bring other customers in here, too?'

'You are only man here who say no when I offer company. *This* is strange.' She smirked. 'And that man would have beat you into—how do you say, keema?'

'Yes,' I admitted.

In the middle of the bed was the gold and blue cabaret apparel she'd worn tonight. I ran my hand over it. 'Don't you ever feel exposed dancing the way you do, in front of all these, all these ... *men*?'

'*Exposed*?' she raised her pitch in surprise. 'What you mean, *exposed*? I'm *per-for-mer*. Like these ones here (she picked up the *Illustrated Weekly*). It's men, you men, sitting there drunk and your tongues out like, like this, *you* are exposed.' She watched me rub my forehead. 'Okay?'

'Yes,' I replied. 'Little dizzy, maybe.'

'Ahh. That's *nor*-mal.'

'Normal? Why?'

'Because, my darleeng,' she pointed to the empty glass on her bedside table, 'there was opium in that.' She turned off the overhead light, and we were now in the more intimate enclosure of a red lamp she had on the floor in a corner.

❧

'What would your boss, what would the brigadier say?'

But the sentiment that what we were doing was somehow *wrong*, like the guilty, beautiful bond of two children spying on an elder undressing, had filled the room. Another spell of vertigo curled in my head. 'You've drugged me, you evil woman.' I laughed, and reached for the *Illustrated Weekly* and leaned toward the light. I flipped the pages under the rouge of the lamp, not really reading. But something in one article made me stop, a reference to the Rawalpindi Conspiracy of February 23, 1951 when, according to the version I had in front of me and now read out loud to Malika, a handful of military officers and Communist Party leaders met in the home of Major General Akbar Khan to plot the overthrow of the government. The governor-general and prime minister were to be arrested upon their arrival in Rawalpindi, and Major General Khan would form a new government committed to land reform, ending corruption, holding elections, and so on. 'But news of the meeting leaked to a policeman,' I read, 'who told his superior, who then told the governor who, in turn, told the prime minister—the plot was thwarted and the conspirators went to jail.'

'What?' she said.

'My father was part of this,' I said.

She turned her head towards me. 'Yes?' Her eyes were closed.

'So they say. He and Faiz Ahmed Faiz—you know Faiz? The poet? They said he and Faiz were at that meeting.'

'They were?'

I paused.

'I don't know. But that's why we left. All of nineteen years ago.' She turned on her side now, facing me. 'But maybe we get to the bottom of this. Maybe you could do a performance of the whole thing?' I said. 'Ask your brigadier. A reenactment of the Conspiracy, on stage, for the good customers of the Agra.' I was standing now, the magazine in my hand. 'Ladies and gentlemen, the Rawlpindi Conspiracy! With the ravishing Malika from Cairo.'

'What part I'd play?' she asked, her head raised and propped on her fist.

'We'd create a part for you. A general's wife, perhaps, with good breeding like yours. Malika as Begum Shahnawaz, lustful, power-hungry, who talks her husband, the Major General—played by the brigadier so-and-so—into organizing a coup d'etat, a Lady Macbeth for our modern day.' I sat back down. 'Perhaps we'd need roles for some of your friends, more women in the Conspiracy. And a corpse or two by the end of it, demand being what it is.'

'Blood?'

'Oh yes, plenty,' I said.

'And you will play your father.'

I tossed the magazine aside. 'Now you've ruined the fun!'

'Your father.' Her voice was thin from fatigue. 'Tell me.'

'About my father?' The thought exhausted me. 'He never allowed birthday cakes onto the dining table,' I finally said. 'It was too Western for him. When we used to live here, he didn't allow anyone to wear trousers or skirts at home. In his presence we had to be dressed native, kurtas, kameezes, saris. He was hard on his actors and actresses, too—'

Malika had turned again on her back, her hands meeting behind her head. The dim light didn't hide the tiny, pointy hairs emerging on the soft tissue of her armpits, this public figure so vulnerable now. I wanted to touch her, to put my hand on her thigh. 'Yes, he made films. You know, movies? Cinema? Yes. Have you heard of the actress Zeba? No, probably not. She was one of his. He introduced her to cinema. Her career almost ended because some general or politician, big man, courted her. You know? *Wanted* her. She was flattered of course, but then my father told her that she could either be an actress or a whore, not both.' I stopped myself, but too late. It struck me that Malika herself was likely negotiating a similar bargain, and to put it in such candid, untoward language ... I got out of bed again.

On the floor, below the window, was a stack of framed drawings the size of postcards, each with the same two characters, a boy in an Afghan pugri and a girl in a veil. Spider grass crawled out of two clay pots on either side of the window and looped around the glass. The night behind them was rich navy and I thought I heard the gentle brush of high tide. I paced her room. She was still living out of suitcases, one set on the hotel desk, the other on the floor, both of them exposing piles of unfolded clothes. I stood before the suitcase perched on the desk. Cabaret material lay on top, at least three outfits. I fumbled through the rest—more caftans, shawls, underwear, two beige envelopes, small boxes of tea, more underwear, another cabaret outfit, this one turquoise. I pulled it out, its metallic frills jangling, electric and half-alive in my fingers; I held it in front of the long mirror leaning against the adjacent wall, placed it against my own body and seeing the absurd image in the mirror, I laughed. Another small surge of vertigo filled my head and limbs and threatened my balance.

'What you are doing?' Malika murmured.

I turned around. 'Nothing.' I placed the cabaret uniform back, returned to bed. Malika's eyes were shut. I lay down, put the *Illustrated Weekly* with Bhutto and Mujib on the cover behind me, out of the way. 'Where was I?' I asked.

'Actress-whore.'

'Yes, of course.' I wanted again to put my hand on her thigh, but that hesitation filled me again, and I did nothing.

∽

The taxi that took me back to my hotel from the Agra smelled of the pulp of some dead fruit. 'Bhai jaan,' I said to the driver, a boy. 'A question for you.'

'Ji sir, tell-tell,' he smiled, his widely spaced teeth scattered across the rear-view mirror.

'I hope you don't mind . . .'

'Nahin sir, nothing like that, tell-tell.'

'Where can one find a larki, a foreigner, this time of night? Not local woman. Foreigner. From outside.'

He covered his smile with his hand and ducked his head. 'Sir, I don't know about these things. I just drive my taxi.'

'No problem,' I said. 'Sorry. No problem.'

'How much?' I asked him when he dropped me at the hotel.

'Whatever you want, sir,' he said, embarrassed. I gave him the coins I had in my pockets, and climbed the long steps of the Khyber. Another day and another night, filled.

5

I sat in a leather booth in an Elphinston Street bar and ordered a beer. I hadn't slept much, thinking of the orchard, one sleepless night spent remembering those other sleepless nights, long ago. And in the Khyber Hotel bed I remembered numerous occasions when, after the others were asleep, when inside the abode of adults the card games had stopped and all the lights were off, I tiptoed away into the orchard's cool black world of insect noises and silhouettes and night-time deformations of the shapes I took for granted in the sun. Walking barefoot, despite the night, and loving the earth's touch against my soles, even when muddy. And then I decided on a spot with the mysterious rationale of a four-legged animal and settled there. From the second or third time, I took off my clothes, flung them to the base of a tree and sat down, bare ass against grass and tweeds and pebbles and mud. Sat there for what felt like hours, with my legs raised, crossed at the ankles, heels on the ground, hands enveloping knees. Nervous, of course, scared of the rustling nearby, but immobile, thrilled, not getting up and putting my clothes on and returning to my charpoy. On one occasion—and I don't remember how many such nights there were—sitting in the same position, in a different spot, without moving I succumbed delightfully to the light spasm in my groin, and felt the warm endless stream pass around and under and on my heels. Watched and heard the stuff collect and course away, and just sat there for a while longer, until I felt I could sleep. On another, or the same, night the ground was wet from early evening rain, and I delighted in the sogginess against my skin. On yet another occasion, feeling particularly daring, I took my pajama off *before* walking off, leaving it on the charpoy, so that if I got caught, if someone else was also having a sleepless night and happened to be up when I returned, they would see a naked child with no explanation for what he was doing. In the mornings that followed these nocturnal adventures—for that's what I saw them as, adventures—I was quiet, sated with my secret that nobody else knew. So when I thought back to the orchard, the day belonged to the others; the midnight to me. There was no place in the city that was like it, that midnight in the orchard.

But there was a night—and I've still not determined whether this is a false memory, or really happened—there was a night when, sitting there in the black, I realized there was another figure there, nearby, sitting probably like me, but dressed. 'Be careful of snakes, bachai,' the voice said. Was it real, and if so who could it have been? It sounded in my head like a pure Urdu, uneducated voice—did we bring servants with us to the orchard? *Be careful of snakes, bachai.* Could the figure see me, or just a vague silhouette? Could he tell I was naked, could he tell it was young Shahbaz and not one of the other kids? In this memory, or false memory, I pretended I was looking for a lost tennis ball and ran back to the veranda, seized my charpoy, put my pyjamas on, and didn't dare move. Was that the last time I ventured into the orchard's depths at night?

I finished my beer slowly, paid for it, and at the counter asked in the lowered tone of brotherhood where I could buy some opium. I didn't know the Urdu word. The barman frowned.

'Paan?'

'No,' I said. 'O-pee-um. What people have, like charas ...'

'You want charas?'

'No, *like* charas. Stronger than charas.'

'Ah, *afeem*. You're talking about afeem?'

'Afeem.'

'You do this, you get out of here, walk just four doors to the right.'

'They'll give it to me?'

'Why won't they give it? Just ask for afeem, they'll give it.'

Four doors down there was a small kiosk, a khoka, where an old man with glasses large and thick as goggles, and a mouth of toothless pink gums sat cross-legged on a stool, handling the hard, cracked skin of his heel. His hair was henna-coloured. Nervously, I made my request.

'You want afeem?'

'Yes.'

'Achha?' The old man seemed uncertain and moved reluctantly. He searched a small cabinet, then looked back at me, closed the cabinet door without removing anything from it. 'Your name?'

'My name? Shahbaz. Shahbaz Ghazanfar.'

'You have a certi-fi-cate?' He struggled with words.

'No,' I replied. I addressed him deferentially, 'Bhai sahib, do it for me, na.'

He nodded and produced a long hardcover notebook. 'Write your name and address in this,' he said. He turned its cover, and went through the lists of names with frustrating calculation, licking his aged fingers and turning the pages one at a time. My impatience grew almost unbearable with every page he flipped. 'Here,' he said, then fumbled for a pen.

'Thank you,' I said. I looked at some of the other names—the addresses were vague, such as 'PECHS, Karachi', or 'Clifton'. I wrote, 'Agra Hotel'. The old man went back into the cabinet and brought out a small rolled-up cellophane packet with a dark, almost black, paste. He named a price, and I didn't argue even though I was sure it could be brought down. I closed the book of Karachi's opium buyers and pushed it forward on the counter. He took it and put it away with the same slow precision with which he'd brought it out. 'This is in case the police ask,' he explained, apologetically. 'Obviously, we don't want to lose our licence.'

'Obviously,' I replied. But the old man went on explaining, repeating that he wasn't trying to inconvenience me, that he simply didn't want to lose his licence. I assured him again, grew more restless, but felt obliged to stay until he was finished. Finally the man said, 'Achha ji,' and with that I left him, elated, the episode a success, a sign of independence in this city. I walked back to the Khyber, where Ghulam Hussain was waiting dutifully to take me to Mona Phuppi's.

The smell of high tide reminded me, most of all, of

Mona Phuppi's home in Bath Island, where the high tide brought the sea right up to the roads and houses and one had to either leave before it hit, or wait until it passed before driving on the roads again. Mona Phuppi, of course, never let us swim on the streets with the other naked 'street kids', though there were times when we'd do so anyway, for as long as we could before getting found out, and then my aunt would reprimand all of us, make sure we bathed and in my cousins' clothes, send me home with the driver or ask my father to come get me.

It was comforting coming back to the house, a place that carried the scent of the past. Her driveway was crowded with cars, more than one household could need, two of them preserved under white sheets like new furniture. A male servant met me at the front door, and led me to the drawing room. This room had wood panelling that was capped by three neat layers of exposed red brick. Three hexagonal windows, too small to admit much sun, left the task of light to two lamps that extended a carrot-coloured shade on the room. I sat down on a two-seater, double layers of wicker on the sides and back, and cylindrical cushions against the armrests. Next to me on a lectern was a portrait of the Founding Father, Jinnah, sitting cross-legged in a greenish suit. On the wall facing me was a framed inventory of the ninety-nine names of God, written in ornate golden Arabic against a black background; the most used, 'Allah', was in the middle, in larger letters than the others. On a table below the ninety-nine names was a framed family photograph: my father on the far right in a dark sherwani, Mona Phuppi in the middle, and their younger brother, Ifti, who lived in Lahore, on the other side. On the adjacent wall, within a small black frame, a Koranic prayer was sewn into beige Egyptian papyrus. Of the Arabic words, I could make out only the 'Bismillah-e-Rehman-e-Rahim' at the top. Despite the bits of theology in the room, the carrot glow made it all look damned.

But so trapped I felt at the Khyber Hotel, that I was happy to be here, happy to have a night out. I heard the flapping sounds of a woman's slippers, and turned around to see Mona Phuppi enter the drawing room. I stood up. 'Oh, look who's here!' she exclaimed, feigning surprise, walking from the drawing room entrance to me with a sweet, frozen smile and squinted lids.

'Mona Phuppi,' I said, standing up and raising my hand to my forehead. 'Adaab.'

'Jeetai raho, beta, jeetai raho!'

She held me at a distance for a moment, with both hands at my shoulders, as if examining me after many years, before closing in on me with a hug and a parched kiss on the cheek. Her light brown eyes were similar in colour to my father's. She sat down and gestured me to do the same. 'Oof, I am ex-*hausted*. I just got back from my florists' class, this thing I'm a part of, we meet twice a week.' Her speech was slow, every word given undue weight. Her patrician English accent sounded tenuous.

'I see. How nice,' I said. 'How long have you been doing this?' I found myself adjusting my tenor when I spoke to her, to make my voice less adult.

'Three months.'

'How nice.'

She asked about my father, sent him love; I did the same for her kids, one in Manchester, one somewhere in America. The servant rolled in a tray of appetizers. I smiled when my aunt's hands shook as she raised her glass to her lips. Even when she passed a bowl of namak-parras, her actions seemed as taut as a drunkard being tested for sobriety. I'd heard so much about Mona Phuppi's madness in recent years, brief signs of which I thought I saw the day at the Yacht Club, that I found myself stirred in her presence. Behind every one of her gestures I wanted evidence of a damaged mind.

She walked to the switchboard next to the room's entrance and rang the bell twice. She walked back to her seat, slowly, making a show of her struggle on her feet. She let out a grandiose sigh, 'Oooh, Allah,' as she sat down with one hand at her back, delighting in age and exhaustion.

A servant, this one a young girl, came in to be told to go call sahib and tell him dinner was ready. She cleared the table, put the empty plate and glasses back on the trolley. Once the servant had turned her back to us, pushing the trolley, Mona Phuppi said with a lowered voice, 'Listen, you see the kapra of her kameez? The dark blue patches against the light blue background. Nice, nahin? I gave her that kapra. I still have lots of it left. I was planning on making a skirt out of it. But problem is this girl wears that damn kameez *every day*. You think I should still make it? It doesn't seem right, na, friends coming over and seeing me wearing the same fabric as the servant? I should have never given it to her.'

'Ji,' I said, noncommittal.

Phuppa Jaan joined us at the dinner table. I kept looking at the clock on the wall, and fingering the opium in my pocket. The land issue didn't emerge during dinner, except as a passing reference when she mentioned an imminent trip to Islamabad to meet with the lawyers. Mona Phuppi suggested again that I should stay with them. I asked them about Brigadier Alamgir. Haan, haan, of course we know him, they said, why did I ask.

After eating, Mona Phuppi excused herself to catch up on a round of prayer she'd missed. Phuppa Jaan assumed the role left suddenly vacant, asked some of the same questions that Mona Phuppi had asked during dinner. Voice raised, I gave him the same answers, could almost hear them reverberate in that familiar buzzing from his earpiece. He played with his thick, unbrushed beard, and then, with one hand in his mouth and the other covering it from view, he picked bits of food from his teeth, examined them, and then replaced them on his tongue. I distracted myself with the large painting of the Mohata Palace, framed on the wall behind Phuppa Jaan. He took off his glasses, blew hot breath on the lenses, rubbed them against his napkin and put them on again, a jittery man. Peering toward the dining room entrance and then, leaning forward and dropping his voice to a secretive hum, he said, 'You know, it's actually good that ... ah, in a way, that you're not staying here.' I looked at him surprised, unexpectedly offended. 'It's your phuppi,' he continued. 'Her illness (he tapped his temple softly) has gotten much worse. You can't always tell. And of course she'll insist and insist, but the fact is she wouldn't be able to handle guests, any guest, right now. These next months we have to be very careful with her.' He didn't move his lips much when talking. 'Very careful.' When Mona Phuppi returned, he went back to being the half-deaf husband.

My aunt, looking a tad weakened from prayer, lit a

cigarette and spread herself out, moving the chair back so she could cross her legs, one resting over the other more horizontally than vertically, like a man. 'So. Brigadier Alamgir, huh?' I nodded, uncertainly. '*Brigadier* Alamgir. Ha.' She took a long, smooth drag, and blew out a long, smooth trail, ashed the cigarette. 'He was never even *close* to becoming a brigadier.'

'What?'

'Haan-haan!' she hollered with a laugh. 'Call him brigadier in front of someone from the army. They'll laugh at you. Yes-yes! Flat out, *laugh*. His family, corrupt to the core. You know his father was in the railways, hain na? So? Where do you think he got the money to set up a fancy hotel? Where does he get the money to pay those dancers and all that? Oh, you think it's what he's raking in with his business? I see, I see. Ha! Please, you know as well as I do that that place loses money every bloody month. He has all this money because his father was in the railways. You know what that means, don't you beta? You don't? Did my sweet younger brother not teach you anything? The *railways*!' She repeated this as if simply doing so, with this added weight, was evidence alone, would reveal the fact of it all. R. A. I. L. W. A. Y. S. 'Ward-and-Watch. Transporting jute. Coal contracts. That whole industry runs on coal, you know that, na? Whoever you gave the coal contract to was more than grateful. There wasn't a better shop in town to make a killing. What, you think the house he has, he made with his own money? Has the army suddenly started paying enormous pensions, kya?' Again, that pleasure entered and revived her face, the pleasure of prosecuting the world. 'His father, with those enormous nostrils of his—' she turned to her husband.

'You remember how big his nostrils were? Alamgir doesn't have nostrils like that, na? No, didn't get the nostrils but the corruption, that's in the blood.' She took another hard drag. 'Our father, your dada, was the only one who didn't make a penny. He said—this is a true story, you know—he'd rather resign . . . when the people he worked for told him they would have to let him go unless he started accepting bribes. He said he'd rather be let go than take a bribe. It's true, ask your abba, he must have told you this story. Very upright, in his lovely sherwanis. A very literary mind, too, your dada. Those values . . .' She scrunched her mouth and shook her head almost in repentance. 'He would have rather died a pauper than . . . But these other people, no integrity.' And then, just as quickly as she began, she closed her case, left me to draw my conclusions and then with a smile got up and said she wanted to show me her display of flowers before I left. So in the downstairs bedroom I was shown the arrangements she made at whatever florists' group she was a part of. Delphinium, gerberas, daisies, gladioli, sharp colours, surrounded by greens. And it occurred to me that this activity, the fruits of which she displayed with such satisfaction, was part of her therapy, that there were indeed efforts underway to make her more sound and manageable. 'Very nice,' I said with each bouquet. 'Very nice.'

'Did them all myself. Aren't they pretty? Your bloody Phuppa Jaan is colour-blind so he's useless, but aren't they . . .'

'Yes, very pretty,' I repeated. I wished her the best with them.

❧

'Should I stay?' Ghulam Hussain asked, as I got out of the car at the Agra's entrance. I'd already had him for a couple of hours, and thought it unfair to keep him here, for I imagined how eagerly he looked forward to getting home, settling into whatever routine he settled into every night when he returned. As soon as I saw my affection growing I should have told him to leave and not ever come back.

'I've brought you a bouquet,' I told Malika when she opened the door. She stood in the doorway, barefoot, one leg bent, the foot positioned vertically, based on folded toes. She stared at the packet in my hand, looking puzzled. It was late, her performance, if she performed at all, over.

'Well?' I said.

Finally, she took the opium from me, but as I followed her into the room, she put a strong hand at my chest. 'No,' she said. 'You, first, you go to three-one-three.'

'*Room* three-one-three?' She nodded. 'Why?'

'You go. Then you come.'

Three-one-three. Standing outside the door was Quinn, the man who'd assaulted me the last time. The sound of a radio came from inside. Quinn knocked when he saw me, and after the loud 'Hmm!' from the room, opened the door. Facing us from a beige one-seater was the retired brigadier, or whatever he was, with something white pressed between his lips, not a cigarette. He gestured for me to come in, which I did hesitantly, and then raised his hand to his aide to suggest all was well, his duty done. Quinn shut the door, leaving me alone with his boss. The brigadier beckoned me closer with an impatient gesture, like an immobile family elder on the verge of a tantrum. This room was similar to Malika's, but the carpet was a rusty brown. The first time I saw him in proper light. It was a thermometer in his mouth, which he presently removed, inspected its reading, rinsed in the glass set on the arm of the couch, wiped dry on his shirt and put in its cover.

'Haan ji, jenaab!' he declaimed. The little hazel circles of his eyes were surrounded by small bursts of red. Only the two lowest buttons of his shirt were fastened, revealing a flare-up of white wiry chest hair. I started to speak, but he lifted his finger, moved his ear close to the radio, from which Omar Kureishi, the cricket commentator my father followed from Paris, analysed the day's play. 'Hanif's gone,' the brigadier said, shaking his head and tightening his lips, as if describing a man's death. 'We need some batsmen or we're fucked. Hopefully this kid, Zaheer Abbas, can do some damage. Believe it or not, he proposed to my wife's sister.' He lowered the volume, and gestured towards the bed. 'Please, have a seat.' Loose sleeves hung off his forearms. He set an ashtray on one arm of the couch, next to the glass of water, took out a cigarette from a thin silver case and lit it.

I remained standing.

'Why don't you make yourself a drink?' He pointed to the bottle of Royal Salute on the dresser.

'What can I . . .?'

'You should have told me you were Ghazanfar's son.'

I sat down.

'Though I should have guessed,' he added. 'The eyes and the cheekbones are unmistakably the old man's.'

'You're well-informed,' I said. Sweat collected on my forehead, under my arms. I wanted to piss.

'That's the army's occupation,' he replied. 'Or *pre*-occupation. Now fix yourself a drink. Since you're not a teetotaler like your father, thank God—speaking of which, you ever want to buy me a bottle again, Royal Salute, not Chivas, for God's sake.' He pointed again to the bottle. I walked over to the dresser and poured myself a little, filling the rest of the glass with water. I sat down. The brigadier's nails, white pointed thorns, extended perilously from his fingers. With the one on a little finger, he scraped the outer flap of his ear and wiped it on the arm of the sofa. 'So what brings you back—it's Shahbaz right?' I nodded. 'What brings you back, Shahbaz? The whiff of democracy? You could smell it all the way from, where it is, France?'

'Paris,' I replied.

'*Paghee.*' He shook his head. 'It's amazing. Ghazanfar going to France to become a sand-nigger for the rest of his life.' He leaned back, turned his face one way, applied pressure on his chin until he heard a small crack of his neck, then repeated this for the other side. He took a swig of his whisky.

'How well do you know him?' My voice had thinned.

'*How well do I know him*? Ha!' He stood up, went to the dresser, looked at himself in the mirror as he buttoned up his shirt. 'I was the only Establishment man who stood up for the devil. They would say his pictures were obscene, that he was uncivilized. I myself used to tell him, you're too bloody civilized.' His shirt now buttoned, he retrieved his drink. He sat back down, leaned forward and clutched my hand with his cold fingers. 'So how did it feel over there? Being a sand-nigger? That's what you are to them, my boy. A sand-nigger. *Pied noir.*' He placed his hands on my knees, and in a tone that betokened a convergence of interests, a new partnership between us, asked, 'So what would you call *them*, the imperialists themselves? Huh, what kind of niggers are they? *Ice* niggers, I suppose? Ice-nigger.' He stared into blank space, his moniker for white man dangling comically before us. A small smile stretched across his face. Then, he tightened his grip on my knees, shook them forcefully, and said, 'But we'll have to discuss all that the next time.'

'Next time?' I asked.

'Yes, Wednesday night. I want you to have drinks with me. Downstairs. Nine o'clock sharp.'

'I was actually wondering, sir, if . . .'

'Now drink up, young Shahbaz,' he demanded. 'I have a meeting in a few minutes, and I think I'm *just* about drunk enough to bear the company. If we talk any more you'll kill the buzz.' He chuckled, a wheezing chuckle straight from his lungs. He glanced at me, as if expecting the same from me. I smiled. 'Wednesday,' he repeated. He got up again, went back to the dresser, picked up a bottle of cologne, and worked a couple of dabs along his jaw line. I finished my drink in an unpleasant gulp and stood up, the whisky thick and hot in my throat. The brigadier walked me to the door, holding me by the elbow. Lowering his voice, resuming his tone of partnership, he said, 'By the way, Malika's not dancing tonight. I think she's going to be upstairs in her room.' At the door, he moved his grip down to my forearms, framing me for one last valuation, then pulled me into a family friends' embrace. His cologne smelled like gin.

∾

'Never make the fire too much,' Malika instructed me. She lit a low flame on her gas burner, placed a mini wok over it. 'Give the packet,' she said. I gave it to her, and she emptied the seal-brown liquid into the wok. 'Wait for water to go.' The liquid soon gave off tresses of smoke. The host of Hit Parade, Eddie Carrapiett, made small talk with his listeners from the radio before playing Neil Diamond's 'Solitary Man'. Malika got up, flicked her cigarette out the window, and coughed a spiteful cough, full of phlegm. She turned the volume up. The opium thickened into paste.

'So, who else?' I asked.

Moving about the room, she reeled off a series of names and, where required, their professions: business families, political families, painters, an information secretary, and others that she cited too quickly for me to hear.

'That's an impressive clientele,' I said.

She bent down in front of the plate with the mosquito coil, struck a match and lit the coil.

'Why you're so interested in who come to the cabaret?' she asked.

'Just seeing what kind of job your brigadier's done.'

'He had luck.'

'Yes?'

She sat down on a single seater, crossed her legs under her caftan, the red paint on her toenails starting to shrink and fade. Malika told me the story of Aida, a dancer at the Metropole, by far Karachi's most popular belly dancer, according to Malika. 'You know of Mian Kamal?'

'No,' I said.

'A cousin of Ayub, I think. He fall in love with her. With Aida. One day at last she run away with him. The Metropole go down, like that,' she snapped her fingers, smiled, gloated.

'It *went* down,' I said.

'Went down.'

'And that's when they all came here?'

'Everyone was very angry with Metropole.'

'Nothing like that has ever happened here? Dancers running off with a client?'

She shook her head. 'The brigadier! *Very strict.*'

'You're all afraid of him.'

She shrugged. She stood up and paced in small, slow circles on the carpet, her hands behind her back, playfully lifting her feet high like a soldier.

'What's his wife like?' I asked.

'They say she was very *desirée* when she was young woman. For many, many men.'

Malika lay down next to me, sighing as she did, '*Ayo.*' She looked up at the ceiling. 'He doesn't care about men who are not im-por-tent. Alamgir. Or women who are not beautiful.'

'What if they're the wives of important men?'

She turned her face to me. 'Can you feel it yet?'

'Yes,' I said. I turned on my side, propped my head on my hand, and looked at her from this elevated angle, at her dopey eyes. 'So did you ask your brigadier about the act, the Conspiracy Play? I've thought of it some more. Four men in a room: a poet, a filmmaker, a major-general, a Party leader. Stuck in a room, in a small hill station kind of place in the middle of a large orchard. Plotting their communist coup. Outside . . . standing half behind a tree . . . waits our Lady Macbeth. Begum Shahnawaz, played by the ravishing Malika.'

She put her finger on my lips. 'Shhh, no more.' She removed her hand, then turned on her side, facing me. I put my free hand on her thigh. Her lips spread slowly into a lazy smile. I smiled back. I moved my face towards her face, but just before my lips met hers she put a hand on my chest.

'No, darleeng,' she said.

No darling? I wasn't sure if she was serious, moved closer still; she applied more force to my chest.

'Do I have to pay you?' I asked.

She took my hand off her thigh and applied still more pressure on me to make me lie back down. 'Just enjoy opium,' she said, as the Beatles' 'Get Back' faded and Eddie Carrapiett concluded the Hit Parade.

'Let me pay you,' I said. I raised myself again and gazed at her. 'Why do you have me over?'

'I enjoy your company,' she replied. 'Not fun doing opium all alone.' She closed her eyes to avoid my stare. With one simple gesture, she'd made herself inaccessible to me. A week's fantasies festered inside me.

Later, when I walked down the same corridors that hours earlier had contained such promise, I realized that I'd been grinding my jaw, now stiff and aching, for a while. Shortly after I woke the next afternoon, Doli came to my room with two girls. They sat on my bed, their smiles hardened through years of duty. He asked me to choose between them. Or, if I was willing to pay for it, to choose both. He pointed to the one on the left, the slimmer and taller of the two, and told me: 'This one has no language.'

'No language?'

'No tongue.'

The girl on the right joined in to help clarify, but by then I'd understood that the girl on the left was mute. I remembered my earlier encounter with the whore who'd teased me for my 'reading-writing' ways, the woman who would probably have continued insulting me all night if I'd let her.

There was also something else that tempted me about this silent one. The power of speech had made that first woman more than what I'd paid for. When she said she felt the first signs of a cold, when she asked whether I would have guessed she was a whore if I'd seen her in the bazaar, she'd revealed a life independent of the Khyber Hotel, a life of eating habits, illnesses, companions. *This* girl, however ... I took Doli aside and informed him of my decision, paid him the money, and he made a signal at the plumper of the two, a tilt of the head towards the door. She followed Doli out, and once I'd locked the door the other girl took off her clothes. For the next fifteen minutes, the only sounds that came out of her mouth were the female sounds of copulation, sighs of pleasure, or displeasure, I couldn't tell. Her motions were largely automatic, though she did press her cheek to mine occasionally and, briefly, the tip of her cold tongue touched my neck and shoulder. In the post-coital squalor, I sat up and prepared a mixture of hash and tobacco on a day-old issue of *Dawn*. I lit the joint. The mute girl was still in the room, watching, naked but with her clothes sprawled on her lap, looking unsure of whether she still had an obligation to fulfil.

6

I didn't like the idea of being back at the Agra after Malika rejected me. It had been three days and nights since then. But I spent that time with the same bleak desperation to do something, to get away from my room at the Khyber and fill the day. I tried visiting the racetrack behind the Columbus Hotel just after the Clifton Bridge, but a famous ex-Ascott jockey was racing that day and getting a ticket was impossible without a connection inside. Amongst the few women I'd dated in Paris was one who loved horses, and for her sake more than anything else I was disappointed at being so close but not having the chance to see the famous jockey. I found myself counting the days or hours before my meeting with the brigadier. Or whatever he was.

He was already sitting near the stage with a bottle of Royal Salute in front of him when I arrived. He was lost in thought, staring at his glass and playing with its base between thumb and index. When he saw me approach, his broad smile filled his face with red. He stood up and without a word embraced me. Holding my hand, he ushered me to sit. He signalled to a waiter to bring another glass. Malika wasn't onstage yet, nor anywhere in the saloon. The brigadier's eyes were again red, though this time it seemed less from drink than exhaustion. Nevertheless, they looked on me with an almost scientific interest, searching for facts, signs of my father's blood.

'So! Here you are,' he proclaimed.

The waiter brought over a glass with ice, and the brigadier poured me a whisky. 'You want water with it?'

'I can have it without if it's a problem getting—'

'No, no,' he said. Then he turned and called for more water, which the waiter brought promptly. 'You see, we have tropical livers,' the brigadier explained while he topped my glass. 'The Scandinavians and the Finns can afford to drink this stuff neat. And the Siberians, of course. Good Lord, in the Siberian winters they have to bury their bottles in the snow to keep them *warm*—that at least keeps it at zero. So, the alcohol, by the time it's reached their livers, has already done its work. But in our climate, the liver needs water.' He handed me the glass, sat back down and repeated, '*The tropical liver needs water.*' He had a tone of reproof, a teacher making sure the day's lesson stuck. Despite my tender stomach, I clinked glasses with him and drank. I noticed his nails again—long, clean, white. His neck was thick red. Little dark hairs lined the rims of his ears.

'How's your father?' he asked.

'I'll be booking a call to him in the morning,' I said.

'Do tell him you met me.'

'Certainly,' I said. 'Certainly.'

The brigadier's shirt collars extended outward, the grey wiry mass of hair peering above the top button. He

ran a hand through his hair. 'Ghazanfar amongst the
sand-niggers,' he said under his breath, still relishing the
concept. On stage was a comic in a yellow suit and a
multicoloured tie, a thin face with thick eyebrows united
across his brow. I'd seen him the first time I'd come
here. His inarticulate jokes had included sexual
innuendoes he seemed uncomfortable delivering; the
remarks were rushed, references to body parts mumbled,
quickly followed with masked apology ('Okay, enough
with the sex talk. I see women in the audience'). Tonight
he was making fun of Memons. A few tables away a
woman and a large man with thick white hair and tinted
glasses were in hysterics. They were standing, the man
had his arm around the woman's waist, trying to compose
himself enough to talk, while the couple's seated friends
looked on.

'That's a High Court judge,' the brigadier said. 'And
his foul-mouthed wife. *Clueless* wife, I should say. I've
checked him into a room here—his favourite, on the top
floor—*three* times in two months.'

'Different women?' I asked.

He shook his head. 'One of them was some tart he
must have found in . . .' The brigadier spoke in low
tones.

'*It sort of looks like a nipple*,' the comedian said,
drawing a titter or two from the Central Asians next to
us.

'What a disgrace,' the brigadier said, loud enough for
others to hear. Then he turned his attention back to me.
He started to say something but, looking irritated, he
stopped, like a singer who'd missed his cue and decided
to start over. He shook his head, and said, 'First, where
are you staying?'

'At the Khyber. The Khyber Hotel.'

'Good God,' he shouted. 'You're at the *Khyber*?'

'Yes.'

'You know those places are usually whorehouses?'

'No, I wasn't aware.'

'You shouldn't be seen in them.'

'It's only temporary. I'm waiting to shift.'

He leaned forward and with a conspiratorial smile added, 'Not that a young man shouldn't enjoy his share of whoring. But people see you and word gets around that Ghazanfar's son prowls the brothels of Saddar. Nobody will ever believe that you're just *living* there.'

Loud female shrieks drew our attention back to the judge's table. The judge had lifted his wife onto an empty trolley. She was laughing, too drunk to resist. Her husband, claiming stridently that he was the law, drove her between the tables and chairs. The lady clutched at the sides of the trolley, laughing, wailing, as it bumped and almost tipped over. Nobody objected, most merely smiled and moved aside as the unwieldy trolley came their way. The judge finally took his spectacle out into the hotel proper; the woman's hysterics, his '*Vrooom*' effects, his repeated claim, 'I AM THE LAW,' faded into the depths of the Agra Hotel. The brigadier shook his head and hissed through a smile, then reached over and tapped my hand. 'Oh, this is mild, my young friend. The things that have happened in this place. Once right here, where we're sitting, Bhutto beat the shit out of General Yusuf for making a pass at his wife. This was when he was still foreign minister. Beat up General Yusuf right here, in front of everybody. Oh, a lot of history in this place, my boy,' he continued. 'Right there, I remember, Musa and Bhutto and a few others planning the '65 war.

I used to sit with them from time to time—you know, I *ran* the place, so . . . It started with small conversations, small fantasies that we had the advantage over India, that we could easily take back the Valley if we tried. *Right there.*' He pointed to the same table, entreating me to look again and accept its significance. I didn't know much about that war, only that it happened, in the summer of '65, that it probably ended badly for us, and that my father had tried hard to show that he wasn't the least bit concerned. 'All this talk, Bhutto or Musa saying that they could convince Ayub to cross the ceasefire line. Then the Prophet's hair disappeared in Kashmir, and all the Muslims went nuts. So Bhutto would say, Now's the bloody time! By then they would go hush if I approached. But the others didn't take it seriously, they'd have a drink with me afterwards and tell me what all was said. Joke about it, you know. But,' he looked down and shook his head, 'it happened.'

'But we never got back the Valley?' I asked.

'Never got back the Valley.' He was still looking down, repeating the line unconsciously. Returning to his senses, he pointed one last time to the area in the saloon, 'Right there. In my place. Makes me think I could've stopped it all.'

The comedian on stage said, 'Thank you ladies and gentlemen. Please enjoy your evening and, of course, your drinks. Ha. It's been a pleasure.' He bowed to some reserved and uneven applause.

'About bloody time,' the brigadier remarked. The master of ceremonies announced Malika and her band. The musicians took their positions, and my tormentor climbed the wooden steps to the stage. She was wearing the turquoise outfit that had rested at the bottom of her suitcase. It revealed almost entirely her short, bronzed legs, raised and tensed in high heels. The song was a fast-paced rendition of a Roy Orbison song. How I wished for this to falter, to go embarrassingly wrong. I turned my head again towards the brigadier, who looked set to resume the conversation.

'So you're staying at the Khyber.'

'Yes,' I said. 'For now.'

'But you must still have family here.'

'Do you know my father's sister, Mona?'

'Oh yes,' he said. 'Quite a handful, that one.'

I was surprised by the impropriety. But once it sank in, it felt liberating, opened a way into forbidden turf. 'Yes,' I said. 'Quite a handful. Exactly why I'm not staying with her.'

'Elle est fous,' he said, smiling, a bad blown up French accent. 'Elle est . . . how would you say . . . demented?'

'Dément,' I said.

'Yes. Elle est *day-mon*!' He laughed in the exalted tenor of someone who thought he'd successfully joked in a foreign language. With the smile still impressed on his face he waved with two fingers at two couples walking in together.

He turned once more to me. 'So . . .'

'My phuppi . . .'

'Yes, yes,' he frowned. 'How is Mona?'

'We're actually in the middle of a land dispute.'

A fresh bit of life entered the brigadier's face. He leaned forward, his face right in front of mine. '*Yes?*' He listened with deeper focus now as I recounted the details, his hand against his chin, index finger over his lips. After I was done, his attention again drifted, this time to Malika's performance. His head shook from side to side to the music. Ever the professional, Malika didn't look at either of us. The brigadier poured himself another drink, looked at my glass to see if it was ready for a refill. He shifted in his seat, and then began. 'Well, young Shahbaz. I'll tell you what the issue is. You, with your Western education and your nice accent and your little bits of French, are like a Bentley in this place. A nice, shiny Bentley. But you're driving amongst beaten-down Renaults and Morris Minors, with the windows that don't roll down or up . . . Now, you can't bring a Bentley to a place like *this*.' His tone was decisive, and he accompanied the final words with a tight wave of his fist, like a conductor. 'A Bentley gets scratched here. Forget scratched—broken into, torn down, different parts stolen and sold off like kidneys. You have to leave it locked up, in the garage, save it for Europe. In this place, you want to call someone you don't say, "Excuse me, sir." You say,' he grabbed me by the collar with sudden violence, '"Abhey sisterfucker, get over here!"' He'd switched to the Punjabi patois. '"Excuse me" and "please" and "do you mind" (he adopted a feminine voice, tilted his head coquettishly from side to side with each word)—that will get you nowhere, my friend.'

I laughed warily, as a man must when he's being mocked.

'Now, your Mona Phuppi is clearly a Renault. Precisely right. She has a lay of the land. She knows who to talk to and she knows *who—to—bribe*. What *you* need to do, my friend . . .' The song finished, the third or fourth of Malika's set. She bowed. The brigadier looked at my glass again. 'You're taking your time with that,' he said. Instinctively, I grabbed the glass and sipped urgently. As soon as the glass was empty, the brigadier poured me another drink. 'What you need to do, my boy.' He coughed into his fist. 'What you need to do is take care of those squatters yourself.' He took out another cigarette, tapped its base on the table, inattentively, then put it to his lips with two fine fingers outstretched, the pointy, impeccable nails shooting forth. 'I don't know how, but that's what you have to do.' He lit his cigarette. The orange cherry tightened and relaxed as he puffed. A dead weight hung over the silence. Finally the brigadier said, 'I'll tell you what. Come with me to my office right now. Finish your drink.' His tone had turned terse. I forced the whisky down, recoiled with a scowl. I wanted Malika to see me leave with him, but she was now nowhere in sight. As we left the saloon and entered the hallway, a lady in a black sleeveless top, black pants that stopped an inch above her ankle, greeted the brigadier with a flirtatious hug and a kiss on the cheek. High heels, bright red nail varnish on the toes. The brigadier introduced her as Farhana begum. I smiled and nodded. And as she walked into the cabaret, the brigadier called after her. 'Farhana begum,' he said in a mock-serious voice. 'Be-*have* yourself tonight.'

'Oh, behave-behave-behave!' And she was gone.

I followed the brigadier through the hotel, our encounter now imbued with a higher sense of purpose. The brigadier dispensed history like a professional guide. 'It's not a big hotel, only thirty rooms. We opened in the early fifties. Of course, we weren't as established as places like Palace or Metropole. For years there was one question everybody asked: why no alcohol? Couldn't get a damn licence for years because the bloody Parsi community had everyone in their pocket. The deputy commissioner here was the most corrupt man in government. On their payroll. Those bloody Parsis owned everything, the Palace Hotel, all the wine shops, total monopoly on the city's booze. And it was the army that ended up making the difference, because when Martial Law was announced in '58, we got our licence the very next day. That bloody DC was one of the first ones thrown out. The *very next day* . . . we got our licence.'

We could hear drunken laughter, male and female, in the distance. 'And then, a little luck. First there was the rebellion in Indonesia. The Dutch sent their army by air to quell it. Young soldiers in the hundreds. They'd land in Karachi, spend a day, even half a day, and then be off to Jakarta. Sometimes we gave out the same room three times in the same day. And of course the soldiers were horny buggers. Thank God for the Dutch.' We walked up the mezzanine to the conference room. Squinting, the brigadier said, 'Why do they always have to have this place so fucking bright? It's blinding, this . . .' The conference room consisted of a large oval table that covered most of the space, shelves along the walls with encyclopaedias and books about Karachi, and at the far end, by the window, another table, a little antique secretary. The brigadier opened a drawer, searched it, opened another. 'Then, the Metropole fell into a bit of a crisis when Mian Kamal ran off with one of the dancers,' he said, still rummaging, his words seeming automatic. 'You know Mian Kamal?'

'Ayub's cousin,' I replied.

'She was the most popular one they had. It ruined them. So between the Indonesian rebels and Mian Kamal's lechery, our place became the place.' He slammed the drawer, '*Arrey bhai, where the hell* . . .' and opened a third one. 'Ahh! Here we go. He pulled out a plastic box of contact cards, searched through them and finally pulled one. Taking a pen from his inner coat pocket, he copied the details onto a piece of paper and gave it to me. 'Rahim sahib,' he said. 'A friend of mine. You should see him. You have a car?'

'Yes.'

'You know your way around?'

'I have a driver,' I said, proudly.

'Good. Tell him to take you to Lalukhet, to the police station. Rahim sahib's the SHO there. They moved him out of the Ferozabad thaana, around the corner from my house, because he tried cracking down on the nice little prostitution ring the other officers ran.'

'He can help?' I asked.

The brigadier nodded. 'He was stationed in Mirpurkhas a little while ago. That's where your orchard is, right?'

'Thank you,' I said, putting the paper in my shirt pocket.

'Don't waste time on this, my boy.'

As we left the conference room, the brigadier declared 'Okay, young Shahbaz!', and now even if I wanted to go back to the cabaret I felt I couldn't. We walked down the steps to the lobby.

'Adaab,' I said.

'Jeetairaho,' he smiled, and tapped my cheek. I'd just devolved to him the authority of a family elder. I'd said 'adaab' and now I would have to say it every time. He walked away, and I could still feel his cold palm at my face.

7

The local imitations of Western aromas reached a person on foot at least a block or two before Perfume Market itself, an oasis of sweetness in the guts of hot Saddar. Two lanes, back-to-back, were each lined with small shops. I stopped at one. Its shelves were covered from side to side with little see-through bottles labelled Dare Devil, Cast Away, B-Man, Emperor, other names. I asked the kid behind the counter to give me the most popular imitation he had, and he picked out a bottle labelled Cool Water, administered a small sample on my wrist.

'How much?' I asked.

'Eight rupees ... okay, for you, six rupees.'

'Well then give me one,' I said.

'Right now we only have the concentrate. We'll mix it with alcohol for you. You come back at ...'

'Just give me the concentrate.'

I paid him the six rupees and pocketed the bottle. In the shops further ahead there were entire silver canisters of concentrate, also labelled with local and Western names. What a place. I was hungry for acquisition. It was the only way to avoid being in my room in the Khyber and to stop dwelling on Paris. Already I felt that great city slip away. Taking the metro, crossing the Seine and getting off at La Motte Piquet, buying crepes off the guys in the corner, or sandwiches from the hole-in-the-wall between La Motte Piquet and Duplex—these all seemed oddly elusive memories. I wasn't lamenting the past. No, my nostalgia came from fear of the future, a future in which I wasn't returning to Paris. Mapping these excursions filled my head with longing and beauty and the sense not just that it was all dissolving far too quickly, but that I hadn't taken enough of it in the first place. Now I wanted to discard Karachi as soon as I could and meet Paris with a clearer head.

I bought a few more useless things before I got back to Ghulam Hussain's Morris, which stomped through Drigg Road traffic toward Lalukhet. A traffic policeman stopped us at an intersection and asked to see registration papers. Ghulam Hussain fumbled around in the glove compartment, lifting loose documents, repeating under his breath, 'Registration papers, registration papers.' He closed the glove compartment and reached into the pocket of his kameez. He chuckled as he pulled out his wallet. 'Papers must be in here.' He slipped a finger inside, then looked up at the policeman and said, 'In Punjabi we have this joke. A man says to another man, "Abhey, that man has run off with your ear!" And the man panics and starts running around after his ear, without thinking to first check here,' he put his hand to his ear, and laughed raucously. Then he removed two ten-rupee notes from his wallet, scrunched them in his palm. He placed his arm on the ridge of his half-rolled window, the money concealed in his fist. With a delicate movement of his wrist he tapped his knuckles against the officer's hand. The officer looked at Ghulam Hussain with a more curious gaze, sceptical about entering into this covenant with him. He sidled his head through the gap in the window and inspected me. He closed his hand around Ghulam Hussain's fist, but didn't remove the money. 'You're Punjabi?' he asked.

'Ji, ji!' Ghulam Hussain replied buoyantly. I'd noticed the slight shift in his Urdu towards a rough patois. The policeman looked mistrustful, but ultimately accepted Ghulam Hussain's notes with a swift, practised motion that moved it immediately to his front shirt pocket. He wrote on his pad and stuck a sticker onto the windshield that read, 'Checked'. We drove past the checkpoint in silence.

At Liaquatabad Station a guard told Ghulam Hussain to park outside. I was escorted to Rahim sahib's office, a barren little room with yellowing walls, and chairs of deteriorating wicker, many of the filaments on the backrests missing or undone. I declined the boy's offer of a cold or a hot drink. He brought me a glass of water, from which I took a tiny sip, in front of him, and didn't touch it again. Old folders poured out of two crumbling cupboards positioned at an angle to each other in one corner. Rahim sahib's name was missing from the wooden board on the wall with a list of SHOs, and the dates of their terms, from the '30s to the present day. The first half-dozen were English names. On the desk were more files and papers, the district's crimes, investigations stacked and within my reach. In Paris, such official business was foreign, practised by people we never met. We were exiles, immigrants, in an alien system we had no say in.

Rahim sahib came in, a tall, obese frame concealed under a baggy shalwar kameez. He had a top-heavy cut of grey hair, rising from his cranium in a slanted heap. Despite his physique there was something feminine about him, his arms swung loosely and his broad hips twisted in soft arcs as he moved to his place behind the desk. 'So you're Mr. Shahbaz!' He grabbed me by the shoulder and pulled me into his chest, a one-handed hug. 'From the sound of your voice on the phone I thought you must be forty.' His own voice seemed weakened and roughened by illness. The one elegant thing about him was a thin grey beard that became darker around his chin. As he sat down, he held the back of his neck and with a look of pain on his face he said, 'What I need at this time of day is a massage from one of the nice madams we arrested this morning.' The boy stood in the doorway. Glaring at him, Rahim sahib said, 'Why haven't you offered him anything to drink?' The boy, mutely, tried to protest, but Rahim sahib continued, 'Arrey yaar, just get us some lassi! Immediately. And . . .' He turned to me and asked, 'You have a driver?'

'Yes.'

'And for the driver. Phata-phut!' When the boy was gone, Rahim sahib said, 'Achha ji', as if he were swearing me in. The boy returned with two glasses of lassi. He offered me the first glass, then went around the table to his boss.

'You've given a glass to the driver?' Rahim sahib asked him.

'Ji, sir, I'm about to.'

'Do it, do it! And bring this fan closer, bhai. Not getting one current from over there.'

With the cold lassi tumbling noisily down our throats,

and the fan's scant breeze on our faces, Rahim sahib and I began again. He asked a few questions about my background, I dropped my father's name, to which Rahim sahib frowned and stared in the distance, nodding. 'Yes, I've heard the name, of course.'

'Yes, well like I said . . .'

'Oh, before I forget!' Rahim sahib said, reaching into a drawer and pulling out an unlabelled bottle with a clear liquid. 'Here, have a look at this.' He unscrewed the top and pushed the bottle to my face. 'Have a smell.' I brought the bottle's tip to my nostril and took in a pungent alcoholic smell. Rahim sahib smirked, his eyes blurred with excitement. 'Incredible, right? It's made in the villages. From the bark of the Acacia tree. They try selling it here. The poor man's drink. Incredible. We just seized a whole shipment coming from the interior.' He held the bottle in front of him, looked at it proudly, as if the brew itself was his prize work. Then he put the bottle back in the drawer, looked up at me and said, 'Ji, sir.'

I resumed the story—the full story, in *English*, that I couldn't tell Ghulam Hussain. How most of my father's extended family remained in India after Partition, which made him, his younger brother and Mona Phuppi the few Pakistanis of the family, apart from some distant cousins here and there. So that ours was an unusually small family, no ancestral home to come back to, no citadels of aunts and uncles and cousins and hired help. Head tilted back at a slight angle, Rahim sahib fingered a short strand of hair on his Adam's apple, straightening it over and over while listening to me explain that a small family should have made my father and his siblings closer, but didn't, and that at the heart of this was land:

for when they moved from India to Karachi in 1947 and, like all mohajirs, migrants from India, they were promised compensation by the Pakistani government for the estates they left behind, they were eventually allotted six hundred and fifty acres in the district of Mirpurkhas, which the three of them were to split evenly. But then came Ayub's land ceilings, and those six hundred and fifty acres shrunk. 'My aunt fought the government in court, arguing that each sibling was entitled to so much. And she won. Well, she got some of the lands back, but then she sold it without consulting her brothers.'

'Did your father get any of the money?' the policeman asked.

Yes, I explained, he did. 'But he was infuriated. I think he also had doubts about whether Mona Phuppi pocketed more of the money than she claimed, though his Eastern hauteur prevented him from raising the question. And then the judges ruled in her favour in yet another case, giving us back the orchard ... but with squatters on it, like bugs.'

'So she's trying to sell this, too,' he said.

Exactly.

'And you don't want her to.'

No.

He leaned forward, propped his elbows on his desk, and his chin atop his joined fists. He took a deep breath, like a prelude to a sermon.

'Especially with *land*,' he said, mid-sentence.

'Sorry?'

'*Land*, Mr Shahbaz, *land*. It's what brothers kill brothers over, nephews kill uncles, cousins kill cousins. No relationship is holy when it comes to *land*.'

'So ...' I stammered.

'Now, whose was this land? Initially?'

'My grandfather's, I suppose.'

'Your dada?'

'Yes.'

'He was the owner?'

'I think so.'

'He's gone now?'

'Dead.'

He muttered some Islamic refrain under his breath. The short curl of hair projecting from his Adam's apple was more visible because of his persistent stroking. I wanted him to pluck it out. 'And when did your dada-ji pass away?'

'A year before Partition, I believe.'

'Achha.' The boy came back into the room, picked up our empty glasses and disappeared. 'The reason I ask you this, Mr Shahbaz, is that in Muslim law, when a man dies'—he spread out his hand, and pressed the index of his other hand against the little finger—'one-sixth of his estate goes to his parents if they're still alive, one-eighth goes to the wife, and the rest goes to the kids at a ratio of two-to-one, favouring the sons.' His index moved from finger to finger with each count. 'So of that land, your father, Ghazanfar sahib, should have gotten twice what his sister . . . what is her name?'

'Mona.'

'Mona. Unless they had another agreement, he should have gotten twice what Mona begum got. Of that original plot. By law. Muslim law. That's the beauty of it.' He took another dramatic breath through his mouth. 'So, in my mind, your father has more rights to this than your phuppi. Now . . . *squatters*,' he noted the word ominously, as though it weren't bugs but a terminal disease. 'That's a problem.' He scrunched his face. 'In this country, physical possession counts very much. And if Bhutto comes to power, he'll give those bloody haris more power than they've ever seen.'

'Is there anything we can do?' I asked.

'Well look. I can certainly contact people there, tell you what the situation is exactly, see if—'

'I know what the situation is.'

'—see what we can do about these haris.'

'The moment the government hands over the deeds, I'll let you know.'

He looked at his watch. Before I finally left him, he said, 'Please do pass on my respects to brigadier sahib.'

Shops lined both sides of the main road in Lalukhet. We came again to a bridge under which was a large area of copper-coloured land, a seemingly misplaced part of the countryside. 'That's what this area is named after, Shahbaz bhai,' Ghulam Hussain said. 'That's Lalu's khet. Farum.'

'Farm?'

'Yes, farum. Lalu's farum. He used to be here in English times. A Hindu. Lalu sahib. He owned all of that that you see. May have been dead by Partition. But this is where all of your people came.' He assumed his grandiloquent tone. 'Yes, your people, Shahbaz bhai. Your people. You mohajirs from India. Like you.' He slowed the car, and pointed to some of the graffiti on the outer walls of some of the shops. 'Look. See that one?' A filthy white wall displayed a slogan above a dog's face, declaring 'Ayub kota!' in faded blue. 'That's the work of poor mohajirs. Been there since the 1964 elections. This place still hasn't forgotten the pain.' Slowing down even more, his tenor like a lecturer's, he told me a story of how during the indirect presidential elections of 1964, the mohajirs of Lalukhet had overwhelmingly supported the candidacy of Jinnah's sister, Fatima Jinnah, against Ayub. 'Fatima Jinnah *won* that whole election, Shahbaz bhai. Ayub lost the election at night, and he announced his victory in the morning. And now he wanted revenge on the people of Lalukhet who'd made him look ridiculous. So his two sons—both badmaash, tyrants like their father, even worse than their father—went to the frontier, to Peshawar, put together a small gang of Pathans, gave them bandookhs and all kinds of other weapons, and put them on to a train to Karachi. For two days those Pathans were in that train, waiting to be unleashed on the town, like animals, like cowboys you see in Angrezi films. Six hundred people were killed. Then the mohajirs fought back. So much blood spilled here, Shahbaz bhai. So much blood spilled.' As Ghulam Hussain spoke, I surveyed the streets to see signs of that five-year-old savagery. A little boy on our side of the road helped an older man hammer a cast-iron gate into shape. On the other side, the sun was sinking into vermilion wax. Rahim sahib's district seemed at peace. But a fundamental limit had no doubt been crossed; there must still have been a grudge, a demand for justice, biding underneath. Gestating.

∽

The brigadier's servant, a young Sindhi boy named Sajid, showed me the house. The outer walls were made of light pink concrete, unpainted. Some of the windows were shaped like wine goblets. There were three connected Indo-Saracenic window arches in the front, which gave way to a small balcony. A single onion dome capped the roof. Sajid said the brigadier had been delayed at his bridge game in the Gymkhana. And his wife, unfortunately, was unwell and had gone to bed early. He brought me a Coke, which I sipped on the balcony, against the stone balustrade. The brigadier's neighbourhood was a dark expanse pitted here and there by small lights; in one corner these lights circled a large ring edifice on a distant hill.

The brigadier had invited me over when I'd called to thank him for putting me in touch with Rahim sahib. I couldn't refuse the invitation after his gesture of alliance. But there was more to it. I also wanted access to the brigadier's world. As a child in Paris, I didn't so much yearn for a secret life as feel its pull from four or five years down the line, that darker city waiting for me to come of age. Now in Karachi I seemed to be stuck only in its darker part, engaging pimps and hookers in the very room I slept in. So much of Karachi life, its grandeur and power, was unavailable. I was still living my father's exile.

I came back inside and sat on a couch in the second floor landing. At one end of the landing, opposite the staircase, was a two-part glass door leading to another area of the house. I walked over. The two sides of the door weren't closed all the way, and through the little gap I could make out a small side table with a telephone. By its side, a glass of water with a crescent-shaped object inside. My eyes adjusting to the darkness of the room, I distinguished protruding from that object, small artificial teeth, and realized I was looking into a bedroom. Past the side table was a large figure lying prostrate, breathing the heavy breaths of the elderly, the frame expanding and shrinking in a powerful consistent meter. I promptly returned to my seat in the landing and waited for the brigadier, flipping absently through a magazine from the stack on the coffee table.

After the turn that our nascent relationship had taken, I felt it somehow inappropriate to ask him for a room at his hotel. How do you ask for a favour on top of a favour? And if I did, my presence in his home would seem motivated by something other than gratitude. No, I couldn't ask him, I was stuck with the Khyber until my father cooked up something else.

The light from the room with the dentures came on. Heavy sighs, the ruffle of a plastic bag, and a soft, whining woman's voice calling out to Sajid. I didn't see the servant anywhere. 'Koi hai?' the voice bleated again. I held my breath. I considered looking for the servant, worried about the old woman in there croaking or shitting in her bed.

Was there no way to reacquire the orchard *and* keep the squatters? Impose our own order and government on them? Rebuild the homes to make them firmer and more lasting. Erect statues of saints and angels. Have administrative offices, ordinances, curfews, fiestas, cockfights, funerals, expulsions, suspended sentences, public hangings, a small prison in some dark corner and a power-sharing agreement between my father and Mona Phuppi, brother and sister. An administrator in me, invigilating at night, torchlight in hand, making sure curfews were observed. Aiming the light at crevices, along the boundary walls, making sure no squatter left the compound without permission. Making sure the flag was raised every morning. What else? An anthem in the morning. Processions. Official dinners. Make a glorious nation out of the place. Maybe, I thought, I'd made a mistake by engaging the policeman, Rahim sahib; maybe the brigadier was wrong, the answer wasn't to get rid of the squatters—maybe these very squatters were the key to our future. If I could convince my aunt, I plotted, if I could convince her that the poor settlements on our orchard weren't reason to get rid of the whole thing, but all-the-more to keep it . . .

It was half past ten when I finally heard the brigadier's gate open to let his car in, and Sajid's sudden appearance and subsequent disappearance downstairs to receive him. The light in the adjoining room had turned off again. With his steps rising on the stone staircase, the brigadier's voice fired questions at Sajid about my well-being. And when he came up the landing he scolded Sajid for not seating me in the drawing room. 'Sajid!' he said and stared at him in reprimand.

'Adaab.'

'Jeetairaho.' He held my cheek in his palm. 'Come,' he ushered me through the arched doorway that led to the drawing room. 'Sorry for making you wait for so long,' he said. 'Was in a bit of a predicament; one minute I'll tell you. *Sajid*!' Sajid rushed in to turn on a series of switches, just behind the brigadier, which flooded the room with bright yellow light from the chandeliers. I catalogued the furniture—which spanned from the Victorian onwards—under this more arresting light, and then the brigadier asked Sajid to switch off the chandeliers. So in the milder glow of the wall lights we took our seats, adjacent to each other. A glass table in front of us had on it three fat photo-books, a bowl of ivory fruits, and a small crystal sculpture of a jaguar at rest.

'My father,' the brigadier pointed to the large portrait of a man with a Turkish hat and a long white beard on the wall facing us. In unhappy tenor, he told Sajid to bring drinks, and to then put the food on the table. 'You're hungry?'

'A little.'

'Good. We'll get one in before we sit at the table, just to . . .' he waved his hands towards his face, as if heat was consuming him. After Sajid brought the whisky, two glasses and ice, the brigadier stopped him. 'Sajid yaar, for a minute . . .' he tapped the back of his own neck. The servant stood behind him and, as the brigadier leaned his head forward, massaged his neck and shoulders, obtaining wild approving 'ahhs' from him. The servant had a most serious expression as he performed these ministrations. 'I have a heavy heart today.' The brigadier looked up at me. 'Ahh . . . shaabash, Sajid! Now dinner.' Sajid was gone, and the brigadier reached for the bottle, poured our drinks. 'Cheers.' He leaned back in his seat. Eyes closed, he took a long first sip. 'Mmm,' he sighed, opened his eyes. 'I had to finally throw Farhana begum out of the cabaret.'

'Oh?' I inquired.

'You met Farhana begum, right?'

'Seemed a fine lady.'

'Haan yaar! Fine lady, *extraordinary* lady, but,' he shook his head, 'Incorrigible.'

'Drinks too much?'

'Oh nahin, bhai. *Everybody* drinks too much. It's good for business if they drink too much. But Farhana begum, when *she* drinks . . .'

'Misbehaves?' I asked.

'Arrey bhai, forget misbehaves. Outright *solicits*!' He

sounded irritated that I'd forced him to put it into words. 'She started doing this some months go. That's when we found out, anyway. Once or twice, chalo, we can let that slide. Laikin ek tareeka hota hai. We can't allow it every week. I mean it's not good for us.' His voice turned passive, pleading for understanding. 'I gave her a few warnings. You know, politely. But she was incorrigible. So what could I do?'

I nodded, wanting him to know I was on his side. 'Absolutely.'

'I mean we can't have our guests soliciting at our bloody bar. And she's such a terrific lady. A Punjabi to the core. They want you to either leap off the rooftop, jump in the lake, or get lost.'

Sajid reentered to announce that dinner was ready. Taking our glasses with us, we walked to a small dining room. This was a more solemn affair, with a liver-coloured marble table, scattered ruts on its surface. On one wall was a painting framed in the same liver colour, of a depressing old man hunched on a boat. This room, too, had small windows shaped like wine goblets, looking into the landing. 'My father was a railway man, but a poet at heart. He built this house right after Partition. By then he was in his late seventies, already a little . . .' the brigadier placed his index finger to his temple. 'So he insisted on designing it himself and his grand idea was to have these bloody goblets all over the house. Homage to his favourite art. Dear God.'

I dug into the haleem, followed with urgent sips of water to ease the sting of the spices. 'Thank you for the Rahim sahib thing,' I said.

'Oh, never mind. How did it go?'

'Good. Let's see what he comes up with,' I said, to which the brigadier responded with a diligent nod.

'I'll phone him tomorrow. A reminder.'

'Thank you,' I said. 'But I think he'll be on top of—'

The brigadier shook his head. 'Here, my young friend, if you want things done, you *always* make that extra call. That extra phone call *runs* this country.'

'Uh-huh. Excellent haleem . . . Brigadier sahib,' I coughed.

'Call me Uncle, bhai! No *brigadier sahib* rubbish!'

'Ji, Uncle. I have a question for you. It's been on my mind for some time, I'm wondering if you know anything about it.'

'Haan, haan, bolo.'

'The meeting of February 23, 1953, the communist conspiracy. Can you tell me anything about it?'

The brigadier wiped his lips with his napkin, and I thought I saw a brief smile behind it. 'What does your father say about it?'

'I've never asked.'

He pitched the napkin on the table and sighed. 'Ghazanfar was probably there, I'm not sure,' he said. He looked out of one of the goblet-shaped windows, into the landing. 'He never mentioned it to me. Of course, after that we never really got a chance to talk. I tried to see him when he was shifted to the Hyderabad jail, but he sent a message saying he didn't want to see me there. Ghazanfar and his bloody pride.' He turned his head and made eye contact. 'Then there was the trial and then he cut a deal and was gone.' He called out to Sajid, who came in and picked up our plates. 'Conspiracy to Wage War Against the King,' the brigadier said, once Sajid was back in the kitchen. He turned to me and laughed. 'That's what the charge was. *Conspiracy to*

Wage War Against the King. Arrey bhai, at least come up with a native accusation. I don't think anything irritated Ghazanfar more than being convicted on a British charge.'

'Was it true, though? Was there a conspiracy?'

'Who the hell knows? But if there *was* a communist plot I can tell you your father had no part in it. He was friends with that crowd, of course. He loved Faiz, but not for his politics. That was Ghazanfar's big dilemma. As an artist, he almost had no choice but to be a . . . *comrade.*' He smiled, mocking the word. 'But Ghazanfar was too religious to be one. It vexed him to no end—godless Communism, and that people like Faiz were becoming just as godless. I used to tell him the only option left for him was to rally behind the mullahs.'

Sajid lifted our plates. 'Phal?' the brigadier asked me. 'Sajid, what-what fruit is there?' I interrupted Sajid's inventory saying I wouldn't eat fruit. 'You don't eat fruit?' the brigadier asked.

'My stomach,' I said. 'It plays with my stomach after a meal. On an empty stomach . . .'

'Same here, yaar. I can't take the stuff. Full stomach or not. Ruby buys the fruit in the house, eats like there's no fucking tomorrow, bloody juices dripping from her hands. The thing with me is that I was born ass-first. So, they had to pull me out, backwards, and I think all those fluids just . . .' he waved his hands towards his face. 'After that first trauma I could never handle fruit. Only mangoes.'

After dinner the brigadier took me back to the drawing room, straight through to the door at the far end. Below the staircase that led up to the mezzanine was a small TV room. There were two divans on either side against the wall, at an angle to the television, which was perched on a brown cabinet. In the screen's direct line were two love-seats. 'I want to show you something,' the brigadier said, looking through the row of Betamax cassettes in the cabinet. Giddily, he put a cassette into the video recorder, pushed the 'on' button of the television. With a scheming, adolescent smile he quickly glanced outside the door, pulled the door closed. He pressed play from the remote, and the screen filled with the flesh of a man and a woman, both dark haired and with South Asian skin. 'Locally made,' the brigadier declared. There was crude electronic music in the background, like gunshots in a science fiction film. '*This* is progress, young Shahbaz,' he crowed. 'Even a young Parisian like you should be impressed.'

I smiled and nodded. I was being tested, and didn't know what reaction he expected. 'Where did you get this?'

The camera pulled back to show the couple's embracing bodies, now clear that they were on a carpet in someone's drawing room, gaudy orange flames in a fireplace. The brigadier was shaking his head. 'Incredible!' The man and woman fought each other for the upper position, the camera catching brief peeps at the man's floppy genitals. Eventually the woman relented, and then didn't seem to move at all while the man clumsily licked her neck. Satisfied, a final smile and appeal for a reaction from me, which I gave him in raised eyebrows and slow nods, my host turned the video off and led me out, down the staircase to the driveway. Ghulam Hussain had brought the car in. With the brigadier watching, I got in the back instead of the front, which I felt guilty about—but hell. As Ghulam Hussain turned the ignition, the brigadier tapped on my window. I rolled it down. With an uneasy expression on his face, the brigadier leaned forward and made his offer, extended his invitation. 'Listen,' he said. 'The Khyber is no good for you.' And then: 'We've got half a dozen empty rooms in this house. They're perfectly livable. Why don't you just move your things in here?' These words silenced not just me, but everything else, too, even the engine Ghulam Hussain was revving delicately. I tried to find the right words—of refusal, acceptance, I didn't know—and as I stuttered the brigadier said, 'Yes, yes! Just do it, bhai. I can't let you stay in some godforsaken brothel. I probably owe it to Ghazanfar anyway. So pack your things tomorrow. I'll send the driver over in the evening.' He tapped on the roof of the car, and stepped back. Ghulam Hussain put the gear in reverse, turned his head and backed out of the driveway.

❧

I was startled to find one half of the arched shutter to the balcony ajar. Saddar, what remained of the bazaar, sent dust and odours into my room. I closed the shutter, and looked around for signs of intrusion. My briefcase was where I'd left it, under the bed, upright against the wall. The perfume I'd bought was still on the sideboard.

I wasn't tired. I wanted to go for a walk but it was midnight. I sat up in bed and, using an old *Paris Match* for support, I set out to write a letter to someone in Paris, anyone. But I stared at the empty page, and couldn't find the words, couldn't even put 'Dear so-and-so' down, and instead decided to write to my father. I tried at first to force sentimentality, but then avoided it, and the letter became a simple chronicle of my time so far, the acceptable parts of it, including the meeting with and surprising invitation from Brigadier Alamgir, the meeting with Rahim sahib, and the risk of the whole effort failing if Bhutto and his People's Party came to power. I concluded with questions about Paris, his health, his work on his poetry calendar. I signed off, and put the letter aside. I emptied a cigarette on the same *Paris Match*, burned some hash that Ghulam Hussain had given me, mixed it with the tobacco, filled the cigarette with the mixture. I smoked in bed, the silence broken only by the sound of footsteps going up and down the corridor outside.

Was Karachi safer than Paris? A good question. It had taken me some time before I was confident enough to use the underground walkways in Paris late at night. For years I circled the Arc de Triomphe overland, crossing the half dozen streets to avoid using the long tunnel that took you straight across, under the Arc, to the other side. Even when I finally decided against the circuitous walk, I'd rush through the underpass and feel incredible relief when I was out. The mere echo of footsteps underground, metropolitan horrors, was enough to hasten my pace. There were opportunities, though. To change things. I used to frequent a small bar in the Latin Quarter, far less known than the Left Bank meccas, so much so that its owner could keep it open even when the Events began in '68. The owner called himself Roscoe and, as a result, clients referred to the nameless establishment as Roscoe's. During the riots he'd keep the lights down, added curtains on the windows which he drew after dark. I went in that night wearing around my neck the silver Ayatul-Kursi my father had given me years before, while we were still in Karachi. The piece was small, about two-inches-by-one, but the Arabic letters were legible enough for an up-close reading of the verse. I drank a beer at the bar, then went into the bathroom stall, positioning my feet awkwardly around the puddle of piss marked with muddy footprints. Using a couple of tissues, I put the toilet lid down and wiped its surface. I took out my wallet, removed the little dime bag from one of its compartments. Grinding the bag with the steel ball at the end of my keychain, I emptied some of the crushed powder onto the lid. With a business card I arranged two lines, thin as toothpicks, and with a rolled up ten-franc note inhaled both. I held my head back, sniffled to get in as much as I could, then squeezed my nostrils. And it was around then that the man barged in through the carelessly unlocked door.

'Oh, excusez moi,' he said. He turned to leave, but then saw the closed toilet lid, the contents on top, the half rolled note in my hand. 'Ahh!' he exclaimed. He had dark, rough skin, with patches on his cheeks and a small fungal blot on one side of his lips. 'Et qu'est qu'on a ici?' I'd seen him occasionally at the bar, often seated with one of the hookers who used Roscoe's as a refuge and place of business. 'Soyez pas peur, mon ami. J'ai rien vu. I've seen nothing at all.' I was relieved to hear him say that, but was apprehensive when he didn't leave. 'Ah, qu'est que c'est?' his voice went up to a high, gregarious pitch, as he reached towards my chest and held the Ayatul-Kursi between thumb and index. He passed his finger over the lettering. 'T'es Arabe?' he asked.

'Non,' I said.

'T'es d'ou?'

'Pakistanais.'

He still held the ornament. 'Ca m'interese.' I looked at him, with alarm. 'Remember, I haven't seen anything you did in here.' When I protested, he repeated his refrain, over and over—he hadn't seen the cocaine on the toilet lid. I didn't know what he meant to do with this discovery, but whatever the road he was pointing down, I was sure it wasn't worth it. Those were shaky days, they tilted things in favour of exactly such a man. And the smile on his face told me that by then he knew he'd get what he wanted, knew the mildness of my resistance. When I finally removed it from my neck and gave it to him, he looked at it more closely, under the dim white light above the sink. 'Ah, comme c'est belle!'

'Va-sy,' I said. 'Maintenant, lesse moi tranquile.'

Putting the Ayatul-Kursi in his jacket pocket, my intruder turned to leave. And before finally doing so, he said, 'Don't forget to lock the door.'

As soon as he was gone I forced the door shut, locked it, turned around and leaned my back against it. I'd started sweating profusely, almost immediately, as if finally released from the man's immobilizing terror my body could now discharge its functions. I thought another two lines may help, and I did them, but it was cheap street stuff, and shot a sting through my forehead. Inside I was shaking. I lifted the toilet lid without removing the dime bag and granules that were still on its surface, pissed, washed my hands, my face, breathed in some water from my palm and pinched my nostrils again. There was no mirror to see my reflection in. I touched the area at my breast where the Ayatul-Kursi should have been. It was exactly from such villains that the verses were supposed to protect me. I wanted to hit something, smash something. When I left the bathroom I saw my intruder, my thief, sitting at the bar chatting, laughing, with the old and skeletal Roscoe. He looked at me with the mirth still fixed on his dotted face. I walked past him and left the bar. Outside the smell of teargas, the smell of a warring, rotting city, opened my nostrils.

I knew what I had to do. Across the street was a phone booth, and in there I sat, waiting, a silent receiver hung on my shoulder. When the man finally came out of the bar and walked south in the direction of the Seine, I put the receiver back on its hook, and followed him from the opposite side of the street. This part of the Quarter was lifeless but tense, the unrest no doubt swelling, approaching us like an invading army. It was easy to keep track of my target for his shiny silver shirt. I'd never actually fought anyone in a real fight. But I liked to believe that there was a violent man inside me, awaiting birth, a moment like this. Not violence for its own sake, but for giving life a balance and shape that it otherwise lacked. The second-rate drug now beat powerfully in my veins. I don't know exactly how long I'd followed him, or how far away from Roscoe's we'd walked. But I could always recall the electricity of that moment when he finally stopped and, as if sensing my pursuit, turned around. I faltered in my stride, but I didn't stop moving towards him. I was ready—for my first act of violence, my first act of resistance. Feeling faint, ecstatic. *This is big*, I thought. *This is considerable*.

When my father asked me the next morning about my swollen nose, I'd told him that I'd been in a fight with someone who'd ripped me off. But it wasn't true. The swollen nose was from the coke. I never fought the man.

It was knowledge. That's what I'd seen in him. Knowledge of how it all worked. It gave him exuberance, a swelling of personality, and that's what scared me. Knowledge even about *me*. Many times I'd wondered what he'd thought when he saw me again. I'd followed him for so long with a carefully planned crime in my head, but as we faced each other again he resumed the advantage, the calm, of the aggressor. In this disordered city, the most deviant were at the top of the chain of command. The calm—that's what had gotten me: there was just no alarm in his face, and whatever surprise there was had a certain hilarity to it. *He was still smiling.* No, I didn't hit him. I walked straight past him and, eventually, returned home without the Ayatul-Kursi around my neck. He knew I wasn't of the city, hadn't mastered its codes and its tricks. So I walked, ducked my head and avoided eye contact, went back into the city which had just secured another little triumph against me.

I was annoyed at how much importance I gave this episode, how its every detail still weighed down on me with whatever the hell it was. I got up to make sure my door was locked. Saddar, too, after midnight had to be a place of ghouls. I tested the door, pulled at the handle. The same with the shutters. I threw the remains of the smoked joint into the porcelain hole-in-the-ground, then crouched over and tried relieving my burning stomach. Every time I entered this bathroom, I couldn't overcome the thought that this commode was being used by others in the hotel, the smells foreign and of the poor. Turning off the bathroom switch, I received an electric shock. My heart raced, I slapped the area of the wall where the switch was, angrily. I checked the door one last time before returning to bed.

PART TWO

False Promise

1

A second thing happened the night the brigadier invited me to stay in his home. When we left, Ghulam Hussain drove absent-mindedly, humming a tune at the wheel, and often not really watching the road until prompted by the honks of angry neighbouring cars to straighten out. To crack this absence, I asked him what the song was. A Bengali folk tune, he explained, and translated it to Urdu, which I then did my best to say back in English to myself, something along the lines of: *Let's go, let's go, let's go/From the skies the drums are beating/And the Earth is getting restless/So children of the New Sunset/Let's go, let's go, let's go.* The next thing to trap his attention was a disturbance near Kutchery Road, a procession being broken by the police. Outside a pharmacy, amid the turmoil, four old men sat on stools around a Ludo board, each taking his turn rolling dice from a little cylinder, focused on getting his game pieces home. Ghulam Hussain slowed the car almost to a standstill, watching these four men. And then a puzzled smile occupied his face, and only after I coughed did he return to his senses and speed up. A little concerned, when he dropped me home I asked him whether he was all right.

'Haan, theek hoon,' he answered distantly and unconvincingly. Then he returned the question, how was I doing here, in this hotel. I, too, said I was all right but, realizing that it sounded just as false, I added, 'Man gets bored.' Using the English word for bored, one of those that had become a standard substitute in Urdu parlance.

'Haan, Shahbaz bhai.' And he said that he too was bored but, as one can in Urdu, without refererring to himself as the subject. So that, practically, word-for-word in English: 'Boredom has occurred.' Making it sound like some foreign bug. And *his* idea of boredom was far darker than what I meant. We were talking about very different sentiments. I knew it was my role to console him, that's what he expected of me. In many ways—in most ways—he was so much smarter and more experienced and more able than I, there was everything between us that should have made him the knight and me the squire, but in an unjust city I was now the one who had to lead *him*. I'd learned a new Urdu word recently, for 'hope': umeed, and I rejoiced at this perfect opportunity to use it. Have umeed, I told him. After all, wasn't the country about to change.

'Without umeed, the world can't run, Shahbaz bhai.' He rested both hands and arms against the top of the steering wheel, and now even put his head to it. Umeed— a very different word for him. 'But it's given me happiness to meet you,' he said.

'Haan, to me too.' And I meant it.

'But then you will go back to ... over there. This, too.'

And that's when I said it. 'You also come.' Casually,

imitating the elite, cordial Pakistani insouciance. You also come, why not? The problem is that the rich say it to the rich and everyone knows the artifice—Oh, you're going to Paris? Yes. *You* also come? In a tone that suggests it would be silly not to. An aristocratic luxury, being able to talk like that. But in Ghulam Hussain something, I'm certain, changed. Not that he hadn't heard such things before, but because he'd heard it *from me*, someone who'd sat with him over breakfast in a café on Burns Road, who came to him in his quarters, straddled two worlds. I had no doubt that he thought me sincere. And in his moment of boredom, I came to him like an angel, not an angel from above but, more powerfully, from the West. And is that why I did it, to bind him to me, to neutralize the threat he himself posed? No. It was something far simpler. I did it because of a language constraint. Expressing affection unambiguously in any language isn't easy, in a foreign one nearly impossible, and in a lost language just as much so. And I had, as I said, grown fond of my driver.

Ghulam Hussain often filled in my sentences for me. When things got complicated, my Urdu got me far enough to communicate some general impressions and ideas, which through question-and-answer, like a doctor, Ghulam Hussain then did his part to make out, explain, complete. But affection was more complicated. So, how else was I to demonstrate that I had his interests in mind, that I wasn't listening torpidly, but had *his interests in mind*? How else to say that I wished I could help? So I said it. You also come, with me to Paris, and I put five rupees in his pocket. The onset of my betrayal, my birth as a con artist, with this single victim. You also come, I said, put money in his pocket and got out, closed the door and walked up to my room in the Khyber, where I found half the shutter open, and my driver still loitering down below.

❧

I'd tried calling Ghulam Hussain twice in the past weeks since I'd moved into the brigadier's house, and couldn't get an answer for where he was. I'd recently had a dream about the mango orchard with him in it. Or, if he wasn't a physical presence, he was there at least obscurely. In the dream, I'd been given responsibility over the estate's defence, in front of me were a gang of squatters, in the tens or the hundreds, approaching in leisurely steps, assured in their new power, and for some reason I knew that Ghulam Hussain was in the crowd, too, a smile of recognition in his face, but also an unashamed commitment to overthrow me, regardless of our earlier association. Soon, I knew, I'd be the object of a ritual violence, my death a great festivity and mark of revolution for them. And as they came close enough for me to smell their sweaty passion, I wanted to scream. And what I wanted to scream was a charge at Ghulam Hussain, in English (for I didn't know the Urdu word), of 'Traitor!' But the word never came to my tongue. And I woke up in time, and it was already noon. I wasn't trying to read the dream too literally, but I also realized that I missed Ghulam Hussain, and I didn't want him to feel I'd abandoned him, especially after the remark I'd made about Paris.

But I had to take that remark back. Tell him that I had neither the intention nor capacity to take him back with me. That I wasn't an angel. That the point was to convey my affection. But these were complicated thoughts, they required fluency. And how could I be sure he kept my 'offer' in mind, that he didn't see it for what it was, a false and silly thing said at the end of a long night?

There was no phone downstairs, where my room was. Although it wasn't as grand as I'd expected, this room was a significant improvement on the one at Doli's. It had a queen-size bed, but with a hard mattress and two hard pillows; on the other side of the bed an arched partition divided the bedroom from a small alcove that consisted of a mini fridge (its only items when I arrived were a bottle of tequila and three empty ice trays in the freezer); a mirror with a brown frame hanging on the wall, overlooking a dressing table, which had on it two half empty bottles of cologne and a small pile of old *Newsweeks*; a bookshelf stacked with Urdu books, English novels, translations of the Koran, manuals on how to learn Arabic, *Mein Kamf*, political biographies, including three of Hitler, and a row of unlabelled Betamax cassettes. At the base of the shelf was a three-frame set of photographs of a younger Brigadier Alamgir—probably early-forties, his hair already whitening—standing beside a man with a bushy black beard and sunglasses, against a mountainous background. The brigadier's eyes were squinted, and both men's hair was whisked in one direction by the wind. The bathroom was tiled and had a proper commode, though sometimes when I flushed the water came right up to the rim, and I'd have to notify Sajid, the servant.

It was a famous, imposing house. The balcony, with the three Indo-Saracenic arches adorning it, was once used in a well-known scene from a film as a Mughal ruler's balcony. The pale pink outer walls were of Jaipur limestone, giving the house an imperial look that distinguished it from the other PECHS houses. 'People refer to this house when they're giving directions,' the brigadier boasted, when he showed me around my first day. The brigadier's father was a well-known railway man, with as much love for Urdu poetry as for his mornings on the tracks in old stations like Muree, and he'd regularly made the drawing room upstairs a site for poetry recitals—mushairas, the brigadier called them—drawing many eminent artists and intellectuals from across the subcontinent. Photographs of some of these luminaries lined a board on the walls of the entrance, behind glass. The brigadier had taken me through them, but I barely recalled the names. In the background of one of these photographs my father sat on a cushion next to a large woman, his hand raised, the palm turned inward, fingers loose and separated; his head was tilted downward on one side: this was the poetic gesture of applause, and I could hear the *Wah-Wa-Wa* that accompanied it.

The brigadier's father and his era were done now, and the house had suffered neglect, something the brigadier's wife, Aunty Ruby, repeatedly complained about, pointing to cracks that webbed across the dining-room ceiling. Outside, by the garage, were stacked pieces of rotting furniture, suitcases, covered in dust and webs—'Been there for fifteen years,' Aunty Ruby exclaimed. 'Alamgir's sisters. Move to London and araam se, happily, leave this stuff here.' There remained a survivor of that great zamaana in Apa, the brigadier's aunt, his father's eldest sister and, at ninety-one, the most senior family member. Her room was upstairs, beside the drawing room. During the day and for most of the evening her double door was open; people entered and left as they pleased. To use the phone, I would have to visit her.

'Kaun?' Apa asked in her wasted voice when she heard my footsteps.

I walked through the double door. 'Shahbaz,' I announced, standing in front of her.

'Ah, Shahbaz!' She laughed, in relief, and when I was near enough she reached out to clasp my leg just above the knee, recording my presence. She was blind in one eye, almost so in the other, and watched whatever remained of the world through a thick pair of glasses. She sat at the head of her bed, her old fleshy legs crossed over each other and visible under a slackly worn sari. She patted a spot in front of her on the bed. I sat down. Her feet were bloated, the skin looked smooth and jaundiced, thick layers of nail accumulated on her big toes.

'Apa, adaab,' I said.

'Jeetairaho.' She smiled and again reached out to me, pulled my face so that our foreheads met. Old age had pulled at the weight of her face, collected around the sides of her mouth. Her lips were thick, and bent downward even when she smiled. Always moving, those lips, like a muscle she regularly exercised. The skin below her chin had separated from the bone and muscle of her neck, hung loose like a wilting flag. On one side was a mole from which sprang a single, thick black hair.

At Apa's feet were loose papers with blue text and numbers, and a stack of mint hundred-rupee notes jutting out of a brown envelope. Next to her bottom were a black radio and, finally, the fat black phone.

'Have you eaten yet?' she asked, in Urdu.

And in Urdu, for Apa couldn't tolerate English, I explained that I'd be lunching at my aunt's.

'Why?' Her face turned foul.

'I was invited a little while ago,' I said calmly.

'Eat something before you leave,' she barked, her unremitting Eastern hospitality.

'No Apa, thank you,' I replied. 'I shouldn't fill my stomach.' I eyed the phone, as if it were a weapon I'd have to reach for as soon as I got the chance, for protection.

'You don't like the food here?'

'I do, very much,' I said, repeating the same riposte whenever this subject came up. 'But I don't want to be too full to eat at Mona Phuppi's.'

'But you'll be here tonight?'

'Yes,' I said. 'Certainly.'

She still looked displeased, but relented. And soon she devoted herself again to her papers. She passed a large magnifying glass over her documents with the absorption of a forensic expert. I reached for the phone, placed it on my lap, and dialled. Apa counted the hundred-rupee bills. When the tone on the other end of the receiver gave way to a rough male greeting, I asked for Ghulam Hussain. Apa called out to a servant, and Sajid arrived promptly. She gave him three separate stacks of papers and money. From this bed she ran the house—what food was to be bought, how it would be cooked, which bedroom which guests should sleep in, the servants' salaries, were all decided and overseen from this command centre. Next to her bed was a low, wooden table with bottles of herbal and other luminous liquids, and a small cardboard box filled with vials of Zindatalismat, a thin carmine-red solution that Apa had forced two teaspoons of down my gullet when I complained of a bad stomach. Making sure everyone was in the best of health.

'Shahbaz bhai! Kaisai hain!' I was relieved to hear Ghulam Hussain's voice in the receiver. I asked about his health. 'Listen Ghulam Hussain, you once told me that any time I was in the mood for an omelette I should ask you.' Apa looked up from her papers. I was hoping she'd be too engrossed in her own affairs to hear me, but she seemed to have an antenna designed specifically to pick up references to food. And without waiting for the phone call to end, she poked my shoulder. 'You are *hungry*? Did you not get anything to eat? You can have an omelette here. Sajid!'

'Why not?' Ghulam Hussain said, but sounding puzzled.

'Then you'll pick me up?' I said.

'Sajid!'

'Haan sir, why not pick you up.'

I hung up the phone. A sweeper, one of two women who tended to Apa and her room, came out of the bathroom with a damp rag in her hand. 'Is it all clean?' Apa asked.

'Ji, Apa.'

'Achha. Then finish the rest of your work, and when you're done, come and press my feet, will you?'

'Ji, Apa.' The young woman was gone. Much of the domestic staff schedule was devoted to keeping Apa strong, and as a result there seemed a perpetual panic in the house, a fixation on the matron's precarious condition. 'Achha sunno!' she said urgently to me, as if I could slip away any moment before she could make her case. 'Sajid can make you anything you like. You don't like Sajid's food, kya? Then you can tell him exactly how you want it made. You know how to cook? You can show Sajid.'

'I like the food here very much, Apa,' I said. 'But I haven't seen my phuppi in a while and . . .'

Apa picked at loose threads of lint on her bed and clothes. Frowning, even a little flustered, she reached for her magnifying glass and looked over her sari, picking at the foreign bits with anger and insistence, as if they were insects eating at her. Finally satisfied, she put the magnifying glass down and looked at me. 'Haan,' she tapped my knee, refreshed to my presence. I repeated my lie about Mona Phuppi's invitation. She again registered and accepted this with a frown, before moving to her next question—was I too cold, or too hot at night? Thus began the daily arc of her conversation, starting with a brief warm-up to confirm everyone's well-being. *Had her nephew, the brigadier, eaten yet? Were my clothes warm enough? I should be careful not to get sick.* Then she reconfirmed her facts. *Ghazanfar's son. Did I know Shahbaz was the name of a saint? I've just moved back? In the downstairs bedroom? Ayub is gone. Yahya Khan is in.* And having achieved the right momentum, she launched into a demonstration of what remained of her wits. 'But Yahya is a sharabi! He can't drink all day and run the country. The country's already sinking. They're already making sex films. *Neela Parbat*, have you seen it? Oof, tauba!' She pinched one earlobe, then the other, then back to the first, a gesture she took from the repertoire of Muslim gestures to repent sin. 'Don't watch it!' And finally, she looked to me for some fresh input, which she could incorporate and align to her judgments. 'What did you study in France? Philosophy? What philosophy? What did they teach you? Be careful of those foreign ideas. Fooko-Shooko, whatever his name is. Makes people study sex. After war these people turn crazy.' I spent at least a half hour listening to her take on the world before Sajid came to the room to tell me that my driver had arrived.

'Kaun?' Apa asked brusquely.

'The driver, the car,' I said. When I used the Urdu word for car, Apa corrected me on the pronunciation. 'Ga-*rri*. With a *rray*.' I reached for the back of my palate with my tongue to produce the hard 'r' sound that she required. 'Nahin!' Apa was irritated now. 'Ga-*rri*.'

'Ga-*rri*.'

'You have to go somewhere?'

'My phuppi's.'

'Theek hai,' she shook her head from side to side, acquiescing.

༄

The house in Lyari was still unfinished, the way it stood weeks ago, the empty grey spaces, where the windows were to be, looking like the eye-sockets of a skull. Ghulam Hussain had moved into his brother's quarters here, after being thrown out of his own quarters by the master of the house for not fulfilling his duties—duties to an employer I didn't even know he had. I'd come here once more, since moving into the brigadier's. There were other visitors that day, hippie kids of the Karachi upper class, full of their nasty socialist consciousness, and questions and more questions about me. They'd heard of my father, naturally, and while we passed joints around our own circle in the room, any sense of camaraderie in our little smoking circle was undermined by their caustic questions about why I, Ghazanfar Aslam's son, didn't also take an interest in good civil struggle. I'd pretended I was still staying in the Khyber Hotel, fearing their reaction to Brigadier Alamgir's name and my association with him.

The brigadier's home, grand, full of history, was also full of protocol, adaabs and hands to the forehead, servants' footsteps outside the door, servants to make sure I was fed. Here, there was none of that, and even the thin man with the fat malnourished belly and the long wily nose, who I'd met my first time here and had now confirmed him *not* to be Ghulam Hussain's brother (I still didn't know which one the brother was), sitting on the bed, one leg crossed limply over the other, with his bottle of clear liquor, didn't frighten me as much as before. Between the fingers of the same hand that held the bottle was a cigarette, and he took turns sipping and smoking. No doubt, there was still something unnerving about him, he was in the same league as that one who'd swiped the Ayatul-Kursi from me that night in Paris. But I could live with it.

'Sit, sit,' he told me. He proffered the bottle, ash spilling on the mattress between us.

'Not right now,' I responded.

Ghulam Hussain had already started cutting tomatoes, green chilies, onions, on a wooden board, with an old knife, wiping the tears from his eyes with his dirty kameez. He chopped brusquely. They'd set up a portable stove and frying pan in the centre of the room, which Ghulam Hussain now lit, and put a piece of butter on the pan. He cracked eggs, three, four, five, into the pan, then reached over for the stuff on the chopping board. The steam and smell of eggs and onions rose from his pan. The other man with the bottle now unstuck the cellophane from a piece of hash. Raising and aiming his wooden spatula, Ghulam Hussain forbade him from doing it while he cooked—the only word in the gush of Bengali I understood was 'anda', his celebrated eggs. Ghulam Hussain flipped one half of the egg mixture with his spatula over the other. When done, he split the omelette into two on the frying pan and poured half of it into a glass plate. 'Ek minute, Shahbaz bhai,' he said. 'Let's warm the parathas.'

'*We* people eat on the floor,' the wily one said, taking his place. 'But if you want we can get a chair and table for you from outside.'

'I'll eat on the floor, too,' I replied, moved off the mattress and sat on the cold floor.

'It is the way of the Prophet,' Ghulam Hussain added. Indeed.

As I'd already planned, when I took my first mouthful I exclaimed, 'Ahh! *First* class.' And then, 'Better than any Angrez omelette.'

'Have more!' Ghulam Hussain bellowed.

'I shouldn't eat too much, my stomach is a bit . . .' I put my hand on my stomach and grimaced. 'But it's a first class omelette. The food here—that's the thing a man misses most over there.'

'Achha?' Ghulam Hussain spoke softly, absent-mindedly, his focus on his eggs.

'Haan,' I said. 'It's the food you miss the most.'

'What, over there the food is not good?' Still absently.

'Not as good. Not like the food here. The Western food is good. But Western food is not as good as desi food, am I right?'

He added some salt to his, and passed the little saucer to me. This was frustrating, not getting his full attention, the food getting cold on my plate.

'You know, it's difficult over there. Life. It isn't that easy, Ghulam Hussain. The people look down on people like us. Your own country . . . Pakistan is the country.' What clumsy speech. 'Okay. Listen. What I want to say is . . .' I felt like screaming.

'Haan, haan, zahir hai, your own country is . . .' He used a term I didn't get.

'Exactly,' I said.

'But your father, he doesn't think so,' Ghulam Hussain said assertively, proud of his grasp of this complexity. 'For *him* Paris is more beautiful.'

'It *is* beautiful. That is there. And in the summer you should see . . .' I'd raised my voice but then checked myself against the need to defend my father. Paris was a greater city, of course, but that wasn't the point, my father's exile wasn't the point. 'Nahin, but what I'm trying to tell you is that it isn't *that* good, either. Are you listening? Wherever you go, whatever country, there are problems, theek hai na?' Another long pause. Ghulam Hussain chup-chup-ing away. 'The country is only good for the people who are from there. It's better to stay here, in your own country, where . . .' Where you know who you are. That's what I wanted to say. My weak Urdu was all the more frustrating because there was some truth in what I was saying. *I'm not taking you to Paris with me*! That's what I really wanted to say. *I was lying to you. No, not lying, but it's not what I meant, I meant something else. I meant if I did take someone with me, if I could, if that was the right thing to do, then it would be you.* It wasn't right to be cultivating a relationship with a man to whom I couldn't fully communicate. We finished our omelettes—they were good—more or less in silence.

'First class,' I repeated. Then I asked him to take me back.

Sajid opened the front door for me when I got back home, greeted me with two damp palms and a broad grin, and led me to my room. His walk was slow and hunched, his arms swinging purposefully, and from some angles it looked like he was bending closer and closer towards the floor with each step. Under his breath he muttered short phrases, betraying an active interior life. Other hired helpers I didn't recognize scurried around, with big plastic bottles of Pakola, Fanta, Coca-Cola. Women cleaned floors, dusted the downstairs furniture.

Sajid unlocked my bedroom door and then dropped the key in my hand. The red-tiled floor was shiny, with that medicinal scent of detergent.

'Good,' I said, referring to the clean-up.

'Ji sir,' he said, his huge smile making a messy cluster of a moustache that was too thick for his young, soft face. Sajid was ultimately responsible for the room's order and cleanliness. Under him worked a cleaning woman, who'd come in every two or three days. I surveyed the room, opened drawers, made sure that nothing was missing ('Don't trust *any* of them,' Aunty Ruby had warned me my first day). I noticed Sajid was still standing in the doorway. All told, I trusted him; at the very least, I didn't think him a thief. He was still in that early period of pantomime, the profuse gestures of a new servant trying to gain his patron's confidence. But I needed, nevertheless, to show him I was diligent with my possessions.

'What time will the guests arrive? The big party?' I used the English word for party, which drew a confused smile from Sajid.

'Sir?'

'The guests?'

'Ahh,' He used a word, daawat, which I didn't understand. 'I don't know, nine, nine-thirty.' I made a note to ask Apa about it ('If you don't understand something ask me, but never use English with Urdu like everyone else,' she'd told me).

'Okay, Sajid.' I raised my hand to dismiss him. He approached me, again shook my hand with both of his, bowed slightly and left me.

I slept until four. Outside my bedroom I could hear the industry of servants, 'Idhar-udhar, wahan rakho, idhar lao, abhey jaldi, bhari hai!' Sajid and Aunty Ruby were in the downstairs kitchen, full of steam and raw smells, the stink of onions that had been burnt and had thrown the brigadier's wife into a short paroxysm— 'Baiwakoof-kahinka!' she castigated Sajid. 'Shukur karo, that this didn't happen upstairs.'

At the bottom of the staircase, the brigadier emerged from just outside the front door, bidding someone farewell. He had a bottle of Royal Salute in his hand. At four in the afternoon, he was still wearing his dressing gown over a white undershirt and striped shorts. His legs were thin, almost hairless.

'Adaab,' I said.

'Jeetairaho, jeetairaho,' he said quickly, in his characteristic rush to dispense with formality. He took me by the hand and said, 'Come-come, my boy, I want to show you something.' I followed him back up the steps and to the drawing room. He turned a light on at the far end of the room and, bottle in hand, went straight to it. Standing against the wall, he raised the bottle to the bulb. 'See the colour?' I nodded. 'What colour is it?' Before I answered, he filled in, 'It's clear, right? Not murky.'

'Uh-huh,' I confirmed.

'Good. Because if it's murky, it's been tampered with. Now. The second test.' He shook the bottle twice in vertical shakes. His face was humourless, focused. 'It shouldn't get too frothy at the top. If it gets frothy you know it's crap. Now you see that? Not too much froth, right? So far so good. Next.' Without using much force, he tried twisting the bottle cap. 'Okay. Doesn't *seem* like this has been opened. The cap's fixed fine.' He lifted the bottle next to his ear and unscrewed the cap. 'Hear that? A good crack, hain na?' He placed the bottle on a side table, held the cap to me. 'Feel the inside of this.' I passed my fingers along the cap's interior. 'Sticky?' the brigadier asked. I shook my head. He felt for it himself. 'Doesn't seem so. Which means no one opened it and then tried gluing it back.' He lifted the bottle again, along with the glass sitting next to it. 'Now, the final test!' He poured a tot, brought it to his nose and, closing his eyes and twirling the glass, inhaled deeply. 'Hmm.' He took a small sip, then followed it with a bigger gulp to down the glass. He made loud licks, tongue against palate. 'Seems like the real stuff.'

He poured another tot and held the glass to me. It was far too early for a drink. 'Come on, just one,' the brigadier insisted with an impatient frown. 'This is to develop your skills, my boy.' I took the glass hesitantly from him, the strong smell alone made me queasy. 'Quick,' the brigadier said. 'Do you taste vanilla? No, right?'

I shook my head, not sure what vanilla in whisky would taste like.

'Finish it, finish it.'

I gulped the rest down.

'Bravo!' the brigadier beamed. 'End of the lesson. So we can serve it tonight without shame.'

The whisky was hot and thick in my throat. The brigadier patted me on the shoulder, turned off the light as he left the drawing room and made his way upstairs to his room on the mezzanine. I went into Apa's room. She had a bowl filled with raw keema, which she kneaded, her old hand awash in onions and raw beef and spices. I went straight to her bathroom, turned the tap on and vomited into her latrine. I rinsed my mouth and turned off the tap. If the smell remained, the servants would assume it was Apa, which was fine by me. I came out and sat next to Apa on the bed. She put her bowl up to my face. 'Does it smell okay?'

'For tonight's party?' I asked.

'Smell it, bhai!'

'Smells fine, Apa.'

'I'll ask them to fry a kabab for you right now?'

'I'll have it tonight, at the party.' I left her before she could begin insisting.

❦

Sajid had ironed my clothes for the party the day before: dark brown cotton pants and, at the brigadier's suggestion, a light blue shirt. He'd also brushed a pair of brown suede shoes. When I put these on in the evening, and looked at myself in the mirror in my bedroom's alcove, I felt invigorated, a sense of arrival at last in Karachi, the city of my childhood. I could hear the guests making their entrances from my room. I waited until more of them came before going upstairs, where the glamour, the aroma of cigar smoke and ladies' perfumes washed the landing and drawing room. Rarely-used lights had been turned on, and under this light the upper classes came together. The brigadier and his wife had covered them meticulously—federal secretaries, Sindh Club committee members, Gymkhana chairman and former chairmen, Sui Gas executives, remnants of the old Twenty-Two Families. They all knew each other well, Karachi aristocracy being a small and tight operation.

The Supremes and the voice of Diana Ross came through the speakers that had been set up below the stairs to the mezzanine. I was introduced to many guests as Ghazanfar sahib's son, either by the brigadier or Aunty Ruby. I watched their reactions—my father's alleged act of subversion had made my surname public property, about which opinions and judgments were allowed to form. But even when I detected disapproval in the face of a new acquaintance, it was gratifying, in this company, to have a name at all.

Aunty Ruby played her role, fulsome in her remarks about the appearances and apparel of her guests. She was a big-boned and handsome woman, dressed tonight in burgundy, the sleeve of her kameez stopping halfway along her forearm, revealing on one the burn marks from a decade-old fire. She covered these with her other hand. With the foreigners her accent took a twist to something more drawn out and sultry (her 'O's, for example, more compressed). She stood with a Spanish diplomat and his wife. And while they were still talking to her, Aunty Ruby turned towards a stout man entering the drawing room. 'Oh, Eddie!' she exclaimed. She returned her attention briefly to the Spanish couple, spread her arms and enclosed both diplomat and wife. 'You *must* try the fish. *I* cooked it. You *must* try it.' And then she sauntered over to Eddie. They greeted each other with kisses on the cheeks and compliments and calls of 'darling' in a joint falsetto. She noticed me nearby, reached out and with her strong arms pulled me into their company. 'This is Eddie. Eddie Carrapiett. You must have heard him on the radio. Wednesday nights. The Hit Parade.'

'Yes, I have,' I said.

'You remember Ghazanfar sahib?' she said.

Carrapiett tilted his head and frowned, in the act of memory, then nodded, 'Yes, of course, of course.'

'Well this is his son.'

'Ah, I see!' He reached his hand out.

'Shahbaz,' I said.

'Go get yourself a drink, Eddie,' Aunty Ruby continued. 'Catch Alamgir at the bar, he's still there I think. Get him to make it for you.'

Two bars had been set up, one upstairs in the drawing room and one downstairs in the garden. A man with a bow tie and white jacket they'd brought from the Agra poured at the upstairs bar, occasionally helped by the brigadier for the more important guests. As Carrapiett walked towards the bar, the brigadier rested his cigar against an ashtray, pinched Carrapiett's cheeks affectionately before embracing him; his hand moved to the back of Carrapiett's neck. He picked up his cigar, pulled his new guest closer with his other hand, and introduced him to a man in a maroon blazer, to whom he'd been talking earlier. The brigadier stood in between the two men, one hand on each of their backs, like an umpire bringing two opponents to a settlement. He wasn't a large man, but made up for it with these gestures of large men.

Seeing me unattended to, the Spanish couple approached me. 'So,' the diplomat's wife began. 'Ruby said you were in Paris.'

'You were there in May,' her husband weighed in. 'During the riots, I suppose?'

I smiled.

'Must have been something for a young man like you.'

'Yes, it was,' I said.

'What excitement it must have been,' the wife added. 'You know, we shouldn't say this, because of Stephan's job,' she laughed. 'But I, how do you say ... *envy*? ... you young people.'

'Well,' I said, and stopped there, trusting the power of suggestion, for I hadn't the energy to lie at that moment, to cover up my having deferred service in what they saw as a great battle of our time.

'One of these days we'll have a talk about it,' the wife said. She took her husband's arm and slung it over her own shoulder.

The Supremes record was repeating itself, and Diana Ross' voice was becoming tiresome. I sought out the brigadier to see if we could change the music. He was now standing with a portly white man with a large, flushed face, bald on top, a thin grey band of hair semi-circling from one ear to the other. 'Oh, there was nothing like the Air Force mess,' the brigadier told him. 'They had the best wines! Ah! See, all the other forces, the army, the navy, were all itinerant, so their messes weren't anything special. But their base was always the same, so we had to ...' The brigadier saw me standing nearby, and called to me. I approached the two men, and my host put his arm around my shoulder, and introduced him as Temple. The man said, 'Kaise ho?'

'Theek thaak.' I smiled. 'Your accent is better than mine.'

'Oh forget accent, his *Urdu* is better than all of ours,' the brigadier bellowed.

'Oh, nahin, nahin,' the foreigner begged. 'Bahut kum bolta hoon.'

'Nonsense!' the brigadier put his hand on Temple's shoulder and looked at me. 'He was the chief of police here, our very first Inspector-General of Sindh, until, what, '55?'

'"54. '54.' In English his accent was swanky British, the words delivered with self-important puffs of breath.

'Until '54,' the brigadier continued. 'Retired, and decided he wouldn't go back to his crumbling Empire.'

Temple looked down at his glass and smiled the closed, humble smile of a man being flattered. The host patted him on the shoulder and left the two of us together. 'Well, it's a funny story how we first met,' he said, as if the brigadier were still standing with us. His accent and manner seemed exaggeratedly British, perhaps he hadn't got word that the Empire had fallen. It's a funny story, he said again. But before he could begin this funny story, I said, 'I think I need to change the music.' And he nodded, more like a twitch, blinking. I found a Sonny and Cher record from their earlier days, *Look at Us*, and put that on.

Sajid was racing toward the kitchen in frantic duty, his private utterances louder and more urgent. I knew to avoid the kitchen, a high-activity sector, the servants' domain. With the same tentativeness of my first weeks in the house, I went to the balcony overlooking the front garden. A string of tiny yellow bulbs looped the garden's perimeter. More guests filed through the black gates of the pedestrian's entrance. The street was lined with parked cars and drivers leaning against their hoods, chatting and laughing, their own social event. I leaned against the stone balustrade and saw, at the side of a Chinese-looking man in dark blue, Malika stepping over the ridge of the gateway into the brigadier's compound. And as her companion greeted people in the driveway, she surveyed the place, starting with the garden and then raised her eyes to follow the height of the house. I took a step back so she wouldn't see me. She and her companion made a round of the garden, which was soon filled with the brigadier's loud voice. I peered cautiously over the balustrade. He greeted all the recent arrivals, and when he came to Malika and her companion, he held the man by the back of the head and pulled him into his shoulder. He pressed his palm against Malika's cheek and gave her a quick, miscalculated kiss that landed on her ear and forced her to squint. He spoke in Mandarin to the man. After a moment, he lifted his finger to Malika, said, 'Excuse us,' took her companion by the hand and led him into the house.

I crept back inside, to the chatter of guests sitting in the upstairs landing, all men, all politics: Legal Framework Order, East Pakistan, many more seats than the West, they won't let the Bongs win, never, too many resources in the East, they won't let them have control, Mujib's Six-Point Plan, *if* he succeeds, never will he succeed. Hand in hand, the brigadier and Malika's man came up the staircase, the host eagerly leading his guest past other guests, past me, and into the drawing room. I walked down the stairs, and the midget from the Agra opened the door for me, nodding and saying, 'Sir', in his female voice. Malika was seated at one end of the garden, the opposite side to the bar. I walked straight to the table of drinks. My heart was wild with panic. The barman, another bow-tied import from the Agra, poured me a whisky and water. Pretending to survey the garden arbitrarily, I caught Malika's eye, held up my hand in greeting, then walked over.

'What a surprise,' I said.

She nodded to the empty chair next to her.

'Eddie Carrapiet is upstairs. The guy you listen to on the radio.'

She smiled. 'I met him before.'

'Of course you have.' I sat down. Her eyes were full of thought, control, judgment. 'How's business these days?' I asked.

She scrunched her lips and tilted her head from side to side. 'Comme ci, comme ca.' Her lips were dry and cracked at some places, which she passed over with her tongue. Standing by the front door to the house, now on the outside, the midget watched us with his tiny conniving smile.

'That little plotter,' I said. 'What do you think he's plotting?'

'Plotting?' Malika asked.

'The midget. Why do you think he's watching us?'

'He's my lover.' She pronounced it *loaver*, and for an absurd moment I thought she was serious, until she laughed and put a calming hand on my shoulder. She looked down at my chest, at the buttons on my shirt, leaned over and unbuttoned the highest one. 'That's more better.' There was commotion near the gate. Words, orders were exchanged frantically, and finally the dialogue gave way to the squeal of the brigadier's gate opening. A black car climbed over the hump and into the driveway. The driver and a second man from the passenger side got out immediately. The second man opened the back door to produce a man of average height, with a globe of receding grey and black hair and a grey suit. Many in the garden stood up, including myself. I turned to Malika, who was still seated. 'Is that . . .?'

She smiled and nodded.

'Your performer,' I said.

He'd disappeared inside the house almost immediately, but it was certainly him. Bhutto. The man who'd led the revolt against Ayub, his former patron, who'd been in and out of the dictator's prisons because of the defiant slogans he was injecting into the country: *Roti, Kapra, Makkan.* Bread, Clothing, and a House. The man now fighting to lead.

'Should we go in, meet him?' I asked Malika.

'Wait,' she said. 'Sit down.' Her calm was almost condescending, embarrassing me for revelling in Bhutto's presence.

'You've seen *him*, too, many times, no doubt,' I said. 'At the Agra? Have you ever sat with him?'

'I been to his home.'

'In Karachi?'

'In his village. Larkana?' I waited silently for an explanation. 'It was when Shah of Iran come to Pakistan,' she continued. 'When Bhutto was . . . *foreign minister*?'

'Must have been.'

'Bhutto love the Shah. He invite him to stay in Larkana. They go hunting in the day. At night was entertainment. Us.'

'Us, who?'

'Dancers. From every cabaret in Karachi. He fly some of us, drive some of us, to his village. For two nights.'

'The hotel managers must have been outraged,' I said.

She shrugged. 'What they could do?'

I turned my eyes away from her, shook my head. 'Incredible. The Shah comes so he moves all of you to his village.' I laughed, mockingly, contemptuously. 'So did the Shah touch you?' Her eyes didn't move. 'Huh? Did he? What did you have to do for him? You like these *big men* don't you?'

'Just like you do,' she said coldly. I sipped my drink. More guests poured through the gate. 'Go in,' Malika continued. 'Go in and meet. You want to-want to, I know. Go.'

She was right. Meeting Bhutto, in the very home where I slept, what better indication of my arrival? I left Malika sitting in the lawn and came back in, ambled up the stairs. With the brigadier and Aunty Ruby at his side, Bhutto had naturally destabilized things. The governing impulse had changed, the guests automatically forming rows and half circles as though they'd all been transformed into a welcoming committee. The music had been turned off. I felt it my responsibility to turn it back on. Bhutto was kneeling down in front of Apa, held her hand in both of his, bowed and nodded in deference as she spoke. I couldn't hear what she was saying, but I recognized the affected humility in Bhutto's motions of head and face. And I was entertained to see the lords and ladies of Karachi turn into poor spectators in the sudden presence of real power. When Bhutto rose and left Apa, the lines and half circles broke down. With a clear indicator of prestige now present, the earlier one-upmanship gave way to contests of who could sustain

Bhutto's attentions. The vocabulary of politics that was previously spoken obliviously—elections, Yahya Khan, East Pakistan—was now employed, if at all, with care and discretion. Soon, as the Karachi pecking order took its natural course, Bhutto and the brigadier stood surrounded by men, the key group of the party now, with all others merely supporting cast members. Among the men who stood with Bhutto and the brigadier, was the Spanish diplomat, and Temple, the former police chief. The People's Party leader was listening more than he was talking, with a downcast and often serious face. He held his whisky glass from the base, enclosed in his palm. He had a heavy face, a large forehead full of thought, a long, strong nose and thick, dissatisfied lips. His thinning hair was thickest at the sides, extending into long sideburns that framed his full, baby cheeks.

Someone had removed the Sonny and Cher record and not replaced it. I searched through the shelf on which the player lay, finally settling on the Beach Boys, which didn't seem to fit the occasion but I didn't mind. When Aunty Ruby finally announced dinner, the brigadier and his wife escorted Bhutto to the dining room. The food had been laid out on two long tables, forming a right angle, covered in bleached white tablecloth. The three main players—host, hostess, politician—sat at the dinner table in the middle of the room, the brigadier at the head. They were followed shortly by the Spanish diplomat and his wife, and some of the other men in that original circle, including Temple. Sajid and other waiters circled the table, one by one, with platters and serving spoons. The rest of the guests served themselves and returned to the landing, the drawing room, the garden, some sitting with plates on their laps, others eating while standing.

Once I'd served myself—I received no indication from either the brigadier or Aunty Ruby to sit with them—I went back to the balcony to survey the downstairs for Malika, finding her again in the garden, but now with her Chinese companion by her side. Bhutto's men stood austerely around his car in the driveway, like chaperones. I sat next to Apa in the drawing room. Even with my full plate on my lap, she asked if I was eating, eating enough, and I had to raise my plate closer to her as evidence, show her that I'd helped myself to her kababs. 'Did you meet Bhutto?' she asked.

'Not yet,' I said.

'Why?' Not getting the answer she wanted, her face turned foul. I didn't answer, having learned the tricks of Apa's memory, that she couldn't carry on a sustained line of inquiry with too long a silence. The food was better than what they normally had at home. The Agra midget appeared next to me. 'More food, sir?' he said, with that plotting smile. I gave him my plate. 'More of Ruby begum's fish,' I ordered.

On the landing, which had filled with boisterousness, I recognized Rahim sahib, the SHO of Lalukhet who was to help with the squatters. His eyes were thin and runny, and he was close to barking to his three or four listeners. I stood in the doorway between veranda and drawing room. 'Being a police officer is a *command* performance,' Rahim sahib shouted, and stood up, angry, the roughness of drink. 'They make you do this,' he stomped one foot and raised his hand to his forehead at an angle, a perfect salute. 'Stand to attention, twenty times a day. The shock goes up your spine. *Twenty times a day*. It shatters your nerves. Affects your brain, makes you dumb. Then they send us out to inspect parades, to catch the badmaash.' He repeated the salute once more, wholeheartedly stomped the same foot and raised the same hand for the same perfect salute. He sat down holding his stomach. 'Hai,' he exhaled. He recognized me immediately when I went and stood next to him. I entreated him not to get up.

'Baithein, please.' He shifted to give me space. 'Yeh hain Shahbaz sahib,' he told the gentleman on his other side, an old man in a beige shikari suit with a loose and heavily marked face and glasses with fat, russet frame. I extended my hand.

'Sorry,' the old man said. 'I still don't shake hands.' I withdrew mine immediately, as if there was still the risk of disease with my even holding them out. The midget came and took my empty plate.

'Where's your turban?' I asked.

He giggled with embarrassment. 'Fish was good, sir?'

'Maybe Rahim sahib also wants some,' I said.

'Oh, nahin, nahin,' the policeman waved his hand, and gave his still unfinished plate of food to the midget.

'Usually, this boy wears a turban,' I explained.

Rahim sahib looked exhausted, either from the demonstration he had just made, or from actually saluting too much in his life, the nerves shattered and the brains pureed.

'I can still come to you?' I asked.

'Kya?'

'For the squatters?'

'Ahh! This boy, his family owns that bagh in Mirpurkhas, have you seen? Opposite the DC's office.'

'Full of squatters,' I added. The other man feigned interest. 'Speaking of which . . .' I turned back to my policeman friend. 'Have you had any l . . .'

'Beta, do you know which way is the washroom?' Tonight's guests were to use Apa's. I pointed him to it. Now with Rahim sahib, a line of four had formed outside Apa's room. My policeman friend stood at the back of the line with both hands at the hips, pointed towards his back, a feminine pose. Occasionally, his large frame tilted in one direction and then the other. I was unlikely to get an answer about the orchard and the squatters tonight. I decided I would relieve myself, too, and walked through the drawing room, past all the guests who were slowly recovering from dinner, drinks in hand again. I tried the door to the little television room. It was locked. I sought out Sajid and asked him to find me the key. 'Sir, right now, I'm too busy . . .' he began.

'Immediately, Sajid,' I ordered.

After using the bathroom, on my way back into the drawing room, I picked up my glass from the top of the cabinet where the television was, but stopped in front of it. I opened the glass doors. I put my drink back down, and searched through the collection of Betamax cassettes, found the one that the brigadier had played the first time I came to his house, with the white scratched-out label. I inserted it into the video recorder and turned on the television. I closed the door, turned the volume down, and played the video. From the divan, I watched the screen fill with flesh and hair and the grotesque moustache of the lead copulator. Without the brigadier beside me, I could appreciate the full measure of this national accomplishment he was so proud of. The woman had hair on her legs, too, small unshaven ones, and she lay passively, eyes and mouth both closed, as the bear on top of her, his mouth wide open, plugged away at his task.

The door opened, Aunty Ruby appearing behind it, stomping into the room and suddenly apprehending the lights, my presence on the divan. She put her hand to her heart, closed her eyes. 'Oof! I thought a burglar or . . .' She bent down and laughed dramatically. 'Oof, Allah!' She raised her hand to her heart again. She turned her head towards the television, her face now appealing for an explanation; I wasn't sure if I'd stopped the cassette in time.

'I was just seeing if . . .' I mumbled.

'I came to get some towels.'

'I was . . .'

She smiled and went into the bathroom, opened a cupboard and came out with a bunch of towels. She smiled at me again, uncomfortably, and left the room.

'I'm coming right out, I was just . . .' I said. But she was gone.

In the drawing room there were loud male voices, frantic, important movement, guests standing up and walking towards the commotion, preparing for Bhutto's departure. They collected in the landing. The brigadier walked with Bhutto, obsequious guests following behind. The two security men who were upstairs joined the mass, one walking ahead and one walking behind. Bhutto turned at the staircase, went to say goodbye to Apa. This put me in his trajectory. Bhutto shook hands with Rahim sahib, together with a brief pat on his shoulder. He and the brigadier passed me, before the brigadier stopped, took a few steps back and told Bhutto in Urdu, 'This is our guest, family friend,' then in English, 'he's been living with us for a few months.' I reached out my hand, and Bhutto shook it with a cold palm.

'Shahbaz,' I said.

He nodded indignantly, his mouth closed, his tongue pushed forward against the insides of his lips. I considered saying, 'Ghazanfar Aslam's son,' but Bhutto was already at Apa's feet, bidding her farewell, standing up and putting his hand to his forehead in final salute. Aunty Ruby was standing close, and I avoided her gaze.

Bhutto's men outside opened the car door for their boss. The crowd took small steps forward, with the brigadier and his wife at the fore, while the car reversed out of the driveway. Most of us stood at the gate as the Mercedes drove its illustrious passenger away. We came back indoors, carrying on as before, in anti-climax. Some took Bhutto's departure as a cue, and left as well. I climbed the staircase, surveyed the landing, the drawing and dining room, the garden from the balcony, and couldn't see Malika or her companion. I felt a hollowness. I'd been harsh and insulting, and wanted to make amends with her before she left. I came back downstairs, unlocked my bedroom door; with a different set of keys I unlocked my suitcase, reached into the long polyester pocket at the side and pulled out a packet of opium. While the after-dinner chatter resumed at a distance, in the downstairs kitchenette I boiled the opium in a small pot of milk, waited for it to cool, opened windows to let the smell out. I drank the mixture, rinsed the mug, and then sat on one of the concave stone chairs in the back veranda. I replayed Bhutto's image, his gestures and gait and the words I overheard. The Quetta wind brushed over me. I wished Malika was sitting here with me rather than wherever she was.

～

'What are you doing here?' the brigadier exclaimed, standing in the doorway.

I turned around. 'Oh, just ...'

'Come on, come on,' his voice was impatient but humouring. 'The fun is upstairs.'

I stood up, feeling the quiet vertigo of the opium. I didn't know how long I'd been out there. With his arm around my shoulder, the brigadier said, 'We were wondering where you'd disappeared to. I had Sajid even search the garden for you.' As I followed the brigadier upstairs I had the sense that I was being led to a tribunal that would arraign me for my transgression in the TV room. I thought up my defence, I would argue that the brigadier himself had described that tape as progress, a national gem and landmark. What was left of the soiree was Aunty Ruby, Carrapiett, two other men and, presumably, their wives. 'Did you meet Hammad sahib?' he asked. He brought his mouth close to my ear and in a lowered voice, he added, 'The one with that stiff leg.' He often identified people by a handicap. Before I could respond, the brigadier bellowed, 'Hammad sahib, you have met Ghazanfar's son, haven't you?'

The man who responded wore glasses over Burmese-looking eyes, and had sloppy, jutting lips like a duck's beak. He stood and I shook his hand; he hissed eagerly and nervously, shook my hand with all his strength. He was a professor at Dhaka University, they told me, and as I sat down, Aunty Ruby said, 'Shahbaz, Hammad sahib was just telling us about a legal situation he was just, uh, embroiled in?'

Hammad sahib looked at me and with a piercing, shrill voice said, 'Haan yaar. I just spent a month in jail.' I raised my eyebrows, nodded. He had an awful set of front teeth, protruding and gap-ridden. 'It was small thing,' he continued. 'We live in a rented house. Landlord is complete haramee. It's two storeys, one bedroom downstairs, three upstairs, where my wife and children are. So one day haramee landlord tells my wife that he's going to move his own family into downstairs bedroom. I mean, can you imagine,' he squinted his eyes in contempt. 'So I said, no you're not. So, on and on, back and forth, for two weeks or so. Then one night he shows up in driveway with whole bloody family, seven or eight, who he thinks will fit into tiny room downstairs. I told him, get your bloody family off my driveway. He said, ho ho ho, this is my driveway. But you've rented it to *us*, haramzada! But he wouldn't budge an inch. So I went in and got my revolver out. I fired a warning shot in the air. Still: nothing. Not an inch. So I had no choice.'

'You shot him?' Aunty Ruby asked, smiling.

He wiped his lips with a handkerchief and shook his head. 'In the foot, only. The guy bled all over driveway. Black blood, true haramee blood. So then police came. They're friends of mine over there. They said, bring out your servant, we'll say he did it. I said arrey, why the hell you will arrest the servant for what *I* did? What are you talking? So poor buggers had no choice but to arrest me. Peeing in their pants—excuse me. I told them, arrey bhai, fikkar muth karo, nobody's going to fire you for doing your job. A month in jail.'

'How was that?' Aunty Ruby asked, in a light tone that seemed to refer more to a recently opened restaurant than a prison.

'Oh,' he made a circle of his thumb and index finger, 'first class! The one relaxing month I've had in a long time. This kid they had there, nice kid, would bring me the newspaper every morning with a good breakfast. I had more servants in prison than I do at home.'

The opium was gathering force inside me. I felt itchy, hot. As Sajid, barefoot, went around the drawing room to remove empty glasses and dessert trays, I asked him to bring me a glass of water. His face looked wan, sweated through. Hammad sahib's voice came to me now in flashes. I looked down, avoided eye contact with anyone around me.

'You're lucky, Hammad bhaiyya,' the brigadier said. 'This is not the best time for you Bongs to be breaking laws.'

'Oh, ho ho.' Hammad sahib clenched his fist and then, mockingly, bit into it. When there was laughter, I followed suit. Sajid brought me a glass of more ice than water. I put the glass to my cheeks, became aware of my company again, and gulped it down. I sucked and bit at the ice. I felt the crunching sounds drew everyone's attention to me. I kept the broken cubes in my mouth, unsure what to do with them. I was barely conscious when the hosts and guests rose, accompanied them to the front door and turned away towards my room, out of sight, finally.

2

There was only one other person in my compartment so I stretched out on the green seats for the hour between Cantt Station and Hyderabad. Half lucid, half dreaming, I imagined an old lady at the very centre of the orchard, inside a small dwelling or chamber, the shabby headquarters of the whole project. And this old lady was the matron-saint, the pulse that gave the orchard life, without whom the squatters couldn't continue breathing and building and breeding. I'd come to the orchard, perhaps at night, when all the activity stopped, and all the squatters were inside, cooking, sleeping, fornicating. Creeping through the paths that I'd navigated as a child every spring, into her chamber, putting a knife to her throat. Yes, ending the matter there, restoring the orchard to its old majesty.

I forgot to bring a book, so I had nothing but contemplations to occupy myself with. Mona Phuppi and my father: who were my own sympathies really with?

When Mona Phuppi sent him money from the sale of part of the family properties, he'd put it into the magazine he'd been planning for years, relating to the arts of the Islamic Third World. A fellow ex-pat had suggested that a *politics* and arts publication may be more marketable, even a grand success. 'There's a gap in market,' that friend had said. 'Anything that smacks of a left-wing, progressive publication in Pakistan is being shut down or squeezed because of this bloody Pak-American military pact. Simply for us to show the Yanks how anti-communist we are. But imagine starting one of those *here*, where the government can't touch us.' But my father rejected the idea, his childish principles prevailing over good sense. No politics, ever again. He'd become completely devoted to the arts not because of a particular aesthetic, but as a grudge against politics (his final professional resting place was a publishing house that took out a poetry calendar every year that was distributed throughout Europe, in which he fought to include Muslim poets like Iqbal, Ghalib and even his contemporary and collaborator in the conspiracy case, Faiz Ahmed Faiz. Those calendars, like the old issues of his aborted magazine, lay around the apartment, offered to friends who came over). All of that emphasis on Islamic art, what was essentially a lost world to him, that desire to reclaim it somehow through these works—paintings, films, magazines, poetry calendars—prevented him and, by extension, his son, from becoming a part of the city we were now living in. And while he could handle being a man apart in Paris, for at his age there was no other way to be in a foreign city, he'd made me a child apart.

When his own younger brother had gotten married, my father had declined the invitation to come back to Pakistan for the wedding. 'Because you'—he'd started talking about Pakistanis living in Pakistan as 'you'—

'have a military ruler.' He carried around Paris this decayed Pakistani nobility. But I came eventually to suspect that the talk about not coming back because of military rule was an attempt to give his position a moral pretty costume. Actually, he was too nervous and afraid to come back. Caution, trepidation: that was the legacy of his failed conspiracy. That was his legacy to me. And so this man who took part in a failed communist coup, who should have, for example, embraced the events of May '68 in Paris, instead rejected and recoiled from them. Worse, he'd instilled that same passivity and caution in me. It was because of him that I didn't attack the man who'd taken my Ayatul-Kursi. For example. But I was willing to fight his fight for the orchard. Why? Why was this need to prove myself to him so strong, when he'd proved nothing to me? Or was I fighting for *him*, for *his* return to nobility?

The wait at Hyderabad this time was shorter and quieter than when I'd come with Mona Phuppi. It was a hot and humid day in Mirphurkhas, and the orchard was filled with sun and sharp shadows. Many of the male squatters were shirtless, shiny stripes of sweat on their backs. I thought of myself standing at the mouth of a cave, this place some kind of void—in my father's life, in the country's life. And its restoration seemed far beyond his or Mona Phuppi's or even Rahim sahib's powers. The squatter-demons went on building, composing this dull afterlife, with mud and sheets and bundles of twigs and rope and hammers and ladders and tyres tied to branches of trees for kids to swing from. So far outside the system that the law protected them. Everything seemed so calm and contained, not the place of grotesque disorder and hysteria, the bloated liver of this small town, that I conjured in my thoughts since that day my aunt brought me to see it. I felt a discomfort in my chest, my purpose in Karachi seemed suddenly meaningless, or its meaning was far beyond me. Why was I here, to fight over *this*?

I didn't realize that I'd walked a good way into the plot, and was now well past the first line of trees. If I walked any further, I feared, the whole place would ingest me, and that would be the end of it. The orchard seemed hotter than the streets outside, as if it lay over burning coal. A dark façade prevented memories from coming to me. I couldn't remember that old mango orchard now, those beautiful days and those naked midnights in its depths. Not with this other thing right before me.

But I stood there—waiting for images of that older kingdom to emerge from underneath the destitution and dust and heat. I thought if I fixed a rapt enough gaze it would all come springing, us children and our games and our fresh-lime drinks, the adults playing rummy on the patio. But, no, the destitution and dust and heat sat inflexibly in their place. A group of squatter kids, barefoot boys and girls, had dug a hole and were now filling it with bricks. Closest to me were two little boys, a couple of feet from the ones tending to the little pit, one with a stick in his hand, ordering the other one around and striking him on the leg when he got angry. This Little Chief was wearing brown pants that stopped well above his ankles and choked his waist. His subordinate wore a faded aqua shalwar kameez. They stopped when they saw me. I knelt down, and like puppies they scampered over. The smaller kid pressed his finger into my breast, into the small emblem of my shirt. 'Whose flag is this?' he asked. 'Is it the Indian flag?' His Little Chief hit him on the back of the head. 'It's not a flag!' he hollered. The smaller one hollered back in a patois, perhaps Sindhi.

'He doesn't know anything,' Little Chief explained to me.

'How old are you boys?' I asked.

'Seven.'

'Seven? You, only seven?'

'Seven, eight, nine, ten, eleven, twelve ...'

'All right, all right, Chief,' I said. 'Bas. Doesn't matter. How long have you lived here?'

'You're from outside?' he asked.

'I'm from outside.'

'From the department?'

'I'm the landlord,' I said, using the word 'wadera', a word that conjured ancient feudal power.

'Whose landlord?'

'Yours,' I patted him on the shoulder. 'And yours, too,' I shook the other's arm. If I kidnapped them both, would anyone notice?

'Achha,' Little Chief said, and with his stick he swiped at pebbles and grass. 'How did Ali Khan die?' he asked, still looking at the ground.

'Who is Ali Khan?'

He aimed the stick at a brown cat. I took it from him before he could strike, and tossed it away. *Grab them, one in each arm, and take them away, on the train back to Karachi, hide them in Ghulam Hussain's brother's quarters. Who would notice?*

'How did Ali Khan die?' he persisted.

'How should I know?' I laughed. Behind the kids, some of the elders looked in our direction, though nobody approached us, they went on with their squatters' lives. Who was this man, Ali Khan, whose death they wanted to know about? 'They found him hanging from a fan in the morning,' I said. 'His wife found him. No, his wife's brother. In the morning, he didn't come out of his room.'

'He was staying there? At the wife's brother's?' the other child asked.

'Yes. For one night.' My own inventions amused me. 'But he died before twelve o'clock at night.'

'Not in the morning?'

'They found him in the morning. But he died at night.'

'Who killed him?'

'Maybe he did it himself,' I replied. 'Maybe somebody else.'

'Achha?'

'His mother-father are still alive. The father was in the air force. You know the air force? The people who go in planes. And fight wars. So the father will find out what happened to his son. They'll have a ... *investigation*.' I used the English word, which they clearly didn't understand, but it didn't matter. The smaller boy lost interest in the conversation and moved off to chase some small animal by the boundary wall. It was now just me and Little Chief.

'He had three children,' I continued. 'Three children now without a father.'

He looked forlorn, nodded absently, kicked pebbles with his bare feet.

'Their father, killed. He was killed. The police said he killed himself. But his father's ... *investigation* shows he was killed. By someone else. You understand, Chief?' He again nodded his head gloomily. I wondered if I could make him cry, push the story far enough.

An adult from the heart of the settlement called out, 'Chottoo!' Little Chief turned around. The woman, miniscule in the distance, was clearly looking at us with some sense of alarm. The boy gazed in her direction, absent-minded. I grabbed his arm with force. 'Are you listening to me, little one! I'm trying to tell you about the death of this man, what did you call him?' The boy was silent. I tightened my grip. 'What was the man's name, the one who died!'

'Pata nahin,' the boy said warily.

'*You don't know*? One minute ago, you asked me about him!' The woman in the distance called to him again.

'Go,' I told the boy. 'I'll tell you the rest next time.'

'You're coming back?'

'Yes,' I replied. 'I'm coming back.'

❧

Those kids. Again: was there no way to keep them? Maybe these haris, these settlers, were something to cherish. How does one suggest such a thing to Karachi high society? But I went to Mona Phuppi's with exactly this purpose. The television set in her drawing room carried reports of the devastation from a cyclone in East Pakistan, but Phuppa Jaan, sitting on his rocking chair in front of the the television, turned it off as soon as I arrived. He said my phuppi was resting. The two of us sat first in the television-cum-drawing room, he on his rocking chair. I knew only half of what I said reached Phuppa Jaan intact, the rest deformed in the electric jumble of his earpiece. I spoke slowly, loudly, pronouncing the big words in discreet syllables.

We sat down for lunch with still no sign of Mona Phuppi. I mentioned this, but Phuppa Jaan was looking down at his plate, mixing daal into his rice with vigorous motions of his hand. His earpiece was silent. With a twirling action of his hand, he gathered a mouthful into the small beaker he made at the tips of his four fingers, held in place by his thumb, and made a vulgar sucking sound when he brought it to his mouth. My father ate his daal-chawal like Phuppa Jaan. I never enjoyed watching. I picked at the rice and daal with my fork. My uncle's hollow sucking sounds continued. I put my fork down, lifted my napkin from my lap and laid it next to my plate. 'Phuppa Jaan,' I said. '*Phuppa Jaan.*' He looked up from his plate, his fingers dripping with dark mixture. 'I have to go to the bathroom, please excuse me.' He nodded, and with a full mouth muttered an approving, hmm-hmm.

I turned on the tap at high strength, closed the toilet lid and sat down to rehearse my speech to my aunt in my head. All is not lost if the squatters stay. We can build a glorious mini-nation out of it. I washed my face with cold water, pulled the lever of the flush. When I returned to the dining room I saw my aunt coming from the opposite direction. I was for the first time delighted to see her. But as I walked over to greet her, I noticed the heavy eyelids hung low over the whites of her eyes, hiding half the pupil. Her steps were slow and seemed involuntary.

'Mona Phuppi, adaab,' I said, my hand to my forehead.

She smiled with a small bit of life. 'Jeetairaho,' she said softly. I brought my cheek close to her, expecting a kiss, but her lips barely moved.

'Jaani,' Phuppa Jaan said, rising from his seat, licking his soaked fingers. 'Go lie down.' His tone was paternal.

'I just came for a glass of water,' she pleaded. So pathetic was this figure, it seemed absurd to equate it with the woman I feared.

'You should ring for it,' Phuppa Jaan replied, irritated. 'Go! I'll have it sent up.' Quietly, she turned around and walked back towards the stairs. 'Come,' Phuppa Jaan led me back to the table. 'She's been in a bad spell the last few days. Doctor says to increase her medication. So . . .' We sat back down. Phuppa Jaan's plate was almost empty. I began again on mine. According to my father, these highly medicated states of hers usually followed some gross emotional outburst, most often directed at her husband. I remembered one story when Mona Phuppi had beaten him with her hard, bare hands, telephoned his eighty-year-old mother and asked her to 'come and pick up your son's body'. When Phuppa Jaan's family came to the house, they supposedly found him sitting on the terrace, listening to the radio, downplaying the incident and assuming the blame. I searched him now for some sign of fresh suffering. Clearly annoyed by his wife's unscheduled appearance, he closed his eyes, turned his face down and shook his head. His motions looked self-condemning. We were both but small men in these big events, envoys of the real players in this great game of land, family, justice.

I ate quickly, and finished my green tea as fast as I could, mostly in silence. On the way home, I considered this new vision of Mona Phuppi. This was the first time I'd seen her like that, and it was a peculiar sensation to have everything my father had said about her confirmed like this. What a curious creature she was. How a mind so prone to alteration, so defenceless at times, could be so efficient and abominable when clear. Seeing her in that weakened state did nothing to lessen my apprehensions; if anything I was *more* apprehensive, because I realized that her affliction introduced her to extremes I didn't know. Madness was sharper than anything my father or I had at our disposal. If only we could freeze that broken figure, how easy it would all be. To freeze Mona Phuppi on that one extreme, washed-out. But of course she would recover. If not today, then tomorrow; and if not tomorrow, then the day after. Back to sanity, with who knew what kinds of resentments for the rest of us.

West Pakistan didn't see any of the cyclone, but the weather here was nevertheless grey and melancholy and messy, the roads darkened by a damp slippery layer.

I wanted to know the anatomy of the whole thing, what that moment of breakdown felt like when the madness finally settled inside her. And what majestic tantrums preceded the condition she was in today? One of the things that used to annoy me about my father was his limited temper. It was a problem of capacity, or incapacity, and it often prevented him from staking any proper claim to what was his or ours. Easy targets. But Mona Phuppi was a different proposition altogether. Her partial insanity was probably what gave her her appetite for having things her way, and I regretted that I had to ally not with *this* force, but my father's passivity.

∽

My next stop that day was Ghulam Hussain. This cyclone in the East was serious enough that the elections had been postponed. And if it was serious enough for that then it was likely to have wiped out a good chunk of Bengali life. The men indeed seemed melancholy when I walked in unannounced to the quarters, three of them, including Ghulam Hussain, sitting side by side on the mattress, faces pointed to the floor. 'Aiyai, aiyai,' they said, reluctantly and unsurprised. How to finesse my concern for their, particularly Ghulam Hussain's, families back home? 'Everything okay? Your families'— I used the English word—'your families, all okay?' I learned from Ghulam Hussain and the man to one side that the third man there, an older fellow with a bony face who I'd seen once before, had in fact been unable to locate his sister and nephew for days. The old man himself kept quiet, submitted himself, his anguish, as a subject to apprehend. 'He's very angry at the government,' Ghulam Hussain said. In a tone almost a warning to *me*. I sat crouched in front of them listening and nodding and occasionally, as required, looking at the old man and shaking my head, closing my eyes in sympathy.

The good despondency we were working at was somewhat undone by the entrance of a physically boisterous, pale Pathan with a large carton on his shoulder. He dropped it half-carelessly to the floor. 'Ahh!' Ghulam Hussain rejoiced, crouched next to the carton and parted its flaps. Inside were a dozen or so bottles of clear liquid, presumably the same clear liquid that Ghulam Hussain's friend here drank, the same stuff that Rahim sahib, the brigadier's policeman friend in Lalukhet, said he was cracking down on. The poor man's drink, from the bark of the Acacia tree. Ghulam Hussain moved bottles from the carton to the cabinet built into the wall. 'If I don't have my omelette business, Shahbaz bhai, then I need *something*, is it or no?' He held out a bottle, which I took tentatively. I removed money from my pocket. 'Nahin, nahin, Shahbaz bhai!' he said. 'You take this one. After that, if you want more . . .' I put the bottle, a gift that should never have exchanged hands (I was never to be trusted, my friend), in my pocket. More men walked into the quarters, a ring of smugglers, loud, agitated. One of the men took a bottle from the carton, and Ghulam Hussain objected with his Bengali wrath. He took the bottle out of the guy's hand and put it back in the carton. 'Loh!' wailed the man, looking at me, appealing to me to recognize the injustice here. Then he barked a few lines to me, or at me. It was exactly these types, like the man who took my Ayatul-Kursi, who interfered in the kind of world and the kind of life I wanted. But they were all over the place. Hiding like guerillas, waiting to ambush decent people. The empty carton was pushed to one corner, and Ghulam Hussain closed the cabinet forcefully, then stared at everyone else, as if to warn them that the cabinet was not to be re-opened. You'd lose all this authority if you came with me to Paris, I wanted to tell him. Are you prepared to do that? And just as I was settling away from these troubling thoughts, Ghulam Hussain asked, 'Would people in France drink this?'

I froze. Had Ghulam Hussain reimagined himself a glorious lowlife in Paris, always protected by me and my father, the expat racket? God, what had I done, and how to outdo it?

'No, the French people, their sharab is the world's best,' I explained. 'Sharab from outside, they won't drink. The French people . . . they're very strange people.'

'Kya, they're not good people?'

'They *are* good people.' I couldn't bring myself to go

all the way, though I should have—should have said
they're a rotten race. 'But strange people. They . . .
whatever is French, and whatever is not French, for
them it's . . .'

'Achha, achha!' He laughed inexplicably. 'I've
understood.' No. No, you haven't.

If I couldn't find a way of telling him, then when the
time came I would simply leave. Leave without saying
goodbye. He wouldn't be too hurt by that. Deep down
he knew, as they all did, that the bond between my kind
and his kind was as brittle as . . . But then the thing to
do was probably to stop coming to see him, to stop
seeing him as my responsibility, to get over this infantile
need for absolution and to do as much as I could before
I abandoned him.

I'd stayed my necessary half hour, and asked him to
drive me home. Lyari was Bhutto territory, and
everywhere, shops, buildings, boundary walls, displayed
his party colours and 'Jivay Bhutto' graffiti. But as we
left the area, and reentered Saddar, we got stuck in
another party's jalsa, a furious voice in a loudspeaker
proclaiming the Jamaat-i-Islami as the only party that
would restore religious meaning and virtue to the country
after twenty-three years of Western (something). The
Urdu was sophisticated, but what I could decipher and
condense were accusations that Bhutto sahib was a
sharabi and carouser like Yahya, that Muslims were
being killed by Hindus in India's Gujarat province and
that only a truly Islamic Pakistan could stand up for
Muslims. And he finished by declaring that today was
the Glory of Islam Day. And in the car I realized there
was something else, too, a little more distant to be sure
but still no doubt there: I looked at Ghulam Hussain,

from the side of my eye, and thought, with things changing the way they were, was it possible I'd need him at some point in the future? The thought that he, or any of his friends who were bantering back there merrily in Bengali, might commit an act against me if that's what his people needed of him, had entered my thoughts more than once. If power was going to change hands—and who knew what this democratic experiment would yield?—wasn't it possible I'd need someone like Ghulam Hussain? Oh, my need of people, protectors, knights!

The jalsa continued, a new speaker now chanting the same stuff, anti-Western, anti-Bhutto, anti-feudal, anti-secular, promising to finally make the country the theocracy it was supposed to be at birth. He, too, referred again and again to Yawm-i-Shawkat-i-Islam.

'They say if Mujib wins the election he'll try to create an independent Bangladesh? If he wins.'

Ghulam Hussain shrugged, 'Who knows, Shahbaz bhai, who knows?'

'You think Mujib will win?' I asked.

After briefly contemplating this, he said noncommittally, 'God's will.' He twitched and shivered, as if the spectre of great historical change, good or bad, was too daunting to contemplate. When we arrived at the brigadier's I put a five rupee note in his kameez pocket, which he covered with his hand and smiled in false shame.

3

'Sirjee.' Sajid knocked on my door.

'Aajao!' I called, and he opened the door.

'Sir . . . uh . . . brigadier sahib is calling you.' His tone was hesitant, humourless, and unsettling. I followed him up the stairs. 'Have you met Apa today?' Sajid asked. I hadn't, but didn't like that Sajid took it upon himself to remind me.

'Apa, adaab.'

She looked up from her papers, which she was reading closely under the sharp yellow of her lamp, and the lens of her magnifying glass. She took a moment to record my height, my face. 'Jeetairaho,' she said with a short cackle. She cleared her papers, made sure there was space on her bed for me to sit. 'Haan, toh . . . ah . . .' She was absent still, the pain of returning rising audibly in her throat. 'Have you eaten? Haan, Sajid, make him an egg.'

'No,' I said. 'It's night time.' One day I would have to break it to her that I wasn't that precious thing, a growing boy.

Apa looked up at Sajid, murmuring and confused,

searching for reason. 'Haan, haan, Shahbaz.' More conscious, she asked why I hadn't come to her for my usual hour of everyday Urdu speech—indeed I'd been spending an allotted hour almost every day, sitting on her bed with her, listening, asking questions, getting complicated vocabularly down, and trying to use it in subsequent talks with her. Unless I was forced otherwise, I would use English over Urdu, so the brigadier wasn't an option (besides, I didn't want him to know exactly how deficient my Urdu was). And people like Sajid— how much could I speak to him? With Apa's loathing of the English language, using the awful Angrezi words only when she needed to translate, *she* was the one for me, another in the brain trust.

'Now that you're here,' she said, 'I can ask you. You see Sajid here? Why does he keep that moustache? Arrey bhai, if he wants to keep a moustache it should be thin, thin, and long and like this.' She intimated the design with the fingers of both hands twirling on the two sides of her upper lip.

'Nahin, nahin,' Sajid exhorted. 'Apa, what are you saying? That's a villain's moustache, from the films you watch. A moustache from the old days.'

Apa scowled, screamed, 'Woh zamana tha!' She tapped my knee for confirmation. 'Hain na?' she said expectantly. '*That* was the time.'

'Absolutely,' I said. I rose.

'Arrey, where are you going!' Apa demanded.

I told her I had to confer with the brigadier about something, to which she gave her guarded assent. I asked Sajid to stay with her. Interrupted in her private activities, she now needed company, an addressee, someone to lay her cards on the table for, at the tail end of her life.

I went up to the mezzanine, knocked on the door, and was told by Aunty Ruby, from behind the closed door, that Alamgir Uncle was in the bathroom and would be out any minute. I sat on the sofa outside their room, overlooking the drawing room. I could hear Aunty Ruby through the thin walls, coughing, opening drawers, placing jewellery. The flush sounded, the flick of a light switch, a shutting door.

'These bloody haemorrhoids,' the brigadier grumbled.

'Did you get more tubes of—'

'Arrey nahin, this stuff doesn't do a damn thing! When's Nidal coming back from Manchester?'

'Two weeks, he said.'

'Tell him to bring five tubes of—'

'I've told him,' Aunty Ruby said. 'I told you I told him.'

'Well he better not forget. We'll send him right back.' The brigadier's slow, heavy footsteps, sighs of physical discomfort. 'Official Chinese dinners, bloody hell! Don't accept them from now on.'

'*You* accepted this one.'

'They serve those bureaucratic menus. You know, the menus are decided by their Foreign Office in Beijing?'

'The kid is outside waiting for you,' Aunty Ruby said.

'Will Nidal be staying here, with us?'

'He never stays with us. Apa makes his life hell. My own *brother*, and that bloody woman treats him like a servant. And can you *please* get some money from her, I don't have a penny!'

'Yes, yes. She's been stingy of late,' the brigadier said. 'All of a sudden she thinks she's going to live a while longer. But I'll ask her, bhai. Where's my thermometer?'

'Let me touch you ... Oof, you drama, you're fine! You haven't had a fever in five years.'

'Remind Nidal to get those bloody tubes. *Five* tubes.'
The brigadier opened the door and came out onto the
landing, with a small ice box and a bottle of water. I
rose. 'Adaab,' I said.

'What I'd do to shit without it burning. Jeetairaho,
beta,' he tapped the side of my neck and placed the ice
box and water on the table. He walked to the door of
the library on the opposite side of the mezzanine. 'I'm
going to cook us up a batch of single-malt. In the mood
for a single-malt?' he asked as he went in. He returned
with a bottle and two glasses, sat down with care, a
sigh. 'Let me tell you something,' he said. And as I
expected he launched into a story of Parsis and liquor
licences. He shifted in his seat, and with every movement
uttered a sigh to relieve or reveal the pain in his rectum.
His booze supplier, he was convinced of late, had been
bought over by the bloody Parsis, giving him diluted
stuff so that the Parsis, at war with the Agra since it
began, would reclaim their supremacy in the Karachi
cabaret racket. 'I'll bet my life on that,' he now thrust
his finger in my direction, as if I'd argued against him.
'This country is going to the dogs. Too much tampering,
these days. Tashkent Agreements, peace treaties. Abhey,
let things be. It's the nature of things, it's the times.'
And with that I knew that another of his pet topics, the
'65 war, wasn't far from his lips. 'Nothing more unnatural
to me than a peace treaty, in my books. Bloody politicians
playing gods. Let the chips fall where they may, hai ke
nahin? Let the army do what armies are supposed to do.'

'Bilkul,' I said.

'I mean, they say keep religion out of politics. Well
and good, *start there*. Get rid of peace treaties. Stop
tampering! Which brings me back to . . . what?'

'The booze problem,' I said.

'The *booze problem*, exactly! Ha. Now, your Aunty Ruby in there doesn't think there is a booze problem. But I know someone is tampering with our stuff.' We heard her laugh derisively from inside the room. The brigadier stopped. He leaned forward and said, 'Beta, can you see if I feel warm.' I touched his forehead, told him I sensed nothing unusual. 'Anyhow, I would bring those distributors here, but Apa would complain. She doesn't like people of those ... *low* professions coming to the house.' He leaned back in his seat and stretched out a leg at a slight angle, again to give his sore rectum relief. He rested his leg across my knees. A well-cut strong foot. I envied a man with good feet. My own feet, as a lady in a van once told me, were *terrible*. She told me I had a nice face, nice chest ... *mais des pieds enormes. Big toes toooo big*! 'Anyway forget all that, bhai. The reason I've asked you up, beta, I need you do something for me. This Friday we're having a special evening at the cabaret. A People's Party thing. You know, with the elections coming up—if the East can stop having bloody cyclones—I thought we'd have a ...' I leaned forward in interest, flattered at the opportunity to participate. 'The problem is,' he continued. 'The problem is that a friend from Dhaka is coming that same night. Hammad bhaiyya.'

'I met him. At your party.'

'Oh, haan! So you *know* him! This should make it simpler. He's coming in earlier that same evening. Sort of unexpected. Now Hammad bhaiyya is a great man, but a typical Bong, a big Mujib supporter and what-not. Especially after that bloody cyclone, he's now completely riled up at West Pakistan. So I can't have him coming to the cabaret. He's a bit of nutter, no telling what he'll do. You know he shot his landlord in the foot recently.'

'Spent a month in jail,' I added.

'I don't want him getting drunk and ruining the evening. That night we kept him away from Bhutto, thank God. So I need you to take care of him. Make sure he doesn't leave his room ... you know, entertain him, a bottle of—he drinks Black Dog, like Yahya; he loves Mujib but he drinks like Yahya. A bottle of Black Dog on the house. It'll be waiting in the room. Or— yes!—you can take it to him. You know, normally I would assign a dancer, Malika or one of the others, but I need them all downstairs. It wouldn't make a difference anyway, Hammad bhaiyya's such a bloody prude when it comes to women. He'll shoot his landlord in the foot but he won't touch a girl. Fucking Bongs.'

'Won't he get suspicious ...'

'Hammad bhaiyya—you get one drink in him and he'll be ready to sit and talk your ear off until Sunday afternoon.'

He removed his leg from across my knees, sat forward, scowling in his physical ordeal. He sipped his drink thoughtfully as if to relieve the pain. He scratched his head, those long sharp nails cutting the skin, producing the sound of an onion being sliced. 'So you're becoming friendly with Malika?' This stopped me momentarily. 'A fine lady, hain na? You know she left a husband to continue being a dancer?' The brigadier then winked and waved his own comment off with his hand. 'Well, who really knows? That's what they all say, hain na?'

'Why would—'

'Arrey choro bhai, it's all part of their act.' He sounded impatient, annoyed at my naiveté. But soon he smiled like a rascal, that djinn inside him raising its head. 'There's something more you want out of this.' I denied it, but the sides of his smile rose like wings. He tapped his long, strong fingernails against the table in a crisp horse-gallop. 'Things can always be arranged, my young friend. She's a lovely lady.' He poured himself another drink. Once he'd leaned back in his seat, he said, 'Haan!' to start new talk, real talk, comrade to comrade. Like his ninety-three-old aunt downstairs, this was the time that the brigadier liked to have an audience. I wanted my bed downstairs. 'So, I was telling you before, about the '65 war, hain na?' Yes, he was. He was always talking about it, whenever he was three whiskies down. Now I'd nod again through the details, the Prophet's hair stolen, the Muslims of Kashmir rioting in protest, Bhutto and the others convincing Ayub that now was the perfect time to win back the Valley, how it was all planned at his cabaret and, therefore, how he could have stopped it all. The stupidity of leaving Lahore wide open for the Indian army to come right in.

'Jee, jee, uncle, you were saying . . . please continue.'

∾

The midget held the hotel's entrance door open, and when I walked through he said, 'Ek minute, sir.' He searched for a coworker to man the door, and once he found him—a man dressed in the same red uniform and turban, but three times my friend's size—he grabbed my hand like an eager child and led me towards the reception. It all began with this midget. Malika, the brigadier, my Karachi life as it was today. Five rupees in his pint-sized hand, and Karachi opened up for me. 'That sahib—what is his name?' he said.

'Hammad sahib?'

'He arrived half an hour ago. On the top floor.' My little friend was out of breath already, rushing through the lobby, the brigadier obviously having designated this a high priority. The hotel's circular reception desk was at the centre of the large hall, manned right now by only one attendant, who was on one phone while another rang endlessly. Walking through the hall, towards the cabaret, was that old high court judge and his wife, the duo of the trolley ride and 'I am the Law' mantra, presently sober, beginning their night. A foursome of French speakers, three men and one woman in a suit, the sharpest dressed of the four. My spirits swelled with the sound of that familiar language. I'd find them at the cabaret later, I told myself.

The midget gave me a bottle of Black Dog from under the reception desk, along with the room number on a square of paper. Fourth floor. First, I decided to drop by Malika's. Although I'd taken satisfaction in the insinuations I'd made to her about the Shah of Iran, in the brigadier's garden, there was no doubt I envied her proximity to the business of states, her small part in international affairs.

She was wearing a black T-shirt, a pair of blue jeans and rubber slippers with turquoise straps, holding a small red plastic bowl from which she raised something edible to her mouth. She strutted back through the room indifferently as I walked in behind her, and dropped into a chair swinging her legs like a child. On the bed was a red, black and green outfit. 'Gur?' She proffered the bowl. I broke off a piece and put it in my mouth, sat down on the other chair. She ate in a regular, noisy rhythm, receiving the food in her mouth with a forceful biting down that crackled, chewed briefly with her front teeth and then, as she moved the morsels to the side of her mouth she parted her lips, emitting another noise, this one wet, full of saliva.

'I'm going to be entertaining one of your boss' friends tonight,' I said. 'While you entertain the rest.'

'Yes, now you are Alamgir's puppy.'

'You and me both.'

She put the bowl down, got up to open a cupboard, pulled out a jainamaz, spread it on the carpeted floor. I stood at the door of the bathroom and watched as she turned on the tap, kicked off her slippers, rolled the ends of her jeans back a couple of folds, and splashed water on each foot. She lifted her T-shirt halfway up her torso, and splashed more water at her armpits, then the back of her neck and finally rinsed her hands. I sat back down, and she stood on the jainamaz, facing the Kabbah, made the little prelude gestures of hands and head, then the up-and-down of the body, the prayer in full swing. When she was done she folded the jainamaz and placed it on the bed. She sat back down, quiet, replenished.

'So, they say you were married once,' I said.

She nodded. 'One thousand years before.'

'In Ancient Egypt?'

'Cairo.'

'But you never had any children.'

She shook her head. 'We live in a small apartment. Just one room. The kitchen was in same room.'

'Sounds depressing. Is that why you left him?'

'No.'

'Why did you leave him?'

'Why?' she repeated absently.

'Because he couldn't give you children?'

'He was trying to be politician. Too much.' She picked

up the gur again and broke off another small piece, chewed it in the same lively pattern. The talk of her marriage and life in Cairo seemed to enliven her. For a while she had a distant smile on her lips, and then, swinging her legs like a school girl she talked about being born in Tanta, where her grandfather and father had a sweets shop, and where she knew the family of a famous belly dancer and actress named Naima who convinced beautiful, fourteen-year-old Malika, who was already becoming an expert in dance, to join their circus in Cairo.

'And that's where you met your politician-husband? Married a client, eh? But then he wanted you to leave this world of yours because it looked bad for him, and so you left him. Yes? And where does the brigadier come in?'

'He see a photo of me. He like my photo.'

'Ha. And who sent him this photo?'

She aimed her whole frame at me, realizing I knew so little, and explained sensitively away like mother to child, in a tone of voice to make a shocking story more palatable: every cabaret, dear Shahbaz, has a directory of performers from all over the world. When, as manager, you see one you like, you contact her agency in her home city and make the arrangements, settle on a fee, a time period, accommodation. 'One day my agent, he give me ticket to Karachi. He say, you go to Karachi tomorrow!'

'I can sympathize,' I said. 'That's more or less how it happened with—'

'First, I come for two weeks. Then two month later I come again for two weeks. Then again. Next time, for three weeks.'

'The brigadier can't get enough of you, can he?'

'The clients, they get bored. They tell to Alamgir, we see this one already, too much, too much, give us new girl, give us juggler, give us comedian, give us bigger girl. One month later, they say, *where that girl, that Cairo girl, where she go?*'

'Where, indeed.'

'Cairo, Karachi! Cairo, Karachi!' Her voice now was high-pitched and lost its adult tone. 'Sometimes Beirut. Cairo-Karachi! Sometimes Philippines. Cairo-Karachi! Sometimes . . .'

'A world traveller,' I said. 'I'm envious. I wish *I* could put on one of your outfits and just . . .' I exhaled from the mouth, for effect. I looked down and grabbed the fat of my stomach proudly with both hands. 'Although not sure I have the goods you have. You see this?' She looked, nodded, smiled.

'Hey!' she exclaimed. 'How do you know that I no, I *don't* have children?' She spread her arms and gestured towards her torso. 'Because I'm small?'

'No,' I said. 'You're fine.'

'All my friends, they were so happy with boobs when they were young, now look at them, fat like this—' she created a wide arc in front of her with her hands and arms—'It's better to be small, like this.'

'You're fine,' I said again.

'Yes?'

I looked her in the eye, for the first time I noticed some helplessness in them. I leaned over and put my hand on her breast, first from the outside of her T-shirt and then, pulling the neckline down, I slipped it inside. She wasn't wearing a bra. I sought out her nipple and held it tightly between thumb and finger. Her breasts were small. After getting used to them I raised my face to look at her. Her eyes were vague and distant. She stayed still, avoiding my gaze as I began rubbing her nipple with the tips of two fingers. I stopped rubbing her nipple, and tried to seize the unfilled flesh around it. Malika closed her eyes now, and leaned her head back slightly. I moved my hand to her crotch, worked at the button of her jeans, but she placed her hand inhospitably on mine. 'You must go,' she whispered, and tapped her little wristwatch. 'Be good puppy.'

'I'll see you later.'

I myself was a little nervous about this little assignment. But, for one, I felt that doing this favour for the brigadier compensated to some extent for staying at his house for so long; and secondly I couldn't deny the feeling of new prestige coming on, the brigadier bringing me in, closer to his world, a world denied to me by my father. When Hammad sahib opened his door for me, that beak-like mouth and the fat glasses, white short-sleeved vest hugging his chest, I reintroduced myself. Noticing his bare legs under his shirt, I apologized for troubling him, made to leave, but he stopped me. 'Haan, haan, of course,' he said.

I held up the bottle I'd brought. 'From brigadier sahib,' I said. 'He wanted to come up and welcome you, share a drink with you, but he's occupied right now, but will . . .'

'Aiyai, aiyai!' Hammad sahib said, clearing a path for me into his room. He excused himself for being half dressed. I placed the bottle on the dressing table, which already had two hotel glasses on it. He moved through the room dragging his lame leg—though it appeared more as if it was the leg that struggled with the rest of him, swaying like a coolie with too much to carry on his head. He picked up a pair of pants that lay on the bed. He put his good leg through, then struggled with the disabled one. He sat down and leaned his body back for a good angle, but still struggled, leaned forward now, bent as far forward as he could, but still couldn't put the leg through. 'Beta,' he pleaded, 'do you mind . . .' He signalled with his chin towards his foot. I went to him, bent down on one knee. 'I'm not as flexible as I used to be,' he said, half apologetically, but half resentfully, as if to tell me he didn't owe me an explanation at all. 'Normally my wife, or one of my sons . . . there you are, beta, thank you.' His leg looked unusually dry and had a strong antibacterial smell. I held his ankle where it was covered by sock, hesitant to touch that white, sick skin. Once he could reach, he grabbed the hem of the pants and pulled them up. I helped him to his feet, and he buttoned up, fastened his belt. 'Voila. All set, not difficult at all, was it?'

'No, sir.'

He gestured towards one of the seats, and took his place on the opposite one. Having been on opium the time I met him at the brigadier's, I could now take in more of his face: a long face, thin like the rest of him, but with the memory of old fat in a floppy sac at his neck. His nose was long and curved down sharply at the tip; with the backward slanting chin and the beak-like mouth, he looked like an ancient bird of prey.

I reminded him that I was Ghazanfar Aslam's son. 'Yes, yes!' he exclaimed, distractedly, and immediately at the phone, told the operator to get him a number. 'Yes, yes, Ghazanfar,' he repeated, as if to keep the communication between us from dying out. The phone chimed once and Hammad sahib picked up the receiver. 'Haan, shukriya. Haan! Yes, this is Hammad Rehman . . .' The phone call was obviously to some professional whose service he was irritated by. Finally, he ended his denunciation with a louder declaration, 'You don't speak to a Rehman like that!' He dropped the receiver defiantly. It missed its hook and slipped onto the bedside table, remained there. He sat back down. 'You should always talk about yourself in the context of family,' his tone was soft again. 'It frightens them more. You say, "Nobody messes with me," that's one thing. But if you say, "Nobody messes with a . . .", what's your surname one more time, beta?'

'Aslam.'

'"Nobody messes with an Aslam!" It makes things more serious. Doesn't matter if they don't know *which* Aslam, or what the hell *is* Aslam. You see?' Yes, I saw. 'During the language riots—you know, in the '50s— some Bengali students were killed. By the Pakistani army. Of course, who else? So every year on that day they commemorate them. Some through terror—they come into people's homes and take flowers from their gardens for the boys' graves. One year, they came to my gate in Dhaka. My wife told the children to go upstairs, to one room and lock the door. I said, arrey bhai, I'll take care of this. Went to the gate, who is there—four boys. They say, give us flowers for the boys' graves. I said, no I have no flowers for you kids. So, oh! they start saying this, saying that, you stand with the West Pakistani oppressors, and so on. So I told them, you've got the *wrong guy*, my friends. I was there in those riots, before any of you were born. I knew one of the boys who was killed. Okay? And then I said—and this, beta, this was the real kick—I said, I pointed to the plaque above the bell, which had my surname on it in big letters. I said, I'm *Hammad Rehman*!' He tried to guffaw, but was out of breath, so the laughter sounded like that of a dying man. But his anecdote had gotten him excited, and fluids ran out of his nostrils and mouth. He wiped his chin with his thumb, then took a handkerchief to his nose. 'But the truth is, they know, these people know that if they edit my work like that, I'll leave like that,' he snapped his fingers, 'and that means, of course, they lose half their readers. More than half, hain na?' He no doubt thought I knew all this, that I was a reader of whatever it was that he wrote, that I knew his worth, the hard currency of his name. He drank, and I drank; he gulped with a sense of necessity, and then started a new story. I had before me another raconteur-alcoholic.

∽

Hammad sahib was slouching over his seat. He'd gotten drunk very quickly, and when he took off and wiped his glasses his eyes were startlingly watery and bloodshot. He appeared deep in thought, bad thoughts. He raised the glasses toward the ceiling, examined the lenses against the light, and put them back on. 'You know how in those mysteries, at the same hour, everyone in the manor, from different ends, leave their rooms to carry out their little plans and whatnot. Well, that's what my body is like. A nice manor during the day, everything fine and whatnot, and then at midnight my limbs and nerves go their own ways. Against each other, even. This leg,' he tapped the stiff limb, 'this leg is the only thing that behaves itself. It's the one part of my body I can count on. When I'm having a fit it stays loyal, it stands against all the crazy things.'

When the phone rang—I'd set the receiver back on the hook—Hammad sahib looked at it from his seat with contempt, as though he knew who was calling and why. He didn't move, just stared at it, and with what now looked like sadness, he turned his red runny eyes down. He took his glasses off again and absently wiped them on his shirt at the belly.

'Should I . . .?' I volunteered, pointing at the phone. He looked up at me, with blind curiosity, alert again to the room and the ringing phone. 'I can . . .'

'Nahin, nahin,' he waved off my offer, and tottered to the bedside table. He picked up the receiver, and it seemed without even waiting for a voice at the other end he started shouting into the phone in a mocking, funny accent, and when he finally replaced the receiver he smiled and laughed insolently to himself, pleased at whatever offence he'd just caused. The brigadier had me nursing a madman. He came back to his seat, poured himself more whisky; we were running out of ice and he finished all that was left. I thought about phoning downstairs for more, but for now I didn't want to move, things seemed so tenuous with this man. What time was it? Would the brigadier come up and relieve me when the fun at the cabaret finished, or was I stuck with his crazy Bengali friend all night?

'I know what's happening downstairs,' he said, reading my thoughts. And seeing the alarm and embarrassment on my face, he said, 'Not to worry, young man. Let People's Party have their fun. Then if they win Alamgir can get appointed to . . . It's not even him, it's that aunt of his. What do they call her?'

'Apa?'

'Yes! *She*'s the one. Gives the orders. You know, she owns all of this,' he pointed upward and rotated his hand, 'all of it.'

No, I didn't know. I supposed it shouldn't have surprised me, but it did. Again I felt as if I'd been purposely misled, not told everything. 'Speaking of the brigadier,' I said. 'Why did he leave the army? Was it really because—'

'Because he was passed over.' He spoke fast and potently, didn't wait for me to finish, a correction he was no doubt eager to make.

'Passed over for what? General?' I paused. 'Or brigadier? Did he ever make brigadier?'

'Oh!' Hammad sahib smiled, and said, 'That you'll need to ask him.' He clenched his fist and bit into it, to prevent himself from talking in that comical gesture I remembered from the night of the party when I first met him.

❧

When I came down, the brigadier was on stage, for the first time that I'd ever seen. He was leading a sing-along of the People's Party theme. Almost everyone rose and chanted boisterously with him. There was no place to sit, so I stood by the door. The Party's posters, with Bhutto's face at their centre, were taped on the walls. Red, black and green, the party's colours, curved down from one side of the saloon, then back up to the other, in a cloth banner. Each table had little Party flags on toothpicks—red, black and green downward stripes, with crescent and star in the middle.

I'd left Hammad sahib upstairs. He'd suddenly decided to lie down; though he claimed it wasn't to sleep; he'd insisted that I stay in the room and talk to him. He'd deferred more and more to me to carry the conversation, closing his eyes, absently muttering, 'achha', and 'haan', and when finally there was silence, filled softly with the buzz of his nostrils, I turned off the lights and left the room before he could wake back up. Had I known what was eventually going to happen to him, I would have stayed, taken in more. But that night, I was in a rush.

When the brigadier finished the song, the master of ceremonies replaced him at the microphone. In his laboured British accent, he introduced another man, who read an Urdu poem that supposedly celebrated the principles of socialism that formed the Party's platform. I didn't understand the poem, except a line here and there—'The name that remains is Allah's' (repeated twice), and the final couplet, which ended with, 'That which I am, and that which you are, too' (also repeated twice). But I did hear that the words were by Faiz, the poet who was charged for the communist conspiracy with my father.

The dancers weren't dressed in their typical cabaret outfits. Tonight's outfit, specially designed, was the single-piece of red, black and green that was spread on Malika's bed; on their bodies now it was almost like a diver's apparel. While the speakers were onstage, all the dancers were gathered on one side. Once the speeches and anthems and poems were done, the dancers plotted their course through the saloon. Three of them collected around a mustachioed baldy in dark sherwani, whom the brigadier also eventually joined, at a central table. The man was no doubt connected to the People's Party, one of Bhutto's men.

The band played, and some of the audience clapped metrically to the music. No dances. Malika had attracted the attentions of an older woman, in a sloppy black chemise with short sleeves. The woman was several inches shorter than Malika, overweight, with puffy arms and hands. Her hair was a sharp pumpkin-red, and that red tinge also covered her face and arms. She held a drink in one hand, and she often put the other on Malika, at her lower back, around her shoulders, at the back of her neck. The woman laughed frequently, mostly to her own jokes. I couldn't tell if Malika was interested or not in the things this woman had to say, but she went along regardless. The woman, whom I now realized was a foreigner, put her own glass to Malika's lips. Malika accepted the sip. But when the woman made a second, more aggressive attempt, Malika pushed the glass back and turned her face away, shaking her finger, an embarrassed smile on her face. The older woman laughed, an exaggerated laugh, with her head tilted as far back as it could go, and then she pulled Malika close and kissed her on the temple.

❧

Malika's room was filled with dust and hair and lint on everything and malodorous. Why she didn't have the hotel staff thoroughly clean her room I didn't know. She told me that in the beginning, when the staff knocked, she would time and again ask them to come back later; then, when she went down to perform she told them not to enter the room, so that eventually the staff came in to clean only when she specifically asked them. And she rarely did. Her towels, her sheets, her clothes, smelled, and she left things crudely exposed—urine in the toilet-bowl, blood-stained women's materials in the dustbin. It was possible that this exposure, this indecency, was a project in itself, a statement of principle. And I didn't mind it. Because those smells and fluids came from *her*, there was something rank but also very feminine about it. It seemed all the more that she was extending me a special privilege by letting me in here, showing me what she, a woman, was really like.

She lay on the carpet, on her back, smoking a cigarette. It was raining heavily. I stood at the window, hardly able to see the city outside. I started pacing again. I'd told Malika about the orchard, about Mona Phuppi and my father, about Partition and land reforms, about squatters and democracy. The conversation agitated me, but I wanted and needed to continue, I paced the room with my eyes towards the floor. 'Those squatters are filthy and despicable. Immoral, I'm sure. Eating away at the soil, they've probably made the place barren. They're a *cancer*, that's what they are. But if they could stay, if we could make them stay, if we could *govern* them . . . If some of them are ill, we can have quarantine zones, right?'

'Seeet, Shahbaz!'

I did as she asked and sat down. 'I'll bring you to the orchard,' I said.

'Ah! To see where you play as chi—'

'No, not to see,' I retorted. 'Not to *see* anything. To per*form*. An outdoor performance, with all the squatters in a circle around the stage, obligated—through decree if necessary—to cheer. I'll make good public servants of them all.'

'You want me to dance in the . . .?'

'You went to a village for Bhutto and the Shah, didn't you? Yes, we'll introduce them to new things. Like what, like what? Like role play. You can do that, can't you? Pretend to be a . . .'

'Shahbaz,' she raised her voice an octave, playfully, which made her Egyptian accent more pronounced.

'. . . prophetess.'

'You become maaad!'

'You can even stay at the orchard. It could be a glorious place. Every morning a twenty-one-gun salute, in your honour.'

'Pass the glass.'

I lifted the glass of neat whisky on the bedside table, and reached down to give it to her. She rose to take it, sipped, then lay back down. 'You'll choke if you drink it like that,' I said. 'May go down the wrong tube, enter your trachea—you know what the trachea is?—fill your lungs with whisky.'

'It's okay. My lungs already full of whisky.' She puffed and blew out a line of smoke rings.

'You look like a frog when you do that.'

'What I was saying?' she asked.

I got up again. 'Oh, these decadent times,' I mused. I stood over Malika. 'Who was that woman, the redhead, the one who kissed you?'

She raised herself up and propped herself on her elbows, sipped her whisky. She raised her knees so that her feet now lay flat on the floor. The end of her caftan lifted and showed more of her legs.

'And what if she wants more, what happens when that red-head wants to . . .'

I knelt down in front of her feet. I pushed her caftan further back, it drooped to her thighs, revealing the red panties underneath. Malika blew smoke in my face. She put out her cigarette in the ashtray next to her. I rested a hand on each knee. 'You're perfect for the times,' I said, and parted and closed her legs playfully.

'Enough!' she complained.

I stopped. I slipped her panties off and tossed them towards the bed. The thought that the brigadier had endorsed all this, that I was getting this far because of him, didn't bother me. 'Fuck it,' I said. 'I've earned this.' She reached for my belt and struggled with it. 'Agh, Shahbaz!' she complained, as if I should have already done this myself. I eased her hand away and undid the belt, unzipped my pants. I started caressing her again, moved to kiss her. She moved her face away. 'Take them *off*! Ayo!' Now she sounded angry and impatient. She was eager to make me erect, and skip past the caresses and kisses and tongue. I didn't know if her agitation insinuated passion and high expectations, or repulsion. Only when I was inside her, when her eyes closed, her head tilted back and a small sigh of pleasure escaped her chest, did my apprehensions subside.

4

Malika didn't let me spend the night in her room. A matter of policy—probably the brigadier's. Our first two nights, it didn't bother me because I'm one of those who in post-coital needs to be alone with my shame. But on the third I asked if I could stay. 'No.' She was firm. 'You must go.' Okay, I said, 'I sleep better alone anyway.' But something about being in her hotel room made me feel like I was on vacation, and I wanted to wake up to that feeling, Malika at my side. The next time, as we lay in that temporary—whatever one could call that time between the end of sex and the time I had to get dressed and leave, I lay on my front, watching her sitting up in bed, uncovered, sipping a drink, not bothered in the least about being naked, even after sex. Sucking her own teeth, which distorted and swelled her closed lips. Despite the small breasts, her nipples were thick and long and filled with colour. They'd repulsed me at first, but now I'd grown even keen on them. She shook her head as if she was upset at something. I put my hand on her outer thigh and stroked her with my palm, up and down.

'Elections tomorrow,' I reminded her. 'I don't imagine they give Egyptians a vote, even when they are as beautiful and patriotic as you. No matter how many times you dance for Bhutto in his village. So much for your efforts. But that makes two of us, my love, two of us without a vote. What, you think I'm registered? No, no, no. I'm just like you. Non-citizens, baby, making love, absent from the big things. You and me.'

She raised her leg and put the sole of her foot on my face and pushed gently. I held the foot and kissed her sole from heel to toe. I tolerated the smell and taste of leather. When I looked at her I saw that she was smiling. But the smile disappeared almost immediately, and with sudden bad humour she said, 'Now this one,' and thrust the other foot to my face, again pushing me back. I kissed the heel, sole, and then playfully bit at the big toe. Malika put both feet against my shoulder, pushed me back to turn me over. 'Now you leave,' she said. I rolled over the other way immediately, so that she wouldn't see me from the front, rolled off the bed, picked my underwear from the ground and put it on. Covered, unembarrassed, I walked the room looking for the rest of my clothes from the floor.

'I thought maybe we should spend the day together. Let the rest of the country sort out the big things. We can be like tourists for the day. Ice-cream cones, walk on the beach. I'll show you the old house where I used to live, in Clifton, somewhere near ... anyway, I'll find it. Huh?'

'Your sock is there.' She pointed to a spot below one of the chairs. I picked it up and beat it sharply in the air to straighten it.

'What do you say?'

'What?'

'About spending election day together? I can get your boss' approval if you need me to.'

'Yes, yes, yes,' she dragged the words.

'How convincing.' I tied my belt. 'But I'll take it. I'll mark it on my calendar when I get home so that I remember when I wake up in the morning. Of course, I could wake up *here*, if it wasn't for your . . .' I stood around, my hands at my waist, naked Malika on the bed, the gap between us almost infinite. 'You don't mind for a moment?' I asked.

'Hmm?'

'Lying there like that, while I'm here . . . like this. There's something humiliating about this. For *me*. You understand? *You* are humiliating me. The very least you can do is cover yourself.' I walked up to her and held out an open hand. 'Here, why don't you tip me? Let's make this humiliation total. A small fee for services rendered. Come on, I'll even bow before taking leave.'

She smiled, like a toddler fresh out of a bad mood, with those inward slanted teeth. In my open palm she placed her cold empty glass. I finished the dregs of ice, bent down and kissed her, surprised by the affection she returned, holding me by the back of my head and wagging her tongue through my lips. 'See you on election day,' I said and left her.

I felt lonely when I woke up the next day at the brigadier's, wishing more than ever that Malika was by my side. The elections, once mythic, were here. I felt an unusual resistance, a resistance to getting out of bed, to leaving my room, to getting dressed, to wash or even to go to the bathroom. Most strangely, I desired not so much Malika's but my *father*'s company. It was only ten in the morning. I wished it was later. That there was less of the day left, that elections would come and go, and *then* I would get out of bed, rested and shaved and washed for a new democracy.

Sleep wasn't coming back. Malika was a late riser, I imagined, and wouldn't be ready to leave the Agra for at least two or three hours. How to move time forward? Eventually, still in slippers and the shalwar I used for pyjamas, I walked out of my room, out of the house, out through the gate. There was little life on the streets, and walking on the empty pavement, I felt the combination of the joy and self-reproach of the deserter. The rest of the country, good citizens, deciding the future, and I walking alone, away, embarrassed and gleeful. I came across life in the form of the street barber who occupied a pavement corner on the way to Tariq Road. Two broken pieces of a mirror, side by side, were tied to the bark of a tree with rope, splitting a potential customer's face in two. He offered me a shave. I'd never been shaved by anyone, didn't see the point, always associated it with Chicago mobsters. Nor did I trust this streetman's blade. But hell, I let him do it, sat in his uneven wooden chair, the clouds threatening rain possibly midway through the exercise, the barber seeking cover, leaving me with one half of my face clean, the other covered in foam, the towel still around my neck. But it didn't rain, and this streetman stretched my cheeks and lifted chunks tight between thumb and index and shaved me meticulously. I wanted to ask him how come he wasn't at the polls, if he'd voted already, if he was going to vote, but I didn't want to distract him into a political discussion. Not when he had that blade in his hand. He pinched my skin and shaved away, never drawing blood, and wiped me off with a worn-out towel. I dropped a couple of coins into his tin can. Fresh-shaven, I walked aimlessly in the brigadier's neighbourhood, not knowing the time, then thought to rush back to the house and phone Malika before she disappeared to wherever it was she spent her days. But when I came back Sajid gave me a message: Mona Phuppi had called to say that they would be coming to pick me up at one for a day at Hawksbay beach.

Hawksbay beach, the dirty sea creeping up the patios of little huts. I remembered one visit there as a child— not with my aunt or father, because whoever they were they had a supply of beer that never finished, and I remember spending much of that day fetching cold cans from the ice box for the adults and throwing away empty ones, wondering the whole time how come they weren't falling on their faces and dancing stupidly. Later that day I was thrown onto rocks in the sea that scratched the entire surface of my back, and I had to be tended to the rest of the day inside the hut. The way I remembered it, it was a couple of the others who had thrown me into the sea and, perhaps, accidentally thrown me too far. But my elders insisted later that it was an unfriendly wave that had actually pushed me onto those rocks. Whatever the truth, I didn't like going to this particular beach. And I didn't, as an adult, want to go on this day of all days.

But they came at one sharp, aunt and uncle in their yellow Beetle. In a Corolla behind them was the couple from the Yacht Club, the man with the single curl on his pate and his wife. When I got into the Beetle, Mona Phuppi, as if to gloat, held up her thumb with the dark ink stain that the polling officer had given her. She

looked down towards my hand. 'You've got yours?' I
waved my hands, palms facing up, to suggest I had no
such mark but also to reprimand her for even asking me.

The weather was still grey, but nobody seemed to
care. This was a less sophisticated affair than the Yacht
Club—no waiters or servants, just us fending for ourselves
in a very basic hut. Wind, sand in our eyes, plastic cups
and cutlery flying all over the patio. None of which
seemed to fluster Mona Phuppi. She'd recovered from
her recent bout of madness and medication, though
there was new exhaustion in her eyes and cheeks.
Perhaps the madness had run its course, perhaps it had
its own limits, a certain number of outbursts, now spent,
and would go into remission. Maybe my aunt had been
exorcised of whatever it was inside her for so long. For
now, she was in high spirits.

The other couple had brought a big bag of cheeses,
which the wife spread out on a small table on the porch,
along with cheese knives, water biscuits, and bread.
Some hunter beef, too. The baldy was working on
something on the side that, when the air surrendered to
the scent, I realized was a joint. He worked the cooked
hashish into the tobacco, licked and sealed the seams
and then, briefly, looked at me looking at him, before
lighting the thing. I was hoping that he'd offer it, just to
give me a chance to refuse. He smoked in one corner of
the patio. The grey clouds stayed where they were, but
accumulated volume and colour, as if pumped with
blood. The portentous sound of a giant heartbeat fittingly
thumped in my ear for the rest of the day. Mona Phuppi
was barefoot, slightly hunched, and walked with an air
of seriousness or defiance. If her mind was betraying
her, she still had good command over this bulkish frame.
That was nice to see.

There was another hut nearby which belonged to people they knew. Eventually, the man and wife and Phuppa Jaan walked over to visit, leaving me and Mona Phuppi behind. After digging into more of the cheese, aunt and nephew lay side by side, gazing out to sea. My aunt sprawled on the deckchair, her toes again folding inward and out, the little manias at the last extreme of her body.

'Mona Phuppi.' She turned to me with a smile. 'There's something I want to ask you.'

'Haan, bolo, bolo.'

'Did Abba ever ... did he ever ... mention, a ... *woman*, after Ammi's death?'

'Ahhhh. *That*, beta ...' She rested her cheek on her fist, looking downward with a sweet nostalgic smile.

'It wasn't very often,' I said, 'that a woman came alone to the flat for dinner in the first place. It was his Eastern propriety that hid it all, that found it unacceptable to reveal ... such a thing to his son. But I did pick up on things. For example, when he'd say "tu" to a female lunch guest. That's the equivalent of "tum" in Urdu, you know. His excessive decency usually made him use "vous" to any white person, even hooligans on the metro. In fact, I wouldn't have been surprised if he also used "vous" with a woman he was ... you know. But when the "tu" came out in conversation, I was convinced that the woman wasn't an ordinary guest.'

Mona Phuppi still had her chin on her knuckles. 'There was this woman,' she said. 'When your father was still in his early twenties. Long before he met your mother. She used to live down the road, the Delhi days. This woman. Much older, in her early forties at least. Arrey bhai, a proper *lady*. You know where they used to meet? You'll never guess—the *rooftop*! Ha! Every afternoon, when our parents would take their naps. He thought nobody knew.'

'How did you come to find out?'

'Oh, he would *never* tell me. Never. But . . .'

'They'd . . . have their fling . . . *up there*? And you all *knew*?'

She looked at me and chuckled without opening her mouth. The look of late day was congealing in the sky, narcotic, grey clouds filled with the noises of a gentle locomotive.

'I've found a buyer,' she said. She was still looking out to the sea. 'We can consider it done. That bloody orchard off our hands.'

What a woman! The precision, to be able to break silence and warmth in this flawless unforgiving way. But to beat us in straight sets, this was the kind of focus required. I admired her for it. I unstretched my legs, then rotated towards her, put my feet on the ground and sat on the side of the deckchair, bent, my chin in my hand. The vision was sure to give her pleasure. 'We can get rid of the squatters. Or even . . .'

Cigarette between her lips, she shook her head frowning, assuringly, as if to tell me, don't worry about it, bachai. She exhaled away from my face, and said, 'A good price. Better than I expected.'

'I've spoken to a policeman, he says—'

'And we should do it fast.'

'That orchard is family property.'

'He's a school administrator from somewhere, a decent chap, but we can't keep him waiting forever.'

'My father has a right—'

'Have to act fast with these things, bachai.'

'This is crazy.'

'We've been assured that the deeds will be handed over by the end of the week.'

'Abba has more of a right to it than you do!' I shouted. She was silent, and I was out of breath, so soon. I stood up. 'He's not here, you'll say. I *know* he's not here. That's the point, that's what *gives* him the right! He's given everything to this country, the last nineteen years of his life.' I felt a need not to let Mona Phuppi speak, like a boxer who knows if he loses the edge, if he lets his opponent recoup, he'll lose everything. 'You know, I went to the orchard. On my own. This might surprise you, but I did. Some weeks ago. I met them, the squatters. These two little boys, I talked to them, played with them, good kids. But I've had a recurring dream since then, a nightmare. I'm at the orchard, I think either I live there or I live nearby, or I come there often enough that all the kids recognize me, and are excited to see me whenever I *am* there. But the excitement, I know later, is not the natural excitement of kids for an adult. It's obedience. They're told, they're *required*, to be excited. But I don't know that yet. When I'm there, I think these kids are sincere, sincere in their . . . *adulation*. And I love them back. Yeah, in the dream I love them. These filthy, malnourished, stinking kids, and I love them all. I look forward to them running at my feet. But then, on this day—where my dream begins— I come in, and the kids greet me as usual. They lead me by the hand, like they always do, playful kids. But this time it's different. At some point I realize that they're not leading me anywhere to play, but their plan is to beat me, to beat me to death. And by then there's nothing I can do about it. They're kids, yes, but there's too many of them. And I'm thinking the whole time, don't let yourself fall. If you fall you're finished. C'est finis. But I do fall and then I know the end is close. Can you imagine dreaming something like that about one's *own property?*' I leaned down, took her cigarette from her, inhaled deeply. 'But the awful thing of it all is that I still believe . . . in the dream, I still believe, even when they're beating me, even when I fall, is that they . . . they have a *right* to it all. They have a right to stay. They have a right even to kill me, trespasser that I am. And that's why I want to keep the place. Not to be rid of them—no, in the dream, it's to *keep* them. To make sure they *stay* there. And that's what I want to tell them when they're beating me, *I'm on your side, I want you to stay*! The orchard is not just a plot of land, Mona Phuppi, it is a living thing, an organ. You don't just sell *life*. How dare you even try!' I was done, my body felt hot, my tongue was dry, with the awful taste of tobacco. Mona Phuppi's mouth was open slightly as she looked up to me, the tongue resting on the lower lip, like she'd felt a private pleasure in my outburst. I gave her her cigarette back, she held it down, the hand that held it rested on a knee. She lay back on her beach bed, so calm, what a piece of work.

The others came back from the neighbouring hut before the exchange could go any further, all three of them excited by the contact with familiar souls on the beach, filling our own hut with noise, even Phuppa Jaan.

'We've made a decision!' announced the baldy. 'A *binding* decision I should add.' He pointed at me. 'The *men*,' he raised his eyebrows, 'and the *women*,' he pointed at Mona Phuppi, 'are to swim.'

'Aaa!' My aunt burst into laughter.

'Haan, haan, they have a costume for you next door.'
I said, 'I also don't have any—'
'Neither do I, bhai. Those shorts are good enough.
We've got those towels there, you just dry yourself off
and you change when you get home, simple.'
'The water will be freezing,' I said.
But the three of them went squealing and laughing
into the cold sea, while I watched from my deckchair.
The baldy dunked his wife's head under water, and she
came up screaming and scolding and laughing. It had
started to drizzle, too. I thought of Malika. I missed her.
Was she angry that she didn't hear from me today?
Would she require an explanation? The most excruciating
thought was that she wouldn't give a damn. The elders
in the sea shouted once more for me to come in, stop
being a chicken, and after a few of these cries I yielded,
taking off my shirt and, inside the hut, removing my
underwear so that I was wearing only the shorts. They
cheered as I approached the shore, advised me not to
baby-step my way in but to throw myself into the water,
whole body, and I squealed just as they did when the icy
water rushed to my bones. The four of us, all floating
close and looking inward at each other, bobbed up and
down. Mona Phuppi watched me with a clever smile, the
cap tight on her skull which made her face bloated, the
madness squeezed down to her cheeks.
'It's cold, no?' she said.
'Very,' I replied.
'But fun, no?'
She'd seen me rise to the challenge as best I could, and
it was still not up to her standards of conflict, just a silly
fantasy of getting attacked by squatter kids. But I had
more serious things to tell her. That the orchard was the

reason I was here, in Karachi, at this time. If she sold it I would have nothing.

'Dunk your head in,' the bald one advised me, his single curl pasted down his temple like a dead thing. I did, squeezing my nostrils but still coming back up with a head full of salt. The rain gathered force.

'Chalain,' the baldy, today's ringleader, called. And we got out.

'Here.' Mona Phuppi tossed me a towel. I dried my legs, my chest, and as I swung the towel to my back, she stood behind me, took the towel and rubbed my back fervently. When she was done I thanked her and wrapped the towel around my waist. We sat in the patio waiting for the rain to subside before we left. Phuppa Jaan kept the heater on in the car as we drove back.

'Do give our regards to Alamgir.'

I went straight upstairs to Apa's room to phone Rahim sahib. I knew it was Election Day, I importuned him, but things were getting desperate and I would be extremely grateful if he could spare just a few minutes on the phone. To my surprise, he asked me to come to the station. I then called Ghulam Hussain. Apa watched me intently. In my haste, I'd forgotten to say adaab to her. I said it now, and she ignored me, returning her attention to a tiny platter of walnuts in her hand. She looked at the nuts closely, as she did all things, arranged them with her free hand, moving some pieces aside, others to the centre, until she finally found a piece she liked and pressed it between her old pouty lips. Bit down, but didn't chew. Didn't offer me any. To hell with it, I thought. There was too much going on to worry about a ninety-year-old woman's sense of tradition.

❦

Rahim sahib was in uniform this time, his whole comportment more grave and burdened with duty. His tone was as sombre as a doctor's to a patient. He had the boy shut the door, and then asked me to pull up my seat closer to him, to the side of the desk. His thumb, too, had the polling officer's ink stain. 'So, time is running out.'

I sipped my lassi. 'She says she has a buyer.'

There were again files stacked on either side of his desk. Somewhere, stored away in some office in the country, there must still have been files like that on my father. Detailing the charges against him, suspicions about his Communist Party ties. How could I get my hands on them? Just for a look. Not to keep or destroy.

'Any progress on the squatter issue?' I asked.

From a drawer, he pulled out a sheet of paper and gave it to me. The writing was in Urdu, and the bold black lettering of the header was too ornate and cursive for me to read. I focused on the text, but although I was picking up spoken Urdu, I still could read only very small words. There was no point trying. I passed my finger at a pace over the letters, from right to left, moved my lips as if mouthing the text. And I nodded occasionally. I returned the paper, Rahim sahib searched me for a reaction. 'So what does this mean?' I asked.

'Well.' He raised his eyebrows and clenched his lips, and I knew the document wasn't good news. Rahim sahib brought his chair closer to mine, lowered his voice and, his face leaning towards mine, he said, 'You know, this is not for me, of course, but it's just the way . . . you understand of course?' I nodded. 'In this country,' he continued, 'things move faster when there is . . . *some incentive*.' I had two hundred rupees in my pocket.

'Around how much would it ...'

He smiled and looked down, embarrassed by the whole business.

'Would a hundred be ...' I asked. He nodded, his head still inclined forward. I took out two hundred-rupee notes, and before I separated one, Rahim sahib reached out and took both. 'Just give me this,' he said. 'This should be fine.' I left the station convinced that I was finally making the right moves, the necessary moves, things my father would never have done.

'Clifton beach,' I told Ghulam Hussain. I still had the taste for the sea, and I knew everyone at the brigadier's, Mona Phuppi's, and probably even Ghulam Hussain's quarters, would be watching or listening to election results, reports from the democracy experiment. I gazed at and smelled the town from my open window, remembering the story Ghulam Hussain had told me the first time I'd met Rahim sahib, about the massacre of Urdu-speakers in Lalukhet, about the Pathans from the Frontier who'd been assembled and armed by Ayub's badmaash sons. I imagined them on that train, the thirty or so hours from Peshawar to Karachi, burning in their compartments, restless as wild horses, salivating and sweaty. There were so many Pathans in Karachi who would have been jubilant about killing Urdu-speakers—why did the sons have to get a band from the Frontier? It was exactly to work them up into that state, through hours of fever. Killing on that scale needed a long prelude, a certain metabolism and metamorphosis. They were geniuses, those two sons, and how they produced their militants! No training, no propaganda. Just some old tribal antagonisms to begin with, and then guns and thirty hours in a hot culture dish passing from one end of the country to the other; on the other side an altered, almost feral specimen, out of its habitat, crazed. Under military government perhaps they'd all metamorphosed, and now were let out into the open air of democracy . . .

There were a fair number of families at Clifton beach. The air was cool but couples and families ate ice cream and kids rode camels across the sand. We sat on a stone bench between road and beach. Ghulam Hussain rolled two joints, we smoked and talked. He, too, must have felt out of place, not being able to vote in East Pakistan where his people were. I wanted to tell him, *Let's just roam the streets, you and me, until the votes are counted and a government is formed.* And I really did want to share something with him, something that I otherwise couldn't because of my weak Urdu. I let him talk, I let him tell his stories. And he told them. For almost an hour, he told me his stories of Dhaka during the riots.

He and his cohorts stopped a car at about ten at night, the only car on the street. They asked the driver to roll down the window. Right away, they understood that he was an Urdu-speaker. For thousands of Bengali rioters, finding an Urdu-speaker at that time of the Dhaka night would have been a great triumph. But these men were polite, according to Ghulam Hussain. They asked him where he was coming from—apparently he worked at Lever Brothers, had parked his car there in the afternoon, and went to a relative's home near the office after he was done for the day. Now he was going back home. 'You shouldn't leave your car outdoors for so long,' Ghulam Hussain warned him, in Urdu. 'And you shouldn't be driving this late. We're burning cars, and we'll burn yours.' One of Ghulam Hussain's cohorts called from behind him, aggressively, 'You're an Urdu-speaker, huh?' The man in the car timidly replied that yes, he was an Urdu-speaker, but that he'd been in East Pakistan for years and had also learned Bengali. The man who'd asked the question, and one or two of the others, started pressing for some kind of action. 'At least, let's burn his car. Tell him to get out, walk back, and we set fire to haramee Urdu-speaker's car!'

'Bechara was completely frightened,' Ghulam Hussain told me. 'I asked him where his home was. When he told me, I told him which streets to take and which streets to avoid—*without doubt*, avoid, otherwise they would burn his car. And who knows, maybe even burn *him*.'

I imagined this gang, armed with sticks, petroleum, lighters, and a conviction in their violent virtues, walking the streets of the East Pakistani capital like the Magnificent Seven. On another occasion the gang *did* burn a man's car. 'We made him get out—him and his son, a little boy this big—and in front of him we poured petrol and burned it.' On yet another, they saw a group of students surrounding a car, banging on its roof and bonnet and back, and then all collected on one side to try to tip the car over, with the people still in it. The car at first was barely tilting, an inch off the ground at most, before some onlookers joined the effort. Ghulam Hussain said he watched for a while, got closer, all the attention on the block now directed to this one endeavour. And as the car looked set to finally turn over, with just a little more force, he ran to it. He found and grabbed an accessible corner. And he found, too, a line of vision into the car and saw the horrified family inside, a husband, a wife and two young children. 'They were looking around like they didn't know what was happening,' Ghulam Hussain said. 'Like they didn't know it was *man* doing it. Like it was a storm. Like God was doing it. Ha!' Was he concerned for the family, the children? 'At that moment, Shahbaz bhai, a man is in a different—' he put a finger to his temple and then rotated his wrist to signal a mental or spiritual shift. 'I saw the children, but it didn't matter. Tipping the car was more important. When it happened, we all laughed and jumped and hugged, as if after months of heat the rain had come. Dancing in the rain, that's what it was like.' And the family in the car? 'They were okay, like this.' Ghulam Hussain contorted his legs and arms and upper body to imitate the victims in the car. 'Ha, ha! In such strange positions, Shahbaz bhai. Like in—what are those you have over there, in England, where they put . . . where people come to look at models, or . . .'

'Museum,' I said, in English.

'Haan, haan. Just like that. They looked like those things in a *moozeem*. In a glass case. I thought to myself, if I had children I would bring them to show them the glass case with the people inside in such strange positions. Or maybe buy a little . . . what do you call it, *model*. A little model, this small, that we can put in the room, next to window, something like that.'

'If I was in the car? Then?' I asked him.

He compressed his lips and swayed his head. 'Haan, there's that, too.' He leaned to the side of the bench and spat onto the road. 'Another time, Shahbaz bhai, we were all standing, meaning in one big group, on a road that went uphill, meaning that we were at the lower part of it, and the police people were above us. With their masks and bandooks and big sticks. Some of them were standing on this, you know those—' he used words I didn't understand, and so I shook my head. 'Meaning—

what do you call them?—those grassy . . .' Embankment, I understood. 'Haan, toh, some of them were standing on *that*. And *nobody* was moving, Shahbaz bhai. Not us, not them, absolutely frozen, like today they can do in those videos, nah, where you push a button and everything stops moving? It was like that. I was thinking, who will move first, someone from their side or someone from our side?'

'Were you scared?'

He frowned and nodded. 'Haan, little bit, I'm sure. Fear of course there must have been. Sometimes in a situation like that, one of them would say, either you leave right now or we'll start that tears-wali gas, or we'll fire, or whatever it is. But this time, khamoshi. *Silence*,' he used the English word. 'Then, one bhainchod policewala from up above, his foot must have slipped a little, so he lost balance and fell down the embankment, rolling—' he revolved his hands one around the other to describe the movement of the policeman's body, 'with his shield and his stick and his mask, everything. Ha ha ha! Then fell onto the street, dhuz!' He laid out a flat hand and then slapped down on the palm with the other. 'So much we laughed, Shahbaz bhai, you wouldn't believe it. Then we all left. We'd had our, what you say in English, our *veektory*. So we went, looking for the next veektory.'

Ghulam Hussain wandering the Dhaka streets with his army, looking for Urdu-speakers to attack, cars to overturn and burn. The beautiful focus of this group of men, the beautiful dementia in it. Dhaka on fire. My father had lived in Dhaka as a teenager, and was still fond of the city. I remembered his expression when he listened, far away in Paris, to news of the Dhaka riots, stunned that the same monster that had overcome Europe had overcome his old city.

I tried again to see myself through Ghulam Hussain's eyes. I liked to imagine that he saw something uncommon in me, none of the entitlement of the wealthy. I made it a point to remind him often that we never had a live-in servant in Paris, relying on this fact alone to separate me from the likes of Mona Phuppi and the brigadier and Aunty Ruby. And yet, I wasn't fulfilling the promise of such a temperament, that combination of an upper-class background and sympathy for the poor. This temperament, the very existence of it, was supposed to yield something for him. He was waiting, waiting, waiting. When I talked of Paris, he was always elated. Why? Did he really believe, based on a casual remark a hundred nights ago that I could, or would, take him back with me?

Before getting into his car, I looked up with special interest at a monument that had been another major vision of the Karachi of my childhood, the Abdullah Shah Ghazi shrine. Men, women, families, climbed the long steps to the mausoleum, to the tomb of the saint, Abdullah Shah Ghazi, one of the several saints who supposedly kept the city from sinking into the Arabian Sea. My father had taken me up there a few times. I recalled some things: donkey cart after donkey cart bringing the vistors to the shrine; the guys with their bags of rose petals harassing us (my father had a favourite stall that he'd always buy petals from); taking our shoes off at the entrance, checking them in in return for a numbered chit (I remembered being worried that we'd come back down and our shoes would be gone); the barefoot climb up cold and grimy steps; the strangers' shoulders against mine; entering the little chamber, where the saint's body lay covered in cloth and some kind of plaster, like a mummy. The short prayer everyone would say, hands meeting and raised near the mouth (I would move my mouth to something or other then, in conclusion, move my hands over my face as if throwing water on it); and finally throwing some rose petals on him. These memories came lucidly. When we'd come back down, before we got our shoes back at the stall, I always noticed a small pathway that many men followed to somewhere behind this big edifice.

'Ghulam Hussain,' I called to him from the other side of the car. 'Let's go there.'

'You want to go up to the mazar?'

'Not up. I want to go behind it, and see what's there.'

He slanted his head to get a view of how I was dressed and grimaced with doubt. 'Sirji, are you sure tonight you want to . . .'

'Yes, I'm sure.'

'Theek hai, Shahbaz bhai.'

He led me with heavy lethargic steps across the dirt street where the petal and garland vendors made their rowdy promotions. We walked past the shoe stall without leaving ours behind, then walked along the muddy path to the rear of the premises. On this side of the shrine was an open field full of people, people of the streets. Small businesses prospered here and there: a corn-on-the-cob man standing by his wheelbarrow; a man selling watches, encouraging me to take a fake Rolex; fake fat ruby rings, necklaces; roasters handing out chanas in cones made from newspaper; the thick scent of hash. Many looked at me, sizing me up, calculating my worth, and immediately I understood why Ghulam Hussain had reservations about bringing me, in my pants and shirt. I had premonitions now of being stabbed. Ghulam Hussain had walked on, looking back once in a while to see if I was still behind him. I chased him eagerly, disquieted every time another body touched mine. I contorted my body to avoid the dirty shoulders pressing past me.

Ghulam Hussain waited for me at the doorway of an open-air quad at the other end of the field. The outer walls were muddy white stone. Inside a hundred men were sitting on white sheets on the ground, their backs to us, watching a group of qawals perform. I followed him into the quad, and we stood just behind the last row of the audience. The group included a hefty lead qawal who handled his harmonium with puffy hands. The main backup vocalists were three men with identical long, curly hair and thick black moustaches. Behind them was a string of percussionists and minor backup vocalists, some of them just young boys. They were chanting the chorus line, over and over in a slow, fading anti-climax. Clapping in unison. The beat intensified and now the lead qawal launched into a shrill incantation. He held it for a while, and just before he stopped his group recited the chorus line again softly, three or four times. A deferential silence followed, except for the single note of a harmonium and the metrical claps of three members in the back row. The lead qawal threw himself into another piercing, wordless frenzy. Again, the chorus rang three times, after which the leader led with short, cadenced phrases, all ending with the word, 'Ho'. Each successive phrase was more passionate until finally, as if in a fit of temper, he raised his voice and issued an urgent challenge, a pointed question to an absent lover or absent god. The group members and the audience responded with almost fanatic claps, hand gestures, shouts of appreciation.

'Va!' Ghulam Hussain joined in.

When the music ended, people in the audience shouted names of qawalis they wanted to hear. Ghulam Hussain, too, shouted some title or the other. The group decided on one, it began, slowly. I felt the first stares from members of the crowd, turned heads, red eyes. As the music, vocals, clapping, picked up pace a man in a long black robe, with a grey beard going halfway down his torso, a white prayer cap on his head, and enormous necklaces and armlets and other spiritual paraphernalia approached the stage with three escorts helping him, as if he was in too much of a stupor to make it on his own. With the man in black standing in the centre, the three men stretched out and joined hands, along with this bearded man's, in front of the lead qawal. There was a stack of coins and rupee notes in Black Robe's hand. Others from the audience also gathered around him and added their own little notes to the pile. Then Black Robe, with his friends still holding him, began swinging his upper body in theatrical forward-and-back shifts, his friends supporting his precariously shifting weight. 'That's the haal,' Ghulam Hussain said. The trance. He moved closer to the stage, and we were standing now to one side of the crowd, far more conspicuous. The man in black was still rocking violently. From somewhere above I heard the shouts of women—on a balcony overlooking the quad, two women with scarred faces, watched, hollering spiritual stuff. Black Robe's haal lasted some minutes, after which the group threw all the collected money onto the stage before dispersing, Black Robe back in his original place.

'Shahbaz bhai,' Ghulam Hussain said, 'Do you have a rupee, or so?' I reached into my pocket, looked at the value of the coins I had, and collecting one rupee, I dropped the coins into Ghulam Hussain's hand. He took the money and left me standing alone. I met several more turned heads and red eyes, everyone in shalwars, me in pants and shirt. Ghulam Hussain placed the money on top of the qawal's harmonium, saluted him. He stood at the side of the stage, watching the performance from up close, swaying his head in rhythm, raising his hand in appreciation to a particular couplet. A member of the public, Ghulam Hussain. I was nervous without him here at my side, and I tried signalling to him. When he finally came back I said, 'Chalain.'

'You want to leave?'

'Yes.'

The crowd outside had grown. More bodies. There was a muddy embankment next to the quad, which scaled the outer wall of the Abdullah Shah Ghazi shrine and overlooked the crowd in the field. People sat on the two or three different levels of this embankment, drugged, watching, smoking cigarettes and joints, the cherries shining on and off like luminous insects.

'Chalain?' Ghulam Hussain said.

'No,' I replied. 'I want you to find me some opium. You must be able to find it here, na?'

Ghulam Hussain tilted his head from side to side, uncertainly. 'Should be able.'

'Then you do it. I'll be here.' I pointed to the mound. For the first time that I'd seen him, Ghulam Hussain appeared tentative amongst a crowd but, at my insistence, manoeuvred through the bodies. I took a seat on the mound, first at a level close to the ground, but then shifted to the very top. I gazed down at the crowd, which looked like an enormous centipede. How close was this place to events? Had Bhutto come to them, stood up there at the top level of the muddy embankment, injected his furious slogans into their heads? I had an idea, to go down there again and, one by one, like a ticket inspector, check their thumbs for the ink marks, and rebuke and expel anyone without.

It was chilly, and the men near me sat crouched within their chadors, sadly bringing their cigarettes to their mouths like starved children. Ghulam Hussain was down there somewhere, murmuring his request for afeem. It had been a long day, and I was tired. But I felt I'd accomplished *some*thing. Properly bribed, my policeman ally would now cut through the system, the offices and commandments, and get to the heart of things. The squatters. My money was a little quantity of energy, stripping things to the core, eating its way to the family orchard. In some ways that was more important than a vote. Because if all the people in this place *had* voted, then my vote didn't matter. In this immense human pool, I would be a single tiny molecule, nothing more. But I'd given Rahim sahib those notes, with the photo of Jinnah and the crescent and the moon, and that *would* make a difference. The orchard would be ours and the little molecules would add up. Governments could come and go, rise and fall, but we'd have the orchard. And Rahim sahib was going to get it for us.

I liked the idea, itself, of bribing Rahim sahib. That I could afford to bribe, that I was the *type* to bribe. A hand in the pocket, a secret transfer to another hand, and new things suddenly opened up and were put in motion. My father had for so many years claimed that he'd never agreed to bribe or receive a bribe, as if it was his major achievement in life, the core of his character. He talked as though there was something sacred about it. It was a joy to flout all of that, come down to a more real life, a world where things happened. *You wouldn't have been able to get it done, old man. This is it, this is the way this world of ours works. Means and ends. You were right to send me.* Again and again, I replayed the episode, in the greatest detail: the way Rahim sahib and I sat at angles to each other, the hushed, secret tenor of our voices, the play-acting, the money leaving my hand for his.

I looked up the mausoleum, people were going in to pour their petals and prayers on the saint. I imagined now that it was all a front. There was no dead, holy body under the cloth and clay. No, in that little chamber were the people who ran things out here, the ones who made sure there was enough opium and hash and music and fake watches and jewels circulating to keep this little heaven going. They didn't need to vote, and neither did I. I thought of my father. It was approaching evening in Paris. What was he doing? Surely, the elections here affected him, possibly harassed him with a sense of nostalgia. What would he do to overcome that sadness? One night, in one of those vans in Paris, after I'd dressed again and sat back down on the bedding, frozen, when the woman was about to open the sliding side door, I shouted, 'Non, attendez!' Because I had a very real fear that I would come out, spent, and find my father standing outside, awaiting his turn.

Ghulam Hussain was at the base of the mound, calling my name and waving. I raised my arm and twisted my wrist to inquire from a distance. He motioned for me to come down and join him where he was. I got up and stumbled over the feet and legs of hunkered bodies. I forced my way into the crowd greedily. Hot, wet arms and shoulders and chests rubbed against my own arms, shoulders, and chest. Where did I get my repulsion to filth? Out with it! I thought. I wanted these bodies now, these stinking bodies wrapped in damp kameezes. Every time someone touched me I closed my eyes, tilted my body as immodestly as a glutton in that body's direction to prolong contact, welcomed the sensation of their sweat spreading on my shirt.

Where we stopped, a long-bearded medicine man held up a needle, a thin syringe more than half of it covered in grunge. The man pointed the needle toward my arm. I glared at Ghulam Hussain accusingly, as if the time had finally come, the time for him to betray me, hand me over to this man, inject me with whatever was in that thing, and keep me here. I pushed Ghulam Hussain aside and hurried away, into the mass, towards the quad where the qawali was being performed. Up the steps by the wall, to the upstairs gallery from where the women had watched the performance. It was a narrow gallery with the same dirty white walls. A woman, the same one I'd seen from below, was walking in my direction, and as she passed me she stopped and said, 'Sharam karo, jao yahaan se!' I walked past her. Ahead was the part of the balcony that permitted a view of the quad below, with a bench seating a woman, an old and fat terror with no front teeth and barely any pupil showing in the whites of her eyes. She was wearing an ornate green kameez, whose cheap golden embellishments had faded with the rest of it. Her face had been sweating for a long time. She was rocking back and forth and from her mouth came a robust lament, which had lost its melody long ago and sounded more like a death wail now. With her was a boy of no more than six or seven, who leaned over the balustrade watching the qawals. As the music intensified the kid, too, rocked, with head and neck in motions that began slowly as he tilted to one side, then hastened with a sharp exclamation downward. Such practised, professional movements in a kid so young.

There was a sound of collision behind me. The ugly woman had collapsed and lay on one side on the floor, the bench similarly overturned. Her eyes were closed and her mouth agape and contorted in misery, two flies on her lips and cheek. She was breathing out of her mouth in heavy gasps. 'Oye,' I called to the kid. 'Your mother has fallen.' He continued his motions, in the haal. I stood over him and grabbed him by one shoulder, turned him around to face me. 'Check if she's dying,' I said in English. The boy didn't even look in the woman's direction. Instead, with my hand on his shoulder, he let his feet give way and abandoned all balance, falling backward and forcing me to hold him tighter, now by both sides. 'Kya kar rahe ho!' I shouted. He had his eyes closed, and a small smile appeared momentarily. Then he rocked his head from side to side in those fierce motions. The smile merged into a look of suffering. I looked behind him to the qawals downstairs and their rapt crowd. And this boy in my arms swaying with his eyes barely open and a little bit of heaven on his lips. I searched his arms for injection marks. What if I threw him over the edge, down into the quad? He freed one arm from my grip, raised it with a finger pointing upward and yowled a holy invocation. I looked around like a guilty party, afraid for anyone to see this drugged, hollering boy in my arms. I also felt uneasy letting him go, but now I had to, things seemed about to get frighteningly out of control. I positioned him gently on the floor, his back against the wall, like a brittle ornament. The expression on his face didn't change, so completely had he left his body. He seemed to sink into the concrete, or to want to sink into it. Two figures on the floor, mother and son, I left them there and went briskly down the steps to the field. Perhaps Bhutto *had* really been here, made his promises of redistributed honour and wealth, and they were all waiting patiently, killing time pursuing smaller goals, discarding their little possessions, before a new age.

The bodies, the warm kameezes with their warm patches of sweat, pressed me again on my way out. Back on the street, the cool air felt like freedom. Within that boundary wall was a place just like the orchard, separate, heated by coal underneath, where nothing from the outside world applied. Ghulam Hussain was still in there and that was fine, he belonged there as well as the others. I got back into his car. A man came to my window, a big head, an upward curled lip, a missing eye. How was a face like that possible? What an Age. I gave him money, then got out of the car to avoid any more like him. I walked back to the Clifton beach, sat close to the water. Ghulam Hussain would find me when he needed to.

I hadn't asked my father or Mona Phuppi where our old house was, partly a little embarrassed that I didn't remember. It was near here somewhere. I walked on the dirt road, away from the beach, in the direction of the Old Clifton residential streets. They were farther away than I thought, and I'd walked a lonely quarter of an hour at least, not a soul on the streets, the restless screeching of insects' wings and teeth outlining the silence. I was in the side streets, in the distance I thought I could hear the qawali. I found an elderly servant holding a tin of milk from its long handle. He gave me directions to the ocean. 'Achha, tell me,' I said. 'There was a gentleman who used to live in this area many years ago. He was a filmmaker. Ghazanfar sahib. Have you heard the name?' Yes, he said vaguely, the name was familiar. 'You don't know where he used to live? What street?' He looked upward, put his hand to his mouth in contemplation, then turned his head down, as if in parody of his role as a man of knowledge. Finally, with an expression of deep regret, he shook his head and said, 'Sir this I don't know.' 'Theek hai,' I said, thanked him and followed his directions back to the Clifton beach. It was a relief to find the familiar monument, people climbing the long steps to Abdullah Shah Ghazi's tomb, with bags of rose petals and wreaths in hand, their heads clear, their prayers ready. All of this to keep Karachi afloat.

PART THREE

New Friends

1

I soon came to know that the gentlemen in the drawing room were Jamaatis. It was early evening, just before dinner, and these two men waited below the mezzanine. It was Sajid the servant who told me their first secret, which wasn't an actual secret but I took it in as such: that the two sahibs sitting below the mezzanine with their backs to the window were members of none other than the Jamaati-i-Islami. This was the party that during the elections had attacked the corruption of the generals and the Western decadence of Zulfiqar Ali Bhutto, whose election rally, calling for an Islamic state, I'd witnessed briefly when driving somewhere with Ghulam Hussain. Of course, I recalled the grammar school lessons about Maulana Maududi founding the party in 1941, and I even remembered—because my father was one of them—that many Indian Muslims who migrated to Pakistan after Partition believed that this was the party that would defend their interests in the new state, against the Punjabis and Sindhis and whoever else. What I didn't know yet, but know too well now, was what they were up to that patriotic summer of 1971, the

things they did, the *extent* they went to to keep Pakistan—
East and West—intact, one nation under God—which
meant that, for them, Bengalis like Hammad Rehman,
with whom I'd had several drinks one night at the Agra,
and my own friend and benefactor, Ghulam Hussain,
had treason within them. And long before I knew these
things, that evening in the Spring of 1971, two of its
officials, it turned out, were waiting for the brigadier.

It wasn't unusual for people to show up unannounced.
In fact, a new era seemed to have been inaugurated at
the house. Guests had started showing up in nightly
packs, men and women with the comportment of power
makers. The bottles and glasses and ice trays were
arranged, the brigadier would finish his dinner and have
Sajid bring him a Coke and cigarette in the drawing
room, where he'd sit on his usual seat, his legs propped
on a foot stool, and wait for the night's visitors, whoever
they turned out to be. They'd start coming in shortly
after ten, and by eleven the drawing room filled with
conversation about cricket, politics, the new parliament
still to be convened. Aunty Ruby, too, participated,
often in private conversation with one big wheel or
another, whose words she'd eventually relay out loud to
the wider group. She'd taken a particular liking to one
man who often came, with thick perfect white hair and
a dark moustache, who'd won a senate seat on a
People's Party ticket. One evening, after a secluded
quarter of an hour in conversation with him, she
announced exuberantly: 'Senator sahib says that Bhutto
sahib has told them he'll break their legs if they attend
the National Assembly session.' The brigadier, red eyes,
red face, interjected, 'Haan haan, bhai, it's all a bloody
sham.'

The guests always came after dinner. But it was not even dark yet, and there were these two Jamaatis in the drawing room.

I stopped at the drawing room's doorway, nodded awkwardly to them, got a smile from the thinner man, a raised hand from the other, and moved on to Apa's room. A book lay closed on the old lady's lap, on its surface a sheet of letter paper. She was bent over it, pen in hand, writing as slowly as a calligrapher, large cursive letters, and sighing with every completed word.

'Apa, adaab.' I sat next to her. 'Who are you writing to today?'

She looked up from the page, registered my presence. 'Kya?'

'Who are you writing to?'

'Writing? Haan, I'm writing. This . . . I'm . . . ah.' She was struggling more and more with speech these days. 'This . . . I'm writing a letter.'

'To *whom*?'

'To who? To, uh, um . . . Nasser. Nasser of Egypt.'

She couldn't continue with me there. She sat uneasily with the letter in front of her, pen in hand, the magnifying glass next to her. Like an artist, needing privacy to create her art, or a spy selling secrets. I took the letter. The quality of English, the mere fact that she was using English at all, always surprised me in her letters: *Dear Colonel Nasser, I am your sister in Pakistan. When you announced resignation, I would also have been in streets, I also would say, 'We shall fight.' But I am old woman. Howver*—I took her pen and squeezed an 'e' where it was missing—*in Pakistan, these day*—the letter stopped there. I placed it back on her lap.

'Have you got an answer from Brezhnev yet?' I asked.

'Brezhnev?'

'The Russian. You wrote to him two-three weeks ago.'

'Haan, haan, Brezhnev. He, toh, is, uh . . .' She looked suddenly despondent and ashamed. 'No, he . . . until now, no letter. But it must have come to the . . . what do they have, the Russians, here . . . their, uh . . .'

'Consulate,' I said, in English.

'Haan, haan, con-su-late. One of these days I'll go. To the con-su-late.' Poor woman, forced to speak an English word. 'They'll give me the letter.' She'd been saying this for days. In that letter, she'd requested politely of the Russian leader that he end the Cold War, since we were all brothers and sisters and all wanted peace. She signed it, *Your sister, Ayesha*. This was the first time I saw her real name in use. Now she smoothed the letter to Nasser with her slow crooked hand, and looked at it tensely, considering taking up the pen again. Next door I heard the brigadier coming down from the mezzanine, exclaiming 'Haan, haan.' I stood up and inclined toward the wall that separated us.

'Is there someone here?' Apa asked.

'Two men,' I replied.

'Which two men?'

'A thin one and a fat one.'

'Eh? Thin one-fat one?'

'Guests.'

'Which guests?'

'A thin one—this'll go on forever,' I said in English, under my breath. I sat back down. 'Why don't you send Sajid?' I asked.

'Sajid?'

'Send him to the Russian consulate, get your letter from Brezhnev.'

'Nahin!' she snapped. 'What good will Sajid be? To him, you think they'll give the letter?! Kabhi nahin.'

'If the letter's there, they'll give it to him. Why don't you call them right now? Tell them you're sending Sajid.'

'Oh, let it be, bhai.'

'Brezhnev will be most upset if you don't get his letter.'

'That there is,' Apa said, shaking her head from one side to the other and back again like a pendulum until its natural momentum subsided. Next door, the two men and their host talked so low that only a melodic secret hum came through to Apa's room. Apa tugged at my leg as I stood. 'Don't go. Abhey, sit for a while!'

'I have to meet the guests. They're waiting for me.'

'No!' Apa keened.

'Write your letter to Nasser,' I said.

The thin man, in pants and shirt, rose for me as the brigadier introduced us. He was a professor at Punjab University in Lahore, clean-shaven and with wavy hair combed as far back as it could go, breathing bulky on his small head, his mouth wide open and shaped for a laugh, urging me to make a quip. He looked too young to be a professor, no more than his early thirties, with the swollen snoopy-like eyes of a dope fiend. His fat companion, in white shalwar kameez, only half-rose, squatting over the sofa when I took his hand. The brigadier didn't say anything about this larger man, except his name, Khwaja something. He had small sunken eyes, a pear-shaped nose that wanted to end early, dipping but then giving another little bump that leaned over his upper lip before finally rounding off. His was a big beard not because it came down far so much as climbed up his cheeks almost to the cheek bones.

'His abba, a very old friend, made films,' the brigadier said, as we were all seated again. 'You remember Ghazanfar sahib?'

'Achha, achha.'

'But I was saying, Khwaja sahib,' the brigadier continued, in Urdu. 'Please forgive me, but it was Allah who interfered in this one. If it wasn't for that cyclone ... that cyclone made Mujib a king. He blamed it on West Pakistan, and now he's won the elections.'

'Nahin, nahin, brigadier sahib,' the Khwaja replied. 'Before that, much before that.' He leaned forward, and now struck the table with a hard eloquent index finger at every important word. 'It was when Ayub put him in *prison*'—thump of the mighty index—'If you want to make a man a hero ... you *put* ... *him* ... *in* ... *prison*!' Thump, thump, thump, thump. The Khwaja's neck, his whole frame was rigid—it was his eyes, the pupils that scampered while he spoke, little brown balls bouncing almost chaotically in white space that was too small for them.

'We have this acquaintance, a Foreign Office man,' the brigadier explained quietly. 'He was here the other night, with a group of others, you know coming just like that. He said he went to Dhaka with a delegation, those Foreign Office things that they have. And he said the Bengali members—the minute the plane landed, he said, a complete change in them. More bossy. And these people are the ones who usually don't open their mouths. As if it was *their* turf, na?'

'Can you imagine if they saw the whole *country* as their turf?'

Our host now turned to me. 'Tampering again,' he said, switching to English. 'Too much bloody tampering.

Arrey bhai, why so much hullabaloo about a new constitution? Who do they suddenly think they are, Jeffersons and Hamiltons all of them? This country, my boy—you think our people will know what to do with a constitution?' He leaned forward and eyed me intensely. '*Blah . . . blah . . . blah*! Government by knife and fork. Our people eat with their *hands*, and *that's* what you've got to let them do.' I was startled by this sudden vigorous attention on me, as if I had made the offending argument, and I was relieved when the conversation turned back to Urdu, back to the three of them. Without excusing myself I got up and went back to the landing, where I loitered for a few minutes before deciding to go back to my room and have some biscuits to ease the hunger. I was at the top of the steps when I heard the brigadier's voice. 'Son,' he called, and I stopped, turned around. He approached me, and said quietly, 'I need to find these gentlemen something, some papers. Why don't you just keep them company for a few minutes, okay.'

He walked through the drawing room to the steps of the mezzanine, and I sat down on the same seat as before, left alone with them. The thin professor watched me with that expectant, gaping smile, a guffaw trying to blow its way out. I waited for Urdu to fill my head and settle on my tongue. The silence was tough. The professor's flared nostrils were packed neatly with coiled hairs, as if to staunch a nosebleed. The big man, the Khwaja, was more sober; but the professor had something of the child in him, waiting to be entertained, told a nourishing tale. I had no such tales. Just a closed saccharine smile that began to ache. A question, a question, I sought a question. How long were they in Karachi for? 'We'll see, maybe two-three weeks.'

'Inshallah,' the other added. Achha, achha, I said. I strained my neck to look up towards the mezzanine for signs of the brigadier's return. Had they had tea, did they need anything else? I asked. No, they said they were quite all right. When our host did come down, a light brown A4 envelope under his arm, my lips relaxed. The brigadier pulled out just a couple of inches of the pages inside on the flap of the envelope, like the butt of a cigarette, and offered it to them. The larger man took the whole envelope and passed it to the professor without looking at him. The professor pushed the pages and the flap back in, and placed the closed envelope on his narrow shaky lap.

'Okay, ji?' the brigadier asked, leaning forward, his arms tensely resting on his knee. The big Jamaati nodded solemnly. 'Come,' the brigadier said. 'Meet Apa.' His Urdu was deferential, using the formal verb conjugation, the equivalent of the French 'vous'. We all stood. Apa in her room was bent over her letter to the former Egyptian ruler. I stood outside, heard the brigadier similarly complaining to the old woman about Mujib and the elections, and Apa in her tired voice reaffirming her nephew: 'This is the Angrez's work—*parliament, rule of law, Westminster.*' I hadn't heard so many English terms from her Urdu tongue. She spoke them poisonously, especially the last one, as if it was the tower on a hill spreading evil across the land below. *Westminster.* The professor stood behind the other two men, half in and half out, a pencil behind the ear. His hand found a glass on the table by the door, and with long lovely fingers he spun it slowly and inattentively from the rim. This was the glass where the old lady's dentures would go at the end of the day.

I crept away to the kitchen where Sajid was standing around, the dishes all prepared, the dough mixed and kneaded in a bowl, the stove and tawa ready for chapatis to be made. 'You sit,' Sajid said courteously, pointing toward the dining room. I did. He transferred plates and silverware and napkins to the table, placing them around me. 'Sir, those men, you know who they are? You don't know?' He chuckled, as if embarrassed, setting a quarter plate to the left. 'Sir, they are Jamaatis.' I looked at him to make sure he was serious. 'Jamaatis?' 'Yes sir,' he confirmed. I got up and out of the dining room. From the balcony I watched the brigadier see them off. The question of what they were doing here, at the brigadier's, hadn't begun to harass me yet. The professor and the Khwaja stepped over the bump of the gate, bade farewell to their host. And I imagined that that was the last of them. They'd received their papers and now they were gone, God bless them both. I loitered at the top of the stairs, waiting for the brigadier to come back up and lead me to the dining table.

∽

The house behind the brigadier's was being reduced with a thousand terrible blows every morning. This had been going on for days, beginning at around seven, and I awoke cursing that the damn thing was still standing. I had complained once, walking outside and scolding the workers for being so insensitive to the people living in the surrounding houses. They'd stopped, but shortly after that the contractor was at the brigadier's door, and later that day my host, with mild ennui, told me that there was nothing we could do about the timing, that it was important for them to get as much done in the morning as possible. So I suffered the sounds, which forced me out of bed, and spent the mornings with Apa upstairs. Although the smallest rattle from the kitchen, a utensil falling, so disturbed her that she would call out to Sajid or send me to check on what had fallen, those thousand blows didn't appear to mean a thing.

This morning, it was precise metallic clinks as the workmen chipped away at the top part of the boundary wall. I gave up on sleep, dressed and went out of my room. There were two small suitcases at the entrance to the house, right outside my room. The door of the downstairs bedroom down the hall was open and cleaning women swiped the floor with grey cloth. Sajid stood over them like a warden, his hands against his hips. I hadn't seen this room properly before. It was smaller than mine, the same dark red tiles which the women now worked over with their powerful liquids. A transportable closet, made of thick lime green plastic and with a zipper opening, stood open in one corner, filled with naked hangers. Sajid murmured salaam.

'Who's coming?' I asked.

'Sir, those two men who came.'

'Who came when?'

'Two, three days ago, sir.'

'The Jamaatis?'

'Sir . . .'

'The thin one and the fat one?'

'Ji, ji, those.'

'They're staying *here*?'

'Haan, here. Where else?' He said this softly, with a smile, but I didn't like the nerve of it.

'When the work here is done, make me two fried eggs and toast,' I instructed.

'Sir, two toasts?'

Before going back towards the stairs I asked how long the men were staying.

'Sir, nothing is known.'

I looked again at the two suitcases at the entrance, wanted to pick them up to gauge their weight, even to open them and see what those clergymen were bringing with them. There had been many guests at the brigadier's but these were the first since I'd been here who were actually moving in. The two Jamaatis, on the same floor as mine.

Apa had been following a story in the papers about a brothel in PECHS that had been busted by the police. She'd taken a strong interest in the case, greeting me two days in a row with updates, new discoveries in the case, each of which seemed to trouble her more—when it turned out that the hookers were foreigners, not locals, she'd wailed, 'Then why did they first say they were Karachi girls? Abhey, you can tell when a girl is Pakistani and when she is from, wherever this is, Kazakhstan-Fazakhstan, or wherever. Their girls don't look like our girls, hain na? So then?' Then, when it turned out that it wasn't the police but a vigilante squad that had originally broken up the joint, Apa said, 'Who is keeping law and order in this country? It's obvious, if we have a sharabi as a ruler, others have to govern, keep peace.' Today it was revealed that of the seven people taken into custody, one of them was a well-known politician. 'Why didn't they tell us this before? You can tell who is the prostitute and who is the customer, is it or no?' Her lips were scrunched and pulled up toward her dilated disapproving nose. One of the girls who tended to her was pressing her leg around the knee. The pallu of Apa's sari had fallen from around her shoulder and lay idly on her forearm. She was irritated by it, repeatedly lifted her elbow to throw it upward, but seemed unwilling to make the final little effort to place it back on her shoulder. I did it for her. She put the magnifying glass and the Urdu newspaper aside, lowered and leaned her forehead onto the symmetrical frame constituted by index and thumb of each hand. Poor lady, having to deal with so much change, so many corrections to one simple story.

There was a *Dawn* issue by her side, too, which I took and folded back so that the front page was again in its normal place. Some party or committee in East Pakistan was calling for a 'Constitution in line with the verdict of the People'. Bhutto was being urged to attend the National Assembly session. Students were rallying. Apa coughed and grunted and made all the noises of a dying interior. 'Have you eaten?' she asked. I told her no, that I would check on my breakfast immediately. And as I made to leave her room, I found them approaching on the landing.

'Ah, Shahbaz sahib!'

Both wore shalwar-kameez today, because it was a Friday, and each greeted me with the half-hug of comrades, a confirmation that it was really happening, the professor and Khwaja sahib were indeed moving in a door away from mine. 'Come,' said the big man. 'Let's sit.' The three of us took our places in the sitting area on the second floor landing, the two of them, side by side, their backs to the Indo-Saracenic window arches, me facing them and the metallic gold of sunlight behind them. The professor wore closed-tip shoes, but the Khwaja wore sandals: labourer's feet, bloated grey toes, especially the big toe, the nails almost disappearing in so much hard bulging skin; black deposits on at least six of ten toenails, a contaminated creature. He occasionally held the two sides of his jawline between thumb and middle finger, and then exercised the big jaw, opening and shutting his mouth as if to unblock his ears. Immobile drops of sweat flecked his forehead evenly like the marks of a small shoe sole. He put a white handkerchief to it, pressed every little spot, careful to wipe away all traces of insult.

The Jamaatis sat close enough to resemble, in their identical beige baggy shalwars, a two-headed turtle. Then the two heads, two necks and torsos, parted as the professor leaned forward, his hands to his knees. 'Yes, sir?' he exclaimed, looking at me giddily, expecting, expecting, his thick wavy hair brushed back with thin fuzz extending from the top as if he'd been rained on or electrocuted. Sajid rolled his trolley to me, my eggs-on-toast and a cup of tea, even though I had told him twice in as many days that I liked having my tea *after* my breakfast. I looked at him and shook my head. Sajid asked the men if they wanted anything. 'Nahin, bachai,' the Khwaja said, already addressing Sajid like a son.

'Please,' I said, gesturing to my plate. 'Have some eggs.'

'No matter, eat, eat,' the professor said with a laugh. I wondered: were they really going to sit there empty-handed while I finished my breakfast?

2

Ghulam Hussain reached deep into the cupboard and pulled out an object wrapped in black plastic. He looked focused, unwrapping the object with the greatest care. Its shape was evident even before the plastic came completely off. The long carton of a single bottle. 'Yeh dekhye!' he said exuberantly. It was whisky. Ghulam Hussain pointed to a white seal that ran across the width of the carton. I took it from him and held it against the bulb. It read: 'Chief of Army Staff.' 'Ayub's whisky, Shahbaz bhai!' He took the carton back, opened the lid and pulled the bottle from it. He placed this before me. It, too, had the Field Marshal's seal, running around the width from front to back. 'Ayub's whisky.' He took the bottle from me and eased it back into the carton, trying to use his puffy hands delicately. 'That bottle, I've had it for . . .' he looked towards the ceiling, calculating, 'maybe . . . five years. Shah Sahib gave it to me.' He sat down, repeated, 'Shah Sahib! He was a Bengali kid, no more than this high. I don't know where he and Ayub first met. Long before Ayub was even head of the army. He took this little boy fishing—Ayub *loved* fishing, they say. So he took him fishing in Kemari. Just two of them. Maybe there were others, what do we know. While they were fishing this little Bengali boy— eight, nine years old—said to Ayub, "You will be the first Muslim commander of the army." And Ayub laughed and said, "Yeh kaise, bhai, I'm nowhere close, there are so many generals before me." The boy said, "Nahin, you will be the first Muslim commander of the army." Then, Shahbaz bhai, the next week there was a big plane crash and all these top generals died, bas, in one minute,' he snapped his fingers, 'all gone, and Ayub is commander of the army.'

One assumed power through stories. Ghulam Hussain had them. They all had them: Malika, Mona Phuppi, the brigadier, Apa, Hammad sahib with the bad leg, even my father. And once you have the stories, I argue, you can demand your right to be silent, to remove yourself, go into exile. What stories did *I* have? None. I'd skipped May '68, I'd skipped just about everything, and now I had to earn my way. Earn my way back to Paris, back to exile. The squatters were still there and I was exhausted. The government had finally shifted the deeds back to our family, and now Mona Phuppi and her buyer were getting deep into talks. Again, I felt the panic of Paris and that old clean taste of the West dissolving.

So it was for his stories—not your hash, my friend, as you probably thought—that I went so often to Ghulam Hussain's quarters. Yes, like a parasite I bled (so to speak—the *real* blood came later) and damned him. I couldn't keep myself away, so selfish and treacherous was my yearning. He pulled out a cigarette box that had a small slab of hash tucked into its plastic wrapper. He removed a cigarette, and began emptying the tobacco into his free hand, twisting the cigarette back and forth between thumb and middle finger, where the white met the filter. 'So Ayub said, "Arrey bhai, how did this happen?" So he started taking Shah Sahib with him everywhere. Wherever he went, this little Shah Sahib was with him. And he became close to Ayub's daughter, she used to play with him, badminton or whatever that game is, the one with rackets and that little . . .' The last of the tobacco trickled from the cigarette and lay in Ghulam Hussain's palm. 'Shah Sahib was good with electronics. He loved electronics. One day he was fixing a radio, Ayub's daughter's radio maybe, and there was a picture of Ayub in front of the radio. In a frame.' He burned the hash on the tip of a matchstick and, once it was hot enough, blew out the flame and flicked it into the tobacco in his palm. 'Maybe the picture was getting in the way so Shah Sahib moved it to the shelf that was on top. Then he said to Ayub's daughter, "Look I've made your father the Badshah." Two days later Ayub threw out the president and made himself the leader of the country. The Badshah!' He mashed the hot black into the tobacco. 'When Ayub became president he kept Shah Sahib, little Bengali boy, right next to him. Meaning, every thing he did, Shahbaz bhai, he spoke to Shah Sahib first.' The hash mixed into the tobacco, he now sucked it into the empty cigarette. He held the cigarette at the tip and shook the mixture down to the base, sucked in some more, repeated this until the joint was ready. He twisted the tip into a thin wick. 'So all the businessmen, all the politicians, meaning *everybody*, came to Shah Sahib. They are the ones who gave him the name, Shah Sahib. *Shah Sahib, please tell the Field Marshall this, Shah sahib please tell the Field Marshall to do that.*' Ghulam Hussain ducked his head and raised his hand to his forehead to imitate these elite supplicants. '*Do this for us, do that for us.* They wouldn't give him money—twelve-year-old boy, what's he going to do with money? So they gave him sharab. Whisky, wodka, gin-shin, beer-sheer. Meaning, whatever a man can drink, they gave to Shah Sahib.' Poor little liver. 'So he started to love sharab. And he'd ask Ayub's daughter to get him bottles from her father. He'd say, "I made your father king, now you give me." So she gave him bottles. *Chief of Army. Chief.*' The English words delighted him. With that, he finally lit the joint, puffed several times. 'One day he tried getting into President House, here in Karachi. I think there must have been new guards, they didn't know Shah Sahib. This bechara Bengali boy, dressed in poor man's clothes comes to President House, of course they don't know him. He had a big fight with them. Let me in, I'm Shah Sahib! They laughed at him. He went away very angry. So when he met Ayub he said, "Field Marshall sahib, don't stay in this house. Everybody who stays in this house meets a bad end. Jinnah stayed in this house, Jinnah died. Liaquat stayed in this house and they killed Liaquat. You'll also be killed."' He handed me the joint. 'And *that's* why, Shahbaz bhai, he moved the capital to Islamabad.'

'What happened to this little boy?'

'I think he's dead. Or maybe he's in East Pakistan. Who knows?'

I took a few deep puffs and handed it back to him. I looked at my watch. It was close to midnight, and I wanted to see Malika tonight. Ghulam Hussain wrapped the chief of staff's bottle back in its black plastic and set it in its hideaway at the back of the cupboard. This second time he opened the cupboard, I was watching more closely and, therefore, noticed the two guns on the upper shelf, their black grips meeting at the inner tips, the barrels facing each other. My friend now grabbed a bottle of his self-made booze, self-made poison that would one day destroy him, and gave it to me. This time he accepted the five rupees I gave him. I didn't ask him about the guns. Instead I looked at my watch again, and asked him if he could drive me to a taxi, which predictably he rejected, saying he would drop me to PECHS himself.

'No, no,' I said. 'Just find me a taxi and I'll be . . .'

'Doesn't matter, Shahbaz bhai. Ten minutes it will take.'

I exhaled a guilty sigh. 'I'm not going straight home. I have to stop somewhere else.'

'Theek hai. You tell me where, and I'll take you.'

Oh! he was going to insist, he was going to make me tell him that I was going to the cabaret, a world he had no part in, never would have a part in. Each time he took me, I felt guiltier about our differences, guilty about the fact that I couldn't tell him to come in with me. 'I have to meet someone at the Agra Hotel.' So preposterous, my guilt, because Ghulam Hussain cared nothing about any of this. It was the way of things, the bigger picture. So he drove me to the Agra. Quiet behind the wheel. He wasn't as euphoric about Mujib's sweep of East Pakistan in the elections as I thought he'd be, about a Bengali soon to be the country's first-ever elected leader. When I asked him about it now, he withdrew into himself, looked out of the driver's window at the black emptiness connecting the old Karachi to the new. Perhaps he did talk about it to his own people, perhaps he didn't trust me enough to speak his heart about this future, a country ruled by Bengalis. And when I asked him if he was troubled by the fact that Mujib's victory in the election wasn't yet being honoured, he responded with his customary, 'Who knows?' After those nights wandering the streets with his gang of rebels, perhaps he was now leaving big matters to others. He'd served proudly. Not for him another scar on the arm. Fair enough, my friend. Recede away. Having already given him money for the bottle of alcohol, I didn't tip him tonight.

∾

I sat at my corner table. The soldiers had occupied a cluster of tables in the middle and grouped them together untidily, but nobody complained. They were in uniform, after all. In Karachi, getting ready to go to Indonesia or Burma or some other friendly country, and from there they were going to East Pakistan, where things were getting out of hand. Mujib wasn't yielding, insisting on his right to become prime minister, and he'd called for a hartal, as they called it, every day from six in the morning to two in the afternoon. Riots, strikes, the mandate of the times. And Yahya was sending in his soldiers in that twisted route to circumvent the thousand miles of India. So here they all were, at the Agra, on standby, giving a retired brigadier some dazzling business. Some of the men, Malika told me, were senior colonels and generals, and often they didn't leave at closing time, demanded that the band play on and the dancers keep dancing.

Malika was back. What a relief! I thought. She'd returned to Cairo, and maybe travelled to a thousand other places, gone for weeks. The cabaret, the whole of the Agra, was almost wretched without her, so that it was I who told the brigadier to bring her back. He'd noticed the dullness in the place, and when he asked me what it needed—a juggler? a magician? a comedy routine akin to the Marx Brothers?—I said: 'Why not bring Malika back? It was so much more lively when she was around, no?' Two nights later, I suggested it again, and it wasn't long before the brigadier told me they'd agreed on another deal and she was coming back soon.

But this time around, she looked more tired, and short-tempered with some of the men, even the soldiers. In these new circumstances, I was as hesitant as ever to approach her during her working hours. Her professionalism was exemplary; she received me after all this time with the same hollow cheerfulness as she did everyone else. When she was dancing or tending to customers, she didn't once turn her eyes my way.

But now I wanted to pronounce *some* claim over her—claim her from these bloody soldiers. I had come to feel more deeply for Malika because she took sex seriously, and I was becoming a better lover to her, *through* her. But this feeling also gave me an appalling sense of urgency, afraid that the energy, my coming into form, could still be derailed. I wanted to make love to her every night.

The plump redhead who I'd once seen kiss Malika's temple was talking to two soldiers, who watched her with great expectations. Glass in hand—she drank remarkable amounts for a woman—her whole manner slowly taking on a more frantic and theatrical air, the lady moved closer to them, her hand movements became unrestrained as she talked and illustrated her topic. It

was two a.m. and there were no signs that the soldiers
were getting too tired or drunk to carry on, except the
two who were asleep on one of the tables in the cluster,
one leaning back in his seat with his arms splayed out,
ready to be sacrificed, and the other with one side of his
face flat on the table, his hands dropped on either side,
dangling like legs and almost touching the floor. With
all these soldiers here, overstaying, the cabaret gave me
a feeling of Karachi slipping from my already weak
grasp; I felt cheated.

It was well past three when Malika and I finally met
in her room. I told her about the two Jamaatis. 'When
did they come?' she asked, changed into her post-
performance caftan.

'A week ago.' I poured myself a drink and sat down.
'I don't like being in that house anymore. These two
men. Theocrats. You know what theocrats are? Mullahs,
beards—well, one of them is clean-shaven, but what I
mean by beard . . .' I sipped my drink. 'First it was just
a suitcase each. Fine. Well and good, as my father would
say. But then two days later, more things.'

'What things?'

'What things, what things. For example, a big ivory
trunk, this long. For their room. Now why would you
bring an ivory trunk to your room if you weren't
planning on staying a while? Ah, *then*! There's this clock
on the wall in the entrance to the house, you must have
noticed it when you came that night, or, well I don't
know *how* many times you've been to the house, but
however many it is, I'm sure you saw this clock. Yes?
Well, the clock is no longer there anymore. Why?
Because it's now in *their* room. Yes, they needed a clock,
they need to know what time it is, after all, despite being

so close to God, and so that clock is now in their room. *Out*-rage-ous.'

'You like the clock?'

'What?'

'You don't have a watch?'

'I do. Of course, I do.' I raised my wrist, pushed back my sleeve. 'But that's not the point. The point is they see a clock, a clock in a *public* part of the house, a part that we all use, and they like the clock, and they decide that because they don't have a clock in their room, and because they need to be able to tell time at all hours of their rotten day, they'll simply move the clock to their room. If you can't see the problem here . . .'

There was a knock on the door, and when Malika shouted, Yes, a boy brought in a highly ornate parcel, a new cabaret outfit delivered for some reason at three-thirty in the morning. Malika took it from him, tipped him a coin, and then unfolded the jangling bits on the bed. 'Hmm,' she said, looking it over.

'Never worn?' I asked.

'It's nice, no?' She held it to her breast.

'Try it on.'

'Yes?'

I nodded. 'If you can stand to put that stuff back on after a whole night of . . .' She undressed, her back to me. 'What I want to know,' I continued, 'is what are they *here* for? I can't bear them, my love. I don't know what it is about them. The bigger one, Khwaja something-or-other, I can hear his body moving in the room down the hall. The whole downstairs moves with him.' She was silent, in her panties, putting on the bottom part. It was the skimpiest outfit I'd seen her wear yet. 'Why does your boss have these men staying in the house? What are they there for? They say their prayers in the drawing room upstairs. Why not in their own rooms? And when they're done they look at me as if I should be saying my prayers, too.'

'It's true!' She raised her voice playfully. The outfit fit her well. Half her attention was devoted to the long mirror, sticking one leg out, then slowly moving her belly in that beautiful snake-like motion of hers.

'You know I have this dream. We're all upstairs in the drawing room, the brigadier, Aunty Ruby, Apa—you know Apa?—me, even you are there. And the two guests, too, these Jamaatis. And we're enjoying ourselves, drinking, talking. And then the Jamaatis want to go downstairs. Which is fine. But then they look at me as if to say, "Chalain." And I look at everyone else, and the brigadier nods as if to say, "Yes, it's time for you to go. We'd love to have you stay but you must go with these gentlemen." And I'm resigned to it—you understand "resigned"? I . . . I *agree* to go with them, but only because I know there is no other way, it's my duty. God knows what they're going to do to me.'

'Why you give so much . . . im-por-tence to this . . . *dreams*?' Malika asked. She was still watching herself in the mirror, shifting her hair around, first creating a big heap on her head, then collecting it all on one side, bringing it over her shoulder so that it went over one breast.

'You know, the other day, I had to have lunch downstairs because the brigadier and those men were having some kind of meeting in the dining room? I went upstairs and the door of the dining room was closed, and Sajid—you know, the servant?—told me to come to the kitchen, that smelly kitchen, to put my food on my plate and eat on the veranda or in my room or wherever. Because the brigadier and the guests were having a ... meeting. And one evening I went upstairs and saw not the two of them, but *three*—Sajid, the poor kid, they'd made *him* say his prayers with them. That kid is caught in this ... this *madness*. He has to take care of the whole house and now he has to say his prayers with these men, too.'

She unfastened the bottom piece, and in panties walked over to me. 'Come.' She tapped my thigh. 'Is getting late. Enough of the two men.' She took the top piece off, placed her apparel on the empty chair. She let her panties fall to the floor and stepped out of them. 'Come,' she repeated, as if calling me to the breakfast table. She lay on her back. I took off my clothes and placed them neatly on my chair and went obediently to her.

'Why is it I only ever meet with you in this room?' I asked, leaning over and, before getting an answer that wasn't coming anyway, I kissed her. She responded well, her hand on my face, the back of my head, the back of my neck, two hands now. Sometimes I felt it was the kissing she liked best.

❧

When I came home that night, I took the bottle out of my pocket and put it in my drawer, next to the other one, both unopened.

3

In Paris I *would* have stories. I'd learned new things, achieved a certain Karachi stature, the close company of powerful people. Yes, I would bring stories with me: of the brigadier; of the police captain; of shaking Bhutto's hand, the man who was now preventing the new parliament from convening; of Malika, who'd performed for the Shah of Iran. I could finally grow into the role that was mine. And we were close to having a civil war on our hands, besides. Yes, in many ways this was the larger world, and now that I'd soaked in it I was sure it would satisfy the people of the smaller world of Paris. I had so much to feed their imagination. My Urdu had improved, thanks to Apa. And I was particularly proud of my new capacity for drink. Those nights on the mezzanine with the brigadier, drinking whiskies-and-water over memories of his father's days in the railways, his own days in the army, the irredeemable failure of the '65 war, calibrated me. I could drink like a man. In fact, those nights on the mezzanine gave me insinuations of the kind of man I might have been had we stayed in

Karachi. Now only in Paris would all this new beauty take its true form.

◌◟

I had to see them again. For months they ran around in my head, with little sticks and a tennis ball or a ping-pong ball or a shuttlecock, bouncing across the bleak grounds in my mind from wide awake midnight to bleary morning. Good kids, both of them. In fact, they wormed their way into my childhood memories of the days and nights in the orchard. So that now when I thought back to those bases in the trees, the kids positioned all day on fat branches like guerilla fighters, somewhere nearby (not exactly *with* all the kids but nearby) were Little Chief and his deputy. And those nights in the deeps, those black spots where I undressed and sat naked, waiting for god-knows-what, the other two were around as well. Sometimes they sat with me, undressed, the three of us sitting in a circle like some quixotic tribe; sometimes I just knew that they were somewhere in the dark, watching me like that adult figure, whoever it was, who told me to beware of snakes.

It was hot but I walked the way to Cantt Station. Another British moment, a cathedral, elongated and only two storeys high, with a flag flying from the triangle roof. There were hot unwieldy cues going through each of the arches to the ticketing booths. I waited in front of a group of three, two women and a man, all three with enormous stainless steel pots on their heads. In this sun, I imagined that the *pot* was cooking, burning, melting the skull on which it rested. These people would go insane by the time they reached the booth. As the line advanced, they stepped through the arch and were now in shade. I got two A/C class tickets, one to Hyderabad, the next to Mirpurkhas. During the stop at Hyderabad I bought three cigarettes from a canteen and then looked around for a place to roll joints. I turned a corner outside the station and found a conductor-like man standing and drinking tea, a reddish-brown uniform on him. I approached him, said salaam, told him I had a favour to ask, showed him the piece of hash. 'If I give you this, can you make two or three hashish cigarettes for me? I don't know how to do it. Not well . . .' The man smiled, laughed, hesitated. I urged him on slyly the way I did the midget at the Agra. He didn't do it himself but, finally, delegated the task to a couple of coolie-like teens. It had already become a bigger operation than I'd conceived. I tipped them a couple of coins when they brought me the sloppily rolled joints. I lit the first, behind that same corner. A couple of other men in the same clay-coloured uniforms came simply to gaze at me, the word having spread through the station of this young man smoking hash in the back. I held the joint out, silently offering them a puff, which they turned down with smiles and heil-raised hands. Feeling exposed, I returned to the platform and boarded the train, found my seat. I put my head against the window and closed my eyes, only to be immediately startled by the sharp sound of a knuckle on the glass tapping thrice. It was the original conductor-looking man. And standing with him were two policemen. They gestured to me to come out. That bastard conductor! My chest heated up, I was drained and dizzy and without a future. Hyderabad—the middle of nowhere, they could do with me whatever they wanted. I wasn't under the brigadier's protection. Why had I been so stupid, so rash, flouting the law this far out? I thought of making a run for it, but where could I go. I got out, stood with my back to the sun and my face to the cop. 'Haan ji!' I said, arrogantly, but the boldness stillborn in a finally sunken delivery. The cop was curt: 'You have two cigarettes on you. When you get to Mirpurkhas, give one of those to the driver. Do bismillah and have a good journey. Why are you looking so worried? There's nothing to worry about, we are all brothers-brothers.' He squeezed my cheek between the caked knuckles of his index and middle fingers. He walked away with a cool swagger, the town's sheriff. Should I get back on the train? What if their demands increased once the train was moving, when there was no escape? But was there any way to get back to Karachi from here, if not by these very trains?

From my seat, I watched the driver get on. He saw me at the window and smiled and nodded. Yes, yes, I'll give it to you. I nodded back. No point arguing, this deep into their territory. The train departed on time.

∾

A vast beige outside, too lifeless and pale to call brown. Thin greenery, which occasionally thickened, but disappeared into the beige again. The wind sometimes produced a floating layer of dust above the surface like steam. The orchard—and this was something that had oddly never struck me before—was in the middle of what was almost desert. How the desert hadn't ingested the plot entirely was a wonder. Were the squatters in fact children of the desert? I had visions of them emerging from these endless empty plains, invading, scaling the walls into the orchard. This is where we would have to banish them back to. There were little concrete structures that appeared sporadically in those plains, sometimes a little block no more than two feet high (at least that's the way they appeared from my window), sometimes the same block but with a small half-globe rising from it. And all these mini structures were painted the same, in red and white squares. I decided they had to serve some military purpose. Later there were black circular patches that I again saw not as some agricultural detail, but the mark of the army, stratagem, testing. This whole vision, of the plains, now changed for me, lost its mute incorruptibility and became something more nefarious, an incalculably secret operation right here in these dry lands that played with the fate of millions. Beyond Bhutto, beyond even General Yahya. Bigger forces, bigger picture. Even the muteness was misleading; the area was in fact filled with sounds, at a non-human frequency, signals dogs and bats but not people picked up. Some greenery again. People, too. I've always been engrossed by the image of a single person alone in a large empty expanse of space, and now I played the same old game I played during the adolescent drives through rural Europe, gaze into the infinite looking for human forms. The time on the train passed quickly like this. A man kneeling over what remained of a small body of water; at another canal a few hundred yards ahead, a shirtless boy raising and tying the hem of his shalwar well above the knee, giving it the look of the sarouel or, once he was in the water, of an inflatable something to prevent drowning; another kid, with another grown man, led by a little cow in front, and followed by a cow at the back. Man and beast. No vehicles anywhere. How did these people get so far in, had they been walking for days, would they ever make it back? I smiled a smile of appreciation, even affinity, for these lost souls.

At Mirpurkhas I gave the driver the joint and walked on at a pace without a word, without giving him time to speak. When I got off the tonga in front of the orchard I realized it was Sunday because the deputy commissioner's office was shut. The gate to the orchard, as before, was distorted and perhaps even more so, one side nose-diving into the earth. That would have to be fixed when the time came. And there they all were, the squatters, carrying on as before. Exposed to the radiation not just of the sun but of whatever military thing was taking place nearby, all of them half-demented at the very least. There was a clay-looking wall of an unfinished, roofless accommodation, with a small chunk bitten off of the top, producing a U-shaped dip along the ridge. A kid sat in this U, his soles to the base, folded arms resting on folded knees. I took out the last joint and a box of matches, though merely touching the joint's tip to the earth for a few moments would probably have been enough. Kids stared while I smoked and that was fine by me. A small group of them had coalesced around a tree, looking up towards a white plastic bag stuffed with things hanging from a branch. Were these Acacia trees, whose bark produced the liquor Ghulam Hussain and his friends made and sold? There was a young girl amongst this group, a young girl in a bright red shalwar carrying a little boy on her hip. Another small boy wore an empty food bowl for a hat. And then there was the boy with the stick. Why a group of kids only seem to find one stick in a place like this amused me. No democracy amongst kids. The leader today, who lacked the easy authority of my Little Chief, wore an eye-patch on one eye. The other kids had collected on either side of him, watching, rapt as he beat the white plastic bag. Finally he managed a tear, and something shiny, metallic, fell out. Nobody seemed to care, nobody picked it up. I walked forward a few steps and gazed down. It was an aluminium leaf of some kind of medicine. Not candy. The leader, egged on by success, now attacked the bag eagerly, and more and more things fell out, little white boxes of medicine. The girl in the bright red shalwar walked back toward the inside, as if what was about to take place was too awful for the eyes of the little one she carried. The boy wearing the bowl on his head knelt down to pick one up, but the leader struck the steel hat with his stick. The boy dropped whatever he'd picked up, but the leader, loving the musical ring of stick to bowl, struck his head repeatedly just as he had the plastic bag a moment ago. Other kids grabbed whatever little boxes they could, their silly fortunes, and made a run for it. I ran after one of them and caught him by the back collar. His little hands tightened around the medicines. I pried a bottle of painkillers out of one hand, had to twist the other wrist to get a distorted box of something called Amytal. I let the kid go, and he ran faster than I'd ever seen anything his size run. I approached the tree. At some point, inevitably, you have to confiscate a child's stick, and this boy readily relinquished his when I asked for it. Then I tested it myself against the upturned bowl on the smaller one's head, which gave back a good treble. I could see why the kid was addicted to doing this. The one who wore the bowl walked away, the last of the supporting cast, so that it was now just me and the pirate. I pulled back his eye patch. The eye under it was closed. I restored the patch, gathered the fallen goods into the gutted bag as best I could, tied the bag from its ripped ends. 'Somebody might need this,' I said.

'You are a doctor?'

'You have sick people in there?' I asked.

'You are a doctor?'

'Yes, why not, I am a doctor.' I stood over him, bag in hand, like a high priest and dismissed him. This boy, too, ran like the wind.

I relit the joint. There were two possibilities regarding how this bag of medicines got here. Some benefactor, delivery man, had left it here, and someone from inside was supposed to come out to get it. I imagined myself one day filling this or a similar role, walking through their squatter town in a purple overcoat and purple hat and a thin gold walking cane, with this bag of medicine in the other hand, distributing sprays and syringes and syrups and pills—stimulants, depressants, barbiturates, hallucinogens. Arriving every couple of weeks, unannounced, humming la-da-dee-da da-da-da, and the workings of this little society would stop and its citizens would come to me for their supplies. Yes, if we didn't get the orchard back to the way it once was, that is what I could do, make sure that at the very least the place was healthy, fully dosed.

Or, these medicines were discarded goods from within, the squatters deciding they had no more use for modern remedies, the people here were well past the point of saving.

Hand across my brow to give me shade, I gazed far

and wide for Little Chief. Perhaps he'd already seen me, perhaps he'd reported back to his elders. *That man who was here before, he's here again. That one over there, smoking the cigarette.* Signalling perhaps that the end is near. The thought that I was their negation was both horrible and breathtaking. I dropped the joint to the ground. Hash had a much stronger impact in this sun. I wished I'd brought water for my dry mouth. I stood a foot away from the tree and took a piss, looking out into the deep. Who was that man who whispered in the dark to my naked ten-year-old self about snakes?

There were two women near the entrance. They watched me with conniving entertained faces. Middle-aged women getting their kicks. As the urine collected, I took a step back, gave the women their view. Then I zipped up and made to leave, walking in their direction, which set them off in mine. Throughout their approach, they eyed me with those same base smiles, which I found promising. Our paths finally crossed. As they grew closer, I saw the resemblance and guessed they must be sisters.

'You are not ashamed of yourself?' one of them said. 'You should be beaten and beaten!' I smiled. 'Get out of here!' she cried. I stayed where I was wondering how serious this mad lady was. 'Wait, one minute, just you wait,' she warned, and with extra charge in her step, she led her sister forward towards the settlements. 'Just you wait.'

'Okay, okay,' I beseeched them. 'Don't worry. I'm leaving. Forgive me. Forgive me.' I turned around and so did they and we walked our separate ways. I stopped. 'Oh!' I called, and they stopped, too, turned their heads. I held out the medicine bag. 'For you.'

The other woman, who had yet to speak, took an abrupt threatening step toward me, more like a kick to the earth, the way one does to shoo away a cat or a child, snatched the bag. 'Jao! Don't come back here!'

I put up my hand and curtsied, in peace and compliance. I didn't know if I'd invented it myself, what with all the heat, but there *was* perhaps a hint of a smile on her and her sister's face. Once on the tonga, I felt an urge to turn back and talk to them some more. At thirteen or fourteen, I'd once asked a hooker how much she charged and she scolded me for being too young, and then fifteen minutes or so later I went back to her van and knocked on her window again and she shouted, 'Degage!' And another fifteen minutes later I went back again, this time provoking her to open her car door and get halfway out, so terribly angry, before I scurried away and stopped this little game. But it wasn't really a game. I wasn't going back to rile her, but to be accepted, to convince her I wasn't a scoundrel. My motivation here, too. And perhaps then they could help me locate the Little Chief. But when I returned the women were nowhere in sight, reabsorbed like particles into the sawdust, the wretched bronze of the settlements swallowed the colours of their clothes, the colour of their devilish faces.

❧

I didn't shower before dinner. The orchard was all over me, my skin and clothes, my hands in particular. I'd waited at the station in Mirpurkhas for more than ninety minutes before my train. A humiliating day. First the cop and conductor at the station. Then the two women in the orchard. Was I ready for this life? Being frightened by two squatter women was hardly a sign of a progress.

It was the brigadier, his wife, and me at the dinner table. The main dish was a mutton karahi, and Aunty Ruby grumbled about the amount of ginger in it. Sajid explained that it was in fact the two guests downstairs who said they preferred these larger quantities of ginger. Aunty Ruby turned her contemptuous head down toward her plate.

'Have you served them tonight?' the brigadier asked.

'Ji, sir, half an hour ago.' This was true—I'd smelled the food in my room. The Jamaatis' chosen meal upstairs was lunch; their dinner was served in the downstairs breakfast room just outside their door. Since this was usually done not long before the main dinner upstairs, the poor servant had to race up and down the stairs delivering chapatis, water, fruit, and then clearing up two tables. Often, a second batch of chapatis for us wasn't ready on time, Sajid attending to the men downstairs, and we'd wait over cooling plates for several minutes.

'Send the mangoes downstairs,' the brigadier said.

'But then come right back up, don't waste time chatting to them,' Aunty Ruby instructed. Turning to her husband, she said in English, 'He can't stop chatting to them. Non-stop. Every time I need him he's downstairs chatting away. Chatting, chatting, chatting.'

After dinner, I wiped the orchard dust off my shoes with a tissue roll from the kitchen. The drawing room was ready, the brigadier in his seat with a cigarette and a Coke. The first guests showed around half past ten. Two couples together, one of the women a news anchor and actress with what looked like fake puffed lips, who I'd seen on Apa's television screen, just as made up and rigid in person. She'd come back from some trip and told Aunty Ruby that so-and-so sent her love, that this person also sent love, and then that person sent love, and that one's kid, too, sent Aunty Ruby love. 'Oh ho! You brought all this excess baggage back with you!' Aunty Ruby exclaimed in Urdu except for the words, 'excess baggage'. Some twenty minutes later came a salt-and-pepper-haired civil servant and his white European wife, followed shortly by two women, who came in laughing, one leading the other by the hand, and one more couple. High minded, high society, the ladies all suffered together, turn by turn: servant problems, servant deaths-in-the-family that caused long servant absences, five rupees less returned from a grocery run than what it should have been, given that the servant came back with three cartons of milk and this many pounds of atta; servants who had to be told every day, the same thing, no memory in these people. One of the ladies played relentlessly with her tooth with the nail of her little finger—not simple distracted picking, but a determined pathological scratching that was rough enough to hear. Stop it, I wanted to say, you'll break the enamel, you'll scrape a gap right into your pretty, smoky smile.

Closer to midnight, the white-haired senator appeared, on average still one of the most frequent attenders, for whom the rest stood up. The brigadier was barefoot, both legs now raised and spread on a foot stool, a gap between them that was all the more noticeable because of the long thick ribbons of his shalwar bunched at his crotch. This nonchalance gave him the look of a patient people had come to visit in his hospital room. (One night a couple of weeks ago—and this amused me the most—he had Sajid press his legs while the guests were around.) Now he stood half-heartedly for the senator. The newcomer sat next to the host (another man, the civil servant with the European wife, gave up his seat). The brigadier put his feet back up, resumed the look of long-suffering. The Jamaatis, phantoms-of-the-opera, were downstairs in their cell, doing god-knows-what. I stayed upstairs simply not to go down to them. I listened. I had little to say in these fanatical times. Tonight, having seized the advantage early during the discussion about servants, the ladies dominated, loud, large, long-winded. I was more interested in the quiet talk between the senator and the brigadier. The senator's tone was typically muted, most of his words seemed to go up the nostrils of his hooked nose. 'No, no, this is as perfect as democracy gets,' the brigadier said, raising his voice. 'You have an elected assembly that never meets. It's beautiful. It's pure. I say, let this go on forever. Talk about a Constitution all you want, but don't ever write one. As soon as you put it to paper you've started the process of corruption. The British have always known that. Now let's do them one better: *have* a parliament . . . but never convene it. As soon as you sit down to meet for the first time, it's the beginning of the end. This is a great moment, Senator sahib, don't be upset, enjoy your purity. Once you let go of it, it's gone for good, the pollutant has entered the body. It's like these bloody haemorrhoids that I . . .'

'Oh!' exclaimed one of the women. 'Did you hear the story about the one-armed kid?'

'Yes! Can you imagine!'

'What one-armed boy?'

'Oof, the most incredible—well, almost dreadful, really.'

'Tell, na! *What* one-armed boy?'

'This one-armed Bengali kid—I don't know, was it a kid, or a grown man?'

'Man, kid, doesn't matter.'

'He was drinking water from a tap outside. During the curfew.'

'So we're talking, in Dhaka?'

'Yes, Dhaka, Dhaka. This kid, only one arm, was drinking water from a tap outside and two soldiers came up behind him and told him to put his hands in the air. So the poor kid obviously had only one hand to put in the air. So he did. And these soldiers screamed, told him to put the other hand up. And bechara, what could he do?'

'He didn't tell them he only had one arm? Didn't show them . . .'

'Arrey, what can one do at that stage? You think the soldiers are in the mood to listen? You think the soldiers can even *hear* anything? The curfew puts you in another state altogether.'

'A more natural state,' the brigadier remarked quietly, less to the women than to me and the senator. 'The state of nature is a state of curfew.'

'So? What *ha*-ppened, bhai?'

'They say that not until they hit him, not until they started to beat him, almost to unconsciousness, did they realize he only *had* one arm. And that, too, a stroke of luck. When you're in that state, I'm talking about the state of mind of the soldiers, they're *so* . . .' The lady clenched her teeth and both fists and shook them tensely in front of her face.

A short while later the senator, looking at his watch

and wiping his great nose, murmured to the brigadier that it was time to go. His departure, unlike the others, caused a little disturbance, stalled conversation, people coming to their feet, including the host, to see off this member of a Senate that still hadn't been convened.

When we were left with two couples (the woman who'd told the tale of the one-armed Bengali kid, the one who she'd told it to, and their husbands), the brigadier did something new: he closed his eyes and dipped his chin into his chest, breathing audibly. The guests lowered their voices. Aunty Ruby continued in her normal volume, even soliciting her husband's opinion on some matter or other, to which he didn't respond. 'Chalain,' said one of the gentlemen. 'Alamgir is getting . . . Poor guy, must be exhausted.'

'Exhausted from what?' remarked Aunty Ruby.

'Khair,' replied the man. 'It *is* late. Jaani, we should . . .'

'Yes, yes,' the other couple said. 'We'll leave, too.'

Aunty Ruby accompanied them down. As soon as they were gone the brigadier lifted his head, opened his eyes, found me and grinned. A self-satisfied grin, as if he'd just accomplished a spectacular trick. He picked up his cigar and relit it, facing the huge portrait of his father on the wall opposite. He was still grinning, now with cigar between small yellow teeth.

∿

Since mine was the room next to the entrance, looking out onto the front lawn, anyone coming up the driveway at night could tell if the lights were on, if I was still awake.

I showered and shaved, at two a.m., felt finally cleansed. I was reading in bed, or not quite reading but sitting up with a book open face down on my stomach. The metal creak of the pedestrian gate was followed by footsteps and whispers and the sound of a key and the sound of a click and the opening of the front door and then its closing. And then, alarmingly, a knock. I could see the shadows of two fat feet underneath the door. I stopped breathing. Three more gentle knocks. 'Ji,' I called, and the door opened. I asked them in.

'We saw your light was on. We thought, okay let's visit with Shahbaz mian.'

'You went out after dinner?'

'Haan, we had some people to see. They said stay for the night with us, but all of our things are here, so . . .'

The Jamaatis stood at the two sides of the same corner of the bed, looking down at me, the Khwaja's index finger at his lips. I was wearing shorts, lying on top of the covers, and was conscious of my bare legs. I thought they were, too. When I get the opportunity, I thought, I'll cover them, my bare legs. They watched as if considering me for adoption. *Don't move too much*, they seemed to say, *Let us have a proper look*. The professor, in a dark red shirt buttoned to the very top button, looked at his party colleague. 'Do you know there was this fellow, he used to manage a group of musicians, they used to travel to many, many places— his name, too, was Shahbaz, no?' The Khwaja had nothing to say. 'I think so,' the young-faced professor continued, 'that his name, *too*, was Shahbaz.' This preoccupied him. 'That is not you?' I shook my head, no, not me. 'I don't *know*,' the professor said with a tone of surprise, his hand covering his mouth, confronting a most baffling riddle. 'Maybe his name was something else. Anyway, we have never met before, you and us?' He spoke low, under his breath so that one couldn't catch everything he said. I didn't know whether by the word 'hum', us, he meant the two of them, or if he was referring to himself in the plural, as one can in Urdu.

'If we had I would have remembered,' I said.

He still looked puzzled. Then, giving up, he laughed from his sinuses. His smiley self-mocking eyes gave him the look of a newly respectable man who was still working to restrain his inner Grammarian or Aitchisonian bastard. He took out a cigarette and without asking lit it and filled the room with smoke. He was one of those smokers who leaked the stuff from everywhere—mouth, nose, pores. But his long fine fingers also made him an elegant smoker. He searched around him, on the bedside table at his end. 'You have an ashtray?' I got up, felt their eyes on me as I turned my back to them and reached the fridge, picked up the glass I used for water at night and handed it to the professor. Both pairs of eyes unsettled, aroused (who knows?), by what I wore, the shorts that showed most of my thighs. I sat back down on the bed and lifted part of the cover over my knees. The professor held the glass in his left hand and sat down at the other end of the bed. He inhaled and held the smoke in, his cheeks blown up and then his closed lips convulsing from side to side as if he was rinsing his mouth. I watched his cigarette and the two fingers that held it. He let it rest for unnervingly long periods, the cherry elongating to some tenuous centimetres, but every time he ashed in the glass just before it crumbled on the mattress.

'Isn't it good that we are not alone downstairs but

have Shahbaz mian here with us?' the professor asked
the Khwaja, who scratched that top portion of his beard
that crept to his cheek bones.

'This is exactly what I was thinking.' Theirs was the
kind of duo that spoke to you through each other.

'Where are you coming from?' the professor asked me.
'Ah, Paris!' He turned back to the bigger Jamaati.
'Because of *this*, his Urdu is a little weak.' His tone was
one of quiet defence, patient explanation. How the hell
did they already determine that my Urdu was weak?
'But you know, Paris is a beautiful city.'

'Achha, *very* beautiful?' the Khwaja said.

The professor, holding the smoke in his mouth,
stretched his eyebrows, contorted and shook his head to
indicate, yes, the highest level of beauty one could
imagine. 'They've had their problems there as well, but
nowadays, worldwide, where is there not trouble? So, a
few years ago they went after the fellow they've got,
Charles day Gaal is his name.' He looked to me. 'You
were there then? Okay, so you, too, did all the—' Here
he used a word I didn't know, but it was safe to assume
he was talking about the riots. And to him, unlike to
others, I could proudly, truthfully, say that no, I had not
participated. He laughed, again from his sinuses, mocking
French youth. 'What is the purpose? Come out on the
street, throw things, break things, take off your clothes,
what is the purpose?'

'What is the purpose?' I repeated.

'You, of course, you've got your roots here, so naturally
you saw that there is *no* purpose. You lived with your
father? Your father was Ghazanfar Aslam?' He turned
back to his colleague. 'Ghazanfar sahib, a *famous* man. He
used to make films, perhaps you have seen one of them.'

'Achha, a filmmaker?'

'Made some films and then, I think there were some problems'—he looked at me and nodded and smiled to assure me we were all friends here—'and then he moved to Paris.'

'When you say problems, professor sahib,' the Khwaja said, '*which* kind of problems?' He took one foot out of its sandal and set it against the calf of the other leg, the fat toes bent backward.

'*Whatever* there was.' The professor feigned losing patience. 'So long ago now. In the days of the Conspiracy, perhaps you remember.'

'Yes, but *my* question, professor sahib, is this—that, okay, you've made some films, you've written some poetry perhaps, mashallah you have a good healthy able son,' he looked and gestured at me, 'Allah has given you all this, now . . . *why* participate in Conspiracy?' While he listened, the young professor held his cigarette down at his thigh and let the collected smoke from the last drag swirl around in the deep cavity below the tongue. He released the smoke. 'Look, ji,' he responded, again lowering his voice to that weighty academic tenor so that one didn't catch all the words. Three or four sentences went by non-received. '. . . A man is sometimes filled with . . . *passion*. Sometimes you're not always thinking. It happens to good men, too. Now, of course, you love your country, it's also a new country, you see someone who wants to destroy the government, and you think this man is a bad man. But look . . . even when a man is in middle age . . . in fact, often this happens at that time, a man gets . . . *confuse*,' he used the English word here, 'confuse about, "In this country, what is *my* role?" Then these people come along with a plan, they say let's make the country the way we want, one of them is a famous poet, one of them is a major general, isn't that right? What I'm saying, this is right, no? So a man who is, absolutely, intelligent . . . well-read, also . . . um, honourable . . . and then, respected, also.' With each of these compliments the professor looked and nodded at me. 'It's because of this that these people pick good people like his father sahib.'

'Achha, achha, it gives *them* respectability.'

'Exactly, Khwaja sahib! So you see, this is what I mean when I say it happens to good men, too. Good men always, poor fellows, become part of these things. And *they* are the ones who end up suffering the most.'

'Yes, naturally,' said Khwaja sahib. And both men pondered this a while. Their low-key histrionics amused me. My first question would have been, How long did the two of you rehearse this? But I was also bothered that my father was in play, and the pressure was now on me. I had things to say, but at this time of night my Urdu wasn't going to come to me. What, for example, was the Urdu word for 'rehearse'? 'Khair,' the Khwaja resumed. 'Mistake was made. It was a long time ago. What happened, that has happened. Now what is the purpose of . . .'

'*What* is the purpose?' the professor concurred.

I nodded in silence, condemned to agreement. The silence continued, and with every beat so did my agreement, my unspoken denunciation of the man who made me. I searched for another topic, something simple. For one, I felt they wouldn't leave until I gave them something. The professor dropped the butt into the glass. 'Ah,' I said at last. 'Did you hear about the Bengali boy with one arm, who was beaten by soldiers in Dhaka?'

The Khwaja frowned and nodded vaguely.

'Over there, problems, too,' the professor remarked, rotating the glass in his palm and examining the dead cigarette. 'Yes, yes, a difficult time . . . over there . . . East Pakistan . . .' His speech was sinking, mournful. 'Okay, Shahbaz sahib! It's late. We thought since your light was on, come and meet our friend. No, no, sit, sit. Tomorrow morning, we'll meet, inshallah.'

'Inshallah,' I assured them.

When they were gone I locked the door, came back to bed, and turned off the bedside table lamp.

4

'Take good care of me tonight. I've been terribly sad.'

'Anything poor Shahbaz want.'

'Sad and exhausted.'

'Karachi too much for poor Shahbaz.'

'Exhausted, overstretched. You're the only one I can talk to. Because we make such wonderful love.' I would have added: which earns me the right to be weak on occasion, to break down even, to stop being a man for a crazy little moment or two. We lay in bed. She wore jeans and a white T-shirt with red hems. We hadn't had sex yet. She wanted to clear her accounts with God first.

'You don't mind praying in front of me?'

'Why I would mind?'

'I don't know, it just seems a little ... exhibitionist, don't you think? But I suppose you're used to that. Oh, don't look offended, sweetheart. I'm the last to hold that against you. A part of me envies you. You know that when I was still a boy in Paris before I was old enough to ... I started to want to ... *expose myself*. I wanted people to see me naked. I would stand in front of, or near, the window and undress. Not a flasher. You know what a flasher is? I was *not a flasher* in that sense. I didn't say to some victim, here look at me! No, I pretended that I didn't know I was being watched. I wanted to make the other person feel like a voyeur, like they were violating my privacy in a way. So it wouldn't be like I was standing in front of the window gyrating like a stripper. No, I would usually have my back turned, or offer my profile, or—'

'But then what happen?' Malika asked. 'What happen later?'

'What do you mean, "what happened later"?'

'Now you are shy.'

'Why do you say that?'

'You not like me to see you without clothes.' She pronounced it 'clothe-ez'.

'That's ridiculous,' I said.

'No, when this is hard, it is okay.' She touched me through my cotton pants. 'But when it's finish, you hide. Is true! You put the, the, what is this thing, the blanket, like this.' Using the caftan that lay nearby as a stand-in for the blanket, and with exaggerated speed, she imitated my covering myself.

'I think you're imagining things. I think the opium . . .'

'I never see you, I never see this'—she again reached for my groin—'when it's not hard, when it finish for the night and go to sleep. When you are inside me I can't see you.'

'Well, let me spend a night here and maybe you will. Hell, even if it's to sneak a glance while I'm dead asleep in the middle of the night, take the covers off and watch all you want. What do you say, it's worth it, no?'

'You don't show me sleeping penis.'

'You want to see it, is that it? Do I need to prove you wrong? That's what you're after, aye? Well ...' I massaged myself a moment and then began to unzip before Malika stopped me.

'Wait,' she said. 'First I pray. You stay here and make it big so that I like you. And I pray.' She went to the bathroom to clean up, water on the soles of the feet, the armpits, and wherever else. I stood at the bathroom door, watching her. Clean, ready, she turned the tap off. She stood at the base of the jainamaz and put her hands to her stomach, one over the other.

'You, too, with your bloody prayers,' I huffed, returning to the bed. 'Maybe you should come to our place, the brigadier's place, say your prayers with the Jamaatis and Sajid in the drawing room. You'd all fit so well together, the four of you.' She was silent and erect on the jainamaz, putting her fingers to her earlobes to commence prayer. 'Look at you, praying two floors above drunk men with their tongues stuck out, you said yourself. You think He has that much forgiveness in Him?' She lowered herself to her knees.

The phone rang, stopped after six or seven rings. Then it rang again. This time, I answered: one of the boys from the cabaret, hesitating at the sound of a male voice, stuttered something about Malika, brigadier sahib, but before he could go on the brigadier's voice intruded. 'Haan, Shahbaz.' He sounded irritated. 'Tell Malika to come downstairs. Quickly, okay?' He hung up.

There was nothing untoward here, really. Malika was a professional, the brigadier was her boss and there was work to be done. But still I felt wronged. When she stopped praying and put the jainamaz away, I told her the brigadier needed her. Without changing out of her

T-shirt, jeans, slippers, she was out of the room. Alone, that sense of injustice swelled in my chest. Would I have wanted the brigadier to ask if it was okay for Malika to come down, or at least explain what he needed her for? That was an absurd idea. And yet, yes, something, some gesture from either one of them to acknowledge that I had a relationship with Malika that wasn't secondary to the Agra. I thought about leaving before she returned, took pleasure in the thought of her disorientation when she found her room empty. But then what? And what if she came back very soon, a matter of minutes? What if it was just a small errand? But after how long would just waiting here become unacceptable?

The jug of milk lay on the floor, next to the portable gas burner on which Malika had cooked the opium. For after we made love and I was gone. I poured myself a glass and gulped it down with a sense of declaration. I lay down, waiting for things to get underway. Malika couldn't be gone for long; after all, her things, her cabaret outfits were here, she was just in jeans, T-shirt and slippers.

The soldiers were downstairs, drunk, dancers on their laps, ready to go East to quell the Bengali rebellion. Be it so. Let them crush it. It made no difference to me. Just get it over with and let things go back to normal. I removed one of Malika's cigarettes and lit it. Its flavour was nauseating. Hash joints still hadn't given me a taste for tobacco, but I smoked the cigarette anyway, and left the butt in Malika's mug. I turned on the television set, which was on a table in the corner, by the window, a recent addition to her room. Some man had quit some senior position in the Muslim League in protest of the postponement. Another, the host of a radio programme, refused to go on the air until power was transferred to Mujib. And now PTV was replaying footage of Mujib's Race Course speech. He was in a white kurta and kameez, with a black vest, speaking from a raised platform. I didn't think I'd ever seen so many people gathered before a single speaker, tens of thousands of them, maybe hundreds of thousands, like a forest seen from a distance, long sticks and flags emerging at several points. Seventy million Bengalis! What did it look and feel like when seventy million rose to one's call?

೧೨

I opened my eyes. It had turned dark and Malika still wasn't back. How long ago did she leave? Was she still in the same clothes or had she come back to the room while I lay drugged, changed and gone back down? I wanted to check her suitcase for all her outfits. I wanted to turn off the television, whose oppressive news hovered in the room like the Malak of Death, watching me, the voice reporting on *my* progress through the night. I didn't have the strength to get up.

೧೨

'Shahbaz.' It was Malika's voice. She was back in the room. She hadn't turned the lights on yet. I could hear and sense her move into the room, fill it up, restore order. At some point I'd stripped off all my clothes, and now I could feel my body again, bare skin covered by blanket. Malika sat down on the bed, put her hand on my naked back. It didn't matter what the brigadier had called her down for anymore, or how long she'd been gone. She was back and I had her to myself. I felt nothing but joy.

'Shahbaz,' she whispered.

'Mmm.' My face pressed into the pillow. 'Hi, my love.'

She leaned in, her bulky hair on my cheek and ear. 'You must leave.' Again just a whisper. I turned my body the opposite direction, facing away from her now. Again her warm hand, on my shoulder, the warmth of her body coming near. 'Shahbaz.' Still a whisper. 'You *must go.*'

I tried to fall back asleep. But from Malika's complete lack of motion, that hand on my shoulder still, it was clear she meant what she was saying. 'Why?' I finally asked. Hearing myself say this confirmed that this wasn't a game, that she really wanted me out. And it seemed to have broken something in her, too, because she was up again, to the bathroom. I closed my eyes and was close to sleep when I heard her again. '*Shahbaz.*' This time her voice was filled with impatience. I turned on my back, and she came into proper focus, still in T-shirt and jeans, her hair damp.

'I'm in no condition to move,' I said.

She bent over and collected my clothes from the floor with an irritated sigh, like a mother cleaning up after a son. She held my pants and underwear out in front of me. 'Take,' she said. When I didn't move she sighed irritably again and dropped them on me, stood back and waited with her arms reproachfully folded.

'Malika, did you hear what I said? I'm in no condition to go anywhere. I've done opium. You understand? You expect me to get up, get into a *cab*? In *this* state?'

She remained frozen, her arms folded, not a mother but a corporal. 'Shahbaz,' she repeated, the simple utterance of my name now denoting something of a pest, and a command, the call to be gone. 'This is no way . . .'

'No way to what? To *behave*?'

'*Shahbaz*.' How I hated the way my name sounded in this punitive elocution.

'You're really serious?'

What a creature, so inscrutable in these moments. Malika watched me dress and search around for a sock. She looked so terribly tired that, as she stood in the doorway and saw me out, I thought briefly of *her* as the victim here. She said goodbye, lifting her drained voice right at the end into a light, pleasant pitch, using the last bit of her strength to make this whole transition seem friendly and routine. It was followed by the crisp, definite metal click of the lock. Our relationship couldn't survive this episode. I lingered there a moment, on the same spot where months ago the brigadier's henchman had knocked me down, and Malika's world opened up, full of possibility, the makings of something. I leaned against the wall and sat down, hoping she would come to the door, and open that world up again.

❦

I sat in one of the booths of the green and black artificial leather seats, and hollered to the front for a Murree beer. A waiter brought me the green bottle with the wet peeling label, and I drank slowly. I had fifteen minutes. The sky outside was congealing quickly into a heavy lapis-blue, in which tourists and shoppers and sellers moved like poltergeists. They'd turned the sad hospital-like white lights on inside the bar. The radio played a qawali to whose chorus one of the waiters jiggled his head from side to side and sang to his co-worker, shrinking his shoulders and raising a horizontal, upturned palm in that poetic gesture of entreaty.

I climbed the familiar steps and found Doli slouched over his radio. When I'd come up here, before going to the bar, he'd greeted me silently, shaking hands only when I held mine out, nodding when I said salaam. He received me now with the same indifference. He stood up, and said 'Aiye'. His radio relayed news of Dhaka, curfews and army actions, and the Mukti Bahini, the new Bengali rebel force. Looking at Doli's black skin, as if I were discovering it for the first time, I wondered if he was in fact Bengali: if Ghulam Hussain pretended to some that he was Punjabi, was it not possible that Doli was guilty of the very same masquerade? He took the radio with him through the corridors. The beer had calmed me down but my blood was still accelerated. I'd relied on Doli in the past, and he'd delivered. But now that I wasn't his guest anymore, I didn't trust him. He knocked on a door, opened by a Chinese woman in a light blue dress that stopped above the knee, who went back to the bed, sat down cross-legged. Her legs were pale and there was a bruise on one thigh. Doli left us, my money in his shirt pocket, but I could still hear the electric wash of his radio. The woman introduced herself as Monglu. She took off her dress. As I took her in my arms, she said, 'Thank you.' That she was not a local woman made me take more time, be gentler, pay more attention to her body. Those electric sounds still reverberated in my ears, as if Doli had left the radio right outside my room, the army crackdown in the East trickling through the door. 'One minute,' I said, and, naked, opened the door to peep outside. There was nothing, no Doli, no radio. 'Sounds?' I pointed to my ear. 'You hear sounds?'

'Aah.' She said something in Chinese. I came back to bed and tried to get hard. The girl held my head, pointed my face to her, and said, 'No listen, no listen.' Once I was inside her, she put her hands at my back and pulled me deeper into her. I couldn't reach climax. The girl said, 'Please, please,' and I knew I was hurting her now. I pulled out. She took me in her hand. My head too full of thought, the only escape was into my own groaning, to fill myself with loud cries of pleasure, noises that were unbecoming to a man during sex. But what did it matter? So I did it, I screamed and moaned at high pitch like a woman, and when I looked at Monglu's face I saw that she was excited by it, she stroked me with an eager obsessed face, speeding up as I moaned more frenetically. And as she brought me to climax, Monglu looked pleased and grateful, even laughing a little from exhaustion. 'Wait,' she said, still cheerful. She went into the bathroom, brought out a toilet roll, cut off a long strip. I reached out for it, but she moved her hand back, out of reach, insisted on cleaning me herself. I lay back and let her do it. She was in no rush to put her clothes back on. I tried to act in the same way, but for what, what did the feelings of a hooker matter? I reached for my clothes, and took them with me to the bathroom, where I dressed, quickly. She followed me in, turned the lower tap of the shower on and started filling the plastic bucket.

'You no wash?' she said.

'I wash later,' I replied. I thanked her and she thanked

me back and we hugged like old friends parting. 'Goodbye Monglu.'

∽

I told the taxi to drop me off a couple of blocks from the brigadier's house. I walked down that long pebbly PECHS road, my bag on my back, big square houses on either side, towards the house with the onion dome and the goblet-shaped windows and all the colours leaking out of it. I crossed the final side street, approaching the brigadier's gate, the first on the right. A car's lights were on inside and the gate now parted open. The car reversed out. The brigadier had come out into the street to see the guest off. And as the car drove by, I realized that sitting in the back on the passenger side was Zulfiqar Ali Bhutto. The bald, polished top, and the neat grey hair on the sides, which was puffed and spread like wings in the many photographs of him at a podium. He was wearing a suit and a scarf. So strange to see him smiling in there, this man who every day was fighting to be prime minister, fighting against Mujib's right to be prime minister, fighting against Bengali autonomy. Fighting and fighting. The brigadier didn't recognize that it was me walking up to the house. He went back in, and I got there just before the driver closed the gate.

5

The light dissolved away, the mosquitoes announced the onset of evening, the bugs outside made noises that sounded like a pencil scribbled on a pad. The big Khwaja sahib was asleep sitting on the couch upstairs beside the balcony's doorway. His face leaned down toward his right breast, his lips parted and twisted in one direction like a baby's mouth signalling for a nipple. His right hand gently clutched his right shoulder. I lit a mosquito coil on the floor near him. This way those damn bugs would die on their way in. I gazed out from the balcony. Downstairs Sajid was talking to someone outside the gate. As he shifted, I was stunned to see that the second figure was Ghulam Hussain. This was the first time he'd ever come at his own discretion. He looked up and saw me, waved, and I waved back like the cinematic Mughal king for whom this balcony was once used. When I came down, Sajid superfluously said, 'Sir ji, Ghulam Hussain has come to see you.'

Shaking Ghulam Hussain's hand, I said, 'Next time, you tell me before you come. This is no way to . . .'

'Sorry sir,' he replied.

'What is it?' I asked.

'Sir ji . . .'

'Speak. Sajid, you go.' We watched the brigadier's servant go back inside the gate. I felt bad reprimanding Ghulam Hussain in front of him. Ever since I'd lost Malika I'd become testy. Sajid himself had suffered for it, scolded for the first time for over-frying the eggs, for my room not being tidied properly, for not coming down from his afternoon break at five, as required, to serve tea and snacks.

'I'm going back, Shahbaz bhai.'

'Where back?'

'East Pakistan. Dhaka.'

'At a time like this? Over there, isn't it . . .'

Ghulam Hussain shuffled, he looked down and back, put his hand on the car's bonnet, swiped it slowly and then examined the dust that collected on his palm. 'Shahbaz bhai, the matter is this. My father-in-law. He's my chacha, father's youngest brother.' So he had married his cousin. 'One day this haramzada says he wants his daughter back. Why? Because he wants her to marry someone else.'

'What does he think is wrong with you?' I asked.

'Nothing. But he told another family that she would marry their son. Shahbaz bhai, matter is this, that he has a son, a haramzada just like himself, father-son, both. Son has a needle in his arm all day. But now his father has found a girl for him. Naturally, nobody wants to marry him, so my haramzada chacha told this girl's family—they also have a son who isn't married—he told them, I will give you my daughter for your son, you give your daughter for my son. He learned that from the Punjabis. This never happens in Bengal. But that haramzada spent a few months in Punjab and he thought, Arrey bhai, this is a very good system. So he's trying to—Shahbaz bhai, what is the Angrez word, when you bring something from outside?'

'Import,' I said.

'Haan, haan,' he laughed. 'Em-port. He's trying to em-port that to Bengal. My brother-in-law is a haramzada like his father. He has a needle in his arm every day, *every day*. Who's going to marry him? But what to do, his father, my bastard chacha, is insisting. He said he would come and take his daughter back with force. So I have to go back.'

'But, Ghulam Hussain, how will you go? I thought now with the troubles, the flights don't . . .'

'Ho jayega, ho jayega, Shahbaz bhai,' he declared, assuring me that he'd find a way. 'Even if I have to go through India. On a plane it's a lot of fun, hain na? Ears become absoutely blocked-blocked.'

'But over there, the . . . *curfew*,' I didn't know if there was an Urdu word for it.

'Haan, haan, karfoo.' Ghulam Hussain nodded vigorously. 'In the karfoo, who knows, my chacha might be even crazier! God knows what he will try with my wife. Yes, yes . . . *karfoo*.' He seemed to cherish this foreign word. At that moment, any resentment towards the political situation in his homeland—the Bengalis demonstrating for their election victory to be honoured, and the army trying to quell the burgeoning rebellion— or any fear of what his mad uncle-father-in-law may do, appeared mixed with a fascination with this word, which he repeated like a child getting to know a new insult. The very idea of not being able to leave the house, of the army patrolling the streets and shooting people simply for being on the streets after hours. 'Did you hear, Shahbaz bhai, last month a one-armed man was drinking from a tap on the street. When the soldiers came behind him and ordered him to stand up and put his hands in the air, and when he put up only his one arm, they shouted that if he didn't put up the other they'd shoot him. He tried telling them, I have only one arm, but they killed him.'

'What!' I said. 'They *did* shoot him?'

'Killed the poor fellow.'

'Achha?' I shook my head.

'Shahbaz bhai,' Ghulam Hussain said, swallowing the words. 'I . . . needed to ask you, please don't mind it . . .'

'What?'

'. . . a little bit of money.' He produced a long excuse that I stopped understanding, related to his going back to East Pakistan. How much was he asking for? Two hundred. The figure stopped me. 'Ghulam Hussain, I don't have much on me right now.' I took my wallet out and held it open. 'You can take . . . how much is this? . . . forty now, and then—'

'Sir, when you have it, I'll take it. Should I come back tomorrow or the day after?'

'Your bottles, that sharaab you make, you're not making enough money from that?' He giggled bashfully. '*Huh?*' My tone hardened.

'Nahin, sir,' he said, and looked to the ground in shame. I realized that that's what I wanted from him: a little shame.

'I'll get it for you, in a little while. But not today. But take this.' I stuffed his breast pocket with the forty rupees. He shook my hand with both of his, bowed, and put his hand to his heart. How absurd it must have seemed to him, me standing in front of this flamboyant house, wearing the brigadier's bleached-white shirt, claiming I didn't have two hundred rupees to give him. I waved goodbye and went back inside. I had the money that Mona Phuppi had given me for Eid. Three hundred and fifty rupees. Yes, I was willing to part with it. And my intentions weren't entirely noble: the possibility that he would be gone when I myself left for Paris, whenever that was, raised my hopes. I could leave the country without having to explain why I wouldn't take him with me. I would bring him that money. Of course I would.

I went back upstairs to find Khwaja sahib standing beside the seat he was sleeping in moments ago, looking out into the garden and wiping crust from his eyes. We exchanged salaams. No hugs today. 'Who was that?' he asked.

'Who? Oh, that's my old driver. His uncle used to be my father's servant.' The Urdu word for servant, naukar, tasted ugly. Why couldn't I simply say Ghulam Hussain was a friend? He was a friend. But to tell the Jamaati that would have sounded absurd.

'Achha, achha.' He kept staring at the gate, as if Ghulam Hussain would suddenly appear again. 'You were giving him money.'

I stopped.

'You were giving him money?'

'A little bit I owed him for . . . his uncle used to work for my father. Many years ago.'

'This money was for his uncle?'

'Whoever the money was for,' I said, and left it at that. The Jamaati sat back down and leaned his head back against the cushion. He put two fingers of each hand to either side of the face, at the start of the jawline, and again exercised that big bone covered in flesh and hair. I sat opposite him and closed my eyes, too, seeing images of a one-armed Bengali boy who'd either been shot or had not.

❧

Ghulam Hussain wasn't the only one asking me for money. Rahim sahib had called me back to Lalukhet. When I thought of my policeman ally, I always conjured a sloppy wreck of a man, shirt sticking out over a mutinous belly, the thick neck and the heavy blue mood of a retired fighter. So that when I met him now I was surprised by how handsome and perfect his face actually was, the thin grey beard probably trimmed by professional hands, thin enough to still show the outline of a beautifully symmetrical jaw cut at a hundred-and-thirty-five degree angle, a nose that didn't extend too far outward like most Pakistani noses, and tired murky eyes that bespoke a sensitive deep soul. This face redeemed the clownish mass it crowned. And to be in this office— big brown desks and shelves and dying wicker chairs, hard brown government folders stuffed with old discoloured pages, first information reports, complaints, accusations, investigations, remedies, reports on accidents and who's to blame, court requests, court injunctions, court orders, demands for more evidence—that soul had to be suffering. So, yes, the perfect face was also filled with anguish, sweat descended the sideburns and hairline, an honest sheriff of a rotten outpost town.

The same boy brought us lassi and the cop gulped his down intensely like scotch, and asked for another. Perhaps his was spiked with the liquor he confiscated from smugglers in the Interior. He hit the fan to get it working, which it did only for a minute; he hit it again. He wiped his face with an unbuttoned sleeve. On one row in the shelf behind were several blue velvet cases of different sizes, stacked one on top of the other, covered in dust and concealing their long forgotten medals.

When he was at his most serious Rahim sahib spoke in complicated Urdu. And now in that Urdu he went straight to the matter, spoke of where one district magistrate was from and therefore where his sympathies lay, what his beliefs were, how one dealt with such a man—the acme of his short speech, arrived at with a histrionic sigh, was that all of this would mean another hundred-and-fifty rupees. Clever man didn't tell me anything on the phone, which he should have if only to ensure that I brought the money—but no, he didn't tell me on the phone because he needed me to see the suffering in his face, this handsome face pulled down by large grief-stricken shoulders. And it really seemed like this was the final degradation that would do him in after a career of thugs, swindlers, hookers, illicit booze, bloodbaths, a million salutes turning his thoughts to pap. This failure to deliver to me, the need for one more payment, took all the strength he had left. I played my part of the disappointed bigwig, sat with arms crossed shaking my head. Inside I was calm: more money, that's what it came down to. But what was I meant to do on the outside? Express outrage, warn that this is the last time?

'Now—*how much*?'

'Hundred-and-fifty.'

A hundred-and-fifty to the cop. Two hundred to Ghulam Hussain. In my desperation, my compassion, the city was squeezing me for three hundred and fifty rupees. Rahim sahib may have been a swine but he was after all my swine, and I still believed he would deliver. I took out my wallet, muttering that I wasn't sure if I had that much on me, then confirming, oh yes, I do, and here you go. He took the money so solemnly it could have been an execution order. I gulped my lassi and with a deep breath I said in Urdu, 'Okay, Rahim sahib. We'll meet again.' As you can in Urdu I said this without using the noun, the 'we', which to my ears made the statement more imposing. We shook hands, half-hugged, shook hands again. I told him not to come out, but he did, dragging beside me his warm ex-fighter's frame, yet with that feminine twist of the hips.

'Your driver?' he asked, looking at Ghulam Hussain behind the wheel of his Morris.

Yes, I confirmed. We shook hands a final time and said goodbye. I got into the car thinking how different the second exchange of money is from the first. The first time one feels supreme, above the law, on the inside where the wheels of government spin, the honoured access of the crook. The second time one realizes that one is neck-deep in a charade, weak, low on the ladder, still far from catching up to that man who took one's Ayatul-Kursi in a Parisian toilet years ago. The second time, an empty act, bribery losing its splendour and becoming corruption for its own sake. This one hurt the soul.

∽

Apa's double door was almost closed, leaving a six-inch gap through which I could see the backs of the Jamaatis as they stood in front of her bed. Apa's limbs, parts of her sari were visible. No one was speaking. Walking closer, I realized that the brigadier was in there, too, sitting on the bedpost. Apa's room was barely spacious enough to fit three people, let alone four, with one especially hefty one in the mix. But there they all were, Apa, her nephew, and the two guests, an unusual shot (I use the word 'shot' because that's how it now comes to me, now that I understand the implications of this meeting, a frozen shot, framed by Apa's doorway). One of the visitors turned around and saw me through the gap. 'That ... Shahbaz mian,' he murmured to the others. The brigadier looked through the two Jamaati bodies and when he confirmed that it was me, he stood up and parted the doors.

'Haan mian,' he said.

'I was just thinking of—'

He tapped my cheek. 'Come with me for a walk,' he said and, holding me by the wrist, an uncut nail digging into my vein, guided me to the stairs. 'It's a nice time of the evening, this. Soon it'll get too fucking hot.' I looked back, the Jamaatis were still in the room, talking low, both of them now on bent knees in front of Apa. 'Wait here, let me put on some proper shoes and get my walking stick,' the brigadier said. He was in brown leather sandals, the feet far better kept than his hands. I stood at the top of the staircase, trying to avoid looking at whatever was going on in Apa's room. The brigadier returned in white sneakers and with a wooden cane, an elegant helix descending from an r-shaped handle. He gently tapped my calf with it, 'Chalain,' and I followed him down the steps and out.

'Ahh, things aren't easy, my boy!' he declared as we stepped over the gate's hump.

'What exactly—'

'Come, come, let's just . . .' He held me at the elbow and led me not towards Tariq Road but in the opposite direction, where the residences were interspersed by large empty plots. The darkness was fresh, with a memory of blue and the expectation of bugs. The brigadier walked briskly, his cane just a matter of style.

'I didn't mean to be intrusive back there,' I explained.

'Haan, haan.' He put his hand now to my shoulder and squeezed. 'We were just . . . you know . . .' He rolled his eyes dismissively and stuttered and shook his head in tiny jerks, a head blocked with thought. The electricity seemed to have gone where we were, the houses exuding blackness onto the roads, and something about the silence and the bugs and the smell of mud in the air reminded me of those nights as a child when I used to walk alone into the heart of the orchard. 'So, business seems to be good these days,' I remarked. 'The soldiers . . . Last time I was there, they seemed to be enjoying themselves.'

'Did I tell you, Yahya himself came the other night? With his little entourage, drunk, demanding bottles of Black Dog and a night of only Elvis songs. He was in a shitty mood, some new general had resigned because he refused to order his men to fire on the Bongs. You know, things aren't going well for our man Yahya. So he comes in and says, Tonight only Elvis. Nothing else.'

'And?'

'I just *pleaded* with the band to do what they could, for surely they knew *some* Elvis. Oh, then, bloody hell: a tedious cycle of poor renditions in that bloody— what's his name, the lead singer?—his awful thin voice. But our dictator was in ecstasy. Oh yes! High-commands for second and third plays.'

'What night *was* this?' I asked. While he was thinking, I said, 'Was Malika there?'

'Of course she was there,' he replied abrasively. 'Why wouldn't she be there? She bloody well works there, doesn't she?'

'Well, I didn't mean ...'

'Haan, haan, she was *there*, bhai. We're not going to have a saloon full of soldiers and not her.' He was walking fast and running out of breath. 'These soldiers,' he continued. 'You've got to give them their last bit of fun. Otherwise you'll never move on. No no, I don't mean in the cabaret. That's just ... that's nothing. I mean over *there*, out East. The Feast in the East, you could call it.' He stopped to laugh at this, that wheezing laugh of his, put his arm in front of me so that I, too, would stop walking a moment to absorb this latest quip. Even in the dark I saw the face swell with blood, the veins thickening on his temple.

'Feast in the East,' I repeated. We moved on.

'This ... *thing*,' the brigadier said after a few steps. 'It has its own rhythm now. It would be foolish to try to stop it. Try to stop it too soon. That would be even more dangerous. We've got to just see now what happens, what comes out at the other end.'

'Don't tamper,' I said.

'Pre-*cisely*-ly right! *Don't tamper*.'

We passed a middle-aged couple who the brigadier paused to greet. I was a few steps ahead and looked in another direction to avoid being introduced. After a stretched farewell, the brigadier joined me again and forward we went.

'See, today we put too low a value on hate. Irredentist hate, I'm talking about. It's a failed sense of history. If

you don't hate a people, you're uncultured. Look at the
Europeans. You can't really be European and not hate
another clan of European. You wouldn't *be* European,
bhai. That's Europe's glory. There's no reason why we
shouldn't be just as glorious. Never mind what they
taught you in Paris. *This* is history. They say 'civil war',
blah blah blah, trying to demean it all. But let me tell
you, we'd be a sorry nation if this ... *whole thing* ...
wasn't happening. We'd be giving history *nothing*. It's
our time to show ourselves. *That's* what glory is. Not a
nice cocktail party, black ties and all that, no, it's pulling
your pants down and showing yourself to the world.
Glory is an ugly matter. If we want it, well ...'

We'd reached Hill Park. The restaurant there was
empty, almost all the lights out. In the dark I thought I
could see a child sitting atop the slide at the centre of the
park.

'You know, uncle, there's this chap who drives me
around, I don't know if you've seen him when he's come
to get me from the house. Ghulam Hussain. A Bengali
fellow. He took part in the riots against the military,
whenever that was. A big souled fellow.' (My admiration
for his role in the riots was belittled somewhat when the
brigadier said sternly, 'I *see*.') 'Anyhow,' I continued. 'I
was talking to him the other day. He said that this army
action, it will just produce more rebels, to the point
where the army won't be able to control—'

'Oh, what does a man like that know!' His sudden
sharpness was astonishing. 'Who is this fellow? The one
who comes to get you now and then?'

'Well ... I'm not saying I believe ...'

'Rubbish, rubbish, *rubbish*.' The conversation was
over, and perspiration was now collecting for both of us.

I felt mine at the hairline and below. The brigadier had developed a patch at his back. 'Chalain,' he said, and we turned and headed back to the house. All traces of blue were gone now, stray dogs circled the streets.

'Do you like Shakespeare as much as your father used?'

'I wasn't aware that he—'

'Oh, a big Shakespeare man in his day. He's the one who remembered all the big speeches. You could ask him and at the drop of a hat he'd start reciting, "Is this a dagger before me," and whatnot.' He was quiet for a few steps. 'Anyway, *I* haven't forgotten all my Shakespeare. The army didn't take it all.' He tapped his skull with his finger. 'There's one line I remember well. "Blood will have blood." I think it's from Macbeth. *Blood* ...' He stopped, again put his hand on my arm to make sure I was listening. '... will have *blood*. Precisely right.' I expected him to say more, but he didn't. His forward-leaning face again seemed stuffed with contemplation, and I would get no more.

'I went to see Rahim sahib in his station today,' I said. 'He asked for another bribe.'

'How much have you given him so far?'

'Three fifty.'

He hissed, shaking his head. 'Incredible.'

'Am I being played?' I asked. 'I mean, how much should I give him, if he asks for more? When do I say, enough?'

'Now *look*,' he blurted, irritably. 'You do what you have to do. That's life. Have you got other answers? No, you've got Rahim sahib. So for now, you go with it. Understand?' He pushed open the pedestrian's little entrance in the gate with his cane and we stepped through.

❧

A new total of three hundred and fifty rupees of mine was out there, *in* there, the first tranche cutting through the skin, the second cutting deep into the organs. But the bureaucracy was a creature that re-formed whatever limb or organ was severed, a fat lizard that governed the country, protected the squatters. I didn't blame Rahim sahib. He had to feed the lizard and the lizard had to feed him back. Once this whole system was properly nourished and happy, the squatters would be removed. I was prepared to pay more if Rahim sahib asked for it, which I suspected he would. The brigadier was right, I had no other options. In fact, I felt sympathy for Rahim sahib. Handsome, honourable Rahim sahib, emissary for the fat lizard, the world he operated to make life better, more peaceful, for the rest of us. God bless him. I would pay up.

I didn't leave my room for several hours. Ever since the two Jamaatis had moved in, I was spending more time by myself in my room, reading the books on the shelf—I'd started one of the books on Hitler—or flipping through my favourite sections of *The Republic*. Some days I would only leave the room for lunch, a snack, dinner, a telephone call. I had even started walking to Drigg Road or Tariq Road and taking a cab or a rickshaw to the Clifton Promenade. Or simply wandered around the Tariq Road shops. Why I gave the two men an undue supremacy in our part of the house, I didn't know—their presence was an impediment, verging on obsession. Today, they were nowhere to be seen.

Apa was having her feet pressed by one of the girls. I said my adaab, sat down with her. The old matron was quiet, watching the girl squeeze her bones as if to supervise the effort and make sure nothing went wrong.

She looked at me from the side of her eyes, not at my face but at my chest, then turned her eyes down again.

'Aap theek hain?' I asked, putting a hand to her shoulder.

She looked up at me, at my face for the first time. 'There was this man, friend of ours, Hammad.'

'The Bengali?'

'Haan, haan, Bengali. You knew him?'

'I met him. Twice, I met him.'

'Achha, achha,' she smiled. 'That bechara has died.'

'Died? Hammad sahib, the man with the bad leg? Has *died*?' She nodded. 'How?'

He was beaten to death, she said, in his neighbourhood in Dhaka, last night or the night before, while he was taking his walk.

'Oh ho.' I sat poised for grief to fill the vacancy. Then, restless, I got up and went to the kitchen, through its decaying banana peel smells from exposed dustbin waste, to the winding stone steps that led up to the roof. The roof itself had two levels, the first an expansive open space, beginning with Sajid's quarters. The easiest path to this open space, once you came up the steps, was through Sajid's room. This part of the roof was the area above the drawing room, and then two sets of steps led to a higher platform, which covered the master bedroom on the mezzanine. Here, there was an external access to the brigadier's library. I stood outside that door, the onion dome behind me, looking onto the streets of PECHS. In the garden below, a tiny brigadier was sitting down to a head massage, his masseur had placed a towel around his shoulders and over his chest.

Hammad sahib. The runny nose and mouth, all that life he tried to contain and carry on one good leg, extinguished in a night. I could have handled the death itself, but it was the beating he suffered that was so difficult. That great life of his, tortured out of him. What kind of a temperament did it require to beat another person to death? The only person to ever strike me hard in the face was my father. It was only ever one strong stroke, and then he'd walk away. And Quinn, the brigadier's henchman, outside Malika's room. But to receive a blow like that repeatedly! What did Hammad sahib's face, that funny face, look like when he was being beaten? How many blows went to his face, how many to his body? More than the face, I wanted to know that place behind it, the new area of the soul when it knows it's being crushed and bled. Poor, poor Hammad sahib. At what point did he—this natural fighter— realize that this was not just another fight, that this one was to the death?

Sajid had come onto the roof and stood at the lower level, looking up at me with a smile. I waved to him. 'Sir ji, you have heard about Hammad sahib?'

I nodded.

'Haan, killed him, they did.' He was still smiling the smile of a kid excited by the very novelty of murder.

'Chalo, Sajid,' I said. 'Let's go back down.'

The brigadier's garden seemed full of the fluids of spring, the grass, the flowers, the air were moist and perfumed with renewal. The brigadier sat on a white garden chair with a cushion under his ailing rear, towel draped on his chest. The masseur, a dark-skinned Christian by the name of Dixon (he wore his name on his breast), was standing behind him, working his oils into the brigadier's scalp. Eyes closed and head back, my host was so integrated into the backdrop that it seemed his body, too, was filling with new life and bubbling fluids. He opened an eye and saw me. With minimal movement of his body he gestured to the chair next to him and said, 'Sit down.' He raised his leg and placed it across my knees. We were quiet for some time, Dixon working his scalp. The masseur himself was bald, and above one ear he had a long curling scar with the imprint of many stitches, a winding track that was unsettling because it took some time to determine what exactly the mark was or how such an injury could have been incurred.

'You know,' the brigadier, said, his eyes still closed. 'I'm thinking of adding something new to the cabaret. Things there are getting a little boring, hain na?'

'Well ... I mean, I've never ...'

'I was thinking of a hypnotist, what do you think?' He opened one eye again and looked at me with it.

'A hypnotist,' I said. 'Sounds interesting. What would—'

'I'd like it if you checked this guy out, let him hypnotize you. It'd be fun for you, no?'

'What if we subjected Apa to him instead?' I said, amused. 'Or, more like, subjected the *hypnotist* to *Apa*.' My laughter petered out nervously when the brigadier didn't join in. He gazed at me momentarily before closing that eye again. The masseur had started the final phase, the peak of his work, ecstatically working the cranium like a pianist in the climax of a score. The brigadier heaved 'Ahh's, and 'Oh-ho-ho, jenaab-e-Ali!' When Dixon was done, the brigadier leaned his head back, smiling, blissfully recovering. He opened his eyes, took in the garden.

'I heard about Hammad sahib,' I said.

He looked at Dixon. 'You need to go anywhere?' He addressed him in the informal 'tum.'

'Nahin, sir.'

The brigadier pointed at me and said, 'Do him as well.' He got up.

Dixon asked if the brigadier could arrange for a fresh towel, which Sajid brought out shortly. He set me up as he had the brigadier. The massage was relieving, but I was distracted by thoughts of Hammad sahib. Dixon was getting more involved, his fingers not really fingers, but instruments—that was the only way to feel comfortable about these foreign, working-class hands touching me so intimately. Was that how Malika did it? Felt men's hands on her belly and thigh as nothing more than little appliances that accompanied the cold frills of her cabaret uniform? He was saying things I didn't understand, and I muttered, 'Mm-hmm', every time he asked me if what he was saying wasn't the absolute truth. I wanted to focus on the massage, enjoy it the way the brigadier enjoyed it. But that scar above his ear threw his person, his hygiene, into question. He finished with a strong flourish. Long after he stopped, the oil still turned around in my hair and scalp.

The brigadier came back to his seat, and Sajid brought a tray of chholas, yellow peas, tea. The brigadier helped himself, then leaned back with that usual grimace of pain, adjusting on his seat. He looked deeply into his bowl as he ate. When he was done, he didn't put the bowl down but held it out, resting his forearm on the arm of the chair. 'You know,' he said into the dimming air. He tilted his head in search of words. 'In Hammad bhaiyya's case it was the exact opposite of psychosomatic. It was *soma-psychotic*. His body was so out of his control that it affected his mind, made him completely crazy at times. That's why he wrote the articles he wrote.'

'What exactly did he write?' I asked. His attention was elsewhere. I repeated my question.

'Oh, just . . .' He scrunched his face and shook his head. Absently, he looked into the distance, then turned his face down and again shook his head. We stayed out there until the mosquitoes arrived in their ensembles, building dancing towers above our heads. At dinner, Aunty Ruby stressed her fondness for Hammad sahib, dropped her face in her hand, covering her mouth and most of one cheek, and then shook her head from side to side, making a show out of her capacity for sentiment. 'Alamgir, you remember when Hammad bhaiyya . . .' But I had a greater claim on him. I'd helped him get his pants on, drank Black Dog with him, and shared conjectures about the brigadier and his political alliances. Aunty Ruby carried on. '. . . I even *told* him that day, be a little careful, Hammad bhaiyya . . .' After dinner, the brigadier changed into shalwar-kameez and sat in his usual seat, lit a cigar, waiting for guests, the first of whom showed up at around eleven. 'Did you hear the story about the armless Bengali boy?' one of them said on her way in.

6

My mother died when I was four years old, of cancer, and I barely remember her death. Or, barely registered her death as a death: I remember the funeral, the hundreds of people and the hundreds of prayers, and I even remember my father taking me to her body before it went to the graveyard, untying the white sheet that covered her so that I could get a final look at her face. I remember her alive, and I remember her dead, underground. Two distinct memories: mother alive, mother dead. But no process of dying itself.

So Hammad sahib's was really the first death I knew. It was the first time I felt close to a life that had prematurely ended. I tried to claim him now, even if only in my head, the way Aunty Ruby had done. The night that marked the first time I had sex with Malika I would now remember primarily as the night I shared a bottle of whisky with Hammad sahib. And I hankered to remember all that I could. When memory slipped it was agonizing. The pale stiff leg, over which I helped him raise his corduroy pants; those Burmese eyes, the way they squinted and filled with pink more and more as he drank; and then that mocking fist-in-the-mouth when he mimed the act of holding oneself back. He did it so well, looking down at the fist he was ingesting with demonic eyes, as if that fist were all that prevented him from unleashing the hell inside him. I would take that gesture from him, I decided. Homage to Hammad Rehman. Nobody else would have any use for it. I wanted to share these reflections, but I couldn't do so with the brigadier, or even Aunty Ruby, for fear of trespassing on their own mourning. I started, therefore, to put some of these thoughts to paper, and thought I might write a letter to my father about the matter.

Upstairs, Apa, too, was writing a letter. I peered at the page on her lap. This time she was addressing Richard Nixon, whom she admired greatly and had once met, when he came to Pakistan as vice president in the '50s. She started the story as if for the first time: the vice president was visiting in the mid-'50s, the envoy of the president—she searched for the old president's name, frowning, groaning, bending forward and putting her hand to her forehead in pain, before I finally offered, 'Eisenhower.' And she said, 'Haan, haan, Eezenhower! You know Eezenhower? He, too, was a general. So he loved Field Marshal sahib' (she was the only one in the house who refered to the former dictator as Field Marshal rather than Ayub). They had a reception for Nixon, over six thousand people came to the prime minister's house (those were the days before the Field Marshal's coup, she explained, when they had appointed prime ministers). Apa was introduced to Nixon by the prime minister himself. I couldn't imagine how they would have conversed, her contempt for English being what it was. But there was no question in Apa's mind that he still remembered her, a decade and a half later. And in her letter she talked about how happy she was when he was finally elected president, something she'd been waiting for ever since she'd met him, and she was sure he would be elected again, whenever the next elections were. 'We have elections also in Pakistan,' the letter read. 'But not like Amerika. We vote bad men. You are good man. Here good men are not politicens . . .' Again my presence disrupted her delicate work. She was frozen, pen in hand, her unfinished words to Nixon in front of her, eyeing me suspiciously from the side of her eye, as if I were here to steal the letter.

'I am thinking a lot about Hammad sahib,' I said.

Apa frowned, looked down. 'Aah! Haan, haan.' She relaxed into a role that she must have played so many times in her long life. 'Hammad sahib,' she said, setting the tone and preparing for this heavy subject. She was silent, but her face was opening up, the frown giving way to arched eyebrows, lips parted, words somewhere in there. 'His father was a very good friend of ours. He was . . . he was in the railways, like my brother. He used to come here, sit and talk to me for hours. He stayed here, this house, for some time in . . . I don't know when. Every day he used to come to this room and talk to me. And when he moved back to Dhaka, he used to write me letters. And if he was ever in Karachi, without fail, he would come to see me. Even if he was here just for the day, even if he was very busy. He would always come and bring me a gift. Soaps, things like that. But then I heard he divorced his wife, and I never let him come here again.'

'Oh? Were you a friend of his wife?'

In the strenuous act of memory, she grimaced. 'I don't

remember her. Maybe I met her. But why did he need to divorce her? Once you are married you stay together. That's what marriage means. You understand?' I was tempted to ask her why she herself never married, whether she ever came close. Had this woman ever had a man inside her in her ninety-odd years? 'But his son. He was a good man. Hammad. When a man dies . . .' She turned to me. 'You're listening? When a man dies, it's all in God's hands.' I was listening. I didn't believe a word of it, but it was oddly soothing to hear about death from someone so erudite. 'There's one kind of trouble that a man gets into because he has no—' she used a word that I took to mean 'control', and confirmed with her. 'Haan haan, kantrul. So . . .' She raised her eyebrows and looked down pensively at her palm and fingers, ready to enumerate. 'There's one kind of trouble that man gets into because he has no kantrul—Allah's choice.' As she said this, she placed her index finger against the little finger of her upward turned hand. '*Then*,' she lifted the index, 'there's the kind of trouble that a man gets himself into because of his . . . *own decisions*.' On the last two words she let the index fall, with more force than before, onto the third finger of that yellow hand. 'When a man goes against Islam, when he goes against Allah's will . . . This is a Muslim country. You understand, hain na? This is a *Muslim* country.' She raised her finger admonishingly. I was jolted by the sudden hardness in her speech. 'When people try to break the country up, it's because they are working with Hindus. You understand, na?' I nodded. 'Theek hai,' she continued, lowering her voice again. 'Then you understand. Not everybody understands at first. But sooner or later, they do. Allah has his ways so that everybody understands. You know about the Mughals, hain na? Did they teach you about the Mughals in ... where were you ... England?'

'France,' I said.

'Haan, haan, France.' She sneered. 'Fooko-Shooko. They have no knowledge. Now ... where are you going? Sit, sit! Where do you have to go? Now, let me tell you. The Mughals ruled India—in those days, you know, there was just India, no Pakistan. Yes-yes, you know. For how many years did the Mughlas rule? A long time. That was the *best* time. *The best time* ... was that. Understand? Why, because they were Muslim. And, what else?' She raised her finger admonishingly again. '*Urdu speakers*. Not Punjabis, not Sindhis, not these, these Bengalis. *Urdu* speakers. Urdu and Islam are like this.' She interwove the fingers of both hands.

'I studied history, too,' I said.

'Where? In England?'

'I was never in England.'

'Haan, haan, France you said. You ... haan, you were in France.' She sunk her chin into the curve between her thumb and index. 'Khair, there, too, they know nothing.'

'What does this have to do with Hammad sahib?'

'Hammad sahib?'

'The Bengali gentleman, who died.'

'Haan, I *knew* Hammad. He was a theek-thaak man. A good heart.' Now she looked down, sad, his death coming back. She looked at me with a staggered disoriented look. She stuttered, sentences creaked in her throat. 'Okay,' she finally said, coherent again. 'You need to go somewhere? If you need to go somewhere, you should go.' If she was dismissing me, it was a first. As I walked away, she called after me, 'But wear a sweater. You will get sick in that shirt!' I went up to the mezzanine. The brigadier and his wife weren't home. I poured myself a glass of whisky in the library, and then through the library's other door I went onto the roof to collect my thoughts, and didn't go back in until the assault of mosquitoes on my bare feet. The guests' door was closed, dark underneath the door. I walked past to the kitchenette. They'd left two plates of mango peels and mango bone on the counter, attracting flies and giving off a now rancid smell. Fools. I picked up the plates and shook them in front of the bin until the peels and bones came unstuck and fell in, then put them in the sink. I found the salt I was looking for, and rubbed some on the swollen flesh of my feet where the mosquitoes had gotten to me.

In my room, in dimly-lit enclosed space, I started making connections. Television told you nothing. The papers told you nothing. But the people who came to the brigadier's after dinner, they talked. That was the whole point. To talk and talk. But things from outside, from the East wing, were breaking in. Government censorship wasn't going to protect the drawing room. And what did that one journalist fellow say a couple of weeks before? A middle-aged man with shiny black-rimmed glasses, sitting on a one-seater with his legs stretched onto the low glass table at the centre of all the sofas and seats. What did he say about some group, ITJ, or ICJ, or IJT, carrying out killings on the army's behalf, killing luminaries across Dhaka and wherever else? And what did he say this group was? A student wing. And the student wing of none other than the Jamaati-i-Islami. It was the brigadier, his face an irritated red, who stopped the conversation. 'Oh, leave it, bhai. Good lord, you journos! This is like a festival for you, isn't it? A jackpot of intrigue.' 'It's *happening*, brigadier sahib,' the journalist had replied. 'If it's happening, it's happening,' the brigadier had barked back. 'What can your little stories do? You know they'll get you, too.' It was now clear as day. The envelope, the papers, that the brigadier gave the Jamaatis the very first day I saw them; their late returns well after midnight from God-knows-where; the meeting in Apa's room the time I returned from my visit to Rahim sahib in Lalukhet; our short walk to Hillside Park and back (yes, even I was implicated); the brigadier's reaction to his old friend's murder ('that's why he wrote those articles'); and now Apa's speech about God and the Hindus. Perhaps it wasn't even a secret, perhaps it was just unspoken, that this house, and those two men down the hall, were responsible for Hammad sahib's death. That's what the brigadier and his old aunt were telling me: that in the larger scheme of things, the Bengali gentleman, great raconteur and friend though he was, posed a threat.

No, not the brigadier. The Jamaatis, yes; Apa, perhaps. But not Brigadier Alamgir. Too good a man, and a man who stood for non-intervention, no tampering. A targeted assassination was tampering, was it not?

I heard the pedestrian gate open, two sets of footsteps, and I turned my lamp off, waiting for the front door to open and close, for the footsteps to continue down the hall and recede, before turning it back on again.

7

Sajid opened my door tentatively, stuck his head through. 'Sir ji, those guests are looking for you.'

'Which guests?'

Sajid grinned and sniggered stupidly from his nose. 'Sir, the ones who are staying here.'

'The Jamaatis? Why do they want to see me?'

'Sir, I don't know anything.'

'Go find out,' I ordered. 'And tell them I can't come right now.'

'Ji, sir.'

I changed into pants and a shirt, spent several nervous minutes pacing the small path in front of my bed. What could those men want from me now? There was no reason for our worlds to meet, other than at the dinner table or at Apa's bed. But now did they know that I was inquiring about the Jamaat, about what the army was using them for, from Sajid, from Apa, even from guests who came over after dinner? Had they heard about my connection to Hammad sahib? Was I, too, a traitor-terrorist in their eyes? I could hear Sajid and the professor in the hallway. I locked my door. There was a door through the bathroom that led out to the side of the house, and there was a small unused gate along that boundary wall that opened onto the side street. I wasn't sure if it was still in use or if it was locked. I had to pull hard, but it did open, with a heavy metal noise that the Jamaatis no doubt heard. I rushed down the side street, in the direction of Drigg Road, through the brigadier's neighbourhood, a centre of the West wing's political life: one of Bhutto's men, a legal expert who they said might become law or interior minister in a Bhutto government, lived in the big green house on this street; nearby was Pakistan's first prime minister's house.

It was too early to go to the Agra, so I went first to my old bar in Saddar and ordered a Murree beer. This time I sat facing the street, and when I was done with the three bottles I paid my tab, but was uncomfortable with the thought of leaving, imagining the two Jamaatis were out there, searching the streets for me. I ordered a fourth beer and by the time I finished it I was drunk. I took a taxi to the Agra, for the first time in weeks, the first time since Malika had expelled me in the middle of the night. It was early; I didn't want to wait in the cabaret with the soldier-assassins, so I asked my midget friend in the turban to get a key and let me into Malika's room, placing two rupees in his little palm. He saw to it. It felt like months since I'd last been in here, the old smell that was only Malika's, that in the beginning was a little foul but now delightful and soothing and feminine. I saw no signs of a new lover. On her bed, under her covers, I was safe. I'd been drifting in and out of sleep for a while when Malika finally entered. She didn't seem surprised to see me. Her cabaret apparel made tin-like noises as she placed the various parts on the side. She shook me awake, as before, but didn't ask me to leave. Just a delicate touch to tell me she was here. She moved away from the bed, drew the curtain, and slipped out of her clothes. It was nice to see her body again. After her shower she lay down next to me and pressed her damp breasts against my back. I felt a virginal pleasure. I turned to face her and we embraced for a while before she finally slipped her cold tongue through my lips. We made love without saying a word. All was forgiven.

The time between the end of the sexual act and her full recovery was always a period of vulnerability for Malika. It was perhaps her only period of vulnerability as far as I was concerned. That was the time she needed me most. Now, bent over on her knees, while I throbbed inside her, she reached back desperately, put her hand on my behind and urged me not to pull out. I loved such moments, where she was so astray, almost fearful of what would come next. She whispered, 'Lie on me.' And as we moved slowly down to get off our knees and lie on our fronts, me following behind her, she kept whispering, 'Not pull out, please not pull put.' She held both my hands tightly. She said she could feel my heartbeat against her back. When I was too limp to remain inside her, I rolled off, and turned my face away from her. Just as she needed contact and intimacy after sex, I needed solitude and a sheet over me. But this time I lay spread out, on my back, like a volunteer tied to a spinning wheel for a clown to throw knives at. My penis, devoid of life, for Malika to see. With a finger to my chin, she turned my face so that I would look at her. There was a little anger in her voice when she said, with her finger now pressed against my temple, 'What going on in here?' I remained silent. She wanted more than my simply looking at her, some deeper, impossible communion. She finally turned her back to me in a small fit of temper. I turned on my side and examined her. And when the moment when I couldn't bear physical contact passed, I put my arm around her. Soon she turned around and slept with her head on my chest, breathing heavily.

∾

'I don't know if you ever met Hammad sahib. Hammad *bhaiyya*, as the brigadier calls—called—him. That means brother, older brother. He was here the night you all were doing your silly People's Party thing. I was with him, in a room upstairs. Drinking. Helping him put on his pants. That sort of thing.'

It was absolute black in her room, God knows what time of night. Malika's head was on my chest, her hair all over me, and I could feel the gentle vibrations of my words against her temples. I explained Hammad sahib's murder. And then I conveyed Apa's spiel, her coming-to-peace with it, God's will, God's wrath, what-have-you. 'But there's an earlier episode that keeps coming to me. The brigadier and the two Jamaatis—no, don't worry, I'm not going to go on about them—they, the three of them, were gathered in Apa's little room, the double doors were partly closed. Which is unusual. And what was more unusual was the brigadier, he had his head down—he was sitting down with his hands on his knees and he was looking down. And it seemed to me that Apa and these two ... *guests* ... were consoling him. But this was *before* Hammad sahib died.' I shifted, moved my head back to look at Malika, moved some of the hair away to see her face. Her eyes were closed and she was breathing deeply again. 'What were they telling him?' I whispered. 'Were they telling him the same thing Apa told *me*, that whatever had to happen had to happen, that it was God's way, that they were doing the right thing?' I stroked Malika's hair. 'And what did Bhutto and the brigadier talk about, that night before Hammad sahib's death?' I sensed from her quieter breathing that Malika was more awake now. 'You know as well as I do how faithfully the brigadier stands with Bhutto. I'm not saying that's ... And he's a good man, and he's done a lot for me. But ... would he give up an old friend to Bhutto's cause?' The accusation was out, and it surprised even me, as if it had been implanted into the quiet night not by me but by some foreign thing in the darkness. 'Were he and Hammad sahib really that close?' I continued, unable to stop. 'They've known, they *had* known each other for decades, the brigadier called him "Bhaiyya". And don't get me wrong, I think he's clearly shaken by his death. His murder. But the army, it's still alive somewhere inside him, right? Do you think that soldier in him was willing to sacrifice a good man, an old friend? Turn him over to the Jamaat?' She put a finger over my lips. 'I know, I know. I keep telling myself to stop thinking.' Malika's sleepy hand moved down to my crotch. The warm fingers felt new. 'It's just, he was ...' I was hardening in her hand. '... such a ... *force* ... Hammad sahib, a wonderful ... wonderful ... ah ...' She was immobile except for the deep breaths and this hand that went on working in the same rhythm, no pause, no change of speed. Gentle, yes, but offering all the life in the world. 'After that ... the brigadier and I went for ... baby ... listen ... please ... you know him just as well as I do, maybe better, who knows? I need you to just tell me . . .' The hand picked up pace, encouraged by the swelling, the swelling. 'You incredible thing.' I whispered. 'You sweet sweet thing.' She moved her hand up my stomach, my chest, to my face, and I accepted her slightly moist finger in my mouth.

༄

Refreshed by sex—having Malika again—I was ready to face the two theocrats. If they were responsible for Hammad sahib's death, I would confront them about it. If they wanted me to repent my fondness for him, I would admit my fondness with pleasure, I would stress my grief and anger at his murder, and my condemnation of those responsible.

I asked Sajid if they were home. They were. I told him to let them know I'd be coming to see them momentarily. After changing my shirt, and pacing my room with a silent pep talk to myself, I approached their room in that same slow motion as on the Paris quay years ago, towards the man who'd taken my Ayatul-Kursi. Tuned into my heartbeat. It was one of those moments when the world was stationary, waiting for me to pass dizzily through. This wasn't going to be easy, I knew. I knocked on their door, and both men simultaneously shouted, 'Ji?' When they saw that it was me, pressing my way through the door, they dropped what they were doing— putting clothes away into bags, the green plastic closet unzipped—and came to greet me with Muslim half-hugs. 'Aiyai, aiyai.' They made space for me, I walked between them and, the room too small for three of us, they coalesced behind me into that single ominous presence again. They asked me to sit down on one of the beds, facing the other bed, and then both of them stood before me like interrogators. The professor well-groomed, the nose hairs clipped and packed tight, his head ducked so that even from higher ground he watched me from the top of his dope fiend's eyes. He was barefoot for the first time; his feet were strong, proportioned but oddly-formed, wide spaces between the toes as if each was deliberately separated from the other, looking like a gummy gap-ridden smile. Khwaja sahib wore an unbuttoned kurta. The big curved ivory trunk stood in one corner.

'How are you? Everything okay?'

Yes, I assured them, 'Thanks to Allah.'

'Good, good.' The professor proferred a plate of biscuits and I took one, looking around the room. The papers that the brigadier had given them: if there was a link between the brigadier, the Jamaatis and Hammad sahib's assassination, I was convinced that those papers would be the proof. Hammad sahib's profile, photographs, addresses, excerpts from his articles, all that the clergy needed to indict and execute him. Poor, poor Hammad sahib. Where were those papers, where was that envelope?

'So, all is well?' Khwaja sahib confirmed, two palms raised at his chest.

Yes, all was well, by the grace of God.

'We were talking a little while ago about you with brigadier sahib,' the professor said, using the word 'zikar', which I'd learned recently and had come to use fondly. A beautiful sounding word, *zikar*. 'He was telling us about your father sahib. We knew a little bit, of course, but he was telling us ... Your father sahib came here from India at Partition?'

I liked how these men always used the courteous 'aap' when referring to me. I nodded, my throat blocked. 'At Partition, my father thought of staying behind, with the rest of our family,' I explained. 'But then he decided—'

'Haan, haan, naturally,' the professor said solemnly. 'Naturally, a Muslim man will come here. Pakistan was made for the Muslims, isn't it?' He looked at his colleague for confirmation. 'Haan, Khwaja sahib? Pakistan was made for *Muslims*?' Absolutely, the Khwaja confirmed, a finger slipped through the open buttons of his kameez scratching the big chest underneath. And there it was, the same lesson Apa had offered when explaining Hammad sahib's death. What would I say when they brought him up? I'd tell them that his death was a tragedy and that the people responsible should be hanged. Yes: *hanged*.

'So, please tell us. What is your connection to brigadier sahib?'

'An old friend of my father's.'

'He knew him in India, before Partition?'

'I think it was here, maybe in school.' There was no polite way in Urdu for me to ask why they wanted this information. 'What is your connection to the brigadier?' I asked.

The professor laughed gently, leaning his head back, as if acknowledging a joke at his expense. He put a hand on my shoulder and sat down in front of me. 'Haan, we should tell you a little about ourselves.' His voice lowered in seriousness, adjusted for explanation. 'Our links in this country are very old. You must have heard the name of Pir Zubair. From interior Sindh, you understand, na?' I nodded. I knew about these pirs, these bearded spiritual types who ruled little fiefdoms in the interior. 'He's a good man,' the professor continued. 'His people, his family, are good people. We are not *close* friends, but, even then, meetings happen, talk-shalk continues between us. Because there is rishtidari—our cousin married one of his cousins. You have spent much time abroad, isn't it, so perhaps you wouldn't know about these things. The Pir sahib, we can always go to his people if some problem or (a word I didn't understand) in the province comes up. You know, our connections are with Punjab, so in this part they are not as strong. Our party—I don't know if you are familiar with our party, the Jamaat—is strong in Karachi but in the interior, there isn't as much. We rely on friendships. You understand? So the Pir's people, they do things for us.'

'So, you were telling us your connection to brigadier sahib,' the other man said. 'Brigadier sahib is not connected to this land that you have?'

'Land?' I gasped.

'Yes, yes, brigadier sahib was telling us about your land, in—where was it?' He looked to the professor.

'Mirphurkhas, isn't it?' the professor replied.

'Yes, Mirpurkhas,' Khwaja sahib said.

'Quite a problem, hain na?' The professor looked at me. 'Brigadier was telling. Your khala, isn't it?'

'Phuppi,' I corrected, but swallowing the word.

'Brigadier was telling us, she's a little,' he motioned to the side of his head with a concave hand, turning an invisible knob to suggest malfunction. The brigadier had gone too far this time! And these men were now trying to rob me blind. I tried getting up but the professor put his hand on my shoulder, a touch that was gentle but pregnant with force. 'Sit, sit,' he said laughing, politely, still using the formal conjugation of the verb. 'Don't be alarmed. You are our brother.' He looked up to his colleague. 'Isn't it?'

'Absolutely,' the Khwaja said, met my eye, frowned and nodded solemnly.

'So tell us,' the professor resumed. 'Problem is . . . what?' This cold incursion; they wanted details. 'Tell,' the professor pleaded paternally. 'Don't worry.'

'We have a mango orchard in Mirpurkhas,' I began. The last time I tried explaining the orchard problem in Urdu, to Ghulam Hussain, I wasn't able to. But now I was surprised by how much I could relay. And, as if trying to exploit this new freedom, I went into as much detail as I could, described the rivalry between my father and Mona Phuppi, the fact that Mona Phuppi had sold some property earlier without consulting him. I wanted to stop talking, but I couldn't, I went on, details and more details, whatever I could manage. My Urdu had never been this fluent. The squatters, the deeds, the bribe to Rahim sahib, my aunt's instability. I was in ecstasy. 'She beat her husband once. Very strange woman, she is.' I gave them all the information they wanted, blurted it all out like a tortured enemy. And now I wanted to say, Yes-yes, take the orchard! Contact whoever you need to contact, and take it, save me from this oppressive task. I felt a delightful exhaustion of betrayal.

'And until now, nothing?'

'Nothing,' I confirmed.

The professor looked at his friend and nodded.

'Look ji,' the larger man explained. 'This policewala, how much has he taken from you? *Whatever* it is, it's just the beginning. And it's not his fault. This is the way it works. Like you say in English, *That the way it works*,

Shahbaz sahib. He'll try with one person, this one will say I need money to give to that one, that one will say he needs to give money to the other one, then something will get stuck here, some paper will get lost there, a judge will say I need this money for this. Then new government will come, and ... who knows what will happen, isn't it?'

'I was thinking,' said the professor, sitting across from me. 'It's a sad affair that we never met sooner, a very sad thing, but khair, we're staying here at brigadier sahib's together. This means that we are brothers, you and us. Isn't it?' I put my humble hand to my heart. Khwaja sahib now sat down next to the professor. 'And, khair, for us this isn't even a question. This land is your father sahib's. Not the squatters.' And your phuppi, we respect her, of course, but you know how it is in Islam.' He bent himself a little towards me, laid out his hand flat, the palm turned upward, and brought the index of his other hand down on it. 'When a man dies, one-sixth of his estate goes to his parents ...'

I interrupted him to say that, yes, I knew the breakdown: one-eighth to the wife, the rest to the kids, at a ratio of two-to-one for the male heirs, which meant my father and his brother technically each owned more of the family property than Mona Phuppi.

'Achha, you know it so well!' The men looked at each other smiling and nodding, like grown-ups proud of an adolescent's erudition. 'Then you understand. We have no (an unfamiliar word) of our own. But what's just is just. It's your land, not the squatters' land. In Islam, when a man owns something, it can never be taken away from him. This *land reform-sheform* is against Islam. That land is yours. It's not up to us, what is in the

Koran is in the Koran, Allah's will, who are we to argue, isn't it? Now, as we said, we have old connections here. With Pir sahib, we have a good connection, a family connection, with him. In our country, these relations are very important. You have been living outside, over there of course they do things differently. But ours is a Muslim country. We will speak to Pir sahib. On your behalf.

'If you allow us,' Khwaja sahib added.

'Achha? That's kind of you,' I said. 'But what will Pir sahib do?'

Both men tittered as if by a single physical impulse. 'You, of course, have spent a lot of time abroad. You don't know about these things.'

'Look, ji,' I said, using the formal conjugation, as they did with me. 'I don't know about this. I don't know what you are . . . *proposing*,' I used the English word, 'I can't give you an answer right away, but if you give me a little time to think—'

'Haan, haan, by all means!' Both men stood up. 'Naturally, you need time to think,' the professor said. One after the other, they extended their hands for me to shake. I stood up. 'But don't take too much time thinking.' They looked at each other and laughed again. 'A man shouldn't spend too much time thinking, Shahbaz mian.'

༄

'They have a right to be there,' I said. 'They've been there for over a decade now, we can't just throw them out.'

'Yes, yes, yes.' The brigadier had no patience for this

talk of rights. He was sitting up on the edge of the bed, a masseur behind him (not Dixon), with one knee on the bed, battering his scalp, creating chaos with the grey wisps. 'But it's your property. It's your father's property ... Ah, ha! Good, good ...' Encouraged, the masseur enhanced his beats. 'Haan ... Beta, it was owed to your family, for the sacrifice you all made when you all decided to join this country. Us mohajirs, from India, we're the ones who *made* this country. It wasn't the Sindhis or the Punjabis or the bloody Bongs. Us mohajirs made this country, and we're the ones who made the greatest sacrifice. Left our palaces and estates behind on the other side. But this is not the West, young man. In this country ... ah-ha-ha, bas, bas, that's good enough.' The masseur stopped, tidied the grey hair with both hands before putting a thin comb to it. 'This is not the West. In this country, you don't just belong simply because you're here, contributing to society and bla bla bla. It doesn't work like that. Everything depends on soil.' He rubbed his fingers on his thumb, handling imaginary grains of sand. 'We need that anchor ... Theek hai, ji, bahut shukriya.' They shook hands, and the masseur nodded to me on his way out. 'Running that orchard will be the best thing for you. You'll *learn* things about this country.' He picked up his cigarette box from the bedside table, took one out and tapped its base on the box. 'Abhey, it's all well and good to care about the poor, but they'll survive. They're the ones who *do* survive. No matter what happens, you know that the squatters will always be just fine. But it's *us*, we're the vulnerable ones. Because we don't really belong here, my boy. We're not ... *sons of the soil*.' He rolled his sardonic eyes as he said this, making a statement one

moment, mocking it the very next. 'We only belong to
what we own. You know this, I don't have to tell you.
Let these people handle it, beta. They know how to get
things done in this place. You, you're still a bloody
Bentley, with these lovely ideas of democracy and
equality. Just like your father.'

'What will they do? How will they get the squatters
out?'

'Simple: they'll go there with their goons, tell the
haris, "This belongs to a very big man, and he wants it
back." And to clear the place in one week, otherwise
they'll come back and slaughter the lot of them.' With
this the brigadier lit up with his frenzied laughter, the
djinn inside him flapping its wings, the mouth stretched
as wide as it could. He wiped his lower lip. 'So that's
that.' He put the cigarette in his mouth and removed a
matchbox from the bedside table drawer.

'What's in it for them?' I asked. 'The Jamaatis. What's
in it for them?'

Now he scowled. He took the unlit cigarette out of his
mouth. 'Who knows? Who *bloody cares*, bhai?'

'Why do these people care about me or my father, or
any of this? All because in Islam—'

'They *don't* care! This is not about you or your
bloody orchard. That's the beauty of this whole thing.
You don't have to give them a damn thing. This is about
the show of force, this is about cementing alliances.
Using idle capacity. There's no point having private
armies if you're not going to use them. It's like having
a Land Rover but letting its engine rot away in the
garage. The pirs want to use their engines. These men
want to cement their alliances with the pirs even if they
don't like the idea of pirs. And you want your orchard.

It's all very simple, my boy. Take it. Think of it as a favour.'

'A *favour*? I suppose it—'

'What do you mean, you *suppose*, bhai? The squatters will be gone, and your crazy aunt will have no more excuses. Ghazanfar will be proud of you. And you'll be back here, and running that thing. A full citizen. You'll do just fine.' He stood up, tapped the top of my head. I wanted to push his hand away, even to bite it. 'Let these people sort it out.' He made towards the door.

I called out after him: 'The squatters have a r—'

'Be a man,' he said, opening the door, turning around to face me, and then leaving me in his room, the door open. Leaving, too, his last three words, like a secret file I was supposed to go through and decode once he was gone. But I suppose one knows who is and who isn't susceptible to those three simple words, put together, one after the other. Be—a—Man. When I came out of the master bedroom, I found him sitting outside in the sitting room of the mezzanine, smoking his cigarette. 'Please, close the door,' he said, signalling with his hand, urgently. 'Your bloody Aunty Ruby will grumble'—he grimaced to caricature his wife's complaining face— '*You fill the room with smoke*, blah blah blah.' I shut the door and sat with him. He offered me a cigarette, which despite my aversion to tobacco I accepted. 'We should move to the library before she comes up. She'll say I'm corrupting you. We can even have a drink before dinner.' He got up and I followed him to the library. I noticed that his cotton pants were padded at the back, to ease his distress when he sat down.

8

My benefactors were sitting in the upstairs landing, waiting for lunch. Always the two together. I imagined pulling them apart and seeing the collapse of that single, intolerable presence. They smiled when I came up, a secretive smile not of welcome but of brotherhood, the awful weight of our alliance. I sat down silently. It still felt like stones lined my soles—I had gone for a long walk late at night, when I couldn't sleep, when I wanted to be away from these men, from the brigadier, from this house, and I'd lost my way and ended on the other side of the church; it took me over an hour to get home. But for once I could say absolutely nothing to them and it would be just fine. I didn't deceive myself about the price of this new freedom: I could get away with not speaking because now I was theirs in a way. And so we sat—the two of them next to each other, me in the seat opposite—and waited for lunch in the silence of our pact. Even Apa's room was closed and completely quiet; she hadn't been well, an infection in her chest. Both were reading Urdu newspapers. Planning their next corrupt act, their next crooked deal, their next targeted kill. The Khwaja sat crossed-legged, and the foot that was raised was bare, its sandal left behind on the floor, and it shuddered nervously as he read, so that no matter where I looked, my eyes couldn't escape this big trembling foot.

Sajid announced lunch. The men looked at me and made a gesture that I lead the way to the dining room. They followed behind, the smell of cigarette on their clothes. It was just the three of us for lunch, Aunty Ruby out for the afternoon, the brigadier making use of what he claimed to be his last month on the golf course before the Karachi humidity turned him into a recluse. The professor pointed to the head of the table and suggested I sit there. Sajid brought out the rest of the dishes and two more chapatis to toss in the bread basket. The men each held up a dish for me to get the first helpings, and I waved for them to first serve themselves. I put too much on my plate.

'Bismillah,' the larger one said, tearing a piece of chapati. They were quiet dignified eaters, even though the Khwaja stretched himself out on his side of the table as if to claim more territory. But his plate was neatly organized, the vegetables, daal, and meat partitioned into small clearly separate clumps.

'Shahbaz sahib, you're not eating,' said the professor.

'Please don't mind,' I said. 'My stomach is a little . . .' I rubbed my belly. 'In fact, I should rest a bit.'

'Oh ho!' The Khwaja cried. 'Did you eat something from the outside? Let's tell the servant to make you something, khitchri or something. Seven-Up. Oye bachai,' he called to Sajid, 'get him a Seven-Up!'

No, no, I told them, I just need rest.

'Of course, you should rest.'

I excused myself, called out to Sajid and told him to take my plate away. I left the two men, walked tentatively down the stairs because now I felt the long hours in my knees.

❧

'I'm worried about those boys,' I said. 'There's one amongst them—Little Chief, he's called. Little Chief's got this other little friend. They're like Quixote and Sancho, if you know what I mean.'

'Why you are worried?' Malika asked.

'*Because* ... well, I can't tell you exactly why. It's probably safer that I don't tell you. Safer for *you*. This is a world you're not ready for, my sweet. I've told you the orchard problem is being resolved and that's good enough.'

Lying on her back, in panties and a T-shirt, she'd lifted both legs straight up, L-shaped Malika staring at her curling toes.

'Maybe I should go and at least get the Little Chief and his friend out of there. But then where do I put them? Maybe I can sneak them into the brigadier's? What do you think? There's that door—I don't know if you've seen it—that leads outdoors from my bathroom. So that's an option. They could ... well, they could hide in the closet. You wouldn't tell the brigadier, would you? Of course, we could have them stay here, in your room, too. I'd pay off the midget, that wouldn't be an issue. What do you say? We'd give them opium at night. They could close their eyes while we make love. Kids that young, it actually doesn't matter if they see anything. But then ... what if *they* started looking for them?

What if they counted everyone up and saw that there were two little ones missing? Well, they'd start looking for them, wouldn't they? Oh yes, these people won't be satisfied until they've slaughtered the *whole* bunch. We'll have to move those boys around, but then I fear I'd put you in danger if we kept them here. These aren't people you want showing up at your door. Yes, *I* showed up at your door. That was different. And maybe if I did that *today*, you'd be better off not letting me in.'

'Dangerous man,' she said. She leaned over to the side, towards me, dropping her outstretched bare legs across my waist. Her panties were soaked. 'I should not fuck you from now. Too dangerous. Maybe you will kill *me*.'

'Not you,' I assured her. 'You're not high-value enough. For you I'd use the midget. He's got the key to every room, right? So he'd come in here in the middle of the night. You'd be too wasted on opium to know what's going on. He'll sneak onto your bed. He'll realize that you're naked, once he gets close. So he'll pull back the covers, look at these little breasts, touch them maybe. Then ...' I put my hands gently around her neck. 'Though his hands would probably be too small. You might be safe. Then again, he could poison you, right? He'll put the covers back and tidy your hair and leave. The end of our lovely, ravishing Malika. Yes, that's exactly how you'd look.' I tidied her hair, straightened her legs, pulled her arms straight along her torso. 'Now you lie there like that, make-believe, practise for the day it happens.' She was very obedient, indulged my silly game, which filled me with affection and I leaned over her and kissed her. 'Listen, Malika. Speaking of acting, there's something I want to talk to you about. About my father ...'

'My father made films, I told you that, remember? If he was still here I could have told him to set you up in the business. You'd like that, to become an actress? Maybe he still has friends in the business, I'll ask him and we'll see what we can do. Maybe he'll come back one day, now with this orchard business sorted out, and start the films again. So here's what I say. You do your dance for a few months, fine, but let's see if I can get you out of it. Yes?' I squeezed her thigh. 'How does that sound?'

'Sounds?'

'This whole ... *thing*,' I gestured outward to her room, 'is holding you back. My father, you know he discovered the top actress and actor in Pakistani cinema. That's why everybody knows his name. Well, *that* and the Conspiracy case, of course. He was a better filmmaker than coup-maker, apparently, which does *you* just fine. But you're exactly the kind he would ... you know, I think it could be you who brings him back.' I moved my hand over her knee, below the knee across the length of her leg. She had her index finger between her teeth, watching me distantly with a slight smile, the way you watch someone you've swindled. 'What I'm saying is ... you leave the brigadier.'

'Aah! So now you are bigger than Alamgir?'

'Not ... I'm just saying—'

'Congratulations! Mubarak, as we say.'

'We say that here, too, my love.'

'So, now you *are* dangerous man.'

'I'm *serious*. You were still in your diapers in the late forties and fifties. If you'd been a little older, if you'd been in the country then, you would have known about this actress, Zeba. And if you'd known about her, you would have known about my father.'

'I know about your father. I know he made you ugly because he not let you shave your little moustache.'

'*Didn't* let me. So you're saying you've never had dreams of becoming an actress?'

'I say *you* have dream. Dream to become bigger than Alamgir.'

'But not if you have anything to do with it—that's what you're trying to tell me?'

'I am not Alamgir's, um, how you say . . . protector. I am just his . . .'

'His what? *Employee*? Please. Do finish your sentence. You are just his . . . what?' She bunched a cluster of my chest hair between her fingers and stretched it out, over and over. 'His . . . employee? Is that what you were going to say? If so, what's the problem? Just say it.' She pulled harder on my chest hair, until I felt the pinch. I put my hand over her hand.

'Say it!'

'I am Alamgir's . . .' She smiled, teasingly.

'His . . . what?'

'I am Alamgir's . . .' She held her mouth open, watched me with devil's eyes.

'I am Alamgir's employee at the hotel. Nothing more.'

'I am Alamgir's employee . . .'

'Exactly,' I said.

'And his . . .'

'No, that's quite enough.'

'His . . .'

'Stop it!'

'But you are now bigger than Alamgir. So is okay. You can know every-thing.'

'Kind of you as that is, my love, I think . . . Well, it all sounds more like wishful thinking to me. The brigadier is a faithful hus—'

'If you like.'

'He's a professional—he doesn't fuck his employees.'

'If you like.'

'Say it: Alamgir. Does. Not. Fuck. His. Employees.'

'Alamgir does not fuck his employees.'

'Correct,' I said.

'Except for . . .'

'Enough! I think we're finished here,' I said, getting up, finding my underwear, socks, pants. 'You've been a pleasure as always.'

'You can stay,' she said.

'It's all right, my dear. Got to get home.'

'Which home?'

'You know exactly which home.'

She giggled, a bitchy giggle. 'Home,' she said. 'To your new friends.'

'Yes,' I said with a smirk. 'My new friends.' I stretched the word, 'friends'. I leaned over the bed and kissed her forehead. I straightened up, stared down at her. 'Okay, I'll give you another shot. 'I.'

'I.'

'Am.'

'Am.'

'Alamgir's.'

'Alamgir's . . .' She was energized, smiling, open-mouthed like a schoolgirl. She'd fuck with my head all night if I let her. I stopped the game there and left her.

∾

My new friends. They came to see me a final time. They squeezed their way into my room, and as they did I wondered what would happen if, as the first came in, I shut the door to the second, locked him out? Just me, the professor and the weapons in the room, the hardcover books, the hangers, photo frames, the nutcracker resting on top of the fridge. But no, in the Khwaja came, too. One behind the other, always walking as if the earth had an exceptional pull on them. They stood awkwardly in the cramped room that with the double bed, didn't fit three. What news were they bringing? Had the horrible operation begun?

'Can I get you anything? I have ...' I pointed to the fridge in the little alcove.

'No, no. It's simply, we're leaving soon, going back. So we thought, meet Shahbaz sahib a little before we go.'

'I wish I had some chairs here for you,' I said.

'No problem, no problem,' the Khwaja appealed. 'Our room, the same.' The professor stood in front of the bookcase, examined the books, the Hitler biographies and all the rest. For the first time, I wondered what subject he taught at Punjab University. And how strong his links were to the party's murderous student wing.

'You know I have this fridge,' I explained, opening the door for them to see inside, 'but it doesn't have anything in it. So I'm afraid ...'

The Khwaja opened the bathroom door and peered inside, turned on the switch for the light, then turned it off and closed the door. The two Jamaatis then reunited, their natural course, in the middle of the room.

'Now what?' I asked. 'After this, after you leave Karachi?'

'Bas, Shahbaz sahib,' said the big man. 'We go home for a while. Then we'll see.'

'And all your work here, it all got done?'

'By the grace of God.'

'Very good, ji, very good,' I said. 'By the grace of God. If you came all the way here, and didn't do what you came for, then . . .'

'What's the purpose, hain na?'

'Exactly,' I said. 'What's the purpose?'

'Better to just stay home.'

'Exactly, ji.'

'But you will be here for some time?' the professor asked.

'Let's see,' I said. 'God's will. What can a man do but leave it to Allah?'

'This is absolutely right, what you've said.' There was, again, a small sound, a snigger from his nose and he looked at me with that smile that seemed perpetually on the verge of breaking into a helpless guffaw. I realized that I could have ended up liking him. Perhaps under different circumstances. Without this other tyrant constantly at his side. His thick nourished hair sat strong on his head, from some angles looking like foam from a head excreting thought after thought.

'And now, Shahbaz sahib, we should stop disturbing you. Whatever you were doing, please continue doing. Sorry to have disturbed you.'

'No, no,' I implored them, standing up and getting to the exit before they did. 'Stay a little while. We haven't even talked yet.' They looked at each other. 'Please,' I said, gesturing towards the room. Perhaps they'd come in simply to reassure me of our alliance, that soon they'd be gone from my life but, certainly, not forgotten. They were honourable men, never once mentioning my debt to them. I actually admired these skills of theirs. Now I decided to prolong the feeling of being violated by them.

'We have to pack our luggage, as well.'

'No-no, you pack later!' My heart was beating in haste and I was unsteady. 'After this, meeting may be a little bit difficult, so . . .' I put my hand on the big man's shoulder and ushered him inward. 'I know I don't have much to offer you, but . . . here.' I gave him the nutcracker, along with a little bowl of almonds, and then searched half-frantically for something to give the other, as if he would start crying if I didn't also find him a toy. 'Ah, one minute!' I went to my bedside table, opened the drawer and pulled out one of Ghulam Hussain's bottles. 'Here, let me get you . . . I want you to try something.'

Sitting on the bed, I unscrewed the top, sniffed the moonshine and shook my head in amazement. 'Come, sit here.' I tapped the place next to me and beckoned the professor the way I would a woman. With a short nod of encouragement from his bigger friend, the professor reluctantly sat down. I proferred the bottle to him. He recoiled with an embarrassed grin, and stood back up. Yes, now I would present myself as scum, vulgar, a low life who'd done too much time in the West. If I had to suffer for our alliance, I wanted them to suffer, too, to make our alliance equal, costly, necessary but that nevertheless tore at their Muslim hearts. I took a small sip from the bottle, tasting the poor man's drink for the first time, and immediately spat it out, almost choking. 'I'm sorry, I shouldn't have been the first to drink. *You* are the guests, here . . . in *my* room.' I stood up again and proposed the bottle to him. 'At least smell it,' I said, switching for the first and only time to English. The professor took a quick whiff and laughed with his mouth tightly shut, put his hand up as if to ward off

evil, and took a step back. I stepped forward with the
poise of a man holding a snake. 'Try it,' I said. 'One sip,
bas ... *one sip*!' I had a vision of my forcing the stuff
down the professor's throat, every last drop.

'What *is* this?' the other said. 'How did you get it?'

'My friend Ghulam Hussain made this, made it himself.'

'Ah, that Bengali servant of yours, who came some
time ago?'

I was stunned, unconsciously tilting the bottle in my
hand, and some liquor spilled on the floor. 'Aai-hai. Let
me clean that.' I got the toilet roll from the bathroom
and started swiping. Bent on the floor, these men standing
over me, I asked, 'How did you know he is Bengali?'

'Oh, brigadier sahib's khansama, what is his name,
the boy?'

'Sajid.'

'Yes, *Sajid*. He told us.'

I stopped swiping but remained kneeling. 'Sajid told
you,' I said softly. 'Okay.' I stood up and threw the wet
roll into the bin. 'Yes, he's an ...' I wanted to say
'enterprising' but it was too clunky an English word, too
English an English word to put in an Urdu sentence, so
the word I happened on was 'chalaak', devious, not at
all what I meant. 'Very chalaak, Ghulam Hussain. He
used to make omelettes for his friends in this begum's
back garden. Taking money from each of them, stealing
eggs from the begum. Now he does this.' I wanted to
take back the 'chalaak'—three other less damning words
came to me now, but it was too late. The word was out
there, spreading like acid. Very chalaak, my friend
Ghulam Hussain.

'They are all chalaak,' Khwaja sahib remarked. 'But
we've been meaning to ask you about that, sir. This, that
Bengali man, what does he *do*?'

I explained the obvious, that he was a driver, a moonshine maker, a grassroots entrepreneur.

'No, but what does he do for *you*?'

'Whatever I need. Driving, mostly.'

'Achha, that is why you were giving him money?'

'No, I was giving him money . . .' What good was this information to them, and what right had they to ask me? Why should I tell them? These, after all, were likely Hammad sahib's killers, and what they wanted with my friend I had no idea. And yet, I was asked a question and felt obliged. These were the men who were going to get our orchard back. 'For some other work, his own work.'

'Achha, you don't ask him what he needs the money for?'

I said, spilling terribly these honest answers, 'He's going back to East Pakistan to find a solution to . . . some problem.'

They looked at each other knowingly, privately. 'Now, sir,' the professor said after a time. 'We must take ijaazat from you now.' 'Ijaazat' was another of my favourite words—literally, 'permission'. The idea of servitude ran deep in the language. I loved it, and didn't want to grant ijaazat to them.

'We haven't talked much,' I said.

'But we'll meet again, inshallah.'

'Inshallah,' I repeated. 'Are you coming back to stay here, again, some time soon?'

'Let's see.'

'I move around a lot. I may not be here when you return, so this is the last chance for . . .'

'Nahin, nahin, sir!' Khwaja sahib responded, bursting with spit and laughter and a stench that came from deep

within. 'Now, we are brothers. True brothers.' He put
his arm around my shoulder, his free hand to my chest.
His thin white kameez had permanent yellow patches at
the armpits. 'You live, where, in Paris? Our journeys,
too, may take us to Paris, who knows? Hain na?' Those
tiny pupils strayed momentarily, ricocheting around the
eyeball. He looked at the professor, who reinforced him
with a nod and a 'bilkul'. 'Yes, who knows what the
future will be.' He tapped my chest once and again
stationed his fingers against it. 'We will come to Paris
and come see you. And your father, of course. We must
pay our respects to your father. And next time you're
here, you come to Punjab! Haan?' To this the professor,
listening attentively to our exchange, got excited, tilting
his head from side to side, saying, 'Yes, yes, to Punjab
you come! We'll show you *our* home. Very different
from here.'

The larger man took over again. 'Karachi is nice, yes,
it's all right, but Punjab—if you haven't been to Punjab
you haven't been to Pakistan. Right or wrong? So the
meaning is, our talook—you understand "talook", na?—
our ... *connection* is very strong.' On the English
'connection', he again tapped my chest. Two uncles
explaining to a young one that they would soon visit
him again. I could feel the sweat from his other arm
collect around my collar. I played my part, nodding
disappointedly, and finally conceding, face downcast,
with a quiet 'Theek hai'. The Khwaja smiled the uncle's
smile. 'Now we take ijaazat?'

'Ji, please,' I said. And they were off, back to their
rooms to pack.

I screwed the top back tightly on Ghulam Hussain's
bottle, wiped the streak that was still on the outside, and
returned it to its place in the drawer.

The next day they left the brigadier's. Their stay complete, their missions done. Hammad sahib in his grave. Myself in their debt. A job well done, even beyond expectation. They sat on the white cast-iron table in the front lawn, with the brigadier. It was noon, and the sunlight sat like a brick in the garden. Sajid took their suitcases to the white van that had come for them. He then brought the ivory trunk out. 'Very careful, bachai!' Khwaja sahib called. He was sitting legs crossed, the raised foot again bare; leaning forward, he held it in one hand, a finger pressed through each gap between the toes. The toes, with black deposits in the nails, stretched out and contracted in, over and over.

'Here, take my seat,' the brigadier said, standing up. 'It's too bloody hot.' He repeated the remark in Urdu for the Jamaatis, adding that, okay ji, they'd meet soon. The departing guests stood, hugged the host goodbye, thanking him, the brigadier replying that there was nothing to thank him for, they'd come for such a short time. They sat back down, now facing me, in the brigadier's seat. The professor lit a cigarette.

'Do classes start soon?' I asked.

Blowing out smoke from his cigarette, and always giggling a little, he replied, 'There's still some time. Students are enjoying their break.'

'Travelling, I'm sure,' I said. Once more I had the sense that I could have liked this man. At a different moment in the nation's life. But times were what they were. And people like the professor had chosen their sides and been designated their roles. A professor at Punjab University, a member of the Jamaat-i-Islami, had his.

At Aunty Ruby's appearance, the men stood again,

and the professor flicked his cigarette into a bush. Sajid
had brought the last of the bags to the van. It was time.
The hostess politely saw them to the gate. I followed
behind her, both of us with our hands behind our backs
and our heads pointed down, the posture of prolonged
farewell, strips of sweat on all of our foreheads. Both the
men bowed to Aunty Ruby and raised a hand to the
forehead, like the gesture of adaab, and Aunty Ruby
smiled and returned the gesture, accompanied by a soft
'Khuda hafiz'. I gave each man a one-sided hug, and
each of them, as they then shook my hand, smiled that
flat smile of secret fellowship: our work continues.
'Meeting will happen again, soon.' I stayed out in the
driveway a little longer than Aunty Ruby, after the
guests' departure, pensive, isolated.

While the downstairs was quiet, I visited the room
down the hall, which was still open and not yet cleared
and cleaned. The green plastic closet was unzipped on
one side, full of naked hangers. The beds had already
been pushed back together and lay bare. There was a
strong smell of cigarettes and sweat. And there had to be
something else, too, some scrap of evidence of what all
had taken place while they were here, the designs for the
end of Hammad sahib's life, *something* they'd either
forgotten or didn't find necessary to discard because
they were after all on friendly soil. No, no, I said again,
not the brigadier. And, anyhow, I found nothing. The
drawers, closets, cabinets were locked or empty. They'd
vacated as wholly as they'd occupied.

I was depressed for hours. Now that they were gone
our agreement was truly irreversible. After dinner, which
I ate alone at the dining table, I walked halfway up the
stairs behind the kitchen. The light in Sajid's quarters

was still on, so I came back down. Sajid was harmless, but still I preferred his light to be off, for him to at least be lying down, when I smoked hash on the roof. I waited upstairs, talking to Apa until she lay on her side and closed her eyes. She was soothing to listen to when I was depressed, talking this evening about a brother's grandson losing his job and getting a 'golden shake-hand', English words she pronounced with such care it seemed they might explode in her mouth, followed by a treatise of how the world was moving forward, how today they set you up for life when they fired you, how Islamic it was. I fingered the hash in my pocket, and couldn't wait until that exquisite smell was released. With Apa putting her head to the pillow at last, I tore a newspaper from her pile and, sitting beside the balcony door, emptied a cigarette onto it.

Upstairs, Sajid's room was finally dark. He lay on his back on a charpoy he'd brought out. He'd started sleeping in the open air. He smiled and said, 'Sir,' half getting up before I told him not to worry, to relax. I felt like telling him to sleep in his room. I climbed the short steps to the rooftop's second level. The sky was black and vacant, waiting to be filled again by morning. The Western wing was perfectly quiet. Over there, eastward, behind a thousand Indian miles, were the curfews, the killings, the riots, the rebels. I squatted, placed the newspaper with the tobacco on the ground, then burned the hash. Ah, that smell! Even as I mixed it in with the tobacco I was impatient to start smoking. And I welcomed the sharp waves when they finally went down my throat and crashed in my chest. I took successive deep puffs.

The gate made its heavy metallic sounds, shrieking on the cement. From the roof, I saw the headlights ignite

against the black gate, which soon parted as the driver
came through, latched each end to the driveway, then
got back in the car and drove it through, turned the
headlights and the engine off. He got out and opened
the rear door on the driver's side. Aunty Ruby stepped
out. Her husband shambled out of the other door,
supported himself for a moment against the second car
that was parked in the driveway. The gates shrieked
again as the driver sealed the residence for the night.
Aunty Ruby waited for the brigadier to come to her side,
and when he did she held him by the elbow and urged
him towards the house. He followed her for a step, but
said, 'Wait,' and turned back towards the garden,
stumbling, working at his zip, and I knew what was
coming. I'd seen this before. 'Oh, God,' Aunty Ruby
gasped. And soon enough, the sounds rose of the trickle,
then a stronger stream, against leaves and flowers and
the boundary wall. 'Alamgir, aap kya kartain hain,
really!' Aunty Ruby wailed. The poor driver stood by,
not knowing what to do, the brigadier's penis exposed.
'Tum jao,' Aunty Ruby commanded, and the driver
bowed and bid her khuda hafiz, then walked humbly
away towards the downstairs quarters. When the stream
subsided back to a trickle, and then dwindled to nothing,
and the brigadier tried to zip his pants, he lost his
footing and fell laughing to the ground. Aunty Ruby had
more angry words; from here they sounded almost like
promises of punishment to a wayward child. And she
bounded vengefully into the house. The doorlock
downstairs clicked, the bolt squeaked: she was locking
him out.

Paris suppressed my anger. That's the best explanation I have. I have countless recollections of French women unhappy with the service in a bistro, in a grocery store, even with a policeman, and shouting at the top of their lungs. As darker-skinned immigrants, neither my father nor I could afford such reactions. Whatever injustice we felt, we accepted. My father played his part, too. Despite meagre attempts at establishing codes of conduct like the ban on birthday cakes, in his eyes a Western celebration, under my father I never developed a clear idea of transgression. He was probably too tired to set rules by then, the failure of his Communist coup having so wasted him. But how could *I* build anything without a sense of transgression, where the one vague rule was to not be too much like the people around us? He placed all the emphasis on language and eloquence. And when he realized that my Urdu would be lost in Paris, he began to stress the French language. It was how we gained power, moved forward, under the British, my father loved to explain, regrettable but true, my boy. Now, with the same lament, he urged me to master French. Grammar, vocabulary, pronunciation: he fed all this to me like the medications to treat a cancer that at the same time made the cancer stronger and my self weaker. English and French moved me further away from Pakistan, and still he'd make sure I was speaking it right, correcting my slang, any unconscious slips the way Apa now corrected my Urdu. My language became my way to his approval and, eventually, his admiration, for at times I surpassed even him in my reading and writing and everyday speech. His friends would call me 'such a well-spoken boy', and later one with 'an unusual command of language'. But with this unusual command came much damage to my relations with the people around me. Now, on this rooftop, I felt something change, the life protected by good language slip away. I'd thrown in my lot with the deviant ones, at the top of the chain. Violent men, their world of force. Rahim sahib, the good-natured policeman, wasn't high and crooked enough. *These* men, my new friends, didn't have to salute to anyone, their outfit didn't have a salute; only a nod, or a half-hug, or a two-handed handshake, gestures with more subtle and open-ended meanings. Would the orchard ever be safe? Would those squatters come back in bigger numbers, armed to the teeth and calling for vengeance? Would we always need the Jamaatis and their violent goons nearby? If we ever wanted to spend a week in the spring in the orchard, sleeping outside, would we have to sleep with one eye open, or with guards at the gates, watching for the former residents? Would my Little Chief one day grow up to take revenge, seek me out and put a knife to my throat? What-oh-what had I started?

～

I unlocked the door, lowered the bolt. The Karachi late-night air smarted like neat whisky in the throat. I was barefoot, and the paved ground rose to the bones and joints of my toes. I felt the garden's cold sweat on my feet, along with faint vibrations, the earth's muscles and tissues rebuilding for tomorrow. Patches of mud beneath the grass stuck to my feet; in my narcotic state this contact felt overwhelmingly sensual. The brigadier, his back to the house, lay in the same spot where Aunty Ruby had left him. I turned him on his back. His eyelids were open just enough to reveal the dead white at the bottom of his eyes. His mouth showed the vestige of a smile. I pulled him up by the lapels, then slipped my hands behind his back. We were frozen in this pathetic embrace for several moments while I thought of what to do next. His pants were buttoned, he'd merely pulled down the zip, and I tried not to look at the thing wilting out. Finally confident of my footing on this shaky ground, I stood, pulling my host up with me. The brigadier put one arm around my shoulder and searched the grass for his own footing. Painstakingly, we made it inside. The staircase was endless, and I spent an eternity with the brigadier's weight and dead Royal Salute breath. He gained a little more footing once we climbed the steps, and I decided to take him no further than the seats on the landing. I stretched him out on the chaise longue, across from the open balcony. I thought of drawing the curtains of the balcony, but the air coming through would do the drunk man good. As I placed him on his back, and made to leave him, he held the back of my neck and pressed my face down to his shoulder. I didn't resist. My nose glued to the top of his lapel, the fragrance of his cologne suffocating me, he tapped the back of my head three or four times, gave me a long kiss on the cheek. His eyes were were still gently shut, his head cocked back, and still that vestige of a smile on a red swollen face. He looked as if he was trying to remember some wonderful detail of a story. 'Sleep,' I said softly. And I left the brigadier there, his zipper undone and his penis exposed, ten feet away from his ninety-three-year-old aunt. I came back to the downstairs that was all mine again. But the ghost of the two Jamaatis seemed to be roving the corridor, following me to my room and dawdling behind the door once I closed and locked it and lay down to sleep.

PART FOUR

The Big Picture

1

Dearest Shahbaz,
  I was most pleased and proud to hear of the success of your efforts with our old family orchard. By the grace of God, we now finally have it back the way it always was. I was also most happy to hear that your Mona Phuppi is not going to cause problems. Do go and see her. I do sometimes wish our relationship was better, but I trust there will now be better times ahead. I am also looking most forward to having you in Paris again. It has, indeed, been a long time, although I am sure you have learned much in your time there, your home country, after all.

The news about East Pakistan is just too awful. I am sure that you have heard about the armless boy who they almost shot because he wouldn't raise his hands. It seems the army has become an insatiable beast out there, but we can talk more about these things upon your return. For the time being I eagerly await your return. Please convey my warm regards to Alamgir. He has been too kind having you stay all this time.

  Much love,
  Abba

I was putting my father's letter back into its envelope when my door was gently pushed open and the brigadier's disembodied face squeezed into eight inches of space.

'Adaab.'

'Haan, haan, jeetairaho.' He peered inside like a clown.

'Please,' I said, gesturing him in, although I wasn't wearing a shirt.

He came tentatively. He wore a long white shirt that he hadn't tucked in and his cheeks were unshaven. 'Thought I'd break my summer isolation. I feel I haven't been downstairs in weeks.' He hated the heat more than anyone I'd met. 'Oh, it's too depressing,' he said. 'I stay on the mezzanine in my dressing gown like a dying man. I can't do a damn thing. But I thought I'd, you know ...' The grey bristles made him look shabby but handsome. This was the first time he'd been in my room, and he moved slowly. He looked around as if discovering the room for the first time, seemed surprised to find a picture of himself framed and placed on a shelf, the one in which he was by a mountain with two friends and his hair whisked to the left. The shirts he'd given me were hanging in the open closet. I should be sure to take them to Paris when I returned, he said.

'Really?' I replied. 'I wouldn't want to—'

'Haan, haan, take them, bhai.' His voice had that bouncy irritation to it. 'You think *I* have any use for them?' He passed his hands down on either side of his torso and then tapped his belly, imploring me to look more closely at what exactly we were talking about. Good, I thought. I liked these shirts and looked forward to walking around Paris in them, sleeves rolled up, the top couple of buttons undone the way Malika had taught me. The brigadier sat down on the bed next to me. He took my father's letter out of the envelope, shook his head while reading. 'Oh, Ghazanfar! So ceremonious even to his own son. I don't know what the hell did it to him. Do *you*? We were at Christian Forman College together, you know that right? Oh yes. And every day the Father would come in,' the brigadier stood up, 'he would stand at the front of the class, say, "In the name of the Father, the Son, the Holy Spirit, Ghazanfar Aslam get out."' The brigadier crossed himself as he said this, and then exploded into hysterics, his hands on his knees. 'He was a rascal, your father. And then . . .'

'And then they threw him out of the whole bloody country,' I added.

He sat back down, put his hand on my knee, the same hand that must have been placed on Malika's knee, Malika's thigh, a thousand times. 'You think that's what did it to him? No, no, the rascal in him disappeared even before that.'

'My mother's death, perhaps?'

He folded the letter and hastily jammed it back in the envelope. 'Maybe. Maybe it was your mother's death. You think so, eh? But hell, you were too young to remember that! If that's when it happened then you really didn't know the old Ghazanfar at all.' We both quietly pondered the thought. My host grimaced and sighed at a memory. 'You know, he once brought this chap, this gardener fellow, to this mango orchard of yours. Have you heard this story? A gardener for the orchard, you know, to sort the grass, plant stuff, kind-of-thing. The chap had a long grey beard, thick, to here. Your father, he was a real prankster in those days. The artist in him was far stronger. So he saw this chap, big grey beard to here, and he told him, "You know, you look like a pir." You know what a pir is, right? Spiritual leader, blah blah blah, theek hai na? So he said, "You look like a pir." The chap, this gardener was embarrassed of course—nahin sir, nahin sir, giggling like a little baccha. But Ghazanfar said, *"You don't believe me? Okay.* You get that charpoy from over there." So the fellow goes, brings the charpoy, puts it down, stares at your father. Ghazanfar tells him, "Sit in it. No, not like that, sit *up,* and cross your legs under you." So the gardener, a complete fool, does as he's told, with his big grey beard lying all over his belly. "Don't move," your father says. Then he goes and calls someone in from outside, from the market or somewhere, brings him to the centre of the orchard where that goon waits on the charpoy, as he's told, his legs under his ass, hasn't budged an inch. And Ghazanfar tells the man, "This is a pir." . . . And before you know it, everyone in town is coming to the orchard to visit this pir, throwing money at him, communing with the Almighty through him. The man, this bugger with the big grey beard, is getting more money in a week than he's ever made as a gardener in his whole life. Your father watches, inside he's going hysterical, this is all his work, a masterpiece, better than any of his films. Then finally he's had his fun, it's gone on for maybe, say a week, he tells the man, "Okay, the fun's over. Now do your gardening." And the man, sitting in that same position, probably couldn't move even if he wanted to, says, "No! I am a pir." Ha ha ha! *Very* matter-of-factly, "I am a pir now. I can't move. The people depend on me." Your father had to threaten him with a lynching to finally convince him. I think by then the man was so stiff they had to lift him off the charpoy and carry him out of the property.'

'That's outrageous,' I said.

'Isn't it?'

I couldn't imagine my father showing the enterprise or humour, the sense of the erratic.

'Should I tell you an incident that often used to come to *my* mind?' I said. 'I think it was shortly after we'd moved to Paris, someone in the Pakistani embassy had had a baby, whom we went to see. When the baby started smiling, and I asked my father what he thought the baby was smiling at, he said, "Nothing. That's not a smile. It's just a contortion of muscles." Even at age ten, I thought this was such a sad remark—much like his films, which were all so melancholic, the work of a sad and uninspired man. I don't know how you all thought his work was so splendid.'

The brigadier was nodding, conceding, refusing to defend his old friend. I took the envelope from him, opened the drawer and threw it in.

'Ah! Ha ha!' He reached over me and grabbed one of the bottles. 'So *these* are the famous bottles!' He held the bottle up and tapped a sharp perfect white nail to it. 'Your friend the Bong.'

'You know about him?'

'Those chaps were telling me about him. The ones who were here some weeks ago.'

'The Jamaatis?'

'A bit of a nutter, hain na? This Bong fellow. Not all there.' He pointed towards his head.

'Well . . . one of the herd, I suppose, no different than any of the—'

He turned the bottle over and over in his hand. 'His little radio on him. Talking about the army operations in the East.'

'How would anyone know what Ghulam Hussain listens to on his radio?'

'You know, those Western services—they're all controlled by the imperialists. The . . . what did we call them?'

'Ice Niggers.'

'*Ice* Niggers! Precisely right. All they really want is to rule us again. So they'll say in their broadcasts, "Haan, haan, the West Pakistanis are killing the East Pakistanis, they're all beasts, see what happens when they rule themselves?" It's easy to get caught up in all that and miss . . . the big picture.' The brigadier looked down at the bottle. 'But this is what I wanted to talk to you about, beta. Apparently he's been talking a little crazy. About the Mukti Bahini, raising money for them, going through India—'

'*Been* talking? How would you know—that's absurd! He doesn't really care all that much about politics, not anymore. He's told me himself. How could those Jamaatis—those gentlemen—know? They saw him from the balcony, that's it!'

'Sajid told them. He's going back to East Pakistan and he's taking money from you.'

'*Sajid*? No, no,' I insisted. 'He's going back East because of a problem with his father-in-law. The mad bastard wants his daughter, Ghulam Hussain's wife, to marry someone else, and Ghulam Hussain just—anyhow, if you talked to him, you'd know. In one minute he'll set your heart at ease. To Sajid—I doubt he said it. Or maybe he's just playing big. These people, they do that you know, like to appear dangerous. But if you met him you'd see, a sweet, sweet man.'

'Hmm, hmm,' the brigadier murmured, absently,

unpersuaded. 'You know, they—people like this fellow—
they need to hear the *full* story. Not just what the BBC
tells them. You know, this country . . .' He went quiet,
almost sad. 'Sometimes we *ourselves* miss the big picture.
So a fellow like this, this Bong—'

'I assure you his rioting days are over. Let alone
joining an *armed* movement.'

'I'd like you to keep a close watch over him.' This
remark was contemptible, and yet I can't deny there was
something filial, fatherly about it, an expression of trust.

'I'll keep an eye on him,' I said, nodding credibly.

'And be careful how much money you give him.'

Did my host have any right to make these demands?
In a way, yes he did. 'Oh, I barely have enough for
myself, so . . .'

'Hmm, hmm,' he said, putting his cold, sickly smooth
hand on my bare shoulder. He was looking down at the
bottle, turning it again. 'The Acacia tree, huh?'

'That's what Rahim sahib told me the first time I went
to see him. That's what these people in the interior do,
make it from the bark.'

He shook his head. 'This really is something. How is
it, have you tasted it?'

'No, no,' I said. 'God knows how they make it, what
they put in it. My stomach would probably just . . .'

'Quite right, quite right. You shouldn't. This is
dangerous stuff. God knows who that rotter is selling it
to. A dangerous enterprise. He should be very careful.'

'Well, it's not an enterprise I expect to last. That's
how it is with these people. That's how it is with my
friend. He'll have one money-making scheme going,
that'll end for some reason or other, he'll start a new
one, and so on.' Even to my ears, it sounded absurd

calling him my friend to the brigadier. But this whole
project was strange, discussing and explaining Ghulam
Hussain in this room, in this house. Two worlds forced
abnormally together, there were bound to be errors.
'Anyhow . . . as you say, I'll be sure to keep an eye on
him, make sure he . . .' The brigadier was still looking at
the bottle, then began nodding, absent-mindedly at first
but with more concentration as the nods became tighter.

'Bring him in here,' he said, non-threateningly. 'We'll
have a chat with him here, in this room.' *We?*

'You . . . want to see him?' My voice was wearing thin
and failing me.

'Just a chat.' He spoke softly, as if to sneak the remark
through, unnoticed. I looked at him, and he turned his
face to me, those sharp hazel eyes meeting mine with
stony tenacity. They wanted what they wanted. The grey
bristles, the paleness of a usually red face now seemed
symptoms not of the heat, but of a burden equal to
Rahim sahib's, people doing what they had to do. He
wanted to talk to Ghulam Hussain himself. The silence
made that perfectly clear. How do you deny a man who
has won you so much? His hand was on my shoulder
again, the long white nails in the corner of my vision.
'Look,' he said, sharply now. 'Don't think I'm thrilled
with what's going on at the moment. You think I liked
what happened to Hammad bhaiyya? Sure, the Bongs
have their rights, but democracy . . .' His tone on this
word was a mix of condescension and disappointment
and exhaustion. 'One has to be . . . *responsible*. These
people are *ir*-responsible. Times being what they are . . .'

'Which is?' I said, prepared to argue.

'*Delicate*. Very, very *delicate*. You've been in the West
for some time now.' (How does one argue against *that*

one?) 'You don't *realize*, you don't see the bigger picture. You think shifts in power are brought about by ballots and polls and primaries and what-have-you. Here they're not. It's still the twelfth century. Birth, death, marriages, wars, *they're* the things that move politics. The Pir who got those haris off your land, he doesn't have that power because somebody voted for him.' I liked the sound when he said 'your land', a beautiful sound. 'And the power you have now because that land is yours again— it's not through some intellectual argument. Dear boy, you can't skip your way from the twelfth to the twentieth century. These things take time. And your fat little friend that you're protecting—'

'I'm not protecting anyone.'

'You think we would have been able to get you your property if your fat friend got his way? Why are you here, what's the point of doing all that you've done for your family, if you're going to go on protecting the one who wants to end the whole story?'

I held my head back and laughed. 'Surely, a man like Ghulam Hussain isn't—'

'I know, I know, beta.' His hand moved to my back. I felt the sweat on it. 'He's full of passion, I'm sure, and it can be very appealing to someone like you who's spent most of his time away. But the story must go on. Our nation's story.'

'The story must go on,' I repeated, in a whisper.

'Then give him a call. The chap needs money from you, isn't it? So tell him to come pick up the money. Have Sajid bring him in here. You and I can have a quiet chat with him. See what his views really are about the Mukti Bahini. I'd like you to do this for me.' Again, crisp, quiet words. It was the eyes, those razor-like hazel eyes, that did the work. And then he smiled his charming scoundrel smile, which brought the blood back to his face and made the single silver vein in his temple pulse. Enlivened, he squeezed my bare shoulder and stood up. 'If you need Sajid to help you with the packing . . .' He pointed to the room, the clothes, my bags.

'I think I'm fine,' I replied. 'But I'll let him know.'

'Do.' He turned to leave, with the bottle in his hand. He stopped. 'Let me keep this one,' he requested. And I said, of course, because what else could I say?

❧

I walked into a small conference in Ghulam Hussain's quarters. He and his friends had a table in the middle of the room and a bunch of his Bengali friends sat around it with the sobriety of bureaucrats. 'Sorry,' I said. But Ghulam Hussain, the chair of the session, said, 'No, no, matters not, Shahbaz bhai. Sit, please.' He gestured to one of the others to give up his chair, but I interjected to say I'd be fine on the charpoy. I climbed on, sat with my back against the wall, waving off one of the men's offers of his chair. I'd clearly come at a bad time, but I also thought it would be awkward for all of them if I now left. Oh, how I thought that I understood all these delicate things! The conference continued. There was a bottle of their liquor in the middle of the table. One man took a swig from it, passed it on like a hookah. Again, I caught the usual terms and names: Yahya . . . Bhutto . . . Mujib . . . parliament . . . constitution . . . and, yes, the Mukti Bahini, too, this term mentioned repeatedly. If they were talking about the politics of the times, how could they not mention the great rebel force?

And then the most consequential of the lot, the one they pronounced with care verging on horror: Bangladesh. The treacherous-glorious word.

Keep a watch over my friend. Keep a watch.

I half expected that my entrance would have urged them to finish sooner than later, and I became annoyed at the meeting's length, the lack of compromise, the neglect of my presence that was—to be frank—an overture, a good deed.

It was the Wily One with the thin chest and large belly who was talking now. Another fellow, a few seats away, took upon himself the task of debating him. The two faced each other, leaning over the poor man in the middle. Wily One was roaring, his index finger raised and puncturing the air above his head. His opponent retaliated with similar force, and when things were on the verge of breakdown, others intervened by importuning Ghulam Hussain, who remained reflective and silent for a minute before saying, 'Okay, okay,' in Urdu, his face tilted down, arms spread wide in front of him like the wings of a plunging seabird: speakers went silent, peace was restored. Wily One reached forward, grabbed the liquor bottle and took a furious swig. 'Look,' Ghulam Hussain said, and then the incomprehensible words again together with intelligible ones: *army action* . . . *Mukti Bahini* . . . *Bhutto* . . . and I thought I heard the word, 'Jamaat', too, but couldn't be sure. I leaned forward, waiting for another mention. Then, Ghulam Hussain himself became louder and angrier, but slowly, in perfect metre, and he finished with a lyrical thrust of the finger, starting on one side of his big torso and then down an invisible ramp to the other side, before rising again slightly at the end, the motion of a swing. A chairman's gesture. I didn't want to leave, couldn't bring myself to leave. If I couldn't understand the words, what I could translate was the indiscretion and poetry of it, the rises-and-falls, the negotiations and hysterics, angels and demons all on one table. And then, always, the turning to Ghulam Hussain for some kind of verdict. This authority never failed to fill me with happiness and affection and a good amount of pride—yes, I was proud of my friend.

And then the Wily One addressed me.

'Shahbaz sahib!' he cried. He tilted his face sideward to see me through the shoulders of two peers. 'Shahbaz sahib, you know what's happening in this country?' A fair question. 'You know what they're doing over there?' He held up his radio as if the spirits of all the dead were trapped inside it. And then he began. He was angry now, the liquor and words flowed unremittingly, cursing Yahya and Bhutto, proclaiming Mujib's right to rule, what was it with us West Pakistanis and so on and so on. Ghulam Hussain protested in Bengali, told the man to behave, pointing to me with an upturned palm, used the word, 'mehman',—guest—but the man didn't stop, kept talking in the same tone and volume as if not even hearing Ghulam Hussain's interjection, which also continued. This twin dialogue amused me, and I wanted to tell both of them never to stop, the Bengali on one level and Urdu on the other, a national whole. Whatever he was saying about the violence in the East was cut into fragments by Ghulam Hussain's pleading and ferocious rebuke, and I nodded agreeably with each fragment I received, never taking my eyes off him. *Why have elections if we don't want to give power to ... this is what you get for not helping the people after the cyclone*

... *why kill* ... *why send in* ... But then something came out of this miscellany that stopped me. I put my hand on Ghulam Hussain's shoulder to get him to shut up. 'Wait, wait,' I said. I squeezed Ghulam Hussain harder. 'One minute, let him speak.' But Ghulam Hussain kept going as did his friend. 'What did you just say?' I asked my adversary. Neither was listening. Everyone was shouting. 'CHUP KARO!' I grabbed a bottle from the carton on the floor and threw it against the side wall. The shards and liquid and alcohol stench went this way and that. I finally had their attention. My adversary brushed his shoulder. 'Tell me what you just said. You said something about the Jamaat-i-Islami?' They looked at me, stunned, suspicious. 'Bolo!' I shouted. 'I need to know what you just said—you said something about the Jamaat. What do you know about what the Jamaat is doing? Somebody answer me!' Ghulam Hussain located and lifted the bigger shards; the other, my adversary, picked up a cloth. 'Leave that for now,' I said. 'I'll do it myself.' I removed a small piece from next to me and dropped it in the small stack in Ghulam Hussain's hand. 'Have you ever heard the name Hammad Rehman?' I asked Ghulam Hussain, then looked up to give the question to the room. 'Used to write in the newspaper, or something. One of his legs was bad, he couldn't move it? Hammad Rehman. No? Speak! I'm your friend. He was killed in Dhaka, it hasn't been too long. Five, six weeks. Bengali man. One time shot his landlord in the foot, spent a month in jail. *None* of you have heard of him? Who killed him? Do you know?' Wily One had started mopping, bent carefully over the floor. 'I'll do it myself, just first answer me.' Ghulam Hussain, also clearing the mess, told everyone, my adversary in particular, to leave the quarter.

News travelled in a city like this, servant to servant. Just as Sajid reported to the Jamaatis, did he also tell Ghulam Hussain about *them*, that they were staying in the house, that the Jamaatis and I had little meetings in our rooms? Was Ghulam Hussain actually warning his friend just now against saying too much in my presence? 'Chhoro, chhoro,' Ghulam Hussain said to the other man, taking the cloth from him and then telling him again to leave the room, which after breathing a curse he finally did. Nothing more was said, everyone seemed exhausted. Ghulam Hussain spotted a piece right next to my foot, and told me not to move.

∽

He accepted the money with an indifference that bothered me. Two hundred rupees was no small sum. But Ghulam Hussain looked at the notes in my hand and took them glumly as if it was less than the agreed amount.

'This *is* what you wanted, right?' He tilted his head in acceptance. He seemed still preoccupied by the pieces of glass. Or perhaps he thought me careless for giving him money where the others could see. Perhaps I was meant to slip the notes through his puffy fingers the way one bribes a cop, secretly. 'Do you need more?' I said softly. 'I can get you more with more time.' We were sitting on the charpoy, now the only ones in the room, the others gathered outside.

'Nahin, nahin, Shahbaz bhai,' he responded, now with a little life.

'Good. Now let's smoke some charas.' I could tell he didn't want to, but I insisted. The dope wasn't for me. It was for him. My friend was sad and I wanted his spirits lifted. A drink may have been more appropriate, but Ghulam Hussain and I never drank together. We could smoke as many joints as we wanted, but never alcohol. So, hash was all we had, but two joints today seemed only to deepen his despair. He was quieter than I'd ever seen him. My friend was sad and that made me sad. Sad and angry that he wasn't sharing his sadness with me. I put my hand on his enormous pulsing shoulder. In the summer, his breathing was heavy and audible. 'Is it because they are beating-killing Bengalis?' I asked. In Urdu the same word could be used for beating and killing, and the ambiguity was useful. 'Is that the reason you are a little . . .?'

'I'm fine Shahbaz bhai. Why are you so worried?' He smiled and laughed, unconvincingly, the energy still drained from his face and his voice. A patch of sweat shaped like a giant egg covered most of his back. 'I'll be going back in two days. Back to East Pakistan.' He explained his route, through India, naming districts or provinces I only vaguely recognized. I asked him when he'd return to this side. 'God's will,' he said, twirling his wrist and his fingers, as if unscrewing a bulb, a tragic little gesture. What would he do over there, I asked. Once his family issues were sorted. His lack of a proper answer annoyed and angered me. I had responsibilities here. I sensed now to my surprise that if he was deceiving me I wasn't going to take it well. But the third-degree interrogation was beyond my level of Urdu.

'Ghulam Hussain, tell me. Have you ever thought of fighting back?'

'Fighting back, sir?'

'Over there. In East Pakistan.'

'*How* to fight back, Shahbaz bhai?'

'Mukti Bahini.'

Looking away, he laughed an embarrassed out-of-breath laugh. The name definitely had an impression on him. I thought again: was the story about his wife and her father and this other man her father wanted her to marry all a lie?

'Why are you looking over there? Look at *me*, bhai,' I said. He did so with great reluctance, looking down, laughing nervously again, before raising his eyes to mine—only momentarily before looking elsewhere, picking little particles of glass from the mattress and then trying to remove them from his fat fingers.

'What will the Mukti Bahini do, Shahbaz bhai?' He was still gazing and picking at his palm, as if reading his own future.

'So you're saying there is no purpose in joining with them?'

'Join them and then what, Shahbaz bhai?' His voice was full of pity and understanding, as if he was trying to get *me* to see the error of it all. But, still, no clear answer.

'Okay, okay,' I said, nodding. 'But you are sad, Ghulam Hussain.' I put my hand on his burning shoulder again. 'Ghulam Hussain, this is not a matter of honour. You and me, we are brothers. So you tell me!' My voice hardened. 'What is the matter?' The poor should never have to explain themselves to the rich. Because in that exchange is something deeper, a promise from the rich, an obligation to whatever comes bursting out when the poor man finally does give in and speaks. Otherwise, it's simply an interrogation, a form of torture. Oh, my friend, don't speak! Don't speak if you don't want to.

'Shahbaz bhai,' he finally said. 'A man gets bored. Bored in life.'

I was prepared, eager to listen. I don't know if the thought that he had been misleading me, that I had been as naïve as the brigadier suggested, made me angry. Perhaps it did. And so the time, the crime, was nearing. Step by step, word by spoken word. 'Ghulam Hussain. I want to talk to you, I want us to discuss this, this . . .' I searched for the Urdu word. 'These *issues*.' I used the English word. 'But not here, not in these quarters. I want you to come to me, where I'm staying.' He was confused, my poor friend. 'I've never invited you inside. I come to you, but I've never asked you to come inside to my place. Now I want you to. This is a time when we need to come together, talk to each other. Do you want that? Will you come?'

Will you come? The words still oppress me. Was I inviting him because I felt confident that he was in the clear, a civilian through and through to put the brigadier's mind at ease, or was it the reverse, was I *not* entirely sure, feeling it was indeed incumbent on me to *be* sure. Because if Ghulam Hussain was mixed in something that was going to hurt him, land him in trouble, shouldn't I . . . These questions are of no use. I was betraying my friend. It is time finally to face it. How careless, callous I'd been. How dangerous a game and at what a time! Yes, I did as the brigadier asked. I gave him a day and a time, and promptly informed my host, from whom the instructions came.

2

I wasn't there when Ghulam Hussain came. After that talk with him, I escaped to see family. It had its uses, my family. The saline smell warned of high tide. It came with the breeze through the windows, which were open but taped over with newspaper, all three of them. When Mona Phuppi's servant brought me my fresh-lime-and-Seven-Up, I pointed to them. 'Why is there newspaper?'

She smiled, hesitated. 'Those, sir ... those windows are broken.'

'Broken? How?' She giggled. 'Tell me, bhai!'

'Sir ji, begum sahib got angry and she broke the windows.'

'With *what*?'

'Sir ji, the broom, the stick to clean? With that, she broke the windows.'

'Why did she get angry?'

The poor fool, I was asking for too much. 'Sir, what do I know?' The servant's thing, the plea of ignorance. I relieved her, she bowed and left. I went to the window and unpeeled one corner of the newspaper: a big hole, like an astonished mouth, right at the centre, surrounded by wrinkles in the glass shooting out toward the corners. I pressed the newspaper corner back to the sill. All three windows, just like this? What a vision it must have been! It couldn't have been quick, in just a moment of rage. These windows hadn't just been cracked, but hollowed out, which would have required repeated beating. I imagined it, Mona Phuppi taking the broom to a window over and over, then satisfied that she'd done enough demolition, moved on to the next. And then the next. And then the next. This woman really did what she had to do. I respected that.

Trailing the sound of her slippers, my aunt appeared in an aqua dressing gown. Her face looked a litte pale and swollen. She was holding a dark green Koran in her hand. She smiled, held my face on one side as she replied, 'Jeetairaho,' to my adaab. She sat with her back to the broken windows, the holy book on her lap.

'Well!' she exclaimed. As the servant returned Mona Phuppi told her to bring her a cigarette. 'I phoned the DC in Mirpurkhas. He says it's true. They're all gone.' All gone! 'Hard to believe. God knows how that happened. But it *has* happened. Whatever you did, I suppose you must have done *some*thing right.'

'Yes,' I said, more to myself than to her. 'I did something right.' I took a sip to kill the dryness in my mouth. 'Does this mean you're going to stop trying to sell it?' I glanced again at the windows covered in newspaper, quickly set my eyes back on Mona Phuppi, like trying to avoid staring at a bad scar.

'To tell the truth, I really didn't think this would come through,' she said.

I relished the taste of my dirty victory, even if something of it made me sick in the gut. And I was tempted to tell

her exactly *how* I had won. The girl brought her a
cigarette and matches. My aunt's hand shook like a
drunk's when she raised the flame to her cigarette. 'So
you leave soon, this means? We'll miss you. Got used to
having you here. Spend a night with us before you
leave.'

Yes, I assured her I would. We talked about seeing
more of each other in the future, on my next stay,
paying visits to the orchard together. We talked about
my father and his artistic endeavours, about whether we
thought he'd ever finally come back if the civilians
formed a proper government after these troubles between
East and West were settled. 'We've hardly seen you in
this time. I should give Alamgir a gift, or a note,
thanking him for having you for so long.' What a
strange thought, that *she* was the one ultimately
responsible for me, that the brigadier had done *her* a
favour. 'He sent us an invitation to a mushaira at his
place next week, so kind of him. Oof, his father! Used
to have wonderful wonderful mushairas, you know the
best poets in the country, in the old days and oh, such
lovely evenings we used to have there!'

We were silent for some time. My beverage was
finished, but nervously I kept sipping at the drops of
melting ice. Mona Phuppi got up and sat next to me, the
side her thigh touching mine. She looked towards the
broken windows, and slowly back at me. She smiled,
sweetly, almost in defeat. 'You know, beta, I'm sure
you've heard that I am mad. You have, haven't you? But
if I'm mad it's your phuppa and his family who've made
me mad. Even your father. But no-no, don't look so
alarmed. I'm not about to go off into a rant. I'm not
going to tell you how the whole world is against me. It

is, but, khair, that's not the point. I have Allah. I have this.' She lifted the Koran. 'You wouldn't know, of course, you've never prayed a day in your life. I know this Book means nothing to you.' She ashed her cigarette and put it out. 'You know. Your father once said that this whole ... *business*, he called it, was a fraud. He said there was nothing wrong with me, that I did it all to win sympathy or ... I don't know, I suppose like some criminal telling a judge he is insane. That's what your father thought I was doing. Other times he would say I'm completely mad, and should not be kept in charge of anything. Abhey, which is it, am I mad or no?'

'Which do you think it is?' I asked.

'There are times when I think I could kill,' she said, matter-of-factly, but then started laughing. 'I never did kill, of course, don't worry. No, I used all that ... *life* in the courts. I went to those bloody courts myself. You know, when I lost the case in the High Court I appealed to the Supreme Court. You know what I did there, did your father ever tell you? I sacked my incompetent lawyer. He was bloody useless. So when the judge said, where's your lawyer, I said *I* am my lawyer. The judges laughed. But I didn't budge an inch. One of them said, you're serious? And I said, do I look like I'm teasing you? And he said, "Begum sahib, you do realize that this is the last place you can go, don't you? If you lose here, that's it, the government has won and you have lost. Now we'll give you extra time if you need it. Find a lawyer, we'll give you time." They were nice men, these judges. But I said, no, I'm fed up of lawyers with their Lincoln's Inn diplomas. *I* am arguing my case. So they said, okay. And the government people on the other side were thrilled, of course, they thought, ahh what an easy one. But I squashed them.' With this, Mona Phuppi raised her palm and clenched her fist, as if the whole government were being squeezed to death in her muscular hand. 'That's why we have this orchard at all. What did your father do? Not much and minus two. If I left it to him . . . good grief. And does your father recognize this? Of course not. Oh, but he'll tell you what Islam says about men and women.' She held the Koran with both hands and again lifted it above her lap. 'What does it say about men who don't do a bloody thing? Who leave it all up to the woman to go to court after court and office after office in the heat?

'You're the only man in this family who has *done* something in this whole business. I don't know *how* you did it, and that doesn't matter. The point is you did do it. You know your mother was part Pathan, her father was from the Frontier, hain na?' I nodded. 'So you have some of that Pathan blood in you. If you were a pure Urdu-speaker, you'd be as useless as Ghazanfar and my deaf husband. It's the Pathan in you,' she pressed her index finger into my chest as she said this, 'that got those squatters out. That's a tribe of warriors, they brought down Alexander the Great. Nothing from your father's genes could be responsible. Me, I have it because I'm mad, after all, isn't it? But what, should I have been deaf instead, deaf like that . . . *man*?' She pointed toward the upstairs of the house. For once, I was disappointed when the azaan sounded, and she stopped to get to the bathroom to wash herself for her prayers. It was true: my grandfather on my mother's side was from the Frontier, something I rarely thought of. My mother died so long ago, and so did her father, that I never considered their blood was still in me. A tribe of warriors. What a lovely detail. I wanted my aunt to talk more about this. I felt another groundswell of warmth for Mona Phuppi, for seeing me in this historical light, planting the seed of what I knew would be a great idea, an idea of me, a descendent of *something*, an inheritor, however far removed, of a great tradition.

When she was done saying her prayers, we said goodbye. She said she'd see me at the mushaira at the brigadier's. She stood in the doorway while Munir brought the car forward. I got in and just before Munir drove away I saw that Mona Phuppi had walked forward and was gesturing to me to wait. I told the driver to brake, and rolled down the window. My aunt placed both hands on the roof of the car, and leaned forward to put her face at the centre of the frame.

'Ji?' I said, smiling.

'Tell me something, bachai. Will you ever be able to sleep there again?'

'Where?'

'The orchard. I mean, even if you fix the place, plant all the beautiful trees you want, build another charming little house like we had before, even if you do *all* of that ... kya, are you going to *forget* these ten-twelve years in between, when those blasted haris sunk their filthy claws into the place? If your wife leaves you and then a little while later wants to come back, only she's been a whore in between'—I was shocked to hear that word from her—'what, do you take her *back*? You think any of us will go back with the same old fondness, take our kids—will you take *your* kids there one day? Will you be able to *sleep* there? To answer your question, bachai, one day we *will* sell that place. Take my word for it. Your father's chasing the impossible. He wants the orchard of the *old days*. That's simply not possible. What we had before is gone and now we have to get the most from it. I'm glad you got those haris out. Now we'll restore it as best we can, and then we'll sell the thing for a *proper* price. You'll have turned us a wonderful little profit, and we'll get this rotten stain out of our family posessions.' She smiled that sick sweet smile, tapped me on the side of the neck, and gestured the driver to carry on. Carry on towards the brigadier's, where an unnatural union, between my friend and my host, was due. I was still shrinking from the prospect of mixing the two. And yet, like my deal with the Jamaatis, I felt I couldn't stop it. I know that this is feeble—I could have called Ghulam Hussain and told him not to come, I could have told the brigadier that I had no idea where the man was, perhaps he'd already gone back to East Pakistan—but, really, I felt I couldn't undo what had been set.

◆

I saw his beige Morris parked outside. Coming home from Mona Phuppi's, about twenty minutes after the time I'd given him. So if he was, say, ten minutes late, as he often was, he'd been in there for ten minutes at that point. Possibly just five. But then again he could have been on time. Which meant he could have been inside for fifteen or twenty minutes. Either way, there was his car outside, and there was another car. Whose car, I've never known, or asked. But there *was* another car, and I knew whoever it was was there for Ghulam Hussain, for the quiet chat that the brigadier described.

As such, I'm not sure to what extent the brigadier himself participated in what happened in there, or even whether what happened, happened *in there*, in the house, in my downstairs room. The point is I never went in. I had Munir turn.

'Turn, sir?'

'Turn. *Now, bhai*!'

❦

Why didn't I go? Nerves, no doubt. But can it be said for certain that I could have changed the outcome? Can a person like me ever change an outcome in the face of something so big, guided by big powerful men, men who wanted what they wanted? It was *their* message, let *them* deliver it. And yet . . . I know that in my absence, I was all the closer to what happened. Nerves, yes: the era required nerves of steel. I went instead to the woman who could soothe mine.

❦

Sweet Malika, dangerous Malika. She could soothe and she could devastate, and that evening she did both. I'd been having the strangest dreams in her room of late. Of myself deep in the orchard, and the ground feels crunchy, brittle shells under my feet like skulls that send a chill through me every time I hear them rupture. From somewhere there is the sound of singing, of women or little boys. And when the Pir's men come, with guns and machettes and blood in their eyes, the squatters scramble immediately for safety or exit as if they knew this was coming, they'd waited for it for years. Some jump over the wall into the semi-urban life outside. Many, of course, do not make it. There's so much chaos that I hope the thugs with the guns know that I'm not a squatter, I'm the one who'll keep this place, the one they're working for. Dreams of those two boys I'd come across when I was there, especially my Little Chief, with his too-short pants, his stick, and the extrovert's authority. Dreams of an ambush, the *Pir*'s army defeated and bled all over the streets on their way back to wherever they came from. Beautiful dreams. Of the brigadier, too, many dreams of the brigadier. And sometimes all these dreams seemed to follow me into the waking world, skulls on the ground, the boys from the orchard, the brigadier's cold white hand on my bare shoulder blade. I was losing my mind. So I don't know if Malika actually whispered it or not. But, after we'd made love and fallen asleep for a little while, and started just barely to come awake again, or at least I started to come awake again, and felt my way towards the springy patch of hair, and then below to her still-damp vagina, I heard her whisper, *Alamgir*. I stopped, moved my face to hers, to listen close.

'Bitch,' I finally said.

Rather than offend, this seemed to excite her. She smiled and droned, *hmm*, in her sleep, reached for my hand and pressed it back to where it was. When I tried removing it, she insisted with a hardened grip, pushing my fingers inside her. 'Oh, never mind,' I huffed, snatched my hand away and turned my back to her. Now, an hour or more later, I turned again to look at Malika's beautiful delicate back, on its side, the silhouette of her ribs, then the curve inward like a sleepy lion's hump. My love, I addressed her in my head, you should give me opium and then just leave me here. Alone. Go downstairs or wherever else you would go, but lock me in, don't let me out. Leave me here with these visions of Little Chief and his little deputy in the short little pants, let them torture me, let them beat me to death on this bed.

Malika had gone back to sleep in anger. I accepted her reasons. She required me to hold up my end of the bargain, whatever the circumstances. When I'd turned on her, she'd reached around my waist, but her magical fingers didn't get the results. To someone for whom sex was a serious affair, mine was a very deep failure. What was more, I now sensed that whatever went on between us was being reported back to the brigadier. I leaned in close again. I shook her, took her hand and slipped it into my underwear. Strange, I found I liked the idea of the brigadier and her, even the idea of being outmatched, even the idea of her speaking his name while I was inside her. Oh, it excited me! 'You want to try again?'

It wasn't our best. And soon after, I left her room. I had other business. Couldn't defer it any longer.

∽

The door to the quarters was held open with a flat brick on the ground. The servants' smell rose toward me. And inside, lying on the mattress, was the man with the wily nose. Just him and no one else. I stood over him, forming a shadow on the shirtless prostrate figure. He opened his eyes, liquid red, rubbed them and sat up.

'What happened?' I asked.

'Sir.' His voice had thinned like blood.

'*What happened?*'

'Police came. They took the bottles.'

I opened the closet. The bottles were all gone. Some kitchenware and small jars of spices remained. That was it. I kneeled down to the man. 'They let you go?'

'Sir, I gave them one thousand rupees so they would not do to me what they did to Ghulam Hussain.'

'What did they do to him?'

'Beat-beat-beat. His head—' he described a kind of injury I didn't quite understand, though the image I conjured was of congealed blood.

'When did they beat him?' He was silent. 'Tell me!'

'When they took me to the station, he was already lying in the lock-up.'

'Which lock-up?' Silence again. 'Who came here?'

'The police, sir.'

'That I know. But what did they look like? Tell me.' He kept rubbing his head, as if his was the head they had bashed. 'Where did they take you?'

'Sir, if you know anyone who can help, please.'

I always enjoyed the polite way of saying 'please' in Urdu: literally, 'there will be pleasure', or 'there will be thankfulness'. I stood still and gazed at this barren room as though trying to revive old spirits. I'd tried to discover their world, simply by coming here, smoking with them. As if experience and manhood and nobility were waiting here to be absorbed. Now I was as far away from that world as ever. What did I know about these people? Why even try? I got up and opened the cupboard again. I reached towards the back to that little space between the bottom shelf and the wall, pulled the plank towards me to pry the gap, then reached down until I felt plastic. They hadn't found this one. What would they have done to Ghulam Hussain if they had? I took the bag out, peaked inside to see that it was still the bottle of whisky with the Chief-of-Army-Staff seal. The man gazed at me and the package in my hands with weak eyes. I wasn't afraid of him. I could take anything in this room that I wanted and he wouldn't do a thing. I nodded and walked out of the quarters, the black plastic bag in my hand. From there I went with my cabbie, as if guided from above, to Lalukhet station, whose jurisdiction didn't cover the brigadier's neighbourhood or this one, but I was certain was where I needed to go.

Rahim sahib received me with more warmth than usual—both the heat of his large body and the embrace that pulled me into it. He was thrilled to see me, but he had the mercy-me look, a once great soul drooping day by day under duty. How many times must he have offered that hard faultless salute today, this week! Even the normally perfect beard had moments of shabbiness along the jawline. The mustachioed kid brought us lassis, salting mine on his own initiative so that it was unfinishable.

'So. Your orchard, I hear, is all done.'

'Yes, bas,' I said, acting humble, 'thankfully—by the grace of God—'

'Mashallah, mashallah!' He gulped, put his glass down and his hand went straight to the hair on his throat. 'You know, I could have done it for you, too, if you had—'

'Oh, I'm sure, I have no doubt of that.' Conciliating the cop, his wounded honour, was a delight, a pure aristocratic delight.

'Just a matter of a few more days, easily, no problem, I would have got it done myself.' His brows, his lips were scrunched, his fingers conjoined at their tips as if to suggest that ridding the orchard of squatters was a negligible bureaucratic procedure.

'I very much know, Rahim sahib. And I wouldn't have had a second thought, it's just as you probably know these men were staying at brigadier sahib's, which is where I'm staying, and one day just in passing I, or brigadier sahib, mentioned, you know . . .'

'*But you're happy, you're satisfied?*' He asked with some force, thrusting both palms forward to say, 'Enough?' 'Because if there's anything you need—'

'I'm enormously grateful, Rahim sahib. Rest assured I will let you know if anything—'

'Oh yes! Anything. I'll do it like this.' He snapped his fingers.

A silent minute passed. I took a polite sip of the salted lassi. 'Oof! oof-oof-oof,' the policeman sighed.

'Busy day?'

'Ji, ji, busy day,' he said, absently.

'Filled the lock-up have you?'

He smiled. 'Kya karain?' What to do. He continued in Urdu. 'Duty, well, must be done, is it or not?'

'This it must, this it must.'

I leaned back and turned my head, as if all his prisoners would be somewhere in the room. 'So where *is* your lock-up?'

'Ah!' He stood up quick, jolted back to life. 'Aiyai, aiyai.' Excited as someone showing off a new home or a new car, kept repeating *aiyai, aiyai, come-come.* I followed him down a yellowing corridor, the wall on both sides occasionally lined with plastic chairs where people sat awaiting justice, now watching me, important man from elsewhere, escorted by the station head. We stepped briefly outside into a courtyard of sorts and then back into another concrete valley. At the end on the left was a turquoise metal door with a rectangular open screen the size of a video cassette, through which one saw a sad cell and its two dozen lodgers. Rahim sahib gestured toward the window, encouraging me to look. He presented the cell like it was a gallery of his artwork. It *was*, in a sense. These people were his output, his vocation, his points of pride. He called out to a subordinate, who appeared in the hallway, and barked for the key. It took time, and Rahim sahib shook his head in agitation as if we were losing the moment. The key came, the door opened, and Rahim sahib ushered me in like a potential buyer. And a diligent one, I went through each piece, man by man, inspecting from a distance, feeling it improper to walk in and inspect them up close (*Please don't touch the prisoners, says the sign. Point to the one you like*). So, one by one, prisoner by prisoner, my eyes scoped.

'It's too hot!' the policeman said. 'I need my fan.'

'Oh yes, by all means. I just wanted to have a look.'

'Haan, thank you! I'm much obliged. You've seen?'

'Absolutely, I've seen.'

I followed him along the same path back, and we said goodbye for the last time. The cabbie was waiting outside as I'd asked him. I was driven out of Lalukhet for the last time. Rahim sahib was right: it was a terribly hot day. I told the cabbie to speed up so that more breeze came through our windows, and then I leaned my head back and closed my eyes and let the wind do its best. Rahim sahib's station receded behind me.

He was there. My friend, Ghulam Hussain. They'd done the number on him, every part of his face deformed with bruises. He lay in a big beaten lump close to the far corner. Eyes closed, head resting on forearm. And then the head rose and the eyes opened, as far as they could. They were bloodshot and sad and gazed emptily at me. Like an animal going into a quiet defensive pose, the eyes closed, the head shrunk into the body, the body shrunk into itself, sealing itself off. *Oh it's too hot!* said the policeman.

I still don't know if he was ever part of the Mukti Bahini. But I was beholden to men who were leaving nothing to chance, in these delicate times. The Jamaatis and, to a lesser extent, the brigadier, got me the orchard; in return, they wanted my Bengali friend. I got home, where Sajid and other servants were running back and forth to prepare for the evening's poetry event, the mushaira. My room smelt of the servants' powerful detergents and everything had the shine of crystal. The scene of a crime, covered up. I had no doubt that this is where they did it. This is where they beat him. Sajid was the only other one with the key. He was integral to the whole thing, and he washed up after. I didn't want to look anywhere too closely, in case there were signs of my friend, the crime, drops of blood and bits of flesh. I didn't want to be in the room at all, but where else was there? I put the army chief's bottle next to me on the bed. I knew even before I opened the drawer that the second of Ghulam Hussain's bottles would be gone, and it was. So, the moonshine: at the end that's what they got him with. The poor man's booze he was making from the bark of the Acacia tree. All those accusations, of his being a rebel, a Mukti Bahini terrorist, undermining the state, threatening the national order, the bigger picture . . . and they put him away for cheap booze, left him with the cop who was going to take down that racket. They beat him and then, to make it legitimate, they arrested him. To take down this great man, they used the smallest offence. A joke perhaps, at my expense. Indeed sometimes I think I was the one they were teaching a lesson. And what was the lesson? That when a man like me and a man like Ghulam Hussain become close, a promise is made from the first to the second, a promise that can never be kept.

I put the bottle of whisky with the army chief's seal, still in its carton and its black wrapper, in my bedside table drawer. And then, for the first time in a very long time, I started weeping. First, sitting there with my face buried in my hands. Then, lying on my side in bed, tears spilling into my hot palms and down the side of my cheeks. Giant, exhausting sobs. I gave myself to them with delight. A cloudburst, and then how it poured! I wept and wept and didn't want to stop.

∽

It was strange to see Mona Phuppi and Phuppa Jaan in the brigadier's home. Perhaps it was simply the time to collapse everything and start from scratch. New roles for everyone. Fine by me. Tonight, for the first time it felt like I was hosting *them*, and I tracked them with exaggerated care, made sure Mona Phuppi had her glass of sharbat, Phuppa Jaan his cognac, jumping to attention the moment I saw either glass empty. The thirty or so guests were packed into one side of the drawing room. Some food was served, but most guests were interested in dessert and beverages. The poet that they'd all come to see wore a grey tweed jacket, red tie and a white hankerchief sticking out of his front pocket. He had the fat Pakistani nose and a thin strip of hair semicircling his strong bald head. He sat on the big divan, alone. The brigadier was on his usual one-seater, his bare feet raised on the foot cushion. Many sat on the carpet. The people close to the poet, up front, were predominantly male; most of the women, including Aunty Ruby, sat a few files back. I sat close behind Mona Phuppi on the floor, shadowing her like a personal servant. She sat with her legs under her, giving me, right behind, a view of those hard grey heels which I could tap without her feeling anything. The poet recited for more than a half hour, always in the same rhythm, speaking the first line of the poem, and the people around him saying, 'Wah, wah, wah!' or 'Ah, ah, ah!' and repeating that line to one another, stressing the parts and connections that made it so brilliant. Then the poet repeating that first line again, this time with others reciting it along with him, sometimes even beating him to the beautiful turn or punchline. Then, much quicker, the poet going through the next series of lines, eliciting the same acclaim; stopping, going back a few lines and repeating the poem up to that point, again. Apa was the one woman sitting close to the poet, her frame leaning forward and her chin resting on her hand. She wasn't looking at him, but down at the floor, responding to the lines with strong nods, little shakes of the head from side to side.

Mona Phuppi at first tried translating the poems, but when that impeded both her enjoyment and of the people sitting close to us, she stopped. Ignorantly, I listened. And, to not seem out of place, I occasionally raised my hand in appreciation when the others did. But there was something I did get. Not the words and their meaning, but something far simpler, the mere sound and

rhyme pattern, punctuated by subtle stretches of the
poet's milky voice. I thought of the qawals I saw behind
the Abdullah Shah Ghazi mazar with Ghulam Hussain.
I missed Ghulam Hussain. I recalled my first vision of
him, at the arrivals section in the airport, calm in the
midst of frantic cab drivers making claims from a
distance on potential clients as if they were betting on
horses. Ghulam Hussain stood holding the sign with my
name down below his waist with one hand, saying, *I
will not hold up this sign.* A proud and noble man.
Tonight, I would do my duty to him.

When my aunt and uncle were ready to leave, they
went graciously to thank the brigadier and Aunty Ruby
and bid them farewell. 'And thank you for taking care
of this one,' Mona Phuppi said, rubbing my arm. 'Oh,
it was our pleasure,' Aunty Ruby said. 'He's like family.'
The brigadier smiled and nodded. I walked them down,
arm in arm with Mona Phuppi. I waited until their car
was well on its way down the block before going back
inside.

Upstairs, the mood was changing. Apa was being
guided by the female servants back to her room. The
poetry was over, the poet was gone, and one of the male
guests, clearly drunk, was saying, 'Yes, it's been such a
lovely time. Isn't it funny how we on this side have such
a fabulous evening, while on the other side—' The man's
wife called his name in complaint. 'Kya? Nahin, I'm just
saying it's been a *lovely evening.* And thank God that we
can have such a lovely evening, because if we were in
Dhaka—' His wife said it was time to go.

'No,' the brigadier called from his seat, an unlit cigar
between his fingers. 'Let him continue. If we were in
Dhaka . . . what?' The drawing room was quiet now, the

feelings elicited from the poetry replaced by something quite sour. There was a free chair across from the brigadier. I sat down. The silence was glaring.

'It's a *massacre!*' a woman finally shouted, from a few rows back, who now stood up from her chair, only to sit back down again.

'And?' the brigadier said.

'It needs to be stopped.'

'Not just yet.'

'Not *just yet?*'

'This ... massacre, as you call it, it has its own rhythm. You can't simply *stop* something like this. Have you ever read Shakespeare? Macbeth: "Blood will have blood."' He looked to me and in Urdu, asked, 'That *is* in Macbeth, right?' He was still looking at me for confirmation, and I nodded. He looked back to the rest of them. '*Blood* will have *blood*. Those soldiers are *alive* right now, for better or worse, but you can't just stop a moment like this. We stop it now, then what next? You've got to see the bigger picture.' He set out the imaginary canvas with his hands raised and spread wide.

'It won't last,' said an older, soft-spoken woman. 'They will get their Bangladesh.'

'Then all the more reason to let this go on,' the brigadier replied. 'Would you interfere in a birth just because the mother is feeling pangs? It will help their new country ... if they ever get it. Just think, if it wasn't for the Jallianwala Bagh massacre, where would we be?' He shook his head in those hard, minute tremors, as if nobody had understood the lesson. 'This—what they're going through now—is *history*. We've got to let it be a natural process.' He was like the poet or qawal, repeating the first refrain of a ghazal. 'I mean ...' He shook his head again, frustrated by everyone's inability to appreciate the obvious. And then he looked at me to make sure that, at the very least, *I* understood. I found myself nodding when he looked at me. 'Look,' he began again. 'Here's the point. If we don't let the army have its last bit of fun, get all that excess energy out, you know exactly what will happen. We'll have a beast on our hands, with a thousand heads and a thousands arms, clawing at whatever it can. At *us*, in *this* part of the country. You want that? No. If you really want the army gone, this is how it happens.'

'It's as if you're talking about kids in a playground, before dinner time or something.'

'Yes, it is a little like that,' he said.

'People are being killed.'

'Well, these bloody Mukti Bahinis are only making matters worse. And you all know, of course, that they're Indian agents, right.' He'd raised his voice to an exceptional pitch, and as soon as he mentioned the Mukti Bahini I felt his words were meant for me. That through his guests, through the careful angles of the drawing room, he was addressing me, explaining Ghulam Hussain's beating. I realized that I no longer owed him any loyalty, not even in this unsympathetic crowd. On the contrary, I felt like the crowd gave me a cushion, that because I would be speaking as one of many, I'd be less conspicuous in my defiance. Nevertheless, I surprised myself when I hollered, 'You're turning a blind eye to it because of your love for Bhutto.' The brigadier gazed towards the floor, a man betrayed, before lifting his head and looking not directly at me, but a little past me, as if with defective eyes.

'Yes, I have a love for Bhutto,' he finally said, quietly.

'But don't take that for an emotional love.' He was looking at nobody in particular anymore. 'This man wants so badly to become our leader, nothing but ambition in him! If you people don't see the beauty in that—'

'Exactly,' I said. 'The man's nothing but ambition.' I was getting excited opposing him.

'It's what's beautiful about him. It's his ... *fever*. Have *you* ever felt anything like it? You who were in Paris for so long and didn't do a damn thing, you who likes to stay well within the margins? Ever felt that fever? You who sat there tonight and didn't respond to, didn't *understand* one line of what this beautiful poet spoke?' He was pointing at the empty chair where the poet had sat. 'Tell me, give me one *line* that you understood. So don't *you* worry. You won't end up in anyone's prison, because you've never felt that. That's what *these* men have. It's the fever of an artist. Michelangelo painting the Sistine Chapel.' He'd almost begun rambling, his small hot eyes were seeking focus, but there was dangerous sense in him, too.

'In blood!' I said.

'Please.' He looked me dead in the eye. 'Don't be so dramatic. *In blood*, ha!' The brigadier laughed, his face went red, and he turned to the men sitting next to him to recruit them to his joke. With that laughter, the people in the drawing room escaped the central discussion. They were still talking about the troubles in East Pakistan perhaps, but now amongst themselves in smaller groups. My argument had been demeaned by that last, 'dramatic' remark. The remaining guests started getting up, they said goodbye to the brigadier, and then Aunty Ruby walked a group of them down. Sajid picked up ashtrays and glasses, the brigadier closed the cap of a whisky bottle and walked lugubriously around the drawing room, searching for something. He stood still for a moment, his head down, the bottle held closely to his breast. Recovering perception, he walked to the staircase that led up to the mezzanine. He didn't look at me when he passed me.

'Uncle,' I said, following him. 'I wanted to speak to you about something.'

'Not right now, beta,' he said, without looking back, moving onto the staircase. I stopped on the second step. 'Uncle, I think we really do need to talk. This is about my friend, Ghul—'

'Yes, talk and more talk, you seem to like that.'

'I need you to talk to Rahim sahib. Tell him to release him.'

'I *have* talked to him. Oh, he had a message for you. "Thank you".'

'*Thank you*!? For what?'

'Your contribution to law and order. Your services to the city. He's rather proud of you.'

'He was in on it, the sonofabitch! That's why he took me to the damn lock-up! Look, this is *absurd*. Did you even give my friend a chance? Give him a chance to say he wasn't part of the Mukti Bahini?'

'Rahim sahib isn't going to give him a chance to keep making that poison, I can tell you that.' He kept walking up. 'It's time for a little order in this country.'

'You expect me to believe that *that*'s why, that it was that bloody moonshine . . . I think you're being totally unreasonable.' He stopped, and turned his head. His sharp hazel glare frightened me. 'You could at least give me the chance to speak,' I said, quieter now. 'A chance to speak after what you've done.'

'What I've *done* is get you your orchard. *That* is what I've done. So slip a thank you note under my door tonight and go to sleep, my boy.'

I didn't move. 'You want Bhutto to give you a ministry, is that it? You'll show him what you did to Gh—'

He laughed his powerful red throaty laugh. 'Arrey bhai, how the hell do I get a ministry, I don't even have a seat. Can you see me handle a ministry? I can't even manage this bloody house. Goodnight, young Shahbaz.' He vanished into his room.

I raised my voice again, walking up a few more steps. 'Hammad sahib knew you well. He knew your innermost heart. He knew you'd do anything to do right by Bhutto. Poor man didn't know how right he was. All for to preserve *the big picture*, huh?'

Aunty Ruby appeared in the drawing room, having said goodbye to all the guests, and was coming towards the stairs. She looked exhausted. When she saw me she smiled a void smile. 'Shabakhair, beta,' she said. 'Sleep well. And please turn the lights off when you're done here, if you don't mind.'

'Certainly. But Aunty, do you mind telling Uncle, if he's not in bed yet, to come out for a moment? I know it's been a long night, but—'

'Haan, bilkul,' she replied, walking up. 'I'll see if he's still up.'

I waited at the foot of the stairs, but neither the brigadier nor his wife came out. I walked away, through the drawing room, past Apa's room. Maybe *she* was the one I should have been talking to. But the old lady was fast asleep on her side, her dentures sitting at the base of the glass next to the black telephone, in liquid. Newspapers, half-finished letters to world leaders on the floor next to her bed. She was breathing heavy, taking in every bit of oxygen left for her. For a moment I thought of putting a pillow over her face. She gave all the orders, after all, it was her words that the brigadier was repeating. I came downstairs to my room, lay down without changing out of my clothes and washing up, felt the time slipping away. But the brigadier was right. It was all just talk.

∾

It was four in the afternoon, when the house always napped. I went through the kitchen. The pots were ready for tonight's cooking, a chicken in a sealed plastic bag defrosted in a bowl of water in the sink. The smells, the grime—how Sajid spent his day in here, God only knew. I walked through the back door to the coiled stone-and-brick staircase to the roof. It was hot, and Sajid kept the door to his quarters open. He was lying on his wafer-like bed in shalwar and undershirt, waving a hand-held fan in front of his face. When he realized I was midway into his room he sat up, alarmed, made to get up, but I told him, 'Sit, sit.' I stood over him.

'Sir?' His room smelled of burnt onion.

'You told brigadier sahib that Ghulam Hussain was joining the Mukti Bahini?'

'Sir?'

'Did you tell brigadier sahib that Ghulam Hussain was going to the Mukti Bahini?'

'Sir ji, that—'

'*Why?*'

'Sirji, I didn't—'

'Don't lie,' I said, calmly. 'No need to lie. I know you

told him and the Jamaatis that. You know what they did to him, right? At the police station? So answer me. Why? What was the need to tell people that rubbish?'

'Sir ji,' he smirked. 'It wasn't rubbish. Ghulam Hussain told me himself that . . .' I slapped him, surprising myself not only that I did, but also by how hard. His mouth was open in shock, his face drained of blood. I struck him again. And once I started I couldn't stop. The shock was gone from his face and replaced by panic at the prospect of a long assault. I grabbed him with one hand by the neckline of his undershirt. 'I can have them put you in jail, too, you little . . . gadha! Rahim sahib is a friend of mine, too. The brigadier won't be able to help you. What do you think, that he'll care if you're in jail?' I grabbed the back of his head and twisted it to bury his face in his pillow. 'I will bury you,' I said in English. 'I will fucking bury you!' I held him by the neck with my left hand, his white innocent cheek exposed. I was overcome one moment by a desire to protect that face, but the very next moment by an absolute rejection of that sentiment. I struck him this time with closed fist and more force than I've ever used. Twice, a third time. That animal panic took over his whole body—he was nothing but a set of thrashing limbs. I went on hitting. And then I backed off and found I was panting heavily, just staring at the boy. I wanted to make sure he wasn't cut or too badly hurt, to coddle him and stroke him and tell him it was okay, I was done. I took a step towards him and was so dismayed by the way his whole body flinched at my approach, the sheer horror that had entered him. This power was intoxicating. I was dizzy and felt something in me trying to break out of my chest. 'Okay,' I tried to say, but the words came out in a raucous gasp, and I didn't know if he heard them at all. I put up a hand, palm facing him, as if *I* was telling him, enough, enough, please relent. The more I stayed now the more damage I would do, the more fear and humiliation I would inflict. I also knew that that desire to smash and bury could return any moment.

His face. Those marks would get darker. There was no way to hide this encounter. The brigadier would know. Good. Be it so. This wasn't a fight between me and Sajid. This was communication between me and the brigadier, a larger affair. He hit one of mine, I hit one of his, and that's how alliances of this sort work. I looked forward to when, later at night, at the dinner table, Sajid would dutifully serve me, get me anything I asked for, fill my glass, ask if I was done with the food, take away my plate and bring me fruits even though he knew I didn't eat fruit. There was pure pleasure in this. Something that was static had broken free, something new, something that should have been there since the start, fell into place. I've nursed that feeling ever since. Even as I lifted my hand to declare the end of my assault on the kid, there was something cruel expanding in my breast, squeezing weaknesses out.

I bolted his door, approached the bed. His eyes engorged and he tried to get out of bed, but I grabbed him by the collar, and started my work again. His skin had broken in several places, his lips, too. He'd have to wash the red from his old-white pillow case. But not just yet. I wasn't finished. And I didn't want to finish, even when I feared I was coming to the point where I might kill him. I wanted to shatter the boy, break him to pieces. That beautiful urge took much effort to subdue. And now that rapture, that haal, never seems too far out of reach. Blood will have blood. Precisely right, Mr Brigadier.

3

Sajid would be okay. Ghulam Hussain, too, would be okay. I'm assuming. I exaggerated my power over them. It only went so far. Even the brigadier's power over Sajid, and Mona Phuppi's over her servants, was limited. The servants were protected by years and decades and centuries of powerlessness and misfortune. They could drink the contaminated water that waiters poured into their filthy aluminium glasses. It was us—*we* were the ones with the weak English stomachs and constitutions. We could beat them up all we wanted, but we'd never win the fight over their soul. We could never shock them the way they could shock us if and when they decided to.

The day I left the brigadier's, Sajid and Munir moved my suitcases to the car. Aunty Ruby and the brigadier accompanied me out, the wife holding me by the wrist as we walked, before turning me over to her husband, who put his arm around my shoulder, and together we walked over the little bump of the gate. 'You come back soon,' he said, then gently tapped his cold palm against my cheek. 'Bring your father with you.' As we hugged, shoulder to masculine shoulder, I murmured low enough that his wife didn't hear, 'Say goodbye to Malika for me.' I then exchanged kisses with Aunty Ruby. I gave Sajid a long hug and put twenty rupees in his kameez pocket, a gesture he resisted at first, then at my insistence accepted with that ashamed smile of the servant. His soft face was still mauve all over. So strange to think of that as my work. Did the brigadier know that it was I who had beaten the servant, that the medical bills that he no doubt had to pay were because of his departing guest? I hoped so, and at the same time appreciated that nothing was said, all was understood. Mona Phuppi's driver, Munir, took me to her house in Bath Island, where I spent my last night.

∾

The brigadier was right: things always worked out for these people. I remember that day on Drigg Road when Ghulam Hussain had to pretend he was Punjabi to the traffic policeman, and the bribe he placed in the policeman's palm. Prison would always be near. I was a fool to think *I* could rescue him from this fate. There were larger forces at play. Things would eventually catch up to Ghulam Hussain. This was no different to when the Pathan woman finally caught him using her eggs to make omelettes for his clients in her back garden. On to the next black business, and it was just a matter of time before the stakes were high enough. Whether it happened now or later, at some point the police would have found him with that poor man's alcohol. And wasn't it better that it was Rahim sahib of the Lalukhet station? A decent man who would, no doubt, eventually protect his prisoner, provide justice, or as close a thing to justice in that world?

∾

Did the brigadier ever meet the two Jamaatis again? I like to think not. I've never figured out what he owed them, what their relationship really was, but I like to think that he allied with those men not because he wanted to, but out of the needs of the time. He knew the traditions he inherited from his elders, from Apa, and he was faithful to them. He had a clear idea of his country and he saw a way to get it. No, the brigadier was a good man. And for all his unruliness, there was something about him that said, convincingly, *I'll get this thing done*. He certainly did so for me. Good or bad, I had to be grateful for that.

I doubt very much if today the brigadier holds the same views about the Mukti Bahini, the Bengalis—the Bongs—and the operations against them. In fact I doubt if he sincerely believed it back then. He was caught in a larger moment, which brought those bigger things into play—patriotism, unity, order. It clouded his mind as it would for anyone who was that attached to the country, who had that much of it in his blood. As someone so detached, unable to *be* attached, I can't possibly apply my conventions to him.

I had brought some of him back with me to Paris. A style of wearing shirts, a swagger, an informality, a bonhomie even with strangers and officials. How do you condemn a man you carry with you? Whatever his flaws, failures, poor judgments, I was connected to him.

Sometimes, certainly, it is that feeling of connectedness that causes me the deepest grief. The feeling that everything that went on in that house is a part of me. And so, I'm often reminded that I also carry Hammad sahib's murder, the Jamaatis, the violence, everywhere I go. I've tried to just let things and events be, to keep Karachi and Paris separate, the brigadier's home where it belongs, at the other end of the world. No doubt I have some of his legacy in me. But the fact is I have no idea what the Jamaatis, Apa and the brigadier were talking about that evening I saw them congregated in the room upstairs, just before Hammad sahib was killed. I saw four people squeezed into a small room, positioning themselves wherever they could. Apa and her nephew were sitting, the other men were standing. Those are the facts. What I told Malika about the brigadier looking forlorn and needing consolation—I barely saw the man's face, how could I possibly know if he was forlorn?

We know today that the Jamaat-i-Islami carried out killings in Bengal. Well and good. But surely that doesn't mean that all the party's members participated. The men who helped me were creeps—but killers? Hammad sahib lived in a dangerous world at a dangerous time. His was a protruding personality. That wasn't anybody's fault. Like Ghulam Hussain, he would have found trouble sooner or later. These men of passion, these *feverish* people as the brigadier described them, they try to move the world and sometimes the world punishes them for it. It's people like me who always remain safe.

Today I don't remember his face. Only parts of it that together don't form a proper whole. I remember the pale cold stiff leg. And I remember that beautiful gesture, when he put his playful fist in his mouth and squeezed down with his teeth, as if that was the only thing in the world that could keep him from spilling his guts. (Guts— not a good word to use for a man who died the way Hammad sahib died.) That's the only time I can see his face clearly, with that fist in his mouth.

⌒

Was mine the unkindest cut of all? When I think back to my time in Karachi, it's not the Jamaatis, the squatters, the Little Chief and his little friend and all the others, or Sajid. No, the one I still think of is Ghulam Hussain. So what is it I think of when I think of him? Not calling him to the brigadier. Not of the day I saw him in jail, beaten. No, I think of another incident. We were in his quarters, I had just broken a bottle, I had given him the money that he asked me for to help with his return to East Pakistan. Already, I knew I had given him to them. But that's not what troubles me. Because sooner or later the law would have got him anyway. No, my betrayal was of a different kind altogether. My betrayal was this:

'A man gets bored,' Ghulam Hussain said that day, when I pressed him to talk. 'A man gets bored,' he said, and I was responsible for this statement; that's the duty I took on when I pressed him to speak. 'A man gets bored,' he explained. 'A man no longer knows what to do next, Shahbaz bhai. He knows he won't be what he was before. That time is gone. Whatever it was, it is gone from his body. Now, what does he do?' After a long silence, I did it, told him once more that I would bring him to Paris with me one day, making the promise as if to a woman I was trying to court ('I'll take you to Paris one day, sweetheart, we'll sleep under the stars above the Sacre Coeur'). But for Ghulam Hussain, this was no fantasy. His head sunk and his face tensed with humility and thanks. I'd said it a second time, so obviously I meant it. That was the naiveté of the poor. So full of wisdom and those street smarts that I envied, but which resided simultaneously with the credulity of a child. Did I relent or retract? No, I kept going, more than the first time, adding that it wouldn't be a problem, we'd contact the embassy there and they'd sort out the papers and permits and whatnot, like that, a snap of the fingers. 'A lot of these old apartment buildings, like my father's, come with servant quarters, right on the top floor,' I explained. 'One little room. These days, people over there don't keep servants, so they rent the room out to students. So you'll be on the same floor with these students. You'll like them. You can learn French from them. No, no, don't worry, they won't think badly of you. In English there's a word: *left-wing*. I don't know how to explain it. But don't worry, they'll respect you. They'll smoke charas with you. But you can't smoke too much when you work for my father. Not during the day. You understand, na?'

∼

And then, I asked him to come to the brigadier's.

If I knew that there was no way I could bring Ghulam Hussain to Paris, why did I make this promise, a second time? Was it because I felt my power over him slipping and I knew this would be the way to restore it? A show of force, was that what it really was? No. It was, like the first time, an expression of affection. He drove me around, he got me hash and whatever else, and then I gave him tips. But there was never a moment that I showed him that I liked him and enjoyed his company. I was restricted not only by Urdu, but also by the life I was living, at the brigadier's, by the history that divided us. Even when I visited him in those quarters, Ghulam Hussain was always doing something for me, making me omelettes, giving me the booze that eventually—inevitably—brought him trouble. Master and servant. How does the master show the servant love? By giving something of himself. In my case, what I had was Paris, the promise of Paris that was as powerful, if not more powerful, than the city itself. Because this city would have treated Ghulam Hussain viciously, if he ever did make it here, forced him to its corrupt corners and made a whore out of him. I would be doing him an injustice if I actually did bring him to Paris. But the *promise* of Paris! What I was irrigating his imagination with was something he could always hold on to, not unsimilar to the promise of an afterlife. That's what I shared with him. It was a final beautiful moment between us. And since I already sensed the fate that awaited him, since I knew that I'd brought him within the brigadier's and the Jamaatis' orbit, I made my promise now to help him through the next phase. It was my atonement. I couldn't protect him physically. I didn't have the authority, I was too beholden to the people who were after him. But in some way I had given him hope. And that hope would always be strong. That's the way it was with these people. Ghulam Hussain knew that in me he'd always have an angel-guide for the Western paradise. I gave him Paris. It was a more powerful weapon than anything Rahim sahib had in his sweating office with the stacks of paper piled on wicker chairs and tables and bursting out of broken closets, having dumb young men salute him the way he'd saluted his superiors, sending shocks up the spine and making a mess of the mind. But I can't stop thinking: if he recognized me that day in Lalukhet station, if he could see me through his swollen beaten eyes, he must have thought: *He's come. My friend at last has to come to get me, to take me away, to take me to Paris.* What dangerous games I played!

The mistake we made, Ghulam Hussain and I, was becoming close in the first place. When rich and poor make friends in that country, there's a promise made, a promise that can never be satisfied. I did the best I could.

❧

I was already back in Paris when Dhaka fell. When it did, my father went into deep depression. Although he never had plans to return, his love for Dhaka remained strong. Even the Pakistani idea itself, buried under exile though it was, was still alive somewhere in his heart. 'Pakistan's broken?' He asked me, repeatedly. Eyes and mouth agape, like a ten-year-old trying to comprehend a purely adult experience. 'It's *broken*?'

I couldn't decipher my own reaction to the country's break-up. I should have felt it more keenly than my father did, having just been there. But I was the one consoling him. Consoling him how? Just with silence, gloominess, a downturned head. Miming despondency in this way, I didn't have the time to discern my real feelings about it. And perhaps something in me resisted the idea of uncovering those feelings, maybe these were feelings better left alone.

❧

I saw the brigadier again, years later. He came to Paris one summer, and contacted my father, who then called me to tell me the three of us were to have Sunday brunch together the next day. I was living alone at Pasteur. I came to my father's house at ten, and was edgy the whole morning, pacing around the bedroom that used to be mine, and the drawing room, looking up at the clock. My father had given the brigadier the time of noon, but by quarter to one he still wasn't here. Occasionally, I simply stared at the intercom phone on the wall by the front door, pleading, *ring ring ring*.

'This is absurd,' my father said.

'I'm sure he's on his way,' I assured him.

When the intercom finally sounded, followed shortly by the bang of the elevator, I froze in my spot in the drawing room, and didn't come to the door until I heard the brigadier's and my father's salutations. When I did appear, he said, 'Ah, jenaab-e-ali!' and hugged me, well-soaked in cologne as always, and then held me at a short distance to study me. His hair might have been whiter, his face a little thinner, but he still retained that old fiendish vigour. He'd grown a thick goatee that suited him. He thanked me for the telegram I'd sent him some time ago, condoling about Apa's death. I lamented it again, repeating what I'd said in the telegram, that she was a noble and extraordinary woman, that I'd learned much from her in that time I spent at the brigadier's. I was genuinely saddened by the news. She *was* a noble old woman. I recalled the last time I met her. She didn't quite grasp that I was leaving for good, and I didn't press the point. I remember her trying to say something, but she couldn't find the words. She slapped her index finger against the palm of the other hand repeatedly, reality quickly dissolving in front of her. And whatever advice she had for me for this time, this era, was dissolving with it. In front of her, her unfinished letters. 'Khuda hafiz,' I said. 'Meeting will happen again, Inshallah, when I come back.' She tried to give me money but I told her I had no more need for rupees.

The brigadier gifted us a small crate of mangoes he'd brought from Pakistan. We'd finally ended up selling the orchard a few years after reacquiring it, when all sides decided they needed the money. The siblings didn't split it according to the Muslim calculations, but evenly. I got my share from my father. It seemed almost as if the brigadier was mocking us with this offering. I took the crate into the kitchen and opened it, set some mangoes aside for after brunch. I brought lemonades to the men in the drawing room. When I handed the brigadier his, he looked at me with an admonishing frown, and said, 'Arrey bhai, you call this a drink?'

'No booze in this house,' I said, gesturing towards my father. The brigadier looked at him with his arms spread out for an explanation.

'As good Pakistanis, we are observing Prohibition,' my father joked.

'Oh, don't bloody start with that!'

'The law is the law.'

Bhutto's Prohibition and ban on cabarets the year before had put the brigadier out of business, an attempt to try to neutralize the Jamaatis, his opposition, the party that had once served his purposes, and of many uniformed others, to crush the Bengalis. And the midget? Where had he gone? The brigadier took his lemonade grudgingly. I stayed away from the topic of the Agra, but did at some point ask him how he was spending his days in Karachi, and he responded by mimicking the swing of a golf club. Eighteen holes, sundowners, and a game of bridge at the Gymkhana in the evening. 'The same old schedule.'

Although my father and the brigadier hadn't met for some twenty-five years, they talked like school friends reunited after a summer or a year abroad. That was a skill that old Karachi-ites had, an informality that matched the decorum and ceremony. The language allowed for it, and now those words—*yaar, arrey bhai, mian, tum, jaani*—rang in the drawing room. They talked cricket. 'The morons should have known the pitch clears high afternoon,' the brigadier carped. 'It was just silly, bhai, to bat first. In weather like that, wait for the damn pitch to clear.' They even talked politics, my father having lifted his embargo on the subject; now he was asking questions about the general who'd overthrown Bhutto, wasn't that general Bhutto's own man, would he release Bhutto eventually and restore the government as promised, or were 'you'—still, not 'we'—in for another long military regime? 'Serves the bloody scoundrel right,' the brigadier remarked about his old prime minister.

I went to check on the food in the kitchen. My father had hired a woman who came from time to time to prepare food and clean up, but she wasn't very competent, he said, and requested beforehand that I keep an eye on things. When I returned to the drawing room, the two of them were standing at the window overlooking the main road and, behind it, the outskirts of the Bois de Bologne. 'Ah, she's got visitors,' my father declaimed. The brigadier watched silently, a smile on his face. 'Here we go, she's getting out,' my father continued. 'She's opening the side door aaaaaaand . . .' he paused, '*in* goes the first customer!' Both of them laughed triumphantly.

'I wonder what the other two are talking about right now,' the brigadier said. 'Poor bastards, standing in the heat while their friend gets blown.'

'They'll get their turn,' my father assured him, patting him on the shoulder. I'd rarely seen my father so impertinent. I stood behind them, and when my father noticed me, he said, awkwardly, 'Just showing him some . . .'

'Yes,' I replied. I looked down at the van across the main road. The two men waited, each to replace the friend inside.

For the most part, the day was more about the reunion between the old school friends than about my own reunion with the brigadier. But after lunch, the brigadier instructed me to bring the mangoes out (I remembered it was the one fruit he did eat). 'The best in the world!' my father exclaimed as he handled and cut one. He cut one for me, too. When I was done, the brigadier looked at the stripped mango skins on my plate. 'Arrey bhai, that's no way to eat a mango! You've still got so much on them.' He'd picked up my plate to look closer at it. 'Oof, here and here and here. That's *mango*, bhai!' He gave me a demonstration with one of his own half-eaten slices, raking the rest in with his teeth until the peel looked completely dry. He held the peel out to me. '*That's* how you do it!' And for that moment, with my father looking on, it was as if we were back in the brigadier's home in PECHS, Karachi, he instructing me on how to operate in this world.

Before he left, I gave him the gift I'd brought, wrapped in a plastic bag. I asked him not to take it out now, but once he was back at his hotel. After seven or so years, seven or so years of not having once opened it, I was letting it go, the bottle of whisky with the Chief-of-Army-Staff label.

The brigadier and I made plans for me to take him around Paris the next day. My feelings on the plan were mixed. How many hours would I have to spend with him, when would he be satisfied that I'd shown him Paris properly? I imagined him saying, 'Arrey mian, we're just getting started!' I imagined him wanting to go on until early morning. Even in Karachi, I'd never actually spent more than two hours just with him. So the thought of a whole day unsettled me. Nevertheless, in the morning I couldn't deny a mild disappointment when my father called to tell me that the brigadier had called to say that he had decided to leave to see his sister in Manchester a day early. We never met again.

My father phoned in the morning. 'They've hanged Bhutto,' he said.

'Uh huh,' I replied, and hung up.

Was it that easy? The death of a giant, by the order of his own general? Could decay spread over a body once so sated with power, driven by the highest appetites, exulted by a nation of a hundred million? I had the sense that something had finally collapsed, and that something in me had collapsed with it. Something that had been in me for the past eight years. It was strange, almost damning, to have shaken hands with a man who met this historic death. Those cold hands, those baby cheeks and lips as sensuous as a woman's. To have had that man in the home in which I slept. It left me exhilarated, anguished, and immobile. It was a long rope that hanged him, and it stretched all the way to me. This damn rope. We were all on it, it made a ring around all of our waists: the brigadier, Hammad sahib, the two Jamaatis with whom I once shared a ground floor, the orchard, the squatters, Mona Phuppi, myself, my father, and at the end of it all, Bhutto's body hanging by the neck. When they kicked the foot support from under him, I think we all fell a little bit of the way.

Even Malika. She danced for him in his village in Larkana.

I'd gone to the Agra to say goodbye, but she wasn't in the cabaret and she wasn't in her room and she wasn't anywhere that the receptionist or the midget knew. I wrote a note of farewell to her. I told the midget I was going back to France, and his confused little face didn't know how to take it in, didn't know what look to give. I put twenty rupees in his minute palm. I bent over and hugged him. 'You've done a lot for me, you've taken good care of me,' I said. He smiled, humbly shook his head from side to side, and put his hand to his heart.

So, it turned out, the last time I ever saw Malika was our first failed fuck. Malika and the brigadier—I never discovered *that* story either. Was she punishing me that night, the night I told her to leave the cabaret, punishing me for trying to be 'bigger than Alamgir'? I suppose it worked. I tried to be bigger than Alamgir, and Malika and I, we never fucked again.

I wrote her a postcard, care of the Agra. I didn't expect a response. But I did one day get one. Written in better English than I would have imagined. And we would exchange occasional postcards for years. Cairo-Karachi, Cairo-Karachi, with some other gay cities in between, the pattern never stopped, she kept coming back to the Agra, right to the end. She wrote me a final one around the time Bhutto announced prohibition. 'No more booze, no more dancing, no more drunk men with tongues on the floor. C'est finis, Shahbaz.' She wasn't coming back. I never found out where she ended up. The image that has stayed with me, more than any other, is of the first night I saw her, when she slowly, theatrically, unfurled her arm and gave me her middle finger.

∾

I went to the quay after hearing about the hanging. The warmest day we'd had so far this spring. And although it wasn't quite warm enough for me to take off my shirt and lie in the sun all day, I did bring a towel with me, which I laid out at the edge of the quay. I took my shoes off and dangled my feet above the Seine. There were two young girls nearby, singing behind me. It took several minutes for me to realize that they weren't being frivolous, but had rather lovely voices that were in perfect tune and synchrony. I felt a pleasure that seemed inappropriate to the day.

I was a man who could speak from knowledge and experience about history, a man who'd been close to events, who saw the big picture. I wanted now to talk to someone, any Parisian, and fill his or her imagination the way I'd filled Ghulam Hussain's years ago, when I told him I'd bring him to Paris. It was a task I was quite happy to perform. I don't know if I could have been called a fake, any more than a cultural attaché can be called a fake. I was a sculptor of two worlds, the meeting point of two cities.